Castle Orchard

Also by E. A. Dineley

*The Death of Lyndon Wilder and the
Consequences Thereof*

Castle Orchard

E. A. DINELEY

corsair

Constable & Robinson Ltd
55-56 Russell Square
London WC1B 4HP
www.constablerobinson.com

First published in the UK by Corsair,
an imprint of Constable & Robinson Ltd, 2014

A copy of the British Library Cataloguing in Publication
Data is available from the British Library

ISBN 978-1-78033-590-2 (hardback)
ISBN 978-1-78033-593-3 (ebook)

Printed and bound by CPI Group (UK) Ltd, Croydon, CR0 4YY

1 3 5 7 9 10 8 6 4 2

For Christopher Bryant

On a clear day, from the top of the hill... one can see the spire of Salisbury Cathedral rise up, viewed as a needle of light. Chalk downlands... rising massively, in this direction or another with little villages running... stone churches in miniature... such a valley bottom there is a particular village... are state perhaps only apparent by a name of... distant past: a wide band of a cheese church... lost in obscurity, impossible to read.

A man that cannot recognize the fact... however, not only does he duly begin... village of Orchardleigh but with the... brother keeps a school for preparing... to Eton or Winchester.

The rectory has a dining room... some rooms upstairs which... and a spacious apartment giving... down. It looks over the widest ground... leads to the big house, the path to... the river. Below, in the cellar, in the wall... among the books and the diminutive... hats and the winter muffling...

On a clear day, from the top of the high chalk downland, the spire of Salisbury Cathedral may be viewed, a sliver, a needle of light. Chalk downland undulates, dipping and rising, massively, in this direction or another whilst holding little villages, running water, manor houses and grey stone churches in its various green indentations. In one such valley bottom there is a particular village, not large; an estate, perhaps only apparent by a pair of gates in minor disrepair; a wide bend of a river, a church and a rectory, all lost in obscurity, impossible to find.

Within that distant rectory the Rev. Hubert Conway, a widower, not only does his duty by his parishioners in the village of Orchardleigh but, with the aid of his younger brother, keeps a school for preparing young boys for entry to Eton or Winchester.

The rectory has a dining room with three trestle tables, some rooms upstairs with several rows of small sad beds, and a spacious apartment given over to recreation on wet days. It looks over the cricket ground, the meadow that leads to the big house, the garden, the shrubbery and the river. Below, in the cellar, in the cold and the gloom, amongst the boots and the diminutive greatcoats, the lost hats and the winter mufflers, the cricket bats, hoops and forsaken clutter, Sam Jackson regales the boys with those things that make their hearts beat faster with emotions a mixture of horror and delight.

Mr Conway employs Jackson to clean the boots and fetch in the firewood. The man is not able for much else but it is not proper, in the eyes of the rector, to ignore and starve those who have returned alive from fighting tyrants, in particular Napoleon Bonaparte. Mr Conway believes Jackson to be a sad, ignorant fellow with his wooden leg and his single eye, but however ugly and unwholesome a sight, however poor in mental powers, he is yet one of God's creatures. The rector reasons thus, but Jackson is a fearsome body and it is safe to say the rector actually knows nothing about him. He, perhaps naïvely, assumes youth to be innocent, the souls of the young to be unsullied and Jackson to be merely unfortunate. Waywardness takes Mr Conway by surprise and sins of a more dire nature cause him confusion. He has no concept of original sin, or certainly not after baptism has put all to rights. He is himself perfectly innocent: his pupils, even his three sons, are well in advance of him.

Now he sits at his desk writing letters. He dates each one 18 June 1825. He is aware of it being the tenth anniversary of that great, decisive battle, Waterloo, but he hopes if no mention is made of it his pupils will not heed it, for it is a matter so distracting they will never be got to attend to their Greek: but he has not allowed for Jackson.

As the boys see it, Sam Jackson has only one fault. He lost his leg and his eye at Toulouse, which precluded him from Waterloo. It is but a small drawback, for was he not at Salamanca, Talavera and Vitoria? In the cavernous space of the cellar he sits on an upturned barrel, a short clay pipe clutched between his teeth and, by the light of a single candle, spreads his arms over the heads of his audience, whose eyes are fixed, fascinated, credulous and incredulous by turn.

'Wide as that, yer vultures were,' Jackson says, for his fields of action are Portugal and Spain. 'Yer dead and wounded were breakfast and supper for they, breakfast and supper for weeks on end. Yer looked up at a sky that only sort o' peeked out from yer rocks, yer rocks being that 'igh an' yer vultures sort o' swooned off the edges an' floated about till they flopped down on yer bodies an' gobbled 'em up.'

Jackson pauses for effect before adding, 'They can't never 'ave known it so lucky: wish yer commissariat 'ad been so regular with the rations, yer lump o' meat, yer biscuit, yer lump o' bread.'

'But Jackson, you buried the dead, you told us you did.'

'When there was time yer buried the dead. They wasn't buried none too deep. Turned up the sods with our bayonets an' the wolves turned 'em up again. Time were in short supply.'

Jackson repeats the last sentence while jabbing his stick at a curly-haired infant in the front row, who half muffles a frightened cry. He then sits back and starts grumbling to himself. 'March here, march there, march back: dizzying it were. Walk across the river, don't stop, don't bend, don't drink, 'old yer piece above yer 'ead, keep yer powder dry, cross yer plain, climb yer mountain: yer mate gets 'eatstroke, screams and dies.'

He has forgotten the children. One by one they sneak away, reluctant, to fight other battles, in Greek and Latin,

3

on the plains of Troy. Jackson continues his mutterings to the greatcoats and boots and yearns for his rum ration to loosen his bones.

Across the meadow from the village, the church and the rectory, lies an old, rambling, misshapen mansion of no great size or pretension. It stands a little back from the winding river which, in its course, winds around an old heap of stones, here and there one upright or one on another, all that remains of the castle; it winds round an octagonal turret, the Philosopher's Tower; round a hot, sleepy meadow in which grazes, footfall by footfall, a stout pied pony, the rhythmical tearing of the grass the only sound beyond the chattering of the water; and it winds round an old apple orchard with the trees leaning every which way, but with no breath of a breeze to stir them, as if they play at statues: such is Castle Orchard, though the orchard could never have been the present one but some other orchard of long ago, or the word corrupted from another word, the meaning of which is lost. Such is Castle Orchard at the approach of midsummer.

Within the house a woman sat at a table, a woman perhaps verging on thirty years old, perhaps a little younger. It was apparent she took no particular care of her dress or her appearance in general, but to any who could overlook a worn garment and a pair of scuffed shoes of the work-aday sort, there was something pleasing about her, though she was tired. Before her were the ledgers that held the accounts for the estate, the home farm and the house. Were these not always tiring? The agent had left them with her that she might understand them before Quarter Day, and when the rents came in, wrest what she could for repairs. Barns must be snug, roofs watertight, gates mended, ditches dug and, not to be forgotten, a pig raised and a barrel of ale provided for the bucolic activities the village, by tradition, associated with 1st May, over for this year but needed for next. Servants must be paid, though these numbered few; tea and sugar bought, salt – the necessities of life that could not be produced at home. The anxiety, the endless struggle, gave her a headache, she who never had headaches. Her mind ran on lists: milk, cheese, butter, beef, mutton and pork, eggs, honey, apples, plums, pears, peas, beans and saladings and sovereigns, half-sovereigns, guineas, pounds, crowns, shillings and pence. It would be easier to let the estate go to ruin.

She closed the books and reached for her pen. It was time she wrote to her half-sister. Louisa was the better correspondent but there were things to be said, especially today. She paused before beginning. Fond as she was of Louisa, she found it difficult to write. She had to practise a certain amount of subterfuge, though without telling lies; gloss over facts; make light of things, though without too much pretending. It was a fine line to walk but Louisa never could be told all: she was too young, and too unworldly, perhaps too happy, to be burdened. Today it should be easier because there was something of which she would like to speak, a recollection, a quiet sadness: there was no one but Louisa to whom she could speak, so she drew the ink towards her, dipped in the pen, started.

My dear Louisa,

It is the tenth anniversary of the Battle of Waterloo. I dare say you don't need reminding. You were but a child at the time, but to whom else can I recall our cousin Charles? Because their house was across the garden from ours, he was my childhood playmate, but that you do know, I have so often said it. Dearest Charles. All those young men. Do you remember the day he came to say goodbye?

She laid the pen down for a minute. What would Louisa remember? What would she have been told? Of the latter, nothing creditable to her older half-sister. Would she remember their house in Devonshire thronged with young soldiers, officers, some already in uniform, hastening this way and that, bidding goodbye to their families, joining their regiments? They were sharing transport, exchanging information, gathering about her cousin Charles, because everyone always did, some going to Cornwall, some to Somerset, some stopping the night, some ready to embark. Two or three were from his own regiment, but there were others who were his mere acquaintance: an engineer, a cavalry officer he had, it seemed, gathered on the road. Would Louisa remember all of that or only the subsequent event, the event that had led to her own, not Louisa's, incarceration, disgrace and all the troubles that had followed? Would she remember Charles finding it a grand excuse for a party, not that Charles had ever needed much of an excuse for one of those, the country dances and the springtime moonlit garden? No, Louisa had probably been sent to bed.

The next thing they knew, Charles was dead. It was the second great sadness in her life. She had lost her mother when she was a child, and at barely eighteen she had lost Charles, who had been to her as a brother. What of that could she say to Louisa? Suddenly the letter seemed harder to write than she had thought. Charles had died on the battlefield. And those other young men, what had been their fate? What carnage, what waste. As a family, they never learnt.

She stood up. Phil should have crossed the meadow and be back from school by now. She went to the window. The river could be seen and the stones of the castle, though Phil always said, crossly, that there was no castle. She could see the orchard. Where was Phil? She then saw Domino, the stout piebald pony, making the most of the June grass. Phil was there, not coming in, making his way towards the pony. He clambered awkwardly onto its back and lay on his front with his fair, curly head facing the tail, his legs hanging down, those skinny legs of which he was inexplicably ashamed. In one hand he held a long stick. She watched him. She looked at the river, the orchard, the view. Phil lay so still he might have fallen asleep. Of what did he dream? All of a sudden he sat up, slid from the pony and half-shouted, though his mother could not hear him, 'They can't, they can't.'

He ran as fast as he could up through the orchard, swinging his stick as if slashing at the buttercups with a sword. He reached the unkempt lawn and ran indoors.

Later that day, Robert Conway, a well-built, square-faced lad of twelve years old, the rector's eldest son, retreated to his own room in the rectory. It was not much of a room, but his own. If your home was a rectory as well as a school, having your own room was an object of importance. His younger brothers slept in the dormitories. Standing at the window, a spyglass in his hand, of the big house he saw nothing but the chimneys, for it was full summer; the surrounding trees were in leaf, and even the garden, such garden as there was, lay hidden by a tall dark hedge.

He had no need of the spyglass to see a woman and a small boy, Phil and his mother, walk out from the garden gate and slowly cross the meadow, hand in hand, the thin, little old dog following behind them. Robert's expression changed from one of nothing in particular to one of derision. He thought Phil too old to be holding his mother's hand. There too was the little girl, meandering like a plump bumblebee from one meadow flower to the next. Robert knew nothing of girls. His knowledge was all of boys – the boys in the school, his two young brothers, his cousins younger still – that even such a little girl was almost disturbing. The sensation was dispelled in a moment and his expression deepened to a greater mockery at the sudden appearance of his uncle, Stewart Conway, his father's younger brother, the schoolmaster, hastening, hastening across the meadow to intercept, to walk and talk. This namby-pamby walking and talking with a woman, a small boy and a little girl was surely food for scorn. Was there also something irregular in the proceeding? Robert, after all the rector's son, had, at least in theory, a correct knowledge of right and wrong. His uncle, like his father, was a widower, presumably able to walk and talk with whomever he liked, so he could not quite pin what might be amiss.

He turned away. On his bed lay his treasure, his dearest possession. Another uncle, an uncle he had never known, had died of wounds received in Spain. He had been a lieutenant in the 95th Rifles and no regiment could have pleased his nephew more, apart from one of a Light Dragoon. He had come home to die. His mother had kept his uniform and all his military effects but, just before her own death, she had given them to her eldest grandson with the words, 'I know, my dear Robert, you will revere them as you should.'

He had taken the uniform from its cedarwood trunk and laid the dark green jacket out on his bed because it was the tenth anniversary of the Battle of Waterloo, so what better day could there be for gazing lovingly on the black velvet collar and cuffs, the black silk cord that lavishly adorned the cloth, looped in horizontal rows between the silver ball buttons, of which there were three rows, rising from waist to shoulder and waist to throat, twenty-five in each. He unfolded the tasselled sash of crimson silk and fingered the black leather shoulder belt, the two silver chains that held the whistle and the lion's head boss. He dedicately touched the silver bugle, the regimental badge, on the shako with the cut green feather. He carefully slid the spyglass to its full extent and, placing it to his eye, again turned to the window. What was he to see? Not, he thought, the chimneys of Castle Orchard, not his Uncle Stewart or Phil and his mother, but rank upon rank of the enemy, mustering on a foreign plain.

Carefully, unwillingly, he put everything away again, left his room, rattled down the stairs and down the stairs again, to the boot room. It was a half-day but Jackson was back there all the same.

He was in full flow. 'I lost me leg an' me eye at Toulouse. I gets yer shrapnel in me knee an' I don't know what in me eye, but it weren't no good from then on. Now me knee is worth sixpence a day in pension money. Done it on the field they did, me leg. Assistant Surgeon Patterson it were. 'E said, "It'll rot, me old fellow, an' kill yer." Well, it were all smashed to bits . . . Twenty minutes that took. Yer leg can come off quicker than that, but mine took twenty minutes.

'Then it's yer hospital with all the stink an' the heat an' the flies. Gawd knows 'ow yer comes out of it alive. Some goes raving mad in there an' screams night an' day. Yer never gets a wink o' sleep. Bloody run yer bayonet through the lot of 'em, I would. Be kinder in the end.'

Jackson was, for a moment, silent, while contemplating his lost limb and the fact that he was still alive, before his mind wandered on. He was inclined to repeat himself; the boys had some of it by heart. He shifted his weight to make his absent leg more comfortable and said, 'Boys nowadays is soft as butter. There were boys in the Army some as young as you young gentlemen.' The sneer in Jackson's voice was evident as he said the word 'gentlemen'. He had been a thorn in the side of every officer who ever had command of him, though capable in battle.

'Sieges, they're nasty things. One o' them Spanish places we did in winter with the river all over ice but we still 'ave to get in it an' walk through it, like pretendin' it were a field o' rye more high than yer bellies an' just as pleasant. Black an' blue yer was when yer got out o' that river, frozen from the ice dandling yer about like a babby an' yer clothes stiff like yer couldn't bend. Then what? Yer 'ave to dig the trenches what is rock solid while the Frenchies blast yer to bits with grapeshot an' such.'

The little boys in the boot room stare and shiver but Robert Conway says, 'Well, what happens then, Jackson?'

'Yer brings up yer siege train, happen you've got it, and blast away at yer walls. A breach is what yer makes. Then yer generals speak an' say an' yer gets yer Forlorn 'Ope. Now yer Forlorn 'Ope is those what is ready to go first through the breach an' yer volunteers are in a rare taking for that sort o' sport. If yer wants to warm yer blood yer goes forward yerself, like, an' yer officers is mad for it an' cheer yer in as if 'twas a party: o' course they die, most of 'em. Still, there is always more what fills their places. Yer die in odd ways, yer know. Some goes round and round like birds afore they dies.'

Castle Orchard must belong to someone. It belonged to a Mr Arthur, known as Johnny to his innumerable friends. He was of that set of gentlemen known as dandies or 'exquisites' and they tended to address him as though he were a child. It was not an era in which a man might call his friends by their Christian names, but Arthur gave the impression of never having grown up. He was a slave to all things fashionable – from wearing a frockcoat with a nicety of gathering at the shoulders, a neckcloth just so ... gloves just so ... snuffbox, dancing pumps, canes, pins, quizzing glasses, all just so ... and exaggerated and ridiculous – to never paying his bills and passing his time at the gaming tables. He was even able to set the fashion. His charm lay in his ability to find his own follies and the follies of fashion all amusing – and he laughed away at his own mishaps and escapades, and was declared a good fellow. As for Castle Orchard, he was estranged from it, this rustic retreat, as a man might be from his wife or even his best friend, estranged but unable to break the link that bound him to it.

He was of medium height and slender, but a little pull-ing in here and a little puffing out there was necessary to retain an elegant slightness of figure. His head was crowned with yellow curls, naturally his own. His face was round and pale and his eyes large, childlike and blue. He had been known to say that as a youth he had been pretty and ethereal – but maturity, for Arthur was past thirty, had made him handsome. He was no longer ethereal except to his creditors, who found in him a curious lack of substance. If he was to be associated with Castle Orchard, it could only be to the little, mostly blue, butterflies that flew, with a dizzying frenzy, over the kidney vetch and trefoil of his native chalk. His nature was that of a butterfly.

It was four o'clock in the afternoon. Arthur had breakfasted and left his lodgings in Half Moon Street. To leave his lodgings was an art, owing to the importunings of the myriads who, able to sneak up the stairs, haunted the landing hoping for some little amount towards their bills. He was making his way to the Haymarket in order to dally in the heavenly delights of the Old Snuff House. He had with him a young friend whom he had decided to patronise. The young friend had the makings of being quite as fanciful a creature as Johnny himself and had lent him a small sum of money, which act needed repaying somehow as it was not at all likely to be repaid in the customary fashion, of which both were aware.

It being June, Piccadilly was thronged with every sort of fashionable vehicle, cabriolets and curricles, each more elegant than the last; gentlemen on the finest horses and wearing the finest coats and boots and waistcoats and neckcloths, and tall hats with curly brims; ladies driving their own horses and pairs of horses matched to the last hair in their tails. Ladies in beautiful habits, with exquisite bonnets, ladies with crests on their cabriolets and liveried footmen and grooms, and the whole conglomeration wishing to be seen in Hyde Park sometime between the hours of four and six o'clock.

Such was fashionable London, aware yet unaware of the other London, a street away, thronged with the working poor, the beggars, the prostitutes, all of whom could arise as one body and become the mob, capable of murder though more often merely breaking windows; the partisan mob either shouting for reform or condemning Roman Catholics, all an excuse to throw stones.

'Why don't you ride?' the younger man asked Arthur, waving his hand in the direction of the mêlée.

'Oh, I have done, I have done, but a horse is a tiresome thing. I have from time to time given my heart to a horse, but a horse needs a groom and a stable and I'm not a rich man. One hundred and fifty pounds a year, at the least, for a horse and a groom. Whenever I have had a horse it has ended up in the bazaar, and next I look round to find it is being enjoyed by somebody else. Never mind. I don't really care for riding. My delicate frame will hardly withstand it.' Here Arthur smiled and laughed, knowing his frame would stand it perfectly well, choosing to make himself ridiculous. At the same time he raised his quizzing glass and stared fixedly at a pretty girl passing by in an open carriage with her mother beside her. His young friend thought this rude, but he knew it acceptable conduct for a dandy, who was expected to be rude to women, to ignore them, leave them without chairs or embarrass them with prolonged attention.

Arthur, as if reading his mind, said, 'What a delicious, timorous creature, wrapped in fifty layers of gossamer. How stupid she would be if you found yourself next to her at dinner, but yes, a delightful child and to be ogled by me will make her quite the thing. I am conferring a favour by noticing her.'

'Put that way, I suppose . . .'

'No need to suppose anything. It is so if I say so. What a horrid crowd. One can hardly get along the pavement. Think of the dust, if the streets were not watered. I should have to retire and live on my estate in order to breathe. What a calamity. What should I do?'

He said no more until they reached their destination. Here, the Old Snuff House provided him with a few cronies, and threequarters of an hour was idled away in choosing and ordering. The young friend felt surplus to requirements and, eager as he was to retain his place beside the august person of Arthur, wondered if it was not the tactful moment to escape . . . but no, he was summoned and told they must proceed to St Martin's Lane for the purchasing of buttons.

'My tailor is making a coat,' Arthur announced.

Silence pervaded while the younger man contemplated the paying of the tailor. Arthur took his arm in a companionable manner. He introduced him here and there. He hesitated before leaving the Haymarket, for he was close to the perfumer's. His mind went to Oil of Roses but he determinedly turned his back. The young friend dodged a Punch and Judy Show and tripped over some ragged little boys.

'Your coat is so much the best,' he said, 'I wonder you can bear to get another.'

He looked down at his own coat and wished he was less plump. The buttons were under stress.

'A gentleman must have a new coat,' Arthur declared, 'or he would be nothing. I shall go into the country, for it's June and shortly Quarter Day. The rents, for I take them on a quarterly basis, await me, and I shall rain pounds on the head of my tailor.' He laughed. 'Everybody owes their tailor. I should be quite ashamed not to owe him something. Only nobodies, like Allington, don't owe anything.'

'Who is Allington?'

'Why, nobody. Didn't I say so?'

They were soon absorbed in buttons. The choice was wide. Arthur thought of silk and then of silver and then of gilt or even of gold while rejecting mother-of-pearl. His friend fancied the ivory, but Arthur settled for gilt.

'Are they not rather dear?'

Arthur gazed at him in mock astonishment. 'My dear fellow, pecuniary interests may be reflected in the case of horses or opera girls, but not of buttons. They are too important.' He then, of course, laughed.

They hired a hackney carriage to take them back to Half Moon Street. While the younger man paid, Arthur searched the crowds about his door and on the stairs for anyone who was likely to serve him a writ. For a moment he was uneasy but it was generally understood that Quarter Day would settle any debt of too pressing a nature. He elbowed his way to his apartments followed by his friend, a chorus of voices vying with the barrel organ in the street.

'Settle our bills, sir, or the law will 'ave yer!'

'Quarter Day, Quarter Day,' Arthur answered, airily waving a glove in passing.

The door being slammed on the press, the younger man reached in his pocket to mop his brow, only to find his silk handkerchief gone.

'Some small urchin will be flogging it, you may be sure, at this very moment. I hope you still have your watch,' Arthur remarked, placing his cane in a stand amongst a host of other canes.

'Indeed, I have my watch,' his friend replied, anxiously feeling his waistcoat, whilst peering at himself in one of the two handsome looking glasses that dominated the apartment. He had been in Arthur's rooms before and was, as usual, amazed and absorbed by the richness of the clutter. Johnny liked to collect things and was never content unless adding to the cabinets of snuffboxes and boxes for tooth-picks; quizzing glasses, watches, rings, bottles of scent and cascades of silk awaited selection. A large dressing case lay open on a table and further bits and pieces spilled out of it.

Arthur's demeanour suddenly changed. He held up his hand and said, 'Listen, is that Allington going up? Open the door a crack. Quick, do as I say, Rampton.'

Thus appealed to by name, the young man, though bewildered, opened the door just a fraction. He saw noth-ing but the debt collectors and duns on the landing, but they then parted like the Red Sea and a voice said coolly, 'Good day, gentlemen.'

All that could be seen was the long shadow of someone going up the stairs to the top floor.

'Did you wish to speak to him?' Rampton asked.

'Certainly not,' Arthur replied.

'Well, he is gone. Did you wish *me* to speak to him?'

'No. As you are not acquainted with him, you could hardly halloo him on the stairs as if he were a servant. He was in the street when we went out. He always gives money to the raggedy one-armed beggar on the corner, late of His Majesty's 299th Foot.'

Rampton wondered why he had been required to open the door to watch the progress of a man, of whom only his shadow could be seen, going upstairs – and to whom Arthur had no intention of speaking.

'I keep an eye on him,' Arthur said. 'Perhaps your father knows him. He frequents the Travellers'. He makes a living in a peculiar way.'

'My father would not know a man who had to make a living in any way,' Rampton replied, laughing.

'Ah, but it would not be apparent. He plays cards.'

'Who doesn't?'

'He wins.'

'Always?'

Arthur shrugged. 'He must occasionally lose, if he is dealt a very bad hand.'

'But he has unbelievable luck?' Rampton suggested.

'It's not luck.'

'You don't say he cheats?'

'I shouldn't dare say any such thing.'

'But you believe it?'

'No, no, besides, he plays no hazard, no games of chance. It is, no doubt, why he prefers the Travellers', because there they play only whist and ecarté, with no cards before dinner. As you are a member yourself, I hardly need tell you this.'

'Indeed, I am a member, but I don't go.'

'Allington will play piquet, chess, backgammon draughts, but chess is his game.'

'It would be difficult to cheat at that.'

'He's clever – he forgets nothing. I myself give him a game if it is unwise to leave my rooms. There are times when I just can't get out. Suppose the bailiffs took my snuffboxes? It is my belief Allington makes so much money he can live off it. He has enough to keep a pretty actress.'

Rampton could not help wondering how Arthur could afford to play with this person. After all, if such debts occurred, they were debts of honour: one was required to pay them immediately.

'It can't be his sole source of income,' he said.

'Oh, he is a half-pay officer but that doesn't amount to

anything. I dare say he got a meagre allowance from his father or his stepfather or whatever he was.'

'And who was he?'

'Lord Tregorn.'

'And he was his stepfather?'

'So it is said.' Arthur rolled his blue eyes and smiled. 'They all say that, don't they? Except Allington. He says nothing. When I find it judicious to stay at home, I send my servant to ask if he will step down and give me a game. Sometimes he will and sometimes he won't. From time to time he's downright rude, which I feel a man in his position has no right to be. If I have a couple of friends in to dine, we ask Allington to join us later in a few rubbers of whist. He won't always come even then.' Arthur paused to reflect. He then said, 'Debts of honour between gentlemen?' He laid peculiar emphasis on the word 'gentlemen'. 'What makes a man a gentleman?'

Rampton had no doubt he was himself a gentleman, but then there was no irregularity attached to his birth.

Arthur continued, 'But I have not told you the half of his peculiarities. It is, anyway, unfortunate to be in the same lodgings as a military man. I sometimes wish I might change them for that very reason, but I have a good understanding with my landlord, whom I always make sure I pay the moment I get my rents in. Some other might oblige me less.'

'What's wrong with a military man?' Rampton enquired.

'They are so superior, they have the attitude of one who has seen all. They forget that the rest of us don't want to see what they have seen, or even to have been to all those foreign places. Think of the blood, the violence, the severed limbs, the floggings, the hardship. We don't want our sensibilities blunted by fields of corpses.'

'Perhaps their sensibilities were not very strong in the first place.'

'How can one tell? Today is the eighteenth day of the sixth month. Had you not considered how we should be celebrating the death of all the young brothers of our friends and acquaintances? I had no younger brother myself, which was a blessing. My father had no one too immediate with whom to compare me. To think a man pays a fortune to buy a commission, say £3,000 for a captain in a respectable cavalry regiment, for a son, solely for the purpose of having the boy's sensibilities totally deadened before he is butchered. Is it not odd?'

Rampton, who had never before given the matter a moment's thought, agreed. They were interrupted by Arthur's servant entering the room with a rose-pink figured-silk waistcoat on his arm.

'To think,' Arthur said, 'when on campaign, they are often unable to change their clothes or wash for weeks. What must that *do* to a man?'

'It must make him unbearable, but I suppose they are all in it together, a stable full of brute beasts.' Rampton was casting envious eyes at the waistcoat as he spoke.

'Not for you, my friend,' Arthur said, laughing. 'You are more full in the figure than me and will do best to stick to a darker shade. Your coat needs altering at the shoulder. The cap of the sleeve could be a little less, I suppose, though it's useless to endeavour to turn you into a seriously fashionable man.'

'Why ever not?' Rampton asked, affronted, for he had been under the impression he was already a seriously fashionable man.

'Not a hope.' Johnny Arthur gave his customary peal

of laughter. He leaped out of his chair, seized one of his canes and darted about the room while making slashing motions, both at Rampton and his valet, the latter dodging and skipping to avoid him. 'If this were a sabre I could cut off your head.'

He sat down as abruptly as he had got up. His servant settled to rescuing the dressing case that had been dislodged.

'Allington has a cane,' he said.

'Don't we all?' Rampton replied abruptly, not pacified.

'We all have canes but we don't need them. They are only for show. Allington's is more of a walking stick.'

'Mine is for show,' Rampton said, picking it up and admiring its fine, flexible length and the little gold knob at the top with his engraved initials. 'My father had it made for me.'

'Your father is a poet. Why could I not have a poet for a father? How he would have understood and appreciated me. Alack, it was not so and my father has been dead these last ten years without ever knowing what a treasure he had in his only child. Oh, the filial piety I would have expressed in exchange for a few kind words.'

Arthur took the cane and examined it closely. He then said, 'The only cane my father gave me was one with which to give me a hiding. Well, that's not true, but it sounds good. I don't recall he ever beat me much, but he was so stern and so dull. He would have made a good soldier, he had so little feeling. They can have no feeling or they couldn't do the things they have to do. You listen to the way they talk. A military man will tell you how a bullet did for his best coursing dog at Salamanca and how he had his favourite horse shot from under him at Vitoria and a couple more after that. He might continue by saying the regiment lost a hundred men that day, or the Army several thousand. What he will not mention is the loss of his best friend and both his brothers. No, no, he is more likely to remark that they had only half a chicken for the officers' mess and nowhere to eat it but a roofless barn while the wolves ate the corpses outside.'

'And such a man is this Allington?' Rampton asked, slightly shocked.

'How should I know? He doesn't say enough to me that I should ever find out. Indeed, I believe some military men may be retrained for civilisation – I know of a few – and we must have soldiers or Napoleon would have translated us all into French by now. Your father never wanted you to be a soldier?'

'Certainly not, though he thought it all very well and good for some.'

'My father thought to be a soldier would make a man of me and I should come home all glorious, if minus a limb or two. If I wouldn't be a soldier I must at least be a fox hunter. Now the fox hunter is a soldier manqué, but his injuries are self-inflicted. He thinks himself a hero all the same and his broken bones honourable. My father would hunt when he was seventy-three and then coming off, as was inevitable, my mother must nurse him, attend to his whims and his bad temper. Allington is, I believe, a fox hunter, and under his circumstance, I doubt he's any safer than my father was in advanced old age. God knows who would nurse Allington. His servant, I suppose, if he was sober.'

Arthur's own servant here emerged from a closet with an armful of clothes and said, 'Excuse me, sir, but you asked me to remind you of the time. You are to meet Sir John.' He spoke with a French accent.

'Dear me,' Arthur said, looking at his watch. 'It takes me hours to dress. I shall be late.'

Rampton stood up to take his leave but there was something on his mind. 'I defy anyone to say I am not up to the mark. My tailor is the best, yet you say you couldn't make a fashionable man of me.' He tried not to sound as peeved as he felt.

Arthur again laughed. 'My dear fellow, it wasn't my intention to offend you. It's just that you are a married man. Whatever induced you to take a wife so young? A married man is nothing, for he's saddled himself with the very worst thing – domesticity. Didn't you tell me you aren't free this evening, for you take your wife to the opera? Domesticity is the end, the bottom, the disaster, the bills, the housemaids, the whooping cough, the child once a year. A mistress one may have, some charming little nothing – I have had one myself when I have been in funds – but a wife is the ultimate rope by which a fashionable man may hang himself.'

Arthur looked teasingly at his young friend, who went away with a long face to take Mrs Rampton to the opera. Arthur himself spent the next hour in adjusting a fresh white neckcloth, a frill of a shirt, a narrow pair of trousers, a coat nipped in at the waist, puffed at the shoulder and lean at the cuff, and the rose-pink waistcoat.

When satisfied, he peeked through his door and finding that most of his tormentors had gone away for their dinners, he went downstairs and into the street and from thence to his club in St James', where he might quickly lose the little bit of money lent him.

Captain Allington was craning out of the window as Arthur walked away down Half Moon Street. The sight of this gentleman, or rather the sight of his very tall, very curly-brimmed hat, evinced no change in his expression. He was not interested in Arthur, though occasionally the words of the Irish songwriter passed unbidden through his head:

'Quite a new sort of creature, unknown yet to scholars,
With heads so immovably stuck in shirt-collars.
That seats, like our music-stools, soon must be found
    them,
To twirl, when the creatures, may wish to look round
    them.'

He was leaning from the window in order to see the trees of Green Park, noting, despite the beautiful blue of the June sky, there was still the wisp of a haze induced by too many coal-burning stoves.

He turned his back on the window and surveyed his room. It contained an armchair, two large watercolours of the Cornish coast, a great many books, a writing desk and a table. On his desk lay an unopened letter, addressed to himself, and on the table a large glass bottle half full of sixpences. He crossed the room, picked up the letter, broke the seal and unfolded it, without any appearance of haste. It was, as such, the third he had received.

My dearest, dearest Allington,

Please allow me to speak. Every hair on your head is precious to me. I love you, I love you. Please, please listen. How could you think so ill of me?

I know it must seem strange to you to find Smythe here at breakfast. He and Sir John Parkes came here last night, and, not finding you, settled to play cards.

23

I offered them what wine I had, which I thought you would wish, for you never have minded my entertaining, but they were soon drunk and would not leave. What could I do? I retired to bed, they fell asleep and caused no further trouble. Sir John left only a few minutes before you arrived. Pray, believe me.

You have never told me you harbour any great passion for me. I assumed you had an affection for me at the least. You may not love me, but have our hearts not beat as one? Does that count for nothing?

You told me you wished to be able to rely on my fidelity. I am innocent, so innocent, of all you think.

Yours, your most devastated,
Lucy Marietti

Allington screwed this letter up and chucked it in the wastepaper basket without anger or excitement, perhaps disgust. He said, half out loud, 'Very theatrical, but what should one expect from an actress? No, I won't see her. There would be tears and she's not telling the truth.'

His servant came in carrying a jug of hot water. He was a small, neat, middle-aged man with a face screwed up in anxious enquiry.

'Did you speak, sir?' he asked.

'Not really, Nat. Pour me out that water.' He was still thinking about the letter. Ending such an affair was for the best. It was an expense and he only really wished to spend money that way if it was to lead to something more permanent. He supposed the whole thing had been in the nature of an unsatisfactory experiment. He was, in some ways, an idealist and it had not been ideal, his emotions

24

remaining unscathed when he had rather hoped they might become engaged.

Allington walked through to the bedroom, stripping off his coat, his neckcloth and his waistcoat as he did so. He had been in the boxing salon in Bond Street, hitting the punching bag, an occupation that kept him fit and relieved his feelings at the same time.

His servant obediently poured out the water. He was thinking about the date and the battle but he thought better of mentioning it.

At his washstand Allington pulled off his shirt. He was a man somewhere between thirty and thirty-five, slim and dark-haired but for an odd streak of white rising from his left temple: his back and his chest were deeply scarred.

Later that afternoon he went to the Travellers' Club. There he played whist. It was not a gambling club, there was no faro, macao or hazard, and no one was likely to lose or gain a fortune in a night's play. It was a club in which Allington could steadily apply himself after the dining hour to winning rubbers of whist and at no one person's expense, for the club was the universal player. He could return the markers to the clerk and collect the money when he fancied, a procedure which suited him well enough. In this, he thought, it differed much to playing chess with Arthur, who had a quixotic brilliance, an eccentricity of play which was amusing, but Allington had long since ceased to expect to be paid.

His was not a popular figure nor yet was he disliked. Men were shy of him. He took no alcohol. His tongue was sharp; he was not talkative, but if his views were sought on some issue of the day, he would give a considered reply, often at length.

There was sport to be had out of him. As Arthur had said, chess, draughts, ecarté, backgammon, piquet, were all grist to his mill but chess was preferred. He never challenged others, yet he could be approached, his glass of lemonade purchased for him and a few hesitant suggestions made as to how he might entertain them. They would choose him an opponent, lay out the pieces, and then wager, not on the outcome of Allington's winning the game but on the time it would take, even which moves might be made. The stake between Allington and his opponent was five guineas a game though he sometimes made it ten if he felt so inclined. From time to time he would take a cut on the general winnings, which could be considerable. Occasionally, if it had been a good game, he refused the money altogether. He would then go over the play, point out what alternative moves could have been made and diversify on the various dilemmas. He did this so rapidly he was rarely understood. Perhaps they traversed the club rules but nothing was said. The bets could be considered as of a private nature and laying wagers of one sort or another was a universal occupation. Captain Allington himself was the exception: he never bet on anything.

On this particular day there were two very young men, mere boys, in the Travellers' Club, who had managed to fulfil the club criterion of having travelled five hundred miles in a direct line from London, and being anxious for further adventures had the notion of visiting the battlefields of Spain and Portugal, to follow in the footsteps of Wellington's army. They had the relevant map pulled down on the wall. Wellington's army had traversed the breadths of Spain and Portugal, back and forth, from 1808 to 1814, rather too long, when the cost was considered, but these two young men had cheered the passing troops, the British Redcoats, when they were children, running beside the soldiers and gambolling like lambs at the thought of war. Now they fell out with one another on the route they should take or which route would be closest to the original.

Someone said, 'Ask Allington. He was there.'

'Ask Allington?' they repeated.

'Why not? He was there.'

'But we are not introduced to him, and even supposing we were, we couldn't ask him.'

The gentleman they spoke to was an old soldier, not afraid of Allington. He got up on two sticks, went to the library and approached Allington himself with the request. Allington, without saying much, entered the map room. The two young men stood back and bowed respectfully. He took up his cane and without further ado said, 'August the seventeenth 1808, Rolica.' He pointed to it on the map. The Portuguese name rolled off his tongue.

He continued swiftly, 'August the twenty-first, Vimeiro. Over December and January, the retreat to Corunna.'

He broke into Spanish, giving the dates of each battle and adding the figures of how many soldiers were lost at each, all the time pointing rapidly to the map. It took him some time to get to the finish, for he covered the sieges of Ciudad Rodrigo, Badajoz and Burgos, before concluding with Toulouse, 10 April 1814. Having done that he said, in Spanish, 'Why go there? Each one is a graveyard. ¿Es que no tienes otro sitio a donde ir?'

As neither young man had understood a word of what he had said, though they had followed the rapid movement of the cane over the map, they looked at him in bewilderment.

Allington relented sufficiently to translate the last sentence: 'Have you nowhere different to go?'

One of them said, 'We thought it would be of interest, sir.'

'Those battles are too new, too young. Go and see where Hannibal crossed the Alps. If you must go, learn Spanish.'

They thanked him, but when he had gone they looked at each other in confusion. Turning back to the map they again began to plot a route but their heads were spinning.

'Now, my young fellows,' the old soldier said, amused, 'you are not much the wiser. You forget the size of the army – seventy, a hundred thousand men. They are in divisions. First you might follow one bit and then another. He gave you the major battles, not all the skirmishes. There is a jack-in-the-box quality to Allington. You never know what will come out of him. Waterloo killed him, but such a man is wasted in civilian life. It's the tenth anniversary. You have set yourselves an impossible task. He was teasing you.'

It was fashionable to be seen at the opera. To go from the opera, to come from the opera, to attend a rout or a ball, even if only to stand on the stair, meant risking one's person, one's horses and coach in the mêlée, the impasse of London's West End at six o'clock in the evening. Should wheels lock and tempers fray, the whole could take hours to untangle.

Young Mrs Rampton thought the opera a bore, but to enjoy it was not a necessity. She gazed with languid fascination at women she supposed to be high-class courtesans and wondered at the impropriety of London society. It was, she considered, the fault of the King: he set a bad example. She tried not to yawn but it was hot and she was tired.

Her father-in-law had taken a box. It was full of people she hardly knew. The conversation was of Harriet Wilson, whose memoirs were being published.

'Who is Harriet Wilson?' she whispered to her father-in-law.

'Don't ask, my dear,' he whispered back.

Her husband then leaned forward and said, 'Who is Captain Allington?'

'The natural son of the late Lord Tregorn, though he's not acknowledged as such.'

'Why does he make Mr Arthur so nervous?'

'Arthur owes him a lot of money.'

'Has he lent him money?'

'They are gaming debts. He never asks Arthur for the money. Arthur gives him IOUs and Captain Allington puts them away in his pocketbook – hundreds of them, it is said. I hope you lent Arthur no money.'

'A tiny bit, a mere nothing.'

Mrs Rampton said, 'Is it not rather irresponsible to be so much in debt?'

'In society, my dear, no one thinks anything of it.'

A tiny frown appeared on the hitherto unruffled brow of Mrs Rampton: she did not like the implication she might be ignorant of society. If association with Mr Arthur, however elevating and agreeable, meant her husband was likely to catch his habits, she would not tolerate it.

They left the opera with a little crowd. The confusion had not abated: the postilions, the coachmen, the liveried grooms, the lads known as tigers, in striped waistcoats – fashionable appendages to cling behind gentlemen's landaulets – the glossy rumps of the fine thoroughbred horses, the shining harness, the brass and the gilt, the top hats, the whips and the emblazoned coats of arms ... it was pandemonium.

Surveying the scene, somebody remarked, 'And any minute now the season will end, the parks will be dry as dust and the chance of falling in with an agreeable acquaintance will be ...'

Arthur, in his club, had abandoned, for the minute, all games of chance in order to eat an early dinner in the dining room. He was in the best of spirits, being at this stage of the evening, in funds. He had won a considerable sum of money.

His companion, Sir John Parkes, was a crony of his, a little older than himself, dissolute, perhaps dishonest, but altogether sharp and shrewd. Arthur viewed him as excellent company and was at that moment listening to, but without heeding, his advice.

'If you would but go home now, Johnny Arthur, you would do yourself a favour.'

'Go home just when my luck has turned? Why, you must be mad.'

'Not mad, merely sensible.'

'Damn sense. What's the news? Tell me the gossip,' Arthur said.

'They say the little singer, Marietti, has left our friend Captain Allington, or he has left her, on account of Smythe. Perhaps you can tell me about that?'

'Allington tells me nothing. We share a roof, but that's all. Why, if I spoke to him more, I should have to ask him to dine. I play the odd game of this and that, to pass the time, but one need not speak. You've often been there yourself. Why ask me about him?'

'Why not ask him to dine?'

'How can one? In public, he drinks no wine.'

'So?'

'Think of having a man at one's table who drinks only lemonade. If one should drink with him, which one must out of politeness, raise one's glass, catch his eye – and what has he got? Lemonade, or worse, water.' The notion, so ridiculous, made Arthur give his usual peal of laughter.

'In public he takes no alcohol. What do you imply by that?'

Arthur helped himself to a cut of rare roast beef. 'On his own, he drinks to excess.'

'How do you know?'

'A simple matter of deduction. He's often ill. He vomits, lies in bed, draws the curtains, can't bear a noise, lets no one near him but his servant. There is nothing so unusual in that, we all know the sensations, but he must think such excesses aren't the thing. In his efforts to control it, he tries to abstain altogether. After all, a man getting an income the way he does can't afford to be drunk. And then he tolerates that servant of his who is quite frequently drunk. Anyone else would have dismissed the fellow years ago, but he has, you see, a sympathy for him. He's anyway odd in his choice of servants, for his groom is a deaf-mute. Maybe he isn't mute, but I never heard him speak.'

'Allington doesn't say much, so perhaps he has a sympathy for him too.'

This made both men laugh. They broached another decanter of wine. It sat on the table, squat and ruby-red. Arthur was slightly tipsy. He had drunk one bottle already.

'Captain Allington is not only of doubtful birth—' he began.

31

'Hush, don't speak so loud.'

'Why not? Everybody knows it.'

'Now listen, Johnny. What everybody knows is often wrong. I told you a bit of gossip just now which is incorrect.'

'About Allington leaving the Marietti? I was going to come around to that. Isn't it true?'

'It wasn't Smythe, it was me. Smythe was drunk but innocent. I was less drunk and guilty. Some instinct for self-preservation made me leave before breakfast. Smythe was less lucky.'

Arthur drew in his breath. He said, 'Allington challenged him?'

'Allington said nothing. He came. He saw. He walked out.'

'But it's not at all a pretty situation. Allington will want satisfaction. Was he not in the Ninety-fifth? Aren't they all devilish fine shots? Maybe the officers don't have to shoot, but only to run in front to show it is good to be shot at. Ah, but then maybe he was a Light Dragoon so he will hack the pair of you to bits with his sabre.' Arthur was momentarily overcome with mirth, but then he said, more soberly, 'I stand your friend.'

'They don't use sabres nowadays, not for duelling,' Sir John said coldly, while contemplating the unlikely role of Arthur as a second. 'If it was so, he is lame – one could outmanoeuvre him. I wouldn't find much honour in killing a lame man because I went to bed with his mistress. If it comes to a fight, it will have to be pistols. It's my belief, besides, you have confused his regiments.' He was leaning anxiously across to his companion, who could see the rouge on his cheeks.

'Allington won't fight you, Sir John. He will look at you with the silent disdain a guardsman would have for a speck of dust on his boot.'

Sir John, not caring for the comparison, said, 'Such a man as Allington wouldn't be cowardly.'

Arthur fixed him with his round, childish blue eyes. A little shudder escaped him, something that disturbed the breast beneath the rose-pink waistcoat. He whispered, 'They say he was brave to the point of madness, that he was an intelligence officer. But I hope you haven't upset him, made him peevish or irrational. I owe him a great deal of money.'

'So I understand. I have frequently watched the procedure.'

'He may suddenly ask for it – and they are debts of honour.'

'Mortgage your estate, mortgage Castle Orchard.'

'But I shall lose all my bets. It is a strange father to make a will so to disoblige his son. Trustees held my estate until I was thirty, as if I were a minor . . . the indignity of it. And then the bets I made, even with you, that I wouldn't mortgage it, sell it, lose it, before I was thirty-five. I have two years to go and then I shall make a lot of money. Otherwise I shall have to pay a lot out – and how could I do that? You see, it is important to me not to have Allington disturbed. Every betting book in every club in London has evidence of . . .' He was going to say 'my folly', but not being in the mood to admit to such a thing, he bit the sentence off.

'You must do your sums and choose the lesser evil.' Sir John knew it was not only Allington to whom Arthur owed money. Could there be anyone more familiar with the shady world of the moneylenders than Johnny Arthur? What were the sums involved – and did Arthur know them himself? The sums were more, perhaps, than the value of Castle Orchard, which Sir John thought closer in size to four thousand than forty thousand acres, a good but not a grand estate.

Arthur said, 'Ah well, it will soon be Quarter Day. I wish it didn't necessitate my going down to Castle Orchard. The rudeness of the country, the inconvenience. You lucky dogs with no beastly land attached to your purses: cottages, widows, barns, ditches, roads, thatch, flint, brick, all like lumps of lead ready to make holes in your pockets, not forgetting the retired servants and your father's wet nurse, all to be pensioned and never dying. Your father's wet nurse never dies. Did you know that? They are immortal if they have a pension. I don't wish to go to the horrid green fields and the horrid wet river.'

'Why go then? Tell your agent to send the rents.'

Arthur sighed but made no reply. After a moment, he said, 'I tried my mother again, but since she had the paralytic stroke, it is even harder to make her understand things. I say, "Mother, I must flee to Calais, my debts are so pressing", and she replies, "Your father always said you were a naughty boy, Johnny. You had better go on to Paris for it is pleasant at this time of year".'

Sir John said, 'And should I kill Allington in a duel, I suppose it would be of the greatest convenience to you? Come, don't look so shocked. I am no hero and value my skin. I'll lend you my coach for your journey to Wiltshire, if go you must.'

There was a little house in Chelsea where a woman wrote letters at a satinwood desk. Her abundant black hair was tied up with scarlet ribbons, which now and again fell over her forehead. She pushed them away impatiently, never raising her eyes from the ink and the paper.

Her first letter was to Thomas Smythe Esq. seeking his protection. Her second was to Sir John Parkes, seeking his protection and, a mere hint, a house more fashionably placed. Her third letter was to the manager of a theatre declaring herself anxious to resume her career. Her fourth letter was to Captain Allington, confused, contradictory, begging his forgiveness and protesting her innocence all in the same breath. She thought of what she had told Sir John, that Allington was a cripple and an invalid. She thought of Allington's cool, dark eyes and of his dark hair, soft as a child's but with that streak of white – she believed the result of a wound to his head, for he certainly did not mention such things. She wondered if he would call out Smythe or Sir John Parkes and if he were peculiarly jealous of his honour. What Allington might or might not do remained a mystery to her and she laid her head on her arms and wept, for had he not been kind?

Allington had returned to his lodgings in Half Moon Street but he was restless and had half a mind to take a walk in the park before changing to dine out. His servant came in and handed him letters. He took them to the window. There was yet another from Miss Marietti. This he barely bothered to read before tearing it up and throwing it away. He then opened the next which was signed *Your most obedient servant, T. Smythe*. It was short, apologetic, humble, but gave word of honour as a gentleman of innocence in respect of a certain lady who had a house in Chelsea. The only solecism Smythe could admit to was drunkenness. He indicated that he would have been too drunk to commit the indiscretion of which gossip accused him. If Captain Allington felt his honour compromised, he was willing to meet him at a time and place convenient to him.

The third letter was from Sir John Parkes. It was haughty in tone but indicated that a certain woman could not be relied on to give evidence or speak the truth, that her motive was one of sour grapes for Parkes having rejected her on a previous occasion; and last of all, unwisely, suggested Allington should believe the evidence of his own eyes as he was known to have visited the premises in Chelsea in time for breakfast.

Allington went to his desk and sat down to write a letter for himself but he paused to think. Of the two, he believed Smythe rather than Parkes, the latter not being a man he could trust. He cared little either way, only wishing he did not have to live amongst such people. He occasionally reflected on the anomaly of having sacrificed his health and very nearly his life, so that Arthur and his like could prink about the streets unmolested by pillaging French infantry. Eventually he wrote to Smythe and enclosed the letter he had received from Parkes, concluding that if they had a need to quarrel, it need not be with him.

He picked up a book but finding his servant still in the room, he said, 'Well, Nat, you must take this letter for me. It seems you have earned your sixpence today. You shall have it now, though the day is not yet over.'

'I got that sixpence every day this week or my name is not Nathaniel Pride.'

Allington said, without looking up from his book, 'So I have observed.'

Pride took the sixpence and dropped it into the bottle on the table. He wondered if his master smiled. He made as if to go downstairs to deliver the letter but as he went he muttered, 'Reading those darned books, it can only do his head a mischief.'

Allington said, 'Did you say something, Nat?'

'No, sir.'

This time Allington did smile but Pride did not see it. After five minutes he closed the book and went downstairs himself. Arthur's creditors were, as usual, occupying the space but they moved aside for Allington.

He walked swiftly, or as swiftly as his slight lameness would allow, to the end of the street and entered the Green Park, turning towards Hyde Park, now rather deserted. Thus he avoided Apsley House, the residence of His Grace the Duke of Wellington. The pavement might be thronging with eminent military men, generals and major-generals, colonels and princes, gathering for the anniversary dinner. Some of them would know him, a man who could pass as a Spaniard or a Portuguese, who spoke languages fluently, who could be got to go behind the French lines. Some would be regretting he was a half-pay officer and wishing a job could be found for him, but most of them would know that the wounds he had received had left him unfit for any sort of service.

He needed to walk. His lameness was more apparent. There were times when he seemed able to disguise it. Now he walked as if he would put London behind him. Customarily he took particular pleasure in the greenness, the trees and the few cows the park offered, but today it was difficult to be distracted. He lost his sense of purpose and walked much more slowly. He watched a pigeon fly, sailing along with its wings outstretched, only occasionally finding it necessary to give them a few casual flaps. It dived and swooped, perfect in motion, free. He had used to feel like that himself, his limbs, his whole body, his very brains, all in accord, and what was more, invincible. At Waterloo his luck had run out. What was an anniversary? In this case it was three hundred and sixty-five days multiplied by ten, minus the leap years. A sum so trifling could hardly be considered a sum, yet his head, as if struck again by the sword of a Frenchman, was utterly confused.

He hesitated and seemed to lose direction, occasionally stopping altogether and covering his eyes with his hand. Now, to a few casual passers-by, he looked not only lame but white and ill. At length, as if defeated, he turned and retraced his steps.

The street door of his lodgings was open. He went up the first flight of stairs. The duns and the debt collectors parted before him. They were staring at him. He reached his own landing without giving them his customary greeting. He fumbled for his key but Pride was at the door and swung it wide. Allington sat down at his desk and seemed to bend over it painfully.

Pride went straight to the bedroom and pulled the curtains shut. He placed a bowl by the bed and then he went to Allington and helped him out of his coat and his waistcoat.

He said, 'Go and lie down.'

Allington went through to the bedroom.

Pride could hear him moving about, slowly continuing to undress before crossing the room to the bed. Eventually he heard him say, 'Nat, you are still sober?'

'On my honour.'

There was a long pause before Allington continued, 'Bring me a pen and paper.'

'Yes, sir.'

Allington struggled to sit up. He looked at the sheet of shining white paper before saying, 'Take it away. Go to my desk. Write me a note.'

Pride, leaving the bedroom door ajar, sat down at the desk and waited.

'The note must go to Major Longbourne at the Officers' Mess. Dan can take it. I promised I would dine there.'

'Don't fret, for Gawd's sake. What shall I say?'

'It is with the . . . deepest regret Captain Allington . . . is no longer in a position to accept . . . the invitation from the officers of the regiment . . . on this day, whatever the day is . . . yes, but we know the day, Nat . . . owing to indisposition . . . Can you write all that? I had better sign it.'

The familiar searing pain on the left side of his head prevented him from considering what Pride might have made of the task, and he concluded by vomiting into the bowl.

Pride threw down the pen, jumped up, took a damp cloth from the washstand and wiped his master's face. He said, 'You ain't signing nothing.' He returned to the desk and picked up his note. On it he had written:

My master, Captain Allington that is, aren't well. It's his head, which is something when it is bad and comes on sudden. Pride wrote this.

He folded it carefully.

Allington said, 'Have you written it all down?'

'Yes, I've done it perfect. When Dan comes round with the mare I'll give it to him. Meantime I'll get the ice, somehow or other. Don't you move or you'll bring your stomach up all over again.'

Pride rapidly disappeared down the stairs. When Allington was ill the servant was aware of his responsibilities: he became brisk and authoritative and not in the least tempted by the gin shops.

He saw a groom, a man even smaller than himself, leading a long-tailed grey mare up the street and called out, 'Oh Dan, Captain's bad as could be.'

Pride took little account of Dan's deafness and addressed him as though he had no impediment, but at the same time he held his head and covered his eyes, next pointing up to Allington's window.

'Take this note. It has to go to Major Longbourne. You know where it has to go. You know the barracks.'

Dan was watching Pride all the time and wishing he did not gabble. He could, to a certain extent, lip-read and he knew where Allington had meant to go. He took the stub of a pencil from his pocket and drew on the outside of the letter, three soldiers. He leaned on the saddle to do it and the three soldiers marched, their guns on their shoulders and their tall shakos on their heads.

'Yes, yes, the Officers' Mess, the barracks. They are all a-celebrating, though God knows what, except they ain't dead and thousands were. I must get some ice and make a cold flannel.'

Dan put the letter in his pocket, got on the grey mare and rode away.

Sir John Parkes had a house in Albemarle Street where he adorned himself in his ridiculous clothes, his wide-striped pantaloons, his drawn-in waists, his puffed-up sleeves and his elaborate gold-topped canes. Now he sat at his bureau

40

wearing a silk chintz dressing gown in green and blue, and Turkish slippers.

It was several days since he and Arthur had dined together but now Arthur was sitting behind him waiting patiently for something to occur. Finding nothing did, he said, 'To go or not to go, that is the question.'

'To Almack's?'

'Of course. It is Wednesday. Where else should we go? We must be seen at Almack's.'

'To eat a little dry cake and a stale sandwich?'

'To admire the lights and the music.'

'To imbibe some barely intoxicating liquor?'

'Oh well, what could it matter? I always go.'

'And to dance a quadrille with some bashful child, her governess not yet expelled from her mind? Indeed, the said governess is such a ghostly presence you almost think you see her ready to dictate "In a cowslip's bell I lie" and peering mistrustfully over your shoulder. No, I am not in the mood for Almack's. Look here, Arthur, I wrote a letter to Allington and have received no reply. It makes me devilish anxious.'

'If it's Allington on your mind, let us go to Almack's for he never in his life was there and you needn't think of him again the whole evening. Besides, he isn't well.'

'He's ill?'

'How should I know? It's the usual thing. His man creeps about, all is silent and the curtains closed across the window. It was the anniversary of all that blood and slaughter, so I dare say he went off to some military dinner, drowned his troubles and suffered accordingly.'

'On lemonade?'

Arthur shrugged. 'Either way, I doubt he sits and writes

a letter. I went to Lady Mills' ball. What a crush. I was stuck on the stairs for an hour and could neither move up nor down, so the *Morning Post* may declare it a great success. Come, Sir John, we can't have you in such poor spirits because you haven't had a letter from Allington. I shouldn't care to have a letter from him myself.'

'Oh Arthur, go away.'

Arthur suddenly leaped to his feet and started to plunge about the room, making the wildest gestures with his cane.

'Allington would never call you out. Don't fret. He would consider you a meagre opponent, not worth the trouble. He'll never have more to do with the pretty Italian. You may go and claim her for your own, you lucky dog, else she must return to the stage. Why didn't Allington let her continue her career? Clarence allowed Mrs Jordan to continue hers, and he a Royal Duke. Royal Dukes are always strapped for cash and Allington must have a fortune. All those military men have been celebrating Waterloo. Why do we celebrate the death and wounding of nine thousand Englishmen? I suppose we are celebrating the death of even more Frenchmen. Some of the English were Germans pretending to be English and some of them were Scots. I much prefer the French to either. Mind you, Allington could pass as a foreigner, he has such dark eyes. His skin is the shade of the birchwood veneer on your desk but only in summer. In winter he is nearly as white as you or I. That desk comes from the Baltic, does it not? Seeing that Allington is to slice you up, you had better write a will and leave it to me, I like it so much. He'll be ill three days, he always is, unless it's the ague. I wonder at his parentage with that skin, eyes and hair, though his hair is brown, not black.'

'You tell me he's a natural son of the late Lord Tregorn.'

'Yes, but pray don't accuse me of telling the truth.'

Arthur took a lunge at Sir John's evening coat that was suspended on a hanger.

'That's new, a devilish fine shade of blue. What a beauty you will be. Had you better not put it on? I never should go to Almack's for one has to wear knee-britches and my poor little legs are nothing when only clad in silk stockings.'

Sir John shook his head. He would not go. Arthur, soon bored, went away without him.

'A gentleman like you, Mr Emill, wouldn't like the life of a soldier. There ain't no niceties attached to it.'

Pride was addressing Arthur's French valet, Emile. They were on far more intimate terms than their respective masters, and the Frenchman liked to sit in Pride's room, for his own accommodation was little more than a cupboard. To redress the imbalance he would bring Pride a glass of French brandy, as he had a brother in the trade. His own wages, when paid, would not have stretched to such a luxury. He was careful only to bring a small glass.

'You think you'll spend the days keeping your uniform as it should be,' Pride continued, 'a job you and I understand – brushing an' polishing an' pipeclaying an' a burnishing of buttons – but once you're off to foreign places an' your clothes are soaked an' bleached an' frozen up solid an' you've been outdoors to bed in 'em for nights on end . . . well, there's little you can do with brushing. Patching is more the answer. I was in the tailoring business, so patching comes easy to me.'

Emile was not so rude as to ask how a good tailor got to enlist, besides which, Pride, when in full flow, was difficult to stop.

'The sights you have to see, they turn your stomach. 'Course, there's nasty things to be seen at home, but they fade away, like, when you've seen a battlefield a few days on. I never could like no Frenchman until I had the pleasure of your acquaintance, though we was friendly enough between battles an' took off our clothes an' got in the river together. Then there's no telling who's French and who isn't. Why, I've parlayed with many a Frenchman when I've been on picket an' had a swig from his canteen, but I didn't like being on picket. Frightens me to death, standing alone in the dark, your mate half out of earshot, hour after hour with the trees all rustling an' a wolf behind every rock or every rock looking like a wolf, an' I stared so much I could make out its eyes an' ears an' teeth too. Then I'd think I saw the moonlight flash on a Frenchman's bayonet an' I wondered if it weren't the whole army an' I'd be spliced down the middle afore I could squeak.

'I was ever so thankful when I got me discharge but I didn't care to leave Captain Allington and I told him out straight I'd stay on as his private servant if he'd be so kind as to keep me – even if I never got no wages, for Captain Allington wasn't rich, for all his grand connections.'

Pride paused for breath. He was sitting cross-legged on his bed in lieu of a tailor's bench, making Allington a waistcoat.

'Lightweight for summer, this is. The Captain won't have anyone make his clothes except me. He says it keeps me out of harm's way and I fancy I still know the tricks of it. 'Course, I had to do some tailoring in the Army. When the regiment was due for a refit, they uniforms would come out to Portugal any old size and shape and the men were any old size and shape, though most of 'em

44

were little fellows like me, and the devil it was to get them matched up.'

'That is a fancy colour for your sober Captain.'

'My master dresses very sober except in the waistcoat. Here he allows a little something extra, not that much of it shows.'

'Soldiers are dandies,' commented the Frenchman.

'No, they ain't.'

'But look at your guardsmen here in Piccadilly, each one a figure of glory.'

'Well, yes, but I don't believe many of them were in Spain.'

'My dear Mr Pride, it is the uniform. The uniform is a dandy thing. How many a time you have shown me the red your Captain wore in its box of cedar? And the blue one too, he wore at some other time. They are beautiful, dandy things, not at all right for killing or for waiting for a wolf to eat you.'

Pride attempted to disagree but he was not clever at it. After a few weak sallies into the enemy camp, he contented himself with sipping his brandy, though he did not like a Frenchman to have the better of him.

After a while, he said, 'Those were what he had to wear for reviews and such. He didn't wear 'em for battle, he had second-best for they. As for what he wore at Waterloo, torn off him that were, for the sake of the buttons and the lace. It can't have been good for much else, not the state he was in. Down to his shirt when we picks him off the battle-field, and lucky to have that, though it was only good for rags. They looters don't care how much they shakes a man up, dead or alive. Much of the time while I was with him the Captain was in the Portuguese service. His uniform was brown: there's not much dandy in that. Tell you what, women loves a uniform. A uniform knocks them right silly. They Spanish women flirt, you wouldn't believe it, and the dancing . . . not at all decent. Women are trouble-some things. Look at the trouble my master had with that Italian. Take one look at her and you knew she couldn't stick by nobody. Just as well Master ain't sentimental. I only once know'd him sentimental. Laid out the better part of dead. Brussels we were in. Do you know the place? Pretty, that's what I call it, but the streets were all over straw and crammed tight with the wounded, which didn't do nothing for it. Took your mind off it, but it weren't forever. Still, first impressions stick. Master were in this merchant's house, once Major Wilder had come out and organised things, and there was a young girl with a big, pale plait right down to her hip and she were always laugh-ing and skipping about. Though he didn't never speak to her, I reckon she kept him alive. Peculiar time to come over sentimental but then he had the wound to the head, which probably accounts for it.

'Now, if we were wintered in a place, when we got our orders to shift, the scenes when we was marching out . . . you wouldn't believe it . . . women a-screaming and crying and jumping in rivers, pickets on the bridges to hold 'em back. 'Twas all on account of the uniforms.'

The weather continued hot. Arthur, having spent much of the previous night at a gambling club in Jermyn Street, lay propped up in bed on a profusion of pillows. It was approach-ing mid-afternoon and he had a headache. Emile tiptoed into the room with an armful of shirts and a newspaper.

'Emile, when is it Quarter Day?' he asked in world-weary

tones, for in a night when thousands of pounds had passed before his eyes and through his hands, he had ended the winner of twelve guineas which, though it might pay the wages of a serving maid for a year, was not much to a gentleman.

'Midsummer Day, sir, twenty-fourth of June, and there's a gentleman to see you.'

Arthur picked up the candlestick from beside the bed and threw it in the general direction of Emile, saying as he did so, 'I know what is Quarter Day. Under my beleaguered circumstances, how could I not?'

Emile picked up the candlestick and replaced it with studied care. He said, glancing at the newspaper, 'Today, sir, is the twenty-third of June.'

'Why then, I ought to be out and about. Sir John Parkes is to lend me his coach. I won't take it all the way. I must find the money for posting some of the journey. I am not suited to the hurly-burly of public coaches. I need no clothes beyond a change or two of shirt. There is nothing and nobody at Castle Orchard. Who did you say was at the door?'

'Mr Rampton, sir.'

'Show him in then, don't keep him waiting.'

Emile, without going immediately to the door, said in his usual precise tones, 'I think Sir John will not lend you his coach, sir. He is no more in a lending position. He is dead. It is in your newspaper.'

Arthur sat up in bed, a look of the most profound horror on his face. Emile proceeded to usher in young Mr Rampton.

Arthur said, 'It is not, it cannot be true.'

Mr Rampton, who had on a new coat and had hoped Arthur would notice it, asked, 'What's not true?'

'That Sir John Parkes is dead.'

'Oh yes, it is more than gossip, and Smythe has gone to France.'

'Smythe killed him? Why not Allington? It's Captain Allington who has gone to France. Tell me it is.'

'No. They don't mention Captain Allington, only Mr Smythe. The dual took place at Chalke Farm, wherever that might be, with not a soul there but the seconds and the surgeon, who could do nothing.'

'Ah, but by this dastardly act I have lost two good friends. One is dead and the other gone to France.' Arthur groped under his pillows for a handkerchief. For a while he wept uncontrollably. Rampton could think of nothing to say beyond remarking, to himself, a preference for France over the other.

Arthur then jumped out of bed and pulled a handsome padded dressing gown over his nightshirt, displaying, as he did so, his pair of little thin legs.

'Allington is to blame,' he said. 'Allington is at fault and my poor, good friend Parkes lies stone cold in some horrid place.'

'But it was Smythe shot him. Smythe accused him of something or another and they say Smythe was quite right. Allington has not been seen these two days.'

'No, he's in his rooms. He's ill, if you can believe that. They call it a megrim but we know about megrims, a fanciful thing for women. It's not the ague. He will be drunk.' Arthur began to rush distractedly about. 'I shall demand to see him. I have a right. Parkes was my friend.'

'I beg you not to,' Rampton said, alarmed. 'You're not in a fit state of mind. Besides, it's rather a crowd at your door.'

Arthur remembered he was in danger of being arrested

if he left his rooms. He subsided into a chair and wept some more.

'There'll be an inquest and some futile enquiry. I must attend to my own affairs. Emile must book me a place on the mail and I shall go down to Salisbury or they will put me in the King's Bench. I dare say my friends will still visit me, those that are not dead or gone to France, but I cling to my liberty. Last night I had five thousand pounds in my hands and this morning I have twelve guineas.'

'A clever man such as yourself would surely do better at the whist table, where your fate, much of the time, would be in your own hands.'

'It's true, it's true, but it doesn't have the allure. Why, I do play it from time to time and win quite a little money. Even Allington says I could win regularly if I paid attention, and that's a compliment from him, though I think I hate a compliment from Allington. One day I shall trounce him at his own game, I shall be one jump ahead of him and it will be my turn to say "checkmate" in those quiet, dismissive tones, which I am sure I shall mimic to a nicety at the time. Now, Rampton, I shall bet you the twelve guineas I won last night that I shall beat Allington at chess before the year is out.'

Rampton said he would like to oblige Arthur in any way he could, but he demurred when it came to a bet on a matter on which he could have no opinion. Arthur, who saw little relationship between a bet and an opinion, began to think Rampton a bore, but he was too much distracted by the death of his friend and his own precarious pecuniary state to do more than suppose Rampton still might be useful to him now and again. The lure of the Quarter Day rents eventually taking precedence in the rag-bag of his mind, he announced decisively, 'I shall leave for Castle Orchard, even if I die getting there.'

Rampton was puzzled. He thought there would have to be some catastrophic accident to the coach that travelled so regularly and reliably between London and Salisbury for Arthur to lose his life on the road.

The rat-a-tat, rat-a-tat of the drum meant charge, and charge little Frankie Conway did. He charged and cheered and screamed and ran and waved his arms, bounding through the copse at Castle Orchard, slithering on mud, on the wild ransom, the dog's mercury, the brambles catching his clothes, the hazel slashing his face; and to him, as to the others, it was never only a game.

Robert had a real soldier's coat, not the smart one that had belonged to their uncle, but a raggedy old coat from the rank and file with the lace torn off and a patch on the elbow. It was a rusty brown, but once, once it had been a glowing scarlet: its glory had to live in the mind's eye. It was not very much too big for Robert and he, despite his coat not being an officer's coat, would always be the officer. Stephen carried the drum and he beat it well, even when he was running along. Frankie only had a stick, but that was all he and the little ones had.

Phil ran through the wood as hard as he could go and his breath hurt as it struggled in and out of his chest. Though it was only a game he was always afraid and they, in the end, always caught him. He could never run fast enough, though he ran and ran and ran.

'I don't want to be the French any more.'

He lay on the ground and the Conway boys stood round him with their sticks, even the twins, only six years old.

'You have to be the French.'

'You are our prisoner. We are going to shoot you, because you are a deserter and that is the worst thing you can be. On goes the blindfold and then you are shot by ever so many soldiers at once. You are blown into so many little bits and nobody ever remembers who you were after that, because you're nothing.'

'You wait for the bang, bang, bang with your blindfold on and your insides drop out and they are like the insides of a rabbit, pink with green bits.'

'And purple bits.'

'But first he must be our prisoner.'

'We will lock him up.'

'And forget him.'

'And the rats will gnaw his flesh.'

'When he is shot, all the other soldiers will look at the little bits of him that are left and remember not to be cowards and run away. You are a coward because you are afraid of the river.'

'And then the birds will peck his eyes out.'

And so it went on until such time as the Conway boys thought of their dinner.

Phil wandered home, ragged and dirty, woebegone, unable to say why he always had to be the French, except that he was a coward and afraid of the river.

Indoors, his mother was writing a letter. She looked up as he came in and said, 'Dearest, what a mess and why so sad?'

He went to her and she put an arm round him. She never said, 'You have been crying,' for she thought this something a boy might not like to have pointed out to him. Instead she said, 'Why play with the Conways if you don't enjoy it?'

Unfortunately, Phil did not know how not to play with the Conways, nor did he know how to explain this to his mother. He said nothing, for he must look after his mother and not tell her all the horrid things the Conways said, in case she got bad dreams.

'Go and change your clothes while I finish my letter to your Aunt Louisa, then we'll have dinner.'

Phil went away and his mother picked up the pen and put it back in the ink. She thought of the length of dusky pink silk sent her by her sister, complete with a pattern for the latest mode: low neck, slender waist, short sleeves ruched and puffed and further ruching at the hem. Whenever did Louisa think she might wear such a thing? But it was not Louisa's fault, for did she not deceive Louisa, skating and sliding over the truth? Louisa knew much but never the whole, for why should she worry her half-sister with the whole?

She wrote, *The silk is beautiful.* This could be stated unequivocally. After a pause she continued:

May I be clever enough to make it up. I have made a little jacket for Phil. He fancies a military cut but he overestimates my tailoring skills. I dare say I can add a little braid without making the thing ridiculous. Phil and the Conway boys only play at soldiers, always the French and the English, the Battle of Waterloo, etc., though he seems cast down by it. Emmy is well and shows no interest in battles. Westcott Park may need an heir but I am glad you have a little daughter even

if she is another little daughter. There is a lot to be
said for daughters, and the heir can come later.

And so the letter went on, everything to be made light of.
Having finished it, she reached for her journal. In it she
wrote:

Midsummer Day, 24 June, Quarter Day and J. not
down yet. He will be here tomorrow. I do wonder how
he thinks we can manage on so little. I told Louisa I
made a coat for Phil but not that I made it from the
better parts of my old cloak.

She then turned to the accounts but remembering it was
time for dinner, she allowed herself only a cursory glance
at the figures.

Allington, seated by the window in his own rooms, was
feeling better. His recovery was accompanied by his usual
sense of euphoria at the relief from the pain, but he sat
quietly reading all the same. In compensation for what he
considered his incarceration in his lodgings in Half Moon
Street, he occupied himself with John Keats and was hap-
pily transported. He read of beeches green and shadows
numberless with intense pleasure: he was light-headed.

Pride came in and announced in tones of the deepest
satisfaction, 'His Lordship is come.'

Allington looked up. He said, 'Tregorn?'

'Yes, sir.'

'In that case, please don't keep him waiting.'

Lord Tregorn was a stocky man with a shock of dark

grey hair and a weather-beaten face, middle-aged. Up from Cornwall, where he preferred to spend his time, his London clothes made him uncomfortable.

'Pride tells me you have had a fit of the usual sort,' he said. 'You had better sit down again.' He eyed Allington keenly. 'How are you? How are you really? You haven't the ague, have you? That does frighten me. Why, the mantle of responsibility falls on my shoulders the instant I step into my father's shoes. Here I am, up to make my maiden speech in the House of Lords, my first and my last, I dare say. I shall be no more effective than my father, who never could bring himself to speak more than once and then only to stammer away about rabbits and the game laws. What are you doing, Allington?'

'Getting you a glass of wine. I keep some, you know, for your visits.'

Tregorn thought, Why do we all call him Allington? Why do we never use his Christian name? Now the old man is gone he takes the riddle of Allington's birth with him, stepson or son, stepbrother or half-brother. Tregorn thought Allington no blood relative, with his dark brown eyes, his long figure and his cleverness. His cleverness had shocked them from the moment they had amused themselves with teaching him card games and chess. A little boy of eight or nine had no reason to be leaning forward and expounding on the last ten moves of the game when he had only just learned to play it. He had arrived in their lives, a young boy, his pretty mother to marry their father, a widower and some twenty years her senior. Allington had not resembled his mother either – a fair, timid creature – but she had been living on the estate for years, her soldier husband first absent and then dead, giving rise to supposition. No, Allington was not a blood relative; he was far too clever to be the product of the late Lord Tregorn and his second wife.

Pride had produced another chair from the bedroom. It was evident Allington was not in the habit of receiving visitors. As Tregorn sat down, the glass of wine in his hand and a plate of ratafia cakes placed beside him, he continued to speculate on the mysterious nature of this relict of his father's estate. There was nothing straightforward about Allington – but then, there never had been. In the eyes of Tregorn and his brothers, Allington, even as a child, was too clever, and being too clever rarely did a man any good.

'You don't have to be responsible for me,' Allington said.

'But you have this wretched ill-health. I shall continue to pay your allowance.'

Allington looked as if he was trying to decide if this was or was not fair.

'After all,' Tregorn continued, 'we cannot approve of your way of life, winning money at cards.'

'It hardly seems gentlemanly, does it?' Allington agreed. 'On the other hand, you could not expect me, brought up as I was in the splendour of St Jude, to live on my half-pay as an officer, not required for duty or indeed not fit for duty. I look fit for duty, I can ride, and if I had just lost an arm, for example, I could be serving at this minute.'

The conundrum of how Allington should live was, as usual, too much for His Lordship, as it had been for his father. Allington's allowance could only be increased at the expense of Tregorn's legitimate, but plentiful, younger brothers, let alone his own innumerable offspring. Even suppose the allowance was increased, it would not necessarily stop Allington winning money at cards or however he did win it.

'Who taught me chess? Who taught me whist?' Allington asked, smiling.

'Now, another thing,' Tregorn said, ignoring this, changing the subject. 'What is it I hear of Sir John Parkes shot dead in a duel? Your name, I understand, is connected with it, which I don't care for.'

'Nor I,' said Allington. 'It was an excessive act. Smythe is an excellent shot. I dare say he could have wounded him and left it at that.'

'You speak very calmly and a man shot dead.'

'I have seen many men shot dead. Death comes to all of us, it seems not to matter when. I wouldn't have shot Parkes myself. I don't believe there are circumstances in which I could be induced to fight a duel. His death is of no great significance, but seeing you question me, I will tell you. I passed a letter written to me from Parkes on to Smythe: what a business it is to behave in a manner suited to my station, whatever that station might be, for again, not the act of a gentleman.'

'I suppose you had your reasons.'

'I considered he had lied. From the content of the letter I think it probable he hoped Smythe and I could be induced to fight one another and he get away unscathed. Perhaps he hoped Smythe would shoot me dead. I don't believe he had any personal animosity towards me, but my death would be a great convenience to the friend he has who lives in the rooms below these.'

'An Italian actress,' Tregorn said, a little confused but still anxious to probe to the bottom of the matter.

'Until of late, my mistress. It was by the way of an experiment, not particularly satisfactory. Do you think your father would have disapproved of my keeping a mistress and curtailed my allowance accordingly?'

'How should I know?' Tregorn said crossly, for he thought the question inappropriate. There was nothing unusual in keeping a mistress, but it surprised him that Allington should do so. He then wondered why he was surprised. He reached forward and picked up the book Allington had been reading as if it might help him solve a mystery, but finding it to be poetry he put it down again with a look of faint horror.

'However,' Allington was saying, 'I don't wish to take another, and as the alternatives are too disagreeable, it looks like celibacy.'

Tregorn, thinking the conversation taking an even worse turn, said, 'Why not marry? If you could support a mistress you might support a wife.'

'When I have a place of my own I shall consider it, but I'm not everybody's idea of a catch.'

'A place of your own?' Tregorn was astonished, disagreeably so. 'These rooms seem adequate, though not if you were married. You don't mean a place out of town?'

'Why not?'

'What sort of a place?'

'An estate.'

Tregorn stared at him. His stepbrother, for that is what he surely was, seemed to be stepping out of place if he thought he would join the propertied classes. The only thing he could think to say was, 'Whatever for?'

Allington looked at him in silence but he then said, 'You are the only person I know who has the temerity to ask me endless questions, but I suppose the Tregorns are the only people I have who could remotely be described as my relatives. What for? To keep a pair of greyhounds.'

Tregorn, realising he was having his leg pulled, said, 'Could you really afford such a thing?'

'I believe so, but not yet. It's not, therefore, necessary for you to pay me an allowance.'

Tregorn jumped to his feet and started to pace about. 'I won't have it said I don't support you now my father's dead.'

His mind had gone back ten years, to the aftermath of Waterloo. His father had received a letter from an old and revered friend, in whose regiment Allington had spent much of his military career, accusing the family of neglect because no one had gone out to Brussels to look after Allington, whom the colonel had described as the most brilliant of all young officers. Agitated at the recollection, he said, 'We were told you would die before anyone could reach you and for days that was said, even months, yet die you would not.'

Further words of this colonel came unwanted into Tregorn's mind, fragments of that letter which he could remember word for word. *To die on the battlefield is one thing. We all expect that. To die slowly amongst strangers is another.*

Tregorn knew why the accusation of neglect had so rankled. It was because it was true. None of them had wanted to go out to Brussels. His own wife was expecting a child. His sister was newly married. It was extremely inconvenient to go to Brussels, especially if Allington was to die while they were on the road. The truth was, Allington had been away since he was fifteen, a boy in the Army. He had taken no leave and they had scarcely seen him again until he returned a war veteran eight years later at the age of twenty-three. Either way, they had made amends, gone to Brussels and fetched him home to St Jude, wresting him from the care of a major in the horse artillery. The colonel had travelled down to Cornwall. When he saw Allington he was so upset he had announced, out of Allington's hearing, it would have been far better had he died, so there was no pleasing the fellow at all.

Allington said, 'No, I lived. I have wondered why.'

'Once we got you back to St Jude, we did our best.'

'But in living, one should have a purpose. I thought I could go back to school, to read for the Bar, but I couldn't do it. The sight of all that small print and I was sick as a dog.'

'Why don't those card games, the games of chess, which must agitate the brain, have the same effect?'

'It must be some other part of my brain. I have wondered that too.' Allington then added, to the discomfort of his stepbrother, whom he knew to be squeamish, 'I have often seen brains on the battlefield. They don't look as if they could be useful at all.'

Tregorn searched for an appropriate reply. His eye fell on the jar of sixpences. 'What on earth is the point of those?' he asked.

'They are the exclusive property of Nathaniel Pride. Every evening he is sober I give him a sixpence. I allow him to take a glass of brandy with Arthur's valet, but he must be sober. They are savings for his old age. He thinks they will be adequate for all his needs, but of course I shall have to do more for him.'

'And if he is drunk when you are sick, what then?'

'He knows better than to be drunk when I'm sick.'

'I should find him a liability but you are indebted to the wretched fellow.'

'I am, and he to me. Besides, he knows how to look after me. It would be unthinkable to have anyone else with me at such times. He is also my tailor.'

'I noticed the cut of your coat. It may be plain, but it's

smart. You soldiers always are dandies. It's a deal better than mine.'

Allington did not think it difficult to have a better coat than Tregorn's.

His stepbrother then said, 'I have the picture. My fellow and Pride can bring it up between them, I suppose. It was a damned awkward travelling companion.'

'What picture?' Allington asked.

'Why yours, of course. My father's last words to me, or nearly so, were, "Let Allington have the picture". He was disappointed you wouldn't allow him to have your Waterloo medal added. He would look at it and say, "Allington would not have the medal put on". He was proud of you, in his own way. As he bought you your commission, I suppose he basked in reflected glory.'

Allington thought there could have been many better ways in which he might have been set up in life, but he only said, 'The portrait? Oh dear, how impatient I was at having to sit for it, in that interim in 1814 between the campaigns in the Peninsula and Waterloo. You could keep it at St Jude.'

'It is too handsome a thing. I should be tempted to purloin it.'

'I suppose when I get my estate I shall have to have something to hang in it,' Allington said, with a nearly imperceptible smile.

'Why a whole estate? What is wrong with a little country house, a villa?'

'I must have occupation.'

'But surely you haven't so much money you could buy one?'

'Not yet.'

Tregorn reached for his hat. He said, 'You continue to baffle me. I must go. Dreadful rabble on the stairs.'

'Courtesy of my fellow tenant. He never pays for anything.'

'Terrible, silly sort of fellow, but good-hearted.'

'I am not sure I find him entirely so.'

'Don't come down with me. You will get a chill on your head or something. Lady Tregorn and I will always be pleased to see you at St Jude. You know that.' Tregorn looked hard at Allington, as if looking could assist him in puzzling him out, ascertaining the state of his health, this man for whom he now felt responsible.

Allington suddenly said, 'Are the lime trees flowering at St Jude?'

Tregorn had no idea. Though a countryman he did not necessarily notice such things. He said, 'Now Allington, I will pay that allowance of yours, whatever your situation.'

Allington, from his window, watched his stepbrother go down the street to where the groom was walking the horses. In a moment his servant and Pride could be seen manhandling the picture, well wrapped, towards the door. Again he sat by the window, but now his mood had changed and he was sombre. He picked up the volume of Keats's poetry, as if to recapture a lost moment, and started to read where he had left off:

> *Darkling I listen; and, for many a time*
> *I have been half in love with easeful Death;*
> *Call'd him soft names in many a musèd rhyme*
> *To take into the air my quiet breath;*
> *Now more than ever seems it rich to die,*
> *To cease upon the midnight with no pain . . .*

Allington said out loud: 'Ah, but only if it were like that.'

He got out his pocketbook. It was bound in green cloth and was larger than was convenient, about six inches by four. Pride made special pockets inside his coats to accommodate it, with a button and a loop to ensure its safety. The pocketbook was not exactly an *aide-memoire* because there was little Allington forgot, but he liked to write things down in it, sometimes a single word, sometimes a reflection.

Now he wrote: *John Keats died from consumption on 23 February 1821. Age 26. The squeezing of life from sick lungs, the coughing of blood.*

He was aware of being so severely wounded at the age of twenty-three that he had been much more than *half in love with easeful death.* So many had died, with lesser injuries than his. For what had he lived, for what purpose, partially incapacitated as he was?

Pride came in and gave him a sharp look. He said, 'You are not starting again, are you, sir?'

'No, I'm better.'

'What shall I do with this here picture?'

'Lean it against the wall. I shan't look at it now.'

'Suppose I send round for Dan to bring you your long-tailed grey. You could ride out to the country. You're strong enough, that's what I think. It would do you good. If you read all they books you'll start thinking, and thinking ain't good for you.'

Quarter Day had come and gone. It was July. Captain Allington had noted the going and the subsequent returning of his fellow tenant, with a slight cessation of the besieging forces of duns and creditors in the house in Half Moon Street.

It was a warm and sultry afternoon. He was seated at his desk, contemplating his accounts. He knew exactly what was in them. He could remember whole pages of figures without difficulty, but he liked to have his affairs in order, and order meant writing things down and making any necessary adjustments.

His one-time mistress he had paid two months' rent and the wages for her servants. She was about to resume her career so that was to be the end of that. He stood up and went to his bookcase. His eye fell on a volume of Wordsworth. He took it down and went to sit in the window, opening the pages at random:

> *My heart leaps up when I behold*
> *A rainbow in the sky;*
> *So was it when my life began;*
> *So it is now I am a man;*
> *So be it when I shall grow old,*
> *Or let me die!*
> *The child is father of the man . . .*

Here Allington stopped and laid the book down on his lap. 'The child is father of the man', he repeated to himself. 'It is a wise father that knows his own child'. How complicated, the web of one's inheritance and the stuff of which one was made. Had his childhood made him what he was? Or was he contrived entirely from that unknown being, Captain Frederick Robert John Allington, whose mother had been Spanish, which accounted for his appearance?

That Captain Allington had died in Flanders fighting the French in 1793, a proceeding he himself had endeavoured to mimic more than twenty years later. The evidence of Spanish blood had been sufficient to convince him he was no son of Lord Tregorn. Even the soldiers, amongst themselves, called him 'Spanish Allington'. It was not useful to cross-examine poets. They led one down unexpected labyrinths.

He got up and walked about the room. It was time he got out of London for a while. His portrait was there, leaned up against the wall. He still had not looked at it. Had he been cowardly for putting off the moment? He took a paperknife and carefully sliced down the wrapping, peeling it back. The process reminded him of a dressing eased from a wound.

A portrait of a young man in a Light Dragoon regiment ought to be neither remarkable nor painful, but painful it was. It jerked him backwards to what he had been, to lost youth, let alone lost health. The uniform was buttoned across the chest so there was nothing more than a rim of the brighter colour against the sombre blue of the jacket. He was bare-headed, cradling the felt shako in his arm, its short plume of red and white barely visible. There was a hint of the lavish gold shoulder belt, the epaulettes and the girdle, but little to distract from the face.

Allington said, in much the same tone as he used to the duns that flocked round Arthur's door, 'Good day, stranger.'

His younger self looked back at him with impatient eyes.

He remembered his mood at the time, impatient at

64

sitting in the Bond Street studio, impatient with having a new uniform, impatient at the loss of his campaigning life and impatient at not being shipped straight to the wars in America. His stepfather had achieved for him the one thing that made him the envy of his fellows, a transfer to a cavalry regiment, but, unlike his fellows, he did not want it. He could not afford it. Lord Tregorn had paid for the uniform and insisted on the portrait, but he needed more horses, a charger, and the sort of allowance necessary for living with a smart set of officers. It was at this juncture he slid into the habit of raising the stakes when he played a game of whist or chess. It was not a perfect arrangement but it enabled him to pay his way.

How young he was, and what risks he had taken. The adventure, the constant activity, how much he had loved it. Looking at the picture, he wished he had been painted, if he had to be painted, in the brown uniform of an officer in the Portuguese service, but it would not have accorded with the grand notions of his stepfather, for whom he might have been some sort of plaything, to be shown off when suitable. He began to think of his company of Portuguese caçadores. Where were they now? Tending their olives, their vines, their sheep and goats, or so he hoped.

Pride came in. He took one look at the picture and burst into tears. After a moment he tried to summon some feeble self-control but, aided by alcohol, he only wept the more.

Allington said, 'Go to your room, Pride. I shan't want any assistance. You may occupy yourself by writing to your mother.'

This was the ultimate punishment and they both reflected on Pride not getting his sixpence. Allington, irritated by the world in general and more particularly by himself and his own servant, took himself away to the boxing salon to give serious punishment to the punching bag, a cure for a variety of ills.

Pride, sent to his attic bedroom, made an attempt to obey orders. He sat in a mild alcoholic haze and reread the last letter from his mother, which had run thus,

> *Dearest Nat,*
>
> *I am hoping you keep well. I do though in my seventy-fifth year. Your sister Sarah keeps well and also the children.*
>
> *I hope you do your duty, Nathaniel, and do not go near the gin shops of which London abounds. Your blessed father, so long now with the Angels, never could mention your name, which he did rarely OWING TO DISAPPOINTMENT, without tears and your going for a common soldier. However, the Good Lord had you in His scheme of things, for you to look after a poor invalid, who can hardly raise himself from the bed, though I never would have thought you a natural at such things and he so stern a master you may never visit your old mother who must ere long be upon her deathbed.*
>
> *I hope you are getting a proper night's sleep.*
>
> *Your ever-affectionate Mother*
> *Susan Pride*

Her last sentence arose from Pride once having written, in an expansive moment, when extolling his labours on behalf of his master, that he slept on the floor by the bedroom door in order to be always at hand. His mother wrote to him at the beginning of every month with sentiments that varied little and always including the welfare, or otherwise, of his sister Sarah and her children, with whom she lived. Her notion of Captain Allington's state of health sprang directly from her son's repeated assurances that his master was too much of an invalid ever to be left. Pride, chewing his pen, had a pang of conscience as a vision of Allington's present activities with the punching bag, let alone long days spent fox hunting or riding the grey round the countryside, rose before him, but the fib served its purpose very well in keeping him apart from his mother. What was more, he reflected, it was not wholly a fib, for it was hard to tell exactly when his master would be as prone as in the vision old Mrs Pride had of him.

He now wrote:

Dear Mother,

Glad you are well and Sarah and all. You don't seem near deathbed and would be best not to mention it in case of bringing it on. Do think my father with the Angels would be proud of his son Nat, now I never do go to the gin shop and am a proper gentleman's gentleman and no mistake. Gentlemen can't get their clothes on their backs unless you stand by an' hold all their things out one after another like they were babies so Mr Arthur's man tells me from downstairs but Captain Allington being a soldier ain't like that. Lord Tregorn, brother to my master, should change his tailor. I wished I could have his coat off him to take a tuck in the sleeve. He sent the picture of the captain and it made me cry to see him like he was when I knew him first and he not much more than a boy and light-hearted. I could no more touch a bottle of gin were it right there in the room for the way he looks at me out of that picture. Of course there is no gin it not being a gentleman's drink and besides which Captain Allington taking no alcohol for it effecting his head very badly which makes him very singular, gentlemen being quite drunk on the whole. Captain Allington puts all my money in the bank so I can't be tempted and when I am old I need not go on the Parish.

Your affectionate son,
Nathaniel Pride

Pride thought a little alcohol a great aid to fluency with the pen. It was true Allington emptied out the sixpences, banked his savings, but he always allowed him a little pocket money for, he said, his dignity, even if it led to undignified conduct. His transgression on this occasion was owing to Lord Tregorn having given him a tip which had sat in his pocket until temptation overcame him.

Determined to do his duty whatever his condition, for his loyalty to Allington was unwavering, Pride crept out of his room in order to fetch hot water and lay out his master's clothes for the evening, thus disobeying orders. The sight of the portrait brought on more tears but he succeeded in accomplishing everything he meant to do and was able to retreat upstairs just as he heard his master return.

Allington came in, washed and changed, making only a few minor alterations in what Pride had decided he ought to wear. He then walked to the Travellers. His presence effectively silenced the gossip and speculation on the subject of the death of Sir John Parkes. He said nothing and enlightened nobody.

Pride, having returned to his own room, sat down and allowed himself to be overcome by the deepest gloom, castigating himself for the drink and Allington's disapproval. After a while there was a knock on the door and Emile came in. He gave Pride a look of such deep Gallic sympathy that Pride once more burst into tears.

'Now, my dear friend, you must support yourself. What is the matter? Your master is not ill?' he asked.

'Oh no,' Pride said, 'but I've gone agin him and he never does care for me to be all in a state. It upset me so to see his picture to the life like he was the day we left for France and every day up to that Waterloo. A battlefield is a horrid place, like I told you, Mr Emill, with so many corpses huddled up over one another as far as the eye can see, and the minute the sun gets on them—'

'Ah yes, so you did tell me,' Emile interrupted him, fearful of receiving the descriptions all over again. 'I beg you to think of something more cheerful. Now, tell me this, how did you come to be in the service of your master? Did you not save his life?'

'So I did, but I'm not sure he wants it saved half the time. To be an officer's servant in the Army is a privilege. Did you know that? A privilege I say, for you gets to look out to the baggage and need never go near the guns, though some servants follow their masters into battle, but my master never would have me do that. I was the worst soldier in the world and folks knew it. I could get out the pipeclay and polish better than any, but when it came to the fighting, I died every death. You mustn't never duck when a cannon ball comes over – that's cowardly, it might hit the man behind – but it's mortal tempting, I can tell you, and what with the noise and the smoke . . . Captain Allington don't think much of me. One night, when I'm on picket, we're ever so close to the French. I has a little chat to the French picket, *parlez-vous*, we often does that, and he gives me swigs of brandy. His canteen were right filled with the stuff. Nicked it, I suppose. Well, you know me, a little goes a long way. Captain Allington is inspecting the pickets that night and I'm fast asleep, drunk as a lord. That may not seem a sin to you, Mr Emill, but it's death to me. "Sleeping or drunk on duty before the enemy" is what they call it. Life is sweet when you're young, even when it's hard, but I'd rather die than be flogged. They tie you up to the sergeants' spontoons and the drummers set about you with the cat, three hundred, five hundred strokes. If the surgeon says your pulse is weak they takes you down and packs you off to hospital, but when your back is healed, like, they straps you up again and gives you the lashes what you didn't have before, and the regiment standing by to witness it. I'd rather be shot and that seems my fate when I wakes up and sees the master doing picket duty in my place. He gives me a cold, hard look and I knows I've no hope in hell but to run over to the French on the spot, but my knees is so feeble I can't do it. Death, being quicker, thinks I, is better than a flogging and I might conduct myself more befitting. Terrified into sobriety I was, and I takes up the duty.

'Pickets are changed. Master says nothing. I goes back to me bivouac but waits to be arrested all the same. Is he tormenting me a-purpose? Don't seem like him. He was the sort of officer soldiers respect and will follow any-where, but he wasn't loved like some are, being so sharp with it. Spanish Allington they called him and everyone knew who he was. He got a great performance out of us and we were proud of that.

70

'I couldn't sleep nor nothing. He's lodging in a bit of a shed, very uncomfortable it looks too. I gets the courage to speak: I asks what he means to do with me. He says, "Nothing." He says, if he had meant to do something he wouldn't have let me wait – and hadn't I known that? I says, "No", and he says, "Well, you had your punishment then."

'I saw his coat laid down with a tear in it. I says, "I'll mend that." I takes it away and I mends it so beautiful, I puts me whole heart in it. I even give that coat a kiss when no one ain't looking.

'When I takes it back I find his servant is gone sick, so I fetches water and makes the fire up and cooks the rations for him for he was alone that evening – rations that weren't no better than ours, beef what the wild beasts might get their teeth round but not much else, seeing as the creature is butchered and ate all in one go. Cook, mend, clean, if that were all a soldier had to do, I'd be grand at it.

'Thanked me he did, but he was writing in his pocket-book, much like the one he has now, and didn't take too much notice. I was shy of him, though he were only a young fellow, a boy. Still, if you've been at war since you was sixteen or so, you're quite growed-up. I won't ever know how he come to let me off. What he risked was his officer's commission. They could've chucked him out. 'Tis in the general orders. "Misplaced compassion" is what they call it. I've seen it written down.'

Pride at last drew to a halt and breathed an alcoholic sigh, before continuing. 'He had a mule and a horse. He shared a goat with another officer. She were called Helen because she were a beauty, Master said, but I never did get to the bottom of that. A little Portuguese lad looked after her. Master kept a greyhound, sometimes two, what could bring in a hare, and he fished. There were trout enough if you could get them. It was a hard life. We moved too quick, see, marched day and night from time to time. The commissariat might never get up with the rations. Sometimes it were burning hot, all the heat of Spain and nothing but rocks as far as the eye could see, then it would be winter, rain and snow and ice. Men just dropped as they walked, officers too: fatigue and hunger don't discriminate. They might give us a portion of wheat and I'd husk it and boil it up in the goat's milk. Folks don't know how it was. Captain Allington's servant never came back. I sort of wormed my way into his place and he took me on official. Even when I got my discharge I never did leave, I turned up just the same.'

Pride leaned back, closed his eyes and repeated, 'I never would leave my master, I turned up just the same.'

Emile, astonished, said, 'Well, I never hear anything so unpleasant as what you tell me. Why do the soldiers go? It can't be worth a red coat and a cockade in the hat. The coat gone dirty, the wages not paid . . .' He drew to a halt. Though Quarter Day had passed and Mr Arthur had been to Castle Orchard to receive his rents, the only journey he undertook without his valet, Emile had not received his salary.

The month of July saw the close of the Season. To be in London was a solecism. Nobody who was in London was anybody. The parks were seer and dry, the streets dusty and unpleasant. Arthur noted that even Allington, unmoved by the habits of society, had retired from the scene, taking his long-tailed grey out into the country. Arthur had

had difficulty in leaving his lodgings. He was besieged. His friends had bailed him out twice; he knew there was speculation his Michaelmas rents would not save him. He had won a thousand pounds at the gaming tables but it was nothing.

His anxiety to be out of London induced him to accept an invitation from the Ramptons to visit their country seat. He would have preferred Brighton, Scarborough or even Bath, but the obscurity of Bell Hill Abbey and its distance from the metropolis gave it practical appeal. He made his escape at dawn and young Rampton picked him up in the commodious Rampton travelling coach. Arthur had a hysterical fear of being arrested that went far beyond reason.

Bell Hill Abbey was on the Dorsetshire coast, and though Arthur professed to enter enthusiastically into plans for altering and extending the park, he was soon bored. The chief occupation was walking to the sea, and he cared neither for walking nor the sea. In the evening he played billiards or listened to his host, Rampton's father, recite his own poetry, Arthur having evinced a polite interest in it and the encouragement taken too literally.

Arthur, incurring no expenses while being at Bell Hill and with his troublesome affairs beyond reach of him, thought his seaside idyll would have to continue for several months, at which juncture he could proceed to Castle Orchard for the Michaelmas Quarter Day. He had not allowed for Mrs Rampton, a fair beauty, whom he found neither interesting nor sympathetic. She ran the household, her father-in-law being a widower, with effortless efficiency, kept a sensible hold on the purse-strings and considered Johnny Arthur a poor addition to the establishment and likely to influence her husband towards unnecessary extravagance. In the last week of August she fell ill. It was nothing more than the troublesome complaint of a woman in the early stages of expecting a child. Though it was commonplace, and the idea of an heir was greeted with a bottle of champagne, she insisted on going to London to visit a doctor her family had previously patronised. Her mother told her it was completely unnecessary and the journey more hazardous than staying at home, but Mrs Rampton always had her own way.

Arthur had no wish to return to London, but if he did not travel with the Ramptons the expense of his journey would fall on himself. He was just contemplating the various choices of evil, when Rampton said, 'If we all go together we could, without much deviation, call at your place.'

Arthur looked surprised, even astonished. He said, 'There's nothing at Castle Orchard to make anyone deviate from anything. My old retainers would have apoplexy if I turned up with visitors.'

'We shouldn't stay. We could drive out from Salisbury. I should be very much interested to see the Philosopher's Tower.'

'It's nothing,' Arthur said. 'A mere heap of bricks.'

'It is my belief, Mr Arthur,' Mrs Rampton said, 'you have no wish to entertain us.'

'You are quite right,' Arthur said, laughing, 'No one goes to Castle Orchard. There are bats in the roof, snakes in the grass, sticklebacks in the river and frogs in the soup. Why, no meal is complete without frogs. They come up from the cellars like little green, slimy soldiers with slippery legs and tiny teeth. Not being French, our digestive systems can't accommodate them.'

Johnny Arthur not at all amusing Mrs Rampton, and it being quite clear he had no intention of allowing them to visit even the Philosopher's Tower, they all returned to London and Arthur was deposited at his lodging in Half Moon Street at a very unseasonable moment and with the fear of never again being able to leave them, except to bide indefinitely in the King's Bench.

He was never one for finding entertainment in his own company and he was almost entirely confined to his rooms, Rampton his only visitor, at a loose end himself while his wife had endless consultations with her doctor. Arthur soon tired of Rampton, of his rooms and indeed of all else, announcing he might as well be in the King's Bench Prison for it must afford greater amusement than anything else his life had to offer. Rampton idly agreed with him, at which juncture he became agitated, shocked and horrified. By the end of a week he was desperate for any distraction.

At the beginning of September, Captain Allington returned. This awoke Arthur's curiosity, Rampton noticed, as could anything to do with Allington. However, Allington went up to his rooms and did not come out of them again.

'Go and ask him to play chess with me, Rampton,' Arthur said, his friend paying him his accustomed afternoon visit.

'Certainly not. I'm not a servant,' Rampton answered, laughing, 'Besides, I have not the pleasure of his acquaintance.'

'It would rectify that.'

'Send your valet, write him a note, go yourself.' He no longer treated Arthur with quite the same respect.

Arthur went to the door and put his head out. 'Perhaps I imagined he was here.'

'Of course he is here.'

'He's probably drunk.'

'Then you may win the chess, if he is sufficiently so, unless you consider that dishonourable.'

Arthur did not consider it at all dishonourable. Despite past experiences he knew he could win a game of chess against Allington should luck favour him: he believed in luck under the most unlikely of circumstances. At that moment he saw Pride coming up the stairs.

Arthur called out to him, 'Will you send my compliments to Captain Allington and ask him to step down for a game of chess.'

'Not today I won't. He's not fit,' Pride said, far from politely. He was bustling and busy; knowing Allington despised Arthur, he despised him too.

Arthur, indignant, said, 'Mind your tongue or I shall go up and speak to Captain Allington myself.'

'Not today, not tomorrow. I wouldn't open the door to you, not if you was His Majesty King George. The day after that he will be well enough to see you.'

Pride continued on his way. Arthur heard him lock Allington's door.

'What a cheeky fellow,' Rampton said. 'Fancy employing him.'

'He is indeed very saucy,' Arthur said, shaking his head sadly. 'He's drunk.'

'But he did not sound drunk.'

Arthur, ignoring this, said, 'I shall catch Allington the day after tomorrow and win a game of chess. I feel it in my bones. I shall win—'

He was about to say 'win back all I owe him' but managed to contain it.

September was hotter than August. There was an Indian summer. Arthur felt like a rat in a cage, neither able to escape his rooms nor his affairs. His landlord dropped him a hint he was tired of the rabble of debt collectors at the door. Arthur was aggrieved: he thought they had reached an understanding with each other. Rampton began to think better of seeing him but, for want of much else to do, he still visited. Arthur constantly changed his clothes as if he had a row of flattering engagements to attend. Ever optimistic, he awaited a miracle and somehow he concluded that Allington, as the only person available, was to provide it. He listened all the time for the sound of his footsteps above, or the noise of his door opening.

On the fourth day he sent a note with Emile asking Allington to play chess or any other game he fancied. He was sufficiently desperate to have asked him to dine, but the notice was short and he thought he could not provide a good enough dinner. He hoped Rampton might offer to fund the dinner, but this he did not do, though he had brought Arthur a present of some good cheese and a bottle of wine.

Allington not immediately appearing, Arthur said, restlessly fidgeting about his room: 'It's certainly better he doesn't come. I don't like the fellow above half.'

He was just resigning himself to Allington neither replying to his note nor coming in person, when Emile said, 'Captain Allington, sir.'

There was nothing more incongruous than Captain Allington in Arthur's rooms. Despite a short bout of his usual complaint, he looked well. He had been riding his long-tailed grey on a perambulation round the south of England, thirty to forty miles a day in three stages, starting before breakfast and breaking the journeys wherever he found good stabling. He had spent a week or so with that friend of his, Major Wilder, who had come out to Brussels to attend to him after Waterloo. The sun had browned his face. He was dressed plainly in a lightweight, dark grey coat, a cotton waistcoat and loose trousers. Arthur introduced Rampton to him; the young man was reduced by the utter indifference with which Allington surveyed him, though he gave him a small, polite bow. Rampton had always known himself to be a superior being.

'Well, Arthur,' Allington said, 'you are a sucker for punishment.'

'But will you oblige me? I should like a game of chess.'

'I shall do nothing unless we open the window.' Allington went himself and pushed up the sash as high as it would go, for the room reeked of Arthur's perfumes. He leaned out for a moment before turning and adding, 'And we will not play for stakes.'

'But we can't play without stakes,' Arthur said, indignant.

'Why not? Are we not playing to amuse ourselves?'

'Oh, but we must have some sort of a stake to put an edge on the game.'

'It may put an edge on your game, but it does nothing for mine. I don't object to playing with you, but it is a farce if we play even for a penny, unless you are disposed towards honouring your debts.'

Arthur looked uneasy.

Allington said, 'It is my intention to leave London.'

'I am a little short at the minute,' Arthur said awkwardly.

'It is not quite convenient.' He wished Allington would leave London forever and take the IOUs with him.

'Oh, I am not expecting you to pay, but I refuse to continue the farce. A debt of honour is not a debt of honour when left in your hands.'

This insult stung Rampton more than it did Arthur. He wondered how Arthur could stand there without defending himself.

'Where is the board?' Allington continued. 'Are we to play or not?'

'By all means, but we must have stakes. I shall set them. If you win you shall have Castle Orchard. If I win you must forgive me my debts.'

Rampton gasped with horror. He jumped up and cried out, 'For God's sake, Arthur, you must be mad!'

'Not at all. I might owe Allington the worth of the property, or thereabout. I am not sure of the actual amount.'

'Neither am I,' Allington said, surprisingly. 'It's a long time since I troubled to count. I have the IOUs, of course. Eight years is a long time for you to play losing games.'

'Is that the length of time?' Arthur asked.

'Yes.'

'Well, what do you say to my stake?'

'Not much. What precisely do you mean? What do I know of Castle Orchard? There must be land, I suppose – farms, cottages, a house, things inside the house. Where is the line to be drawn?'

'You shall have all of it. There are three thousand acres and a house. If I have no house, I will not rescue my ancestors off the walls, for where should I put them? Besides, they might look at me spitefully.'

Allington seemed to pause for contemplation. He had

never had reason to believe a word that Arthur said, and what he now proposed went beyond belief.

Arthur now said, 'We have a witness.'

'That is true. What sort of a witness would he make?'

'An honest one,' Rampton replied, nettled, wishing he was anywhere but where he was. He started to walk anxiously about the room, picking up an ebony cane from a stand and swishing it about in his agitation.

'How can I know I want your estate?' Allington asked. 'It's probably falling down.'

'No, it is in good repair. My trustees, who managed it until the last three years, saw to that. It is a few miles from Salisbury, on the river. It has every amenity, even a Philosopher's Tower.'

Rampton could not see Allington had anything to lose. As he could not take Arthur's money, for Arthur had none, he may as well take the estate. For Arthur, if he lost, it would be the end. Castle Orchard was his only source of income.

Arthur got out the chess set. It was exotically carved, top heavy and inconvenient. 'Today my luck will turn,' he said.

'It's not luck but application that's required,' Allington replied. He moved the little table so that he could keep a seat by the window. 'Perhaps Mr Rampton would like to write down the wager. We will sign it and he will witness it.'

Rampton said, 'Arthur, this is complete madness. You can't want me to do any such thing.'

'Oh, I do, I do. Get on with it, there's a good fellow. There's paper on my desk. Write two copies. We must both have a copy.'

Rampton, with extreme reluctance, did as he was told. He would have done almost anything to escape but was at the same time, mesmerised. Allington read the agreement carefully before signing it but Arthur scrawled his name with apparent indifference.

Now excitable, Arthur put the pieces out, knocked a few over in his haste, put them up again. Allington said, 'I will allow you the first move.'

'You are too confident, Allington. This is to be my hour of glory. You can take the red, as befits a soldier.' Arthur, sure his luck had turned, seizing a white pawn, started to play at random, though his brain could be agile enough.

Rampton watched the game in acute discomfort. He never played chess himself so he had no idea of the proceedings. All the same he hung over the board in a state of anxious speculation, as if looking could enlighten him. He noticed Allington took longer over his moves than Arthur.

Suddenly Allington said, 'Pay more attention. I will allow you to reconsider your last move.'

Arthur looked swiftly at his opponent. Allington's face told him nothing. Turning his attention to the board, he repositioned his Queen.

'A slip,' he said. 'Very kind of you to overlook it.'

His voice was not steady. Suddenly, for the first time in his life, he knew it had nothing to do with luck, that Allington was right. He also knew if he engaged his mind he was clever, that he was fighting for his very survival. Allington knew this too. Arthur began to deliberate long and carefully. Allington moved a little more swiftly. His opponent was now giving him time to work out each possible move that could be made. He thought of nothing else, not even of how much he disliked Arthur's room, which had preoccupied him when he had been in it on many previous occasions.

Arthur's game was one of attack. Allington let him run away with the idea that he was doing well. Arthur thought of many possible moves to be made by his opponent, but Allington could think of more. There was not a single moment in the game when Allington was in the least danger of Arthur winning.

Eventually Allington said, 'Checkmate.'

Arthur was not stupid. He had seen it coming.

Allington said, 'Do you wish to make it the best of three?' It was as if he too wished to put off the actual significant moment.

Arthur said, 'Yes.' He was exhausted, his hand unsteady, but he put the pieces out again. Allington's allowing him a second chance was surely luck, and if he made a supreme effort, he could win.

Rampton, sitting uneasily on the edge of the chair, thought them both mad. He realised Arthur was incapable of keeping up the necessary length of concentration, and that even in this hour, with his whole livelihood at stake, his attention would start to slip.

Arthur began looking at Allington instead of at the board. Was not chess a martial game? Had not Allington been in a line regiment, Cornish probably, and worn a scarlet jacket with silver lacing? He saw the scarlet jacket, the epaulette, the belt and some tall, peaked hat on his head, but no, was it not the dark green of the Rifles, with black cord, lacing and silver buttons? Arthur preferred the scarlet. He had a sudden image of death and blood. He would run steel into Allington's red breast and the blood would run red upon red. Ah, but he was wrong, confused. The red would run on

82

the darkest blue and stain the white belt, the gaudy lacings, the sash of an officer in the Light Dragoons. And what was he, Arthur? Surely not a miserable little Frenchman whose sword had rusted in the rain and stuck in its scabbard, so, when the enemy advanced, when the cheers rang out and the drums rolled, he could do nothing but wait . . .

When Arthur looked again at Allington, Allington was looking out of the window. Arthur studied the board. He thought of various moves. Twice he put his hand out and then withdrew it. Eventually he took the edge of the board and tipped the pieces on the floor.

He said, bouncing up, full of mock bravado, 'Well, I shall be glad to be shot of the place. It is a millstone round my neck, wanting this, wanting that, wanting the tithes paid. What do you say, Rampton? I am fairly beat.'

'I know nothing of chess. It is barbarous. Your family have been at Castle Orchard for several hundred years.'

'What should that signify? They have been there long enough. Property is responsibility. My father said it over and over again until he seemed never to say anything else. I feel quite light-hearted to think it gone. Open a bottle, Rampton. We will celebrate.'

'I think that most inappropriate,' Rampton replied, primly. 'Besides, I believe Captain Allington not to drink. I wish I wasn't here. It is not the way for grown men to behave. I am surprised, Captain Allington, at your not taking a more responsible attitude.'

Allington turned from the window and gave Rampton half a glance. He said, 'What difference does it make to Castle Orchard if I have it or the moneylenders. Is it Howard and Gibbs, Arthur, or a string of them? The latter, I dare say. While the deeds are in your hands the property remains yours. If you tell a lie and Mr Rampton another, you may jog on a little longer, for all I know, though I have my copy of the agreement.'

Arthur, stalking about the room, said, 'No, no, the property is yours. You shall have the deeds tomorrow. My lawyer can have nothing else to do at this time of year. I ask of you both only one thing, to let it be a secret until after Michaelmas Quarter Day, and Allington – will you allow me those Michaelmas rents? On my honour I will claim nothing else. I need go there only one more time.'

Allington looked at him. He remained silent. Arthur, thinking again of the soldier, of all the fancy lacing and the buttons made from real bullion, the snug fit of the dark jacket to the ribs, said, 'Aren't you fellows expected to treat your prisoners honourably?'

For the first time Allington gave a brief smile. Arthur could not remember ever having seen him smile before.

'All right,' Allington said. 'You may have the Michaelmas rents.'

'But you shall have the deeds tomorrow, and you will keep it a secret.'

'Of course. Whose business is it but yours and mine?' Allington stooped to retrieve the chess pieces. 'Here is the rook that won the game. It's appropriate.'

'Why a rook better than a bishop or any other piece?'

'Because the word rook comes from *rohk*, which is Indian for a soldier. It also means to plunder or cheat, so it is a two-edged sword, depending on how you look at the profession.' Without looking up he added, 'Perhaps Mr Rampton would like it as a memento of the occasion, though it would spoil the set.'

'No, I should not!' Rampton replied, almost shouting.

'This whole thing is ridiculous. Arthur, you are mad. You should see a lawyer.'

'A doctor is more the ticket for a madman,' Arthur said.

'But you are ruined.'

Allington sighed. For the first time he properly addressed himself to Mr Rampton. 'Really,' he said, 'I think you not very clever. Can't you see it makes no difference? It's either I or his creditors.' He then turned to Arthur and said, 'They will be scrambling for the betting books in White's and Brooks'. You are not yet thirty-five and you have lost the estate. Did they not bet on it?'

'They did, but I am meant not to have mortgaged it. I never did that. They must argue it out.'

'But what did you give the moneylenders as security?'

'Promises, fibs, fictitious grandmothers with fortunes, everything but Castle Orchard. I told them it was entailed on the male line.'

'And how am I to know it's not?'

'I wouldn't lie to you, Allington. To lie to the Jews is quite another thing. My lawyer has the deeds. They tell all and I have never given them in surety, I promise. Oh, I shall be had for fraud as well as debt. What do they call it, "obtaining money under false pretences"?' A curious look passed over his face, for such fraud was a hanging offence, and he lost what colour he had, but then he poured himself a large brandy, saying as he did so, 'It must be an exceptional circumstance for such an affair to be conducted when all parties were sober.'

Every morning Phil went to school at the rectory and in the afternoon returned. Sometimes he would dawdle across the meadow, sometimes he would race, but now he dawdled because there was no sign of the Conway boys. To one side of him there were further meadows, the river, cows in brown and cream; and on the other, fields of corn rippling all the way to the foot of the chalkdown. Red poppies grew amidst the yellow corn, the red of soldiers' jackets, but within a week or two the grain would be cut and after that, autumn. Leaves would soon lie in banks and drifts, rust red, the rust red of the soldiers' jackets after days and days in the rain, the sun and the snow. The jackets were only red for a little while, when they were new. There was nothing smart about soldiers; their clothes were the shade of dried blood.

'How many days did you march? Tell us again, Jackson.'

Jackson would blink his one eye. 'The retreat to Corunna was over yer mountains in Spain. It was winter, see, Christmas Eve, think of that, and we marched four days and four nights without rations. We was flogged if we stopped. The skin was tore off our backs. Many couldn't stick it. They dropped where they was, and if it were yer own brother you walked on by. There weren't no graves. The wolves tore the limbs off 'em.'

Phil could always see Jackson in his mind's eye. He could have mimicked his exact tones, had he wanted. Jackson would go on and on, his 'yer' that stood for 'you' or 'your' punctuating the deathly drama of his foot-soldier days in Spain. He rarely spoke of victory or loyalty, courage or kindness, for that was not his way, but only of the cruelty of the officers, the floggings and shootings, the cascades of enemy fire and the bloody ends of his companions.

Seated on his empty barrel in the cellar, his face grimly distorted by the loss of his eye and lit by the single candle, transporting the boys who gathered around him from the smell of boots and grease to the grisly battlefields.

Phil, caught like the rest of them, unable to take flight, relived the dreams and the nightmares, the screams of the wounded, he and the Conway boys re-enacting all in their games at Castle Orchard, clinging, despite Jackson, to their visions of glamour and romance, though it did not preclude the Conway boys from savagery. Now and again they shut Phil up in the Philosopher's Tower where it stood on the bend of the river. They would wait until school was over and follow him across the meadow, catch him up, threaten him with this and that if he declined to go with them.

The Philosopher's Tower was built of soft red brick, octagonal in shape with small latticed windows to face north, east, south and west. It had a ground floor, rather dark and murky, and a flight of steps to an upper floor, pleasant, with a table and a chair. One could open a little window and look down on the wide, swift river or open another and gaze at the trees in the orchard, at Domino grazing and at the drive with encroaching brambles, shadowed with beech and elm. A third gave a view of the house and the fourth looked across the river to the downs.

Phil thought the tower his, as he had, it seemed, been named for it, though he knew, of course, his name was really Philip, like the Spanish king who never gave wicked Queen Mary any babies and so successfully prevented England from being Roman Catholic and everybody having to pray for the Pope, who was a foreigner, instead of for King George, who was not, though he had been German once, a long time ago. He supposed the tower could have a whole name like his, Philip Osipher's Tower, but it was a bit too long to say. He had begun to say it in a different way, giving it a different meaning.

He did not mind being locked in it in the summer, but in the winter it lacked charm. As evening approached, vapours rose from the fearsome river and owls screeched, though, as his mother reminded him, they were only birds and had never been known to attack.

Now it was August, late August, not at all a bad month, except for darkness setting in sooner. Yesterday he had been ambushed and locked in, but as usual they let him out before night. They had crept up and unlocked the door without his noticing, running away, so he thought he was locked in when he was not, and he was late for dinner.

He had said, 'I was locked in the tower.'

His mother replied, 'Not locked, Phil.'

'No, not locked,' he had answered, feeling confused because, truthfully, he had not been locked in all the time. It was best to give no explanations for lateness.

There was a drawer in the table in the Philosopher's Tower containing paper and pencil, left there by his mother for writing down thoughts, but Phil never found he had any. He wondered if he should bring a real pen and ink. His Aunt Louisa had sent him some steel nibs, but his mother said they would rust, being too modern and the Tower not respecting them as it should. Once, not long ago, he had thought of something he might write. It was probably not of sufficient importance but he had written it all the same, despite his poor, wobbly writing spoiling the snowy whiteness of the paper, because it was important to him, and his mother had said that was what counted. He could not understand why nobody was on his side, why he always had to be the French and the explanation was no

88

explanation at all, so he had written: *Robert says I have to be the French unless I can tell Jacky from James. Well, I can't tell Jacky from James. They are just little twins and are really the same person or nearly.*

He had signed it *Philip Osipher.*

Now Phil reached the gate that led through the tall hedge into the Castle Orchard garden. He glanced behind him. There was not a Conway boy in sight. He started to run.

Captain Allington did not have great faith in ever receiving the property of Castle Orchard, and certainly Arthur's lawyer fought a rearguard action against such a flouting of ordinary practice. He saw no necessity for Arthur to part with the property, but Arthur did not go back on his word: the written agreement stood. Much of September passed before the necessary documents were prepared and Allington required to sign them.

The day before this occasion he dined at home. Pride cooked him a simple meal. The evenings had drawn in but he ate at the table by the window in the last of the light. Soon the lamps would be lit and Pride would bring him a candle. He was half-expecting to see, in the street below, Arthur make a bid for freedom, taking the deeds with him. All he could see, however, leaning on a gaslamp, was the mildly sinister figure whose task it was on behalf of Howard and Gibbs to see Arthur did no such thing.

Allington's mind unaccountably went back to Wordsworth. He supposed if nothing made the heart lift, not even the rainbow, 'Then may I die' was most appropriate. What made his own heart leap up? The sight of the sea, a skylark, the passage of a greyhound, the shining rump and bright eye of a good horse, and the sweet peace of green fields, a peace that he needed. His acquisition of an estate in Wiltshire with a romantic name, without, in a direct way, paying for it, did not make his heart leap up for it was too improbable. He considered Arthur and remembered the countless occasions he had agreed at Arthur's instigation to some challenge or another, at anything from chess to childish card games, exercises for the memory, curious choices to play against a man who was known not to forget things, and at which Allington won, in theory, large sums of money.

The following morning, the lawyer called on Arthur with the deeds in his hands and Arthur instructed his servant to ask Captain Allington to join them.

'My personal affairs are nothing to Captain Allington,' he said to the lawyer. 'He is here to sign the documents and nothing else. Pray mention nothing, absolutely nothing. I want no breach of confidence.'

'I shall be glad, sir, to wash my hands of the whole affair. I shall find it very difficult not to speak out. The whole thing is deeply shocking. Whatever next? Does your conscience never prick you? This Captain Allington can hardly be a respectable person. He will, I suppose, lose the property as quickly as he has gained it. What, may I ask, do you intend to—'

He was cut off by Allington entering the room.

Arthur said, 'No, don't ask me. Well, Allington, Jonas here is put out by the business and supposes you will lose Castle Orchard as soon as you gain it.'

'He may suppose as he likes,' Allington replied.

'This property has been in the Arthur family two hundred years,' the lawyer said. 'However unprofessional it may be, I must protest. Mr Arthur's late father, God rest his soul, for it surely wouldn't rest if he knew a quarter, built the Philosopher's Tower. What would he say to this transaction? He was himself a very astute gentleman. What, now, will be the position of his son?'

Allington thought Arthur's only position was one in the King's Bench or worse, but he did not say so. He merely said he hoped the documents were in order. After examining the deeds for some time and the accompanying map, he checked his name and added his signature. The document included a clause stating he forgave Arthur the money owed him and he would undertake to destroy all the IOUs dated from 1817 and up to the present month of September 1825.

Arthur reminded them the matter was not to become public knowledge until after Michaelmas. 'I hope, I repeat, I may rely on your discretion,' he said to the lawyer.

'My clients can always rely on my discretion,' Jonas replied.

'Arthur is, perhaps, no longer your client,' Allington pointed out. 'Send me your bill. I shall pay it after Michaelmas.'

The lawyer, looking from Arthur to Allington, thought the latter the more likely of the two to pay him. He agreed to send him the bill and took an unhappy departure.

Arthur now stood at a mirror, rearranging his neckcloth and trying the effect of various pins. He said, 'You think of everything, Allington. It would give me great satisfaction to see those IOUs burned.'

Allington had the IOUs in a box. He lit the coals in the grate himself.

'Do you wish to look at them?' he asked.

'I suppose I should satisfy myself it really is the IOUs you are burning.'

'You should. These ashes will make a great deal of mess.'

'Never mind that.'

As Allington fed the papers on to the fire he said, 'You will write to inform your people at Castle Orchard of the change of circumstances?'

'Oh course, but not until after Michaelmas. I don't keep more people there than needed to keep the rats at bay.'

'You have an agent?'

'Yes, but he is not solely my agent. I share him. I had best write down his name and address. How glad I shall be, never to clap eyes on him again. Ah, the rustic horror of a country estate.'

Arthur suddenly let out a peal of laughter and Allington thought how little he trusted him.

'Of course, at Michaelmas I could go down there with you,' Allington said.

'I should dislike that very much,' Arthur replied. 'Think how they will be all a-staring and talking of my father and his grave and how one turns in the other. No, no, but I promise everyone shall know who needs to. You may not care for the place, in which case you can sell it and get something else. Do you like to fish?'

For a moment Allington did not reply; his mind had gone to the rivers in Spain, the Ebro, the Bidassoa, the Aqueda, all teaming with fish. As Arthur seemed to wait for him to speak he said, 'Yes, I can fish.'

Arthur said, 'Oh, a horrid, dull thing, fishing. My father would have me stand there hour upon hour.'

Allington, ignoring him, said, 'It is my intention to pay a few of your lesser creditors.'

'Very good of you, but for what?' Arthur asked.

Captain Allington shrugged. 'It is what I have decided to do if you will give me their bills – your tailor and all those sorts of people. No, not your tailor, the bill would be too much.'

Arthur went to his desk, which was so full of bills they cascaded to the floor as he drew back the front. He said, 'Take your pick.'

Captain Allington sat at the desk and started to set the papers in order. Though he was quick and methodical, the business took an hour and a half. Much of the time Arthur watched him, a look of credulous fascination on his face. He began to think how he envied Captain Allington his figure.

He said, 'Who is your tailor?'

Allington answered without looking up at him, for he was busy, 'Pride. He was a tailor before he enlisted.'

'Why, that's devilish convenient.'

Allington made no reply, as if this detail of his private life was more than sufficient to impart, but Arthur, not liking to be so quiet, announced, 'What I like about you, Captain Allington, is your silence.'

It was the first time he thought he liked anything about Allington and he only liked it upon this occasion. 'Anyone else would be saying how can you owe a thousand pounds to your tailor and five hundred pounds to a coach-builder when you no longer drive any sort of coach, et cetera, et cetera, so tiresome.'

'What I would like about you, Arthur, would be your silence,' Allington replied.

Arthur spread out cards on a little table, still keeping an eye on Allington, and proceeded to amuse himself with a game of Patience. After a while he said, 'If I get this game out, Allington, will you let me have your grey horse? It has such an elegant tail. I wonder why it's the custom to dock the tail of a horse and why yours isn't docked. I'll make it the fashion that horses must wear hairpieces. May I have it?'

'No.'

'But it is certain I can't get the game out.'

Captain Allington did not trouble to reply. Eventually he shuffled together a wedge of bills and said, 'I will pay these.'

'I am sure they will thank you. Those sort of people don't always expect to be paid. It is enough that a man of my position patronises them.'

'Someone must pay a tailor or he will go out of business.'

'Someone always does, but Allington, don't pay all those bills at once. It will look odd.'

Allington paused in the doorway. He saw that the cabinet in which Arthur kept his collection of snuffboxes was half-empty and supposed that he must be taking them away in his pockets, a few at a time, and be hiding them somewhere. If he should leave Half Moon Street with a portmanteau, it would cause suspicion. He would be followed down to Castle Orchard to make sure he intended no escape. At some juncture he must catch his creditors unawares and get the steam packet from Dover to Calais, complete with the Michaelmas rents and his collection of snuffboxes, for they were valuable, one a present from the King. He might subsist for a short while in reasonable comfort.

Returning to his own room Allington sat down at the table and unfolded the map of Castle Orchard. He started to allow himself, for the first time, to believe in his ownership of this estate, complete with its farms and cottages, its house, its woods, its stables and gardens. Though his more practical side acknowledged that the whole place might be a ruin, for he did not believe what Arthur said and a place could go back a great deal in three years, if it was a ruin he was perfectly prepared to spend the rest of his life putting it back into shape.

As he studied the map, the strident sounds of London – the horses, the street vendors, the barrel organ – faded from him: Castle Orchard was enwrapped in the deepest mystery. The map told him of farms and boundaries, of the position of woods and the acreage of fields, but it did not tell him of its essence as a place. It had all the charm of Xanadu's stately pleasure-dome.

'So twice five miles of fertile ground,
With walls and towers were girdled round.'

He went to his bookcase and withdrew the relevant volume of Coleridge's poems. His mind ran on gardens bright with sinuous rills and sunny spots of greenery.

As September drew on, nothing tangible altered in the house in Half Moon Street, for what altered was intangible, the unease and the tension as the month crept towards its end and Michaelmas. All unaware, the girls who worked on the ground floor, employed by the wife of the landlord as makers of gowns for the fashionable, continued their sewing and continued to take sly peeps at the exits and entrances of the two gentlemen lodgers who lived up the stairs, bachelors, and therefore objects of conjecture. Mr Arthur was not above putting his head round the door and making a joke or two, but Captain Allington never did this, and it was difficult to think of a means of catching his attention without also catching the attention of their mistress. Captain Allington's severity filled the young seamstresses with a pleasing alarm, certain it sprang from a broken heart.

As Allington paid off Arthur's lesser creditors, the number of debt collectors besieging the landing grew less and dwindled almost to nothing. All that was left were the ever-watching, ever-waiting employees of the money-lenders, and they were often content to wait in the street. (Arthur had been known to climb out of a window.)

Arthur said, to anyone who cared to listen to him, 'You can see how I'm getting my affairs in order. I hardly owe any money. Sometime after Michaelmas I shall receive a legacy from my late aunt. I am turning over a new leaf.'

Off he would go in all his finery, swinging a cane, dangling his quizzing glass, ruffling his curls, but always in the direction of St James' where the draw of the gaming table beckoned him no less; what he gambled with or how a mystery, unless courtesy of his friends. He was full of talk and laughter on the subject of a reformed life and the economies he was to make. The only economy he was seen to make was the taking of the Exeter mail down to Salisbury, instead of hiring a post chaise, upon the 26 September.

To the surprise of some, he returned, the same conveyance depositing him back in London on 1 October. He appeared to carry on much the same as usual, apart from declaring the experiment to be a failure, the air within the Exeter mailcoach proving foetid, the company not choice and the seats hard and dirty. He did not think he could be expected to repeat the experience at Christmas – but where would Johnny Arthur *be* at Christmas?

He called on Captain Allington.

'I find you very odd, Allington, you have so little curiosity,' he said.

'You do?' Allington replied. He watched Arthur peering about at the austerity of his rooms. He had wrapped the portrait up again. Should he wish to hang it, it was too big to fit conveniently in the available space.

'You don't have much up here,' Arthur said. 'I suppose you live like a soldier, as if you were in a bivouac. Perhaps you don't quite believe in the transaction, think that Castle Orchard is a figment of the imagination.'

'Of yours or mine?'

'Why now of both, I suppose. However, I have returned, as you can see.'

'And is Castle Orchard itself aware of the transaction?'

'No. It occurred to me that there is a usefulness in the matter remaining a secret for another week or two.'

'It's hardly useful to me.'

'I know, I know. You have been very patient. Would you give me a fortnight?'

'Precisely from this day? If I must.' Allington spoke reluctantly. 'After that I spill the beans unless you can assure me you have written.'

'I shall write next week. They will then expect you. The news won't immediately return here. You may go down to Castle Orchard at the end of the fortnight if it pleases you to do so. Shall I tell them you are sending your horses? Haven't you hunters? You can hunt from Castle Orchard.'

Captain Allington left him to write what he liked. He assumed Arthur wished to make his escape to the Continent at a moment when it was least expected, and he must be most preoccupied with that. If it was known the property was no longer his, he would be arrested.

The fact it was not his and could not be sold to pay his debts, would come as an unpleasant surprise after he was ensconced in some Ostend or Calais boarding house, from which it was unlikely he could ever return.

Allington began to consider, cautiously, how he might rearrange his life. The immediate removal of all his horses into Wiltshire seemed rash and premature, despite Arthur mentioning stabling for twelve. For all Allington knew, there might be no roofs on the buildings.

London, from Arthur's point of view, was still empty. The beau monde did not return until January, and that he should be seen, by chance, in the street, during October, made him wish to duck and hide. The Ramptons had returned to their seaside estate and he was at his wits' end how to occupy himself at such a time when he had never before felt more like distractions. The fortnight, for both Allington and Arthur, passed extremely slowly.

With a constant change of horses the eighty-six miles to Salisbury could be done in a day. It had been Allington's intention to ride all the way, but he confessed, only to himself, the riding exercise he had given his lame leg in August had done it no good and he thought it prudent to rest it before the hunting season He had therefore borrowed a britchka, a light travelling vehicle which could be opened or closed according to the weather, from a military acquaintance, with the idea of buying it if he liked it. He sent Dan on with his grey a few days before, showing him maps, listing place names and drawing pictures, concluding with the spire of Salisbury Cathedral. He travelled himself, accompanied by Pride, on 14 October.

On the following morning he instructed his servants to stay where they were, at the White Hart in Salisbury, but he told them where he was going. He had Pride pack him a small saddlebag with a change of linen and, having no idea what awaited him, indicated he would probably stay away one night. Mounting his long-tailed grey, he set out for Castle Orchard.

It was a beautiful day, the trees on the turn and the sky a hyacinth blue, autumn in its full opulence of fruit, the ripeness of plums and apples and the sweetness of leafy decay. He approved of decay that enriched the earth. When expecting death he had asked to be buried not in the neat little churchyard of the Cornish parish, but in some untended plot where he hoped he might add to the greenness: he had thus shocked his stepfather who had assured him he had no intention of carrying out such a heathen request. Allington had pointed out that the bodies of his comrades in arms lay in unconsecrated ground, though he did not add, 'should they have the luck to be buried'. The reply had been that Allington's circumstances did not necessitate such an expedient. Allington suspected him of having in his mind a suitable headstone already written out.

As he rode over the downs and into the valleys, spying here and there the river, the lines of Keats' 'Ode to Autumn' ran through his head.

*Drowsed with the fume of poppies. While thy hook
Spares the next swath and all its twined flowers . . .*

The poet attributed a sleepiness and indolence to autumn.

*Or by a cider-press, with patient look,
Thou watchest the last oozings hours by hours*

Allington knew that harvest was gained by the sweat of men and horses, by long hours and little rest. It was a season of merriment and contradictions. He could see the labourers working the fields, the pale creaminess of the stubble and the darker stooks. When he reached the land which, according to the map, was the outlying portion of Castle Orchard, he got off his horse and rested a moment. He spoke to the men and asked after the quality of the harvest, but he did not delay long. He felt a combination of expectation, pleasure and anxiety. The surrounding country filled him with a quiet happiness and he thought if fate should settle him amongst these grey hills and by the meandering river, he could live out his life more usefully and be content, he who felt destiny had marked for one thing and fate for another.

Arthur had been true to his word when he said that the property was in reasonable order. The farms were tidy and in repair, the roadside cottages snug, their gardens filled. Allington passed a farmer in brown frockcoat, breeches and gaiters, who wished him good day. Allington answered him gravely. He wondered if the man was a tenant of his own. He had looked for signs of poverty and unrest, for agriculture was at a low ebb, but this precise little corner of England seemed to be at ease. The farmer drove a smart cob in a yellow-painted gig. Allington asked him more precise directions to Castle Orchard and, though answering him, the man looked at him with surprise, as if no one ever asked for directions to Castle Orchard. He could instruct him no further than Orchardleigh.

Another ten minutes or so brought him to this small village, and even then it had required his trained eye for the lie of the land to actually happen on it. He noted the church and the substantial rectory. Castle Orchard remained elusive. It necessitated winding along a series of narrow lanes at right angles to each other before coming upon the iron gates which he knew must lead to the house. There was a single lodge in flint and brick, empty, its garden luxuriously entangled with Old Man's Beard. He could see that, where money had been spent to maintain the estate, the immediate environs of the house had been neglected. The drive went away before him through thickly planted scrub and wood, the undergrowth encroaching, some massive limes marking the remains of an avenue, their boughs meeting densely overhead.

The gate being open, Allington urged his grey horse forward. Its hooves made barely a sound on the soft earth and the moss, but it pricked its ears expectantly and then gave a small start as a boy emerged abruptly from the brambles, a boy of eight or nine years old, in a pair of stout boots, trousers too short and a torn jacket.

Allington reined in his horse and stared down at the child who stared back at him with the roundest of blue eyes. He had no hat and his head was covered in a mass of yellow curls. He was the image of Arthur.

Leaning from the saddle, Allington asked his name.

The boy paused before answering. He was out of breath. He then said, looking anxiously behind him and stumbling with his words, 'My name is Philip Osipher but I am not an Osipher – an officer, I mean. I never am, I am only the French.'

Allington said, 'Why can't you be an officer *of* the French? They had some perfectly good ones.'

'The French put their lances in the wounded, jab, jab, jab,' he replied, vigorously poking the ground with the stick he had.

The action made Allington wince and for a moment he closed his eyes, for a wound of his own had been administered just so and he felt it. He then said, 'The Lancers were Polish but that is basically true, though certainly not at all times. It would be unfair to tar them all with the same brush: there was many a good gallant French officer. On the whole, if I were you, I should decline to be the French.'

He made as if to ride on but the boy said, 'Why have you come here?' He looked even harder at Allington but then something frightened him. He nervously backed away, turned round and fled.

The trees opened to reveal the house. It was sunny and mellow, made of red brick, possibly Queen Anne, but with a variety of attachments both older and newer, which gave it a misshapen but not unpleasing appearance, a muddled charm. It was not the orderly house of his dreams, but dreams were adaptable. The unkempt lawn swept up to the door and though there was a carriage sweep, weeds had seeded in the gravel. There was a sundial on a plinth, and to the east side of the house a tall, dark square of yew hedge, in which there was nothing but grass and blown leaves.

Without dismounting, Allington rode up to the front door and gave the bell pull a hearty jerk, but all was silent. He imagined somewhere in the depths of a distant kitchen, an elderly retainer, deaf to the summons even had the bell worked, which he doubted.

He turned his back on the house and looked across to the river. He could see the Philosopher's Tower but all looked asleep in the sun. He wondered if that sprite of a child was the only thing that lived in the place. It had a silence like the fairy-tale castle of the Sleeping Beauty, indolent and heavy. He rode on past the house, the stables and the kitchen gardens, tempted to pause at each but holding himself back. He then saw an orchard, and there, a woman and a little girl busy amongst the apple trees. He made his way in that direction, riding carefully for he was in doubt where garden ended and field or park began. His approach was silent; his long-tailed grey trod the grass softly.

The apple trees were old and crooked, the ground bestrewn with leaves and fruit. The little girl ran about in a pink frock and pinafore, picking the windfalls. A small, pale Italian greyhound, her muzzle grizzled with age, started to bark in a desultory manner, half-turned in the wrong direction, but it made the woman look up.

Allington thought, *She is not entirely young but she is not as yet thirty*, and after that he noticed she wore, such a detail, a small mourning brooch in black and gold. She had a loose, faded apron over her green gown, the sleeves pushed back, and no hat. Her hair was cut rather short but it was a mass of loose, brown curls. The sun had touched her face with freckles and colour. It was lively, her eyes hazel or green, and she looked at Allington with a certain directness, not shy, no false modesty, but frankly as one person to another, though her gaze was questioning. She would, he knew, not be considered more than quite pretty, past the sweetness of youth with those lines of anxiety about her eyes, but he thought her beautiful and when he looked at her his mind went back to Keats: '*Thy hair soft-lifted by the winnowing wind. . .*'

The occasion upon which he had met her before sprung to his mind with startling clarity. So vivid was the memory, it was painful, even shocking. He remembered her name, but then Allington did not forget much. There had been no freckles then, no illicit touching of the sun. The sight of him on his grey horse in the middle of the orchard surprised her – troubled her a little, he thought, but no more. There was no recollection in her gaze. She laid her hand on the dog to quiet it.

Allington dismounted. He tied a knot in the reins of the grey and let it graze. He said, 'I suppose you are expecting me. I rang the bell but got no answer.'

She said, 'I'm afraid it doesn't work. We have few visitors.'

'But you were not expecting me?'

'Not unless you are Captain Allington. I had a letter about a Captain Allington sending horses. It seemed unlikely. I took no particular notice.'

Allington, disturbed, could only think of the need to prolong the moment, to be given time to discern those things he needed to know. He said, in order to contrive this, 'I could reach quite high into this tree.'

She would probably think him strange. He took off his coat and flung it over the saddle, then rolled back his sleeves. There were scars on his forearms, the sabre cuts he had received from a Frenchman when he had lain wounded, pinned to the ground, and had endeavoured to protect his head. Some irrational part of him, and there was not much irrational about Allington, made him want to tell her of such scars, but there was, of course, no occasion to do so. He realised, from her calmness, that Arthur had written but told her nothing.

The little girl had never ceased to trot about, industriously filling the baskets. The old dog lay down. Allington started to pick the apples that had not fallen. It was as good an occupation as any, under the circumstances.

'And you were not expecting me,' he said, but this time it was more statement than question.

'No, unless you are Captain Allington,' she replied.

'Yes, I am.'

'He never sent anyone here before. He said to expect a Captain Allington, but I didn't. I didn't believe him, you see. Are you wishing to stay in this neighbourhood for a while?' She had wondered how Johnny expected her to entertain a single man in a house containing only herself and the servants.

Allington said, evading the question, 'I met a little boy on the drive.'

'Yes, that is Phil and this is Emmy.'

'He told me his name was Philip Osipher.'

This time she laughed. 'I am afraid Phil can be like his father. He never knows where a game ends and real life begins. His name is, of course, Philip Arthur.'

At this Allington knew what he wished to know least, that she was Arthur's wife, but he continued, methodically, to pick apples, while his mind, usually so ordered, ran about in disarray.

She said, 'I am Mrs Arthur. Did he tell you that? You must be a friend of his.'

'Of Arthur's? Of your husband's? Not exactly. We have inhabited the same lodgings in Half Moon Street for the last eight years.' He tried, as never before, to will away encroaching sensations in his head, in his vision.

'Have you come far?' she asked.

'Yesterday from London. Today from Salisbury.'

She noted, uneasily, the odd, abrupt change in him. He looked ill. She said, 'Did you come to see the Philosopher's Tower?'

He managed, she thought with difficulty, to smile. He said carefully, his voice now strained, 'It had not been uppermost in my mind.'

His indignation, his fury with Arthur, was combined with a satirical amusement at Arthur's at last getting the better of him, his ability to wreak his revenge. What was he to do? Who was to tell this woman at his side, who was bidding him leave the apples, who was taking her little girl by the hand, her actual position? And what exactly was that position? He fumbled for the reins of his horse. The low autumn sun was in his eyes. He saw things strangely. The sensations in his head, the dreaded sensations, were not new to him nor induced by the sun, but they were more sudden than usual.

Mrs Arthur wondered if he was going to faint. She certainly did not see how he could get back on his horse. In the distance she saw one of the two boys who worked in the garden. She called out, 'Sam, come and take this gentleman's horse. Put it in a stable. Do what is necessary. Call Annie.'

Allington said, 'I could take the horse . . . I think . . . I'm very sorry but I will have to lie down. Anywhere in the dark will do.'

Mrs Arthur sat in the drawing room at Castle Orchard. She was mending a little tear in her gown with a patch of the same cloth, but the patch was brighter than the gown. The drawing room was long and low – ill proportioned, she knew. There was a large fireplace, ancient chairs, a sofa and cabinets full of china and bits and pieces. It had a genial untidiness, Emmy's doll, a cut-out card soldier, a bowl of quinces and another of apples and pears. There was an ancient spinet and a watercolour of the Philosopher's Tower. The sunny windows looked across the lawn to the river. It was a charming room, full of warmth and pleasing shades, but shabby.

Annie, a redoubtable, indispensable middle-aged feature of her life, put her head round the door. 'Mr Conway to see you, dearie.'

'Which Mr Conway, Annie?'

'Not parson, ma'am.' Annie slipped unconsciously between affection and formality when addressing her mistress.

A fair-haired, boyish-looking man, though probably forty years old, entered the room. He was inclined to play the brooding lover, to which his physiognomy was not suited, as she told him from time to time. She could not take him seriously, for though he was a widower with two little sons, twins, what was she? She was a married woman, as he knew full well.

His brother was the rector, the Reverend Hubert Conway. This was Mr Stewart Conway, who had the management of the school. It was to this school Phil went, his mother thought without enthusiasm, every day, to be prepared for entry to Eton or Winchester, though there was not the two hundred pounds required to send him to either of these places for even a single year, a fact constantly on her mind. She thought a tutor would suit Phil better, but there was an awkwardness in having a tutor in the house when one was a woman on one's own and, just as crucial, no means of paying one.

She disengaged her hand from Mr Conway's and said, 'Why are you not in class today?'

'Because I have sufficient ushers, as you know quite

well. Though I hope you think I do my duty, I have at times more pressing engagements than making little boys understand parameters. Shall we take a turn in the garden? It is very mild. Can I ring for Annie to fetch you a hat?'

'No, I want no hat. If I wanted it I should fetch it myself, for Annie has plenty to do.'

'I wish you would take more care of yourself.'

'You mean you wish I would take more care of my complexion.' She smiled at him, 'It is the least of my worries.'

'Could I but share those worries and have the burden of them.'

'It would be very agreeable if somebody did. However, I think it can't be you.'

They went outdoors and started to stroll in the direction of the river. The little grey hound walked between them, pressing herself to her mistress's skirts. She was jealous; she did not care for Mr Conway.

Mrs Arthur said, 'You look after Phil, and he is one of my worries.' She immediately wondered if he did look after Phil.

'He is a worrying child. Could I but say otherwise. If he could be brought to concentrate . . . however, it was not Phil I came here to discuss.'

Mrs Arthur knew exactly what Mr Conway had come to discuss.

He continued, 'My dear Mrs Arthur, sadly I have no right to care for you, and he who should care for you, whose care of you should be paramount in his heart, shamelessly neglects and misuses you.'

Mrs Arthur, who had heard Mr Conway make similar statements at regular intervals, thought of her husband. He had come down at Michaelmas, gone directly to the agent and this time left her not a single penny. She had a little put by that would pay Annie and Cook and the two lads who worked outdoors. Without the home farm, she thought they would starve.

'I dare say the care of me is *not* paramount in his heart,' Mrs Arthur said, despite herself suppressing a smile at his fanciful use of language.

Mr Conway now said, 'Your reputation is sacred to me.'

She thought Mr Conway much the most likely person to endanger her reputation, but was glad he was coming to the point of his visit.

'Dear Mrs Arthur, it is said you have a stranger here, a gentleman, I suppose, though I doubt he can be, for else he would not have inflicted himself on a single woman.'

'How rumour flies. Yes, I harbour a stranger. How could I not? My husband sent him. It's not that so much, but more that he's sick. Also, I believe Johnny deceived him for I had the impression he didn't previously know of my existence.'

'All the same, it's outrageous. Why didn't he leave immediately? What's the matter with him?'

'I believe, from the way his servant speaks, he has a headache.'

'A headache? I never heard anything so preposterous.'

'His servant, a little talkative fellow, was touchingly aggrieved at having temporarily lost sight of him.'

'Why, he is probably escaped from a madhouse and this servant his keeper.'

'I think him too little to be anyone's keeper. Captain Allington is a man of average size and though he limps, he looks quite strong.'

'And what is his appearance?'

Mrs Arthur, who was not above teasing Mr Conway,

said, 'I never saw such a handsome man before, and very civil. He took off his coat and helped Emmy and I pick apples.'

'Took off his coat?' Mr Conway expostulated, 'He can be no gentleman!'

'He has the manner of a gentleman.' In order to prevent Mr Conway giving her a dissertation on the impropriety of a gentleman taking off his coat, she continued, 'But after a bit it was obvious he was unwell. Annie took him upstairs to the Blue Room. She said, he would do everything for himself but he asked her if she would draw the curtains and bring him a bowl. He wanted no dinner, which was as well as I should have been hard put to know what to give him to eat at such short notice. That was the day before yesterday. I haven't seen him since. Yesterday afternoon he was tracked down by a valet and a groom.'

'A gentleman of means then, if he travels with two servants. I dare say they are paid to look out to him. Remember, madness is very deceptive. He could appear perfectly sane without being in the least so.'

'Perhaps we all could.'

'Mrs Arthur, I beg you to take me more seriously. He's probably hiding from creditors, or worse, the law. You tell me your husband sent him, which I regret is no recommendation. I had better speak to him on your behalf, tell him he must be gone by nightfall. I shall do it immediately.'

Mrs Arthur shook her head. She said, 'No.'

'Why not? It would be most inappropriate for you to go up to him yourself if he is skulking in a bedroom.'

'No. He isn't well. I thought I'd made that clear. I can't refuse him hospitality. As for his being a lunatic, his groom is a deaf-mute, at least I think he is, and I am sure

110

I shouldn't choose one as a minder had a relative of mine been in need of such a person. He has stabled the horses, swept the yard and got in the firewood. One can't tell him anything so he does what he likes, I suppose.'

'Oh dear, it is all very odd and peculiar. I should never forgive myself if some harm came to you.'

'I shall be sure to send Annie to fetch you if I think myself in danger.'

'Now you are teasing me. It is unkind when you know how much I'm attached to you and how I wish your circumstances different.'

'Seeing the vulnerability of my position, you shouldn't express such sentiments. Besides which, you might turn my head, always considered a poorly thing for females.'

Mr Conway accepted the rebuke meekly but he made a last bid to be allowed to at least interview Captain Allington.

'Have you ever had a megrim, Mr Conway?' Mrs Arthur asked.

'Certainly not. It is a thing for the nervous or delicate.'

'A dear friend of mine when I was a schoolgirl had megrim. She told me it was as if the devil poked red-hot irons in her head.'

'Dear me, what a thing for a child to say.'

'It certainly impressed me at the time. Now, be a dear and return to the classroom, even if only to encourage Phil to concentrate.'

Mr Conway took his dismissal in the best spirit he could. When he had gone Mrs Arthur stood and gazed in the river, for they had walked that far. There was an abundance of weed beneath the rush of the water, brilliant green.

Pride reeled under the astonishment of that Mr Arthur downstairs being a married man and not even Mr Emill seeming to know it! Now he waited impatiently, nervously, for Mrs Arthur to come indoors. When she did he approached her and said, 'Please excuse me, ma'am, but I'm bothered about my master.'

'Does he need a doctor?'

'Oh no, ma'am, doctors never do anything for him but make concoctions which he never cares to take. He says doctors don't know nothing and bleed him till he's weak as a kitten. He won't be bled, not ever. They say it's nerves but my master never did have any of them.' Pride began to work himself up. 'Some doctors want his hair thinned, others want it growed. Some want him to take laudanum and henbane in a great big basin of coffee. Laudanum has its point but the coffee would be the end of him. Some say valerian, hartshorn, henbane awashed down with peppermint water. All we does in the end is put a cold rag on his head and wait for it to finish. Anyhows, he couldn't hold none of it down. A sip of water is too much sometimes. That's what I was coming to. When he's getting a bit over it, I give him chicken broth. He's got to have something, I think, or he starves. Now Master says I'm not to trouble the kitchen or inconvenience anyone, and he says it now when he's ill and don't say nothing usually, so he really means it, and if he knowed I'd come to you, I'd get the sharp side of his tongue. I wouldn't trouble no one and I can make the broth myself.' Pride looked at her like a dog waiting for a pat or a kick. He added, 'I never am so bold as when I wants something for him.'

Mrs Arthur said, 'Of course he can have chicken broth. We will have the chicken boiled for dinner. Has Captain Allington always been so affected?'

'Oh no, ma'am.' Pride looked pathetic. 'Indeed not. It was the wound in his head that did it. The surgeons said he'd never survive it, such a hole as it was; or worse, he'd be simple. I knew he weren't simple even if he did think we was in Spain when we wasn't. That bloody battle, begging your pardon, that bloody battle was the worst battle in the world. I wish it had never been, even if it did for Boney.'

Pride searched vaguely for a handkerchief and then wiped his eyes on his sleeve. He concluded more cheerfully, with the words, 'His hair growed over it nicely, though it's a mite pied. I never thought it would.'

The following afternoon, Stewart Conway again walked over the meadow to repeat the conversation he had had with Mrs Arthur the previous morning with the addition of Allington's servants eating her out of house and home, and she saying she had not seen her visitor, who was still sick upstairs, so the circumstances had not altered.

The day after that, Captain Allington had gone.

Two days later, Mrs Arthur was puzzling whether or not he could be made a suitable matter to fill the blank page of her letter to her sister, Louisa, so safely and contentedly married to the dependable John Westcott, the respectable heir to Westcott Park. Mrs Arthur was fond of her sister but the absurdities of her own marriage, her constant concerns over making ends meet, her anxiety for her children's future, were all things so alien to Louisa, so beyond her understanding that she was, as usual, skating around the subject. Indeed, the idea of Louisa's husband sending a strange man to visit Westcott Park while Louisa was alone there, not that she ever was alone there, would be beyond either Louisa or John's imagination. The only thing John

Westcott shared with his brother-in-law was his Christian name.

After the preliminary greetings and enquiries after the little girls, she wrote, for something had to be written, a light-hearted description of the sudden and unexpected visit of a stranger; his illness; Mr Conway's conviction that he was a madman escaping his minders and likely to murder them all in their beds, that being the popular place in which to be murdered; and then his equally sudden departure.

I was standing in the vegetable patch encouraging Sam to dig the potatoes more carefully, not to put a great prong through every one, when he appeared, apparently recovered, though very pale. He apologised for the inconvenience he had caused, seemed much concerned on this point, mounted his horse and rode away.

Mrs Arthur, accosted by Mr Stewart Conway later in the day, when she was walking across the meadow, was able to say to him, 'You will no doubt be pleased to hear that Captain Allington departed before breakfast. We are none the wiser as to why he came.'

Arthur knew, one way or another, much about George Brummell, though it was nine years since the celebrated dandy had fled to Calais, evading his creditors by means of a chaise and four. He did not particularly admire Brummell's style, for he thought it dull in its restraint, for had not Brummell put the starch into neckcloths? He did, however, admire Brummell for his erstwhile power and position. Would anyone remember *him*, Johnny Arthur, visit him and talk of him, nine years on, when he too would be living in discreet retirement across the water?

Arthur would like to have emulated Brummell's flight in detail, as a compliment to so eminent a man, but it was not even the same time of year. It was on a day in May that Brummell had dined on cold fowl and a bottle of claret, attended the opera, left early and made his escape. Now it was October. Arthur would like to have spent his last evening at Almack's, but he could not put off his departure until January, when Almack's reopened. It was a pity he had not delayed losing Castle Orchard until after Christmas. He neither liked cold fowl nor the opera, though he considered one should attend the latter whether one liked it or not. Arthur's only satisfaction was in knowing his own debts greater than the eminent beau's, said to have been a mere forty or fifty thousand pounds, but then Brummell was, in reality, a nobody.

Arthur emulated Brummell in having the coach and four put at his disposal by a friend, in this case Rampton's father. It was packed with portmanteaux containing his favourite clothes, smuggled out under his greatcoat, one by one; his shirts, all thirty-four, which had gone to the laundry and returned elsewhere; similarly his neckcloths and, in a stout trunk, his snuffboxes and the best of his canes. Rampton's wife had agreed to return to the country but Rampton himself had come back to London for the express purpose of aiding the escape, perhaps for the notoriety he would be accorded, for in his heart he now knew Arthur to be too dangerous a friend altogether. He had mundane ideas of how it was to be effected, not being a man for adventures. Arthur was to dine at his house and when it was dark, don a cloak belonging to Rampton's wife, climb into the coach with a pair of horses attached, and be driven away by the family's reliable coachman. The coach would go off to the house of a Rampton daughter, recently confined. It would be assumed Rampton's wife was visiting her sister-in-law. There, an additional pair of horses was to be attached and the journey to Dover immediately undertaken if there was no sign of their being followed. Arthur did not care for the scheme, fleeing disguised as a woman – especially Rampton's wife, whom he disliked – but he knew himself to be watched at every moment, followed everywhere: it was the best they could do.

His signal for departure was to be the day after Captain Allington took the road to Salisbury. Rampton pointed out the expedience of having a fixed day in order to have post horses booked for the entire journey, for they would require many changes between London and Dover. Arthur replied, if he was not himself aware of which day he was to travel, at least nobody else could know it.

Observing Captain Allington to leave Half Moon Street on 14 October, he alerted Rampton to be prepared for the next day. He left his lodging dressed for dinner. Emile, thinking it might rain, ran after him with an umbrella. Arthur had been tempted to take his valet with him, but the risk of disclosure was too great. He thanked him most graciously for the umbrella and wondered who would employ him after he was gone or whether the valet could be persuaded to join him later. He need speak no French if Emile was with him.

The Ramptons had a townhouse in Berkeley Square. Arthur strolled there without a notion he was viewing the familiar streets for the last time. Somebody or something would rescue him from his plight. His sojourn in France was to be just a passing adventure. At some moments he thought this and at others he swung like a weathercock and thought just the opposite and was seized with unreasoning panic. As usual, he was followed.

Rampton, not wishing to appear anything but cheerful, had made certain of the dinner being very fine. There was a raised giblet pie, lobster and venison, syllabub and sweetbreads, a soup and a jelly. The curtains were drawn, the candles were lit and the grave family portraits looked down from the walls.

It was when the cloth was removed and the dessert put on the table, the pears and the apples, the raisins, the iced cakes and the almonds, that it occurred to Arthur he was taking his last English meal in all the comfort of an English house.

He looked up, tears filled his large blue eyes and he said, in a weak, faint tone, 'I don't want to go. I'm not well enough.'

Rampton said, thinking Arthur had made fine work of the meal, 'It's my belief you have to go.'

Arthur repeated it. 'I have to go. What shall I do? They will hang me or send me to Australia.'

'Don't, please, become hysterical. They will not hang you or send you to Australia for debt. You may have a perfectly honourable incarceration in the King's Bench, though in your case, more protracted than you might care for.'

'I have to go, I have to go!' Arthur said, leaping up from the table. 'I should certainly die in Australia.'

'The coach will be at the door in twenty minutes,'

Rampton said, calmly drawing out his pocket-watch. He made Arthur sit down again, ordered coffee to be brought to the table and poured more wine. Time seemed to stand still. The pocket-watch was referred to again and again. At last they got up and entered the hall. There were few servants about since most had gone down to the country with the family, but a footman appeared and announced the arrival of the coach.

Arthur flung the cloak over his shoulders and pulled up the hood. He said, 'I shall be arrested.'

'No, you won't,' Rampton replied, looking forward to seeing the last of him. 'It will be hours before you are followed. Don't disturb yourself unnecessarily. Briggs, our coachman, is as sound as a rock. He will get you there safely. Your passage is booked. It is all so easy and only a few steps from the door to the coach.'

Tears ran down Arthur's cheeks.

The coach was there, an old-fashioned, dignified vehicle and a quiet, middle-aged, sensible coachman in crimson livery on the box and a groom up behind. Arthur peered at it anxiously. He had imagined a postilion to ride the nearside horse and no coachman, but the Ramptons preferred their horses driven, which he knew quite well for it was the same coach in which they had travelled to Bell Hill Abbey.

'Oh, but I cannot go without a postillion,' he said, grabbing at straws.

'Nonsense,' Rampton whispered. 'Get in immediately. It can't make the slightest difference to you. Don't draw attention to yourself, for it's not yet fully dark.'

Arthur drew the cloak about him and stepped up into the coach.

Inside he leaned back on the cushions. It was comfortable and snug but suitably grand with its red Morocco buttoned upholstery and all the little conveniences to make a journey comfortable – a lamp for reading, a box of sandwiches, another of biscuits and a flask of the best French brandy. Ten minutes later he knew they were adding the extra horses. He assumed they had not been followed.

The interior of the luxurious vehicle lulled him into temporary satisfaction and complacency. It gave him the protection afforded a rich man, or so he liked to think. Did he not merit it? Was he not an Arthur of Castle Orchard? Perhaps, or for certain, he was descended from the fabled King Arthur, a suitably fairy-tale prince, and royal blood flowed in his veins. With this half-conviction stirring in his head, so much more agreeable than the reality of the moment, he thought he might sleep and this he proceeded to do, barely stirring when the carriage pulled in and the horses were changed.

It was a few hours before he properly awoke. His first moments were ones of confusion, for the royal connection was still lurking in his mind, but then it occurred to him that the carriage was moving very slowly and his creditors were in pursuit of him, intent on hanging him. Should he escape and get on the steam-packet, he would be addressed in French and he never had been clever at French, or else too idle to learn it. Forever and ever French would be spoken and his English friends would desert him, but if he was caught he might be hanged. He again went from complacency to panic.

The carriage came to a halt. Arthur pulled down the window and peered out. They were at the Bull in Rochester, so they must have been something like five hours on the road. He supposed it about one o'clock in the morning but it was too dark to read the dial on his watch.

They seemed expected, for horses were run out almost immediately and the others led away. Rampton must have alerted the various inns of their need for horses, after all. It had not occurred to Arthur to enquire after such practical details. The groom had been driving to give the coachman a rest but now the coachman got back on the box.

'I want to sit up with you,' Arthur said. The idea of sitting alone in the carriage now made him nervous. He would not be able to tell if they were being pursued. He had abandoned the cloak, preferring to pull on his greatcoat, and he clambered up. It was a night of swift clouds not entirely obscuring a full moon. Rampton had said to him, 'It is fortunate there will be sufficient moonlight, or you would have to delay your going.' He now cursed the moon, for without it he would be back in his own bed.

As soon as they were under way, he urged the coachman to hasten.

'Lor' bless you, sir, we are going at a good even trot, though I declare they have given us a blind horse as the near-wheeler.'

'Have we made good time?'

'Excellent time, sir, don't you fret.'

'I want you to spring the horses to get us on a bit.'

'Can't do that, sir. They have to get up the hill out of Chatham yet. Terrible hill that is. Very pleasant road, the Dover road, apart from the hill out of Chatham.'

Arthur was not interested in the hill out of Chatham beyond thinking it would delay them. The four horses, the wheels on the hard, stony road and the jangle of the bars

120

made plenty of noise but he could hear something coming behind them, very fast, or so he thought.

'We are being followed,' he said.

'If we are, 'twill only be the Mail. Don't know precisely what times they run.'

'We will be overtaken. I shall be arrested. I shall be hanged.'

'Calm yourself, sir. There is nothing behind us.'

'There is, there is, I can hear it.'

Arthur tried to turn round and shout at the groom. He half-stood up and waved his arms but the groom either could not hear him or he had fallen asleep.

'Sit down, sir, do, sir,' Briggs said. 'You'll upset the horses. They are not a very even lot as it is.'

They started to ascend the hill south of Chatham.

'Nasty hill to come down, this,' the coachman said, flicking his whip and encouraging the horses to pull into their collars. 'It ain't safe without a drag chain, an' what if that busts? You're in for a purler.'

'Oh, but I am sure there is something behind us. Can't you hear it?'

'Can't hear nothing, sir. I'd tell you if I did, honest sure. For Gawd's sake, sit still!'

Arthur could not contain his panic. Again and again he twisted on the seat, sure he could hear a second vehicle behind them. For a long while it was a figment of his imagination but then the coachman thought he too could hear something or another.

'Well, sir, the road is a public place,' he said. 'Anyone can be out on it, perfectly lawful.'

He was, of course, quite correct, for the vehicle coming up behind them belonged to a country gentleman returning from a long evening spent dining with friends. He drove a light gig, with a fast, strong horse he was urging rapidly on. At the same time, coming steadily down the hill, four horses, and the drag chain on, was a coach of the Royal Mail.

'I shall be hanged,' Johnny Arthur cried. 'Spring the horses.'

'Don't act so daft, sir,' the coachman remonstrated, as Arthur tried to wrestle the whip from him. 'Mind now, or we'll get under the Mail.'

Arthur, crazy with fright, continued to struggle for possession of the whip. The horses started to weave about the road, the Mail got closer, the gig came up behind . . . and then the nearside wheels of the coach went up the bank and the whole thing tipped and went over. Arthur was shot off the box and into the path of the oncoming horses, though the coachman driving the Mail managed to pull them up before they trampled on him. It made little difference, for Arthur had slipped his creditors for ever, a dribble of blood from his mouth soiling the white of his linen. A rich cascade of snuffboxes from a burst trunk had descended with him.

Between them all, including the passengers from the mail, they righted the coach. The groom and the coachman were not much hurt beyond bruising. They re-coupled the horses and then lifted Arthur's body back inside.

'Best place for him,' the coachman said sourly.

The mail coach then drew hastily away, for the mail must never be late.

Captain Allington returned to London from Castle Orchard. He supposed Arthur would be on the Continent but he intended to follow him there. His inclination was to call him out; he felt sufficiently enraged to do so, though he abhorred duelling and the idea of standing opposite Arthur and shooting him was ridiculous, for he may as well have shot at a rag doll.

When he reached his lodgings in Half Moon Street he found his landlord's wife in tears and all sewing suspended. A guard was at Arthur's door and several grey-faced, rusty-looking gentlemen were making an inventory of what remained in his rooms. Allington was immediately informed of Arthur's death on the Dover road.

He retreated to his own rooms, extremely disconcerted. His indignation against Arthur did not abate. His mind, usually so quick, rational and calculating, he endeavoured to fix on the practical. He thought the deeds of Castle Orchard securely his, but what was the position of Arthur's widow and children? Would she immediately fly to the succouring arms of her family in Devonshire, for he knew she came from there? He supposed she had a jointure, for it was usual, to be used in the event of her husband predeceasing her. Surely no father would have allowed his daughter to marry such a one as Arthur without making sure she had some sort of security in the event of his death?

Allington could answer none of these questions to satisfy himself, and all sorts of other conflicting emotions prevented him from viewing his own position, let alone Mrs Arthur's, with a suitable degree of calmness.

Eventually he took himself off for a long walk. London was still empty but the news of Arthur's death was everywhere, a description of it having been reported in the newspaper. Later, still restless, he went to his club. He took his usual seat in the Travellers', produced his pocketbook and began to draw the landscape that surrounded Castle Orchard, the wood, the meadow and the river. He had been taught to draw as a boy when attending the Military College at Great Marlow, for it was an essential accomplishment when examining a position. He placed the house, the stables and the Philosopher's Tower correctly. He was an object of curiosity, for had he not lived in the same lodgings as Arthur, but nobody disturbed him while he was thus occupied; nobody had the temerity to approach him.

Somebody said, 'How typical of our Johnny to pay his lesser creditors, the ones who would really have suffered.'

There was a pause while others wondered if this were not too generous an assessment of Arthur's character, but the proof was in the pudding.

Another said, 'He was absurd, but charmingly so.'

'He was not fit for the world.'

'The world was not fit for him.'

'To think we will never again spot him swanning down Piccadilly with a cane in his hand, some new toy, as light-headed as a butterfly.'

'He had no enemies.'

'Dogged by his creditors, ignobly run to ground – murdered, one might say.'

'There should be a law against such harassment.'

'Ah, but it's said he gave them the slip, that they didn't know he had gone.'

'Is that so? He was nonetheless harried to his end.'

'The estate must be sold, I suppose, to pay his debts.'

'Undoubtedly.'

'But what sort of a place is it? He never went there, did he, if he could possibly help?'

'Oh, I think he disliked it.'

'Does anyone know it?'

'Not worth a visit, I believe, grounds nothing, house a muddle, shut up for years. It is only known for its Philosopher's Tower and one would not go all the way into the remoter parts of Wiltshire to look at that. Arthur himself said it was a disappointment and likely to fall in the river.'

Someone approached Allington for a game of chess but then thought better of it.

Someone else, who had not previously spoken, now said, 'He was married in his earliest youth.'

'Nonsense.'

'Yes, he was. He married a Templeton from Devonshire. It was, he is meant to have said, at the instigation of his father and quite against his inclinations.'

'But if that is so, what happened to his wife?'

'I suppose she died.'

'Or returned to Devonshire . . . who knows.'

'There was no heir?'

'None ever mentioned.'

'The last of the Arthurs, the estate sold to pay his debts.'

'A Templeton married a Westcott, the heir I believe.'

'A slight connection, if the same family.'

Allington finished his drawing. He was thinking, My own place in the country. He thought of Mrs Arthur whom he had last seen standing in the vegetable garden in a faded blue cotton gown, carefully patched, but the patch brighter than the gown. Would she mourn Arthur? Whose task was it to tell her of his death?

'His funeral?' somebody asked. 'Who is to arrange it?'

'Is he to go back to Castle Orchard? His family must be buried there.'

'All the same, not his natural home.'

'A collection will be made to return him there.'

'No, the collection is to bury him here and to put up a stone.'

A hat was produced. Not everyone had the money they required in their pockets. The hat was passed to Allington. He spoke at last, saying, 'Contribute to Arthur's funeral? Certainly not. Let him be cut up and examined in the surgeon's hall. It would be the first time he had ever been of the slightest use.'

There was a shocked silence.

After a moment Allington continued, 'I have seen many die, though no more than any other serving soldier. Their death, usually, is not important. There is always someone else to take their place. Deserters, the riff-raff, are shot by firing squads. Others are stripped to the waist and flailed, two hundred, three hundred lashes and more, a worthless punishment for often worthless men but none so worthless as Arthur.' He reached in his pocket and dropped a farthing into the hat, saying, 'Even that seems generous.'

After such a speech it would have been judicious to have quit the scene, but he merely abandoned his pocketbook in favour of the *Spectator*. He was not one to walk away from a situation he had himself created. He then said, 'Think with what ceremony you will bury Arthur. They are raking up the bones of those that died at Waterloo to make a mound in honour of the Prince of Orange. Who cares how they were buried, stripped of their clothes and dumped in pits? I dare say you think it a pity I escaped being one of their number.'

Tensions could run high even in the best-regulated of gentlemen's clubs and there were many there who did not lack the courage to challenge Allington. Though he was an undoubted hero of the late wars, these were now ten years old and they did not give him an excuse to speak as he did. They thought it was because Arthur owed him money.

While a hasty debate was in progress and Allington awaited the consequences of allowing his tongue to run away with him, Rampton entered the room. He looked very grave, as was to be expected, but there was also an air of grievance and dissatisfaction about him.

He had of necessity, though he did not see it as a necessity, for surely a man could lend a carriage to whomever he liked, been involved in answering questions, ludicrous questions, such as, had he given the carriage to Mr Arthur or merely lent it, for otherwise it was the property of the receivers? Indeed, his father's carriage and poor Briggs, very shaken and bruised and disgruntled, had all been impounded though subsequently released, the carriage with its red Morocco sliced apart. It seemed Arthur's creditors were particularly enraged, for having sent to his lawyer to obtain the deeds to Castle Orchard, it was learned that the lawyer did not have them, for the estate had not belonged to Arthur at the time of his death.

Rampton began to expound on all this. Then to whom *did* the estate belong? The lawyer had not been prepared to disclose this information, it not being his business to do so, the transaction being perfectly legal and there being no mortgage or other complications. The estate, the house and everything pertaining to it was gone from the Arthurs, and the only comment the lawyer made was that he thought the late Mr Arthur had behaved very shabbily for a man with a wife and two children.

Rampton did, of course, know to whom Castle Orchard

now belonged. He was unlikely to have forgotten it. Nobody else could know. He cast an uneasy glance in Allington's direction and thought better of making further disclosures. He had himself been shocked at the notion of Arthur having a wife and children. He wished he had never had anything to do with the fellow, let alone helped him escape at the expense of the family carriage.

The zest for firing a pistol at Captain Allington died away. He was, after all, a man known to have suffered much for his King and country. It was apparent that Arthur was not all he seemed. Others were speculating on the back pages of betting books. Who might owe money to whom and what provision had been made for Arthur dying before he was five and thirty or for his selling Castle Orchard? If he had sold Castle Orchard, where was the money? This remained a mystery, only the small creditors having been paid and Johnny having with him his snuff-boxes and a quantity of cash amounting to the Michaelmas rents, not the value of a whole estate, the red Morocco having divulged nothing and there being no secret bottoms to his portmanteaux.

The Revd Hubert Conway read of Arthur's death in the newspaper. It disturbed him very much and then it crossed his mind that Mrs Arthur might not have read the newspaper and, being in the strange position she was, could remain unaware of the catastrophe. He thought it a catastrophe for he assumed that every woman must regret the loss of the man to whom she had made her vows, however unsatisfactory he might prove as a husband. It was the duty of a woman to continue in good faith and bear her lot with Christian fortitude. The manner of Arthur's death seemed peculiarly unfortunate, for how could one make one's peace with one's Maker while being hurtled off the box of a carriage going to Dover? The Revd Hubert Conway had not known Arthur well, for Arthur could hardly be said to have cultivated his acquaintance, but he believed no man to be beyond redemption.

'It is a sad, sad world in which we live,' he muttered into his coffee, 'when a man is an undutiful son, an undutiful husband and an undutiful father – and then falls off the box of a carriage. He can't make amends. I must visit Mrs Arthur.'

'What are you saying, Hubert?' his brother asked.

'I must visit poor Mrs Arthur.'

'Why?'

'Her husband is dead.'

'Dead?' Mr Stewart Conway leaped from his chair. 'How is he dead?'

'In an accident. It's most unfortunate to die so unexpectedly.' The rector rose from his chair, his coffee unfinished. 'I shall go immediately to poor Mrs Arthur.'

'Let me go, Hubert, let me.'

'You? Why, how odd you are, Stewart. It is I who am rector. It would be most strange for you to go. Mrs Arthur may be taken ill with the shock and it is certainly my duty to be with any member of the parish grievously afflicted.'

So saying, he hastened out of the room, talking to himself all the way down the drive and across the field. 'Very odd of Stewart, very odd, poor Mrs Arthur, how sudden,' and further words to that effect.

On his way he met Phil, equally preoccupied, going to school. For a moment they stopped and stared at each other. The rector then said, 'Poor child, poor child.'

'I am a poor child,' Phil replied, 'because my legs are like sticks.'

'Dear, dear, what does the boy say?' The rector hastened on.

Mrs Arthur had not read the newspaper. She was seated at the dining table teaching her daughter arithmetic. Emily Arthur was as stalwart as her brother was thin, with round rosy cheeks, green eyes and brown hair. She had the health and shine of a good apple. When the Revd Mr Conway was shown in, her mother gave her a kiss and told her to run outside for a while.

'I hope it's not bad news, Mr Conway,' Mrs Arthur said, taking one look at the rector.

Mr Conway felt unable to proceed. The news was too bad to impart and it was apparent Mrs Arthur was in ignorance of it.

'Please sit down, dear Mrs Arthur.'

'It isn't Phil? He's only just gone off to school.'

'No, no. I passed him on the way here. It is in the newspaper, too dreadful a thing, an accident on the Dover road. Why was he on the box? He needn't sit with the coachman. The carriage was borrowed from a Peer of the Realm, or so the paper said. The coachman's name was Briggs and he said Mr Arthur struggled with him for the whip to make the horses go faster, though there was nobody behind them but a gentleman returning from dinner. The carriage went up the bank and turned over. It is a very dangerous hill, the one out of Chatham, for I had an uncle living there who used to tell me of it. They picked Mr Arthur out of the road but he was no more. Oh, that I should be the bearer of such terrible news. Shall I send for Annie? Dear Mrs Arthur, pray don't faint.'

Mrs Arthur did think for a minute she might faint. She half-stood up and then sat down again, bewildered by the suddenness. She whispered, 'Are you sure?'

'Unless there are two of Jonathan Arthur Esq. of Castle Orchard.'

'He was trying to get to France, I suppose. At Michaelmas he took all the rents and left nothing with which to pay the servants. What is to become of us? What will become of my children?'

Mr Conway said, 'Why, my dear Mrs Arthur, you surely need not go away. There must be trustees and wards and guardians and all that sort of thing.'

Mrs Arthur was not so stunned she could not think the estate must be sold to pay the debts. What were his debts? She had no idea. Maybe the furniture, the library, the plate would suffice, but in her heart she knew they would not and that Castle Orchard would have to go. At the same time she thought of the young man she had married, almost a boy, so like Phil, so charming, a sprite from another world, but so useless, so decadent and so merciless in his intentions.

Mr Conway, seeing her shocked, abstracted air, said gently, 'Would it help to say a little prayer for him, here and now? He can have had no time to prepare himself for the next world.'

Mrs Arthur turned to look at the rector's sad, earnest, innocent face. She said, 'I couldn't say a prayer. Maybe I will one day.' Though she said this, she thought it most unlikely. She added, 'I should like it if you did.' It was said more for the rector's sake than for her husband's.

'Later, later, I shall say a prayer,' he replied. 'Now I must be practical. You should not be alone, Mrs Arthur, at such a time. Have you relations?'

'I have a half-sister, but I don't think Louisa should come and I can't imagine what use she would be if she did. I have a stepmother, but I shall manage well enough.'

'But the funeral?'

'Yes, there must be a funeral, I suppose.'

'He must be returned to lie with his ancestors.'

Mrs Arthur was not sure Johnny's ancestors would welcome him. The puzzling suddenness of death confused her. She said tentatively, 'Where do you suppose he is now?'

'With the angels and archangels, I do sincerely hope, though no time to contemplate redemption. The Lord is merciful.'

'No, I meant his body. That must be somewhere. Perhaps it has yet to be officially identified.'

'You mean it might not be his?' The rector would have preferred not to talk of the body.

'I expect that was established.'

'Dear me, yes, for it was in the paper and they would hardly put it there if there were doubts. Death should not be so unexpected. My wife was a year a-dying and one became quite reconciled to the idea of it.'

Mrs Arthur knew the rector's wife had bullied him from dawn to dusk.

He continued, 'I never could bring myself to marry twice, though for the sake of my dear little boys, perhaps I should have done so. Should I have Phil sent home? He shouldn't be at school today. I will go and have him sent. You will break the news to him yourself, Mrs Arthur? If you feel unable I shall undertake the task.'

'No, I will tell Phil. But you are right, today he must come home.'

'I shall tell my boys and they will be sure to look after him. Robert is most responsible and grown up – he'll be a guide for the others. They know what it is to be afflicted, for did they not lose their mother? They have tender hearts.'

Mrs Arthur was uncertain as to the tender hearts of the rector's three sons. They were polite but when they came to Castle Orchard their personalities eluded her. She thought them a little too polite, a little slippery. Phil would say nothing and squirm, embarrassed, in his chair when they shared his luncheon.

'Now Mrs Arthur, we must try to be practical. There is maybe a lawyer or some man used to dealing with your husband's affairs. Do you have his address? You must ask him about arrangements. He will assist you.'

This startlingly practical notion was as much as Mr Conway could do. He rose to depart, distressed at leaving her alone and promising to return the next day or in the evening.

Phil wandered home from school, dawdling across the meadow. They had told him his mother needed to speak to him. By the time he reached Castle Orchard he had nearly forgotten this. Emmy was playing in the garden. Phil liked Emmy, her intractable will and her solid form. He took her hand and they went indoors together.

Emmy said, 'Mama.' She led him to the drawing room where Mrs Arthur sat in a chair, alone and still. Phil ran towards her and said, 'What is the matter?'

'You know something is the matter, Phil? Yes, something is the matter. It's your father. He has had an accident. He fell from the box of a coach.'

'Is he much hurt?'

'Yes. He is more than hurt. He has died, dearest.'

133

'Died?' Phil chewed the word over in his mind. He knew what it meant. You died and you were gone. In England they put you in the ground, but the soldiers of the Spanish wars were not always put in the ground.

He said, half-aware of his own confusion, 'There are no wolves.'

'No, Phil, no wolves. But why?'

'To eat him.'

'No, of course not.'

'He will have a coffin like my baby brother, Matthew, a wooden box to put him in with the lid shut down.'

'Yes.' Mrs Arthur was surprised at what Phil remembered. It was rare for them to speak of Matthew. It remained too painful.

Phil said, 'I suppose my father being dead doesn't matter very much. Are you sad or happy? I will look after Emmy and you. Well, I'll try, and if I remember.'

Emmy, who had or had not been listening, now said, 'Will the money Papa always took be yours now?'

One could trust Emmy to come straight to the point, but how did the child know about such a thing?

'I am not sure, darling. Possibly not.'

'Shall we have to wait and see?'

It was a matter of waiting and seeing, for Mrs Arthur heard nothing. She felt in a state of limbo. Her brother-in-law arrived in the Westcott Park barouche, tall, dark, handsome, reliable, the epitome of solid virtues. Why had she not married such a man? He asked her questions. He would go to London for her and attend to the funeral if that would be as she wished. He wanted to know if Johnny had left a will and what her financial position would be. Mrs Arthur, over the years, had made light of her situation: trustees had looked after the estate, herself and the children, but when Arthur became thirty the trustees lost their jurisdiction and chaos descended. John Westcott, aware of this, knew the situation was perhaps not good, but his sister-in-law had, he was sure, a jointure set up by her father and her husband's father in the event of her becoming a widow, and she agreed this was the case.

She told him of the likely possibility of the estate being sold. He stood over her while she wrote a letter to the lawyers asking if they could clarify her position and then he departed for London. He thought the death of his brother-in-law a great blessing, but it offended his sense of what was proper to confess. Arthur, whom he had barely known, for their paths never crossed, was everything of which he most disapproved – and surely his widow must be better off without him.

In London he learned that Castle Orchard no longer belonged to the Arthurs. He wrote to his sister-in-law accordingly, but pointing out that no one acknowledged being the purchaser, so perhaps it wasn't true. He gave an account of the funeral and begged her to let him know of what further assistance he could be when she received the lawyer's answer to her letter. He then retreated to the calm and order of Westcott Park.

Of Captain Allington himself there was no sign, for he had gone into Surrey for the fox hunting.

Mrs Arthur received her brother-in-law's letter and one from the lawyer at the same time. Annie gave them into her hand while she was walking round the house, wondering if the odd pieces of furniture she had brought to Castle

Orchard with her marriage might be considered hers or whether the receivers, whom she expected daily, would take everything.

She opened the letter from the lawyer first, with misgiving, but she was quite unprepared for the contents, which even the wildest of her imaginings had not foreseen.

Dear Mrs Arthur,

I was surprised to receive your letter. It is curious you had no information from your late husband, for he disposed of his whole property, estate, house, contents of house, absolutely and entirely last August, vacant possession from Michaelmas Day or the day following.

It was a demeaning transaction, one of which I was most anxious not to be in any way party to. We have closed the file on your husband's family entirely, as without the property there is no business. It is a sad ending when I consider the respect and esteem in which your late father-in-law was held by myself and my partners.

You enquire whether the late Jonathan Arthur, your husband, left a will. I am afraid I cannot say. If there was a will, it was not drawn up by myself. Apart from the estate there was no money, and this being forfeited in a game, there is still no money. I am unaware of the nature of the game. I was not informed. The only surprise is that the gentleman who is now the owner of the property has not come forward to claim it.

Your most humble and obedient servant,
S. Jonas

Mrs Arthur leaned on the table and closed her eyes. Annie ran and put an arm round her, thinking she looked faint, but she rallied sufficiently to read her brother-in-law's letter, which only confirmed the facts.

'The news can't be worse than what it was,' Annie said, for the servants had been informed that they faced an uncertain future.

'I think it much worse,' Mrs Arthur said.

'Why, how could that be, dear ma'am? Is it the gentlemen coming who will take everything away?'

'I don't know. I just don't know. I must have time to think. I will go outdoors.'

Annie ran to fetch her shawl, a poor threadbare thing of which Annie had better herself.

'Don't get cold now, dearie. Annie won't ever leave you and the dear children, not if she should starve.' She burst into tears.

Mrs Arthur still determinedly went outdoors. It was cold and blustery. She walked down to the river.

That they must leave Castle Orchard was certain, but why had the lawyer not mentioned her jointure, for surely he must know of that? She must write again. Of course she had known they would probably lose Castle Orchard one way or another, but to think at this very moment they trespassed on it filled her with horror and bewilderment.

Now she looked down at the river. She wished it were spring and that she could gather huge armfuls of lilac or bunches of daffodils, as if in defiance, but the shrivelled leaves on the bough did not inspire her to so extravagant a gesture, and did they not belong to another? Meg, her old dog, had accompanied her and she thought, Even poor Meg will be homeless.

The folly of her youth must punish her for ever: her determination, against all advice, to marry Johnny Arthur. She thought of her father, whom she had loved and defied. How often had she longed for his presence, his dear, calm, kind face and his moderate, clever advice, but he was dead.

At this very moment she lived on charity, the charity of the owner of Castle Orchard. She had no claim to the house, the garden, the servants, even the food she ate. For want of any purpose, she walked along the edge of the river, passed the Philosopher's Tower and entered the orchard. There were yet a few apples on the trees and she remembered how she and Emmy had been gathering the windfalls in the sun.

Captain Allington, she thought. He is the owner of Castle Orchard, He, of the sweet, perhaps deceptive, smile, for she had noticed it, even though he had only smiled the once, when he had seen her amongst the potatoes. For all his politeness, he was nothing but a gambler too, no better than Johnny, and she lived at his mercy and upon his charity, for it was long past Michaelmas.

In a comfortable posting inn in Surrey, Pride struggled to write to his mother. He acknowledged to himself that he had made a mistake in his previous letter to his only remaining parent, in giving away the information that they were returning to the country for the fox hunting. Had he not made it clear on other occasions that his master was too feeble to get out of bed?

I never have spoken no untruth, honest to God I have not. The constitution of my master must be

understood. When he is up he is up and as good as
the next man, but you can't tell when that will be. It
is not possible for me to leave him at any time in case
he should go down. You might think when fox hunt-
ing he would be very well up and I might leave him
a week, but in this you would be wrong. My master
ought never to be fox hunting, for he has not a sound
leg and no grip, so should the horse tip he will be off
of it. He surely will bust something before very long
– and then who is to manage him? If he gets soaked
through he will bring on the ague, and that is a great
deal worse than the other.

Pride paused here to consider how much of his letter was
true. The importance of truth did not loom large with
him; he remained indifferent to the passing fib, even if
invoking his Maker, but it was sounder policy to speak the
truth where possible. He never told Captain Allington a
lie, for experience had taught him he could not get away
with it. His mother, though as alarming as his master,
could more easily be deceived. Pride's letter gave the
usual impression, he hoped, that he was indispensable.
He continued:

If I could separate him from those hunting horses how
happy I should be for it surely is no safe occupation for
a gentleman what suffered so many wounds. I say so
often to that Dan though he don't hear nothing nor gets
his tongue round no words so it may as well be French.

In the next room Allington was also writing a letter.
Hunting was an occupation close to his heart, for was

it not an activity that mimicked the alarms of war and forced a man to otherwise forget himself? The added hazard of a weak right knee did nothing to discourage him. He had bathed and now sat in his dressing gown in front of a good fire, a small table pulled up before him, the offending right limb on a footstool, his only acknowledgement that it pained him and hunting made it worse.

Captain Allington was usually decisive. He was not accustomed to confusion. His mind perpetually went to the sunny figure of Mrs Arthur with her faded smock, under the apple trees at Castle Orchard or amongst the vegetables. What was her situation, now that Arthur was dead? Her marriage cannot have been a happy one, but did she cling to loving the man she had married? Did she grieve? Did she have anywhere to go? Had she a jointure, money for herself and her children?

At last he dipped the pen in the ink.

Dear Mrs Arthur,

It is with some misgiving that I write to you because I am ignorant of how you are situated. I write to you at Castle Orchard under the presumption that is where you are. Should you have already made other arrangements, this letter can be ignored.

It is my wish you and your children should stay at Castle Orchard until it is entirely convenient for you to remove elsewhere. It would be good of you to let me know what members of your staff would like to stay. Some you may like to take with you. I should prefer the house not to be empty. I shall at the moment retain the agent employed by your late husband so the business of the estate should run much as usual.

I hope this letter causes you no further distress.

Here Allington came to a halt. He would be expected to express a simple condolence on the death of her husband but he declined to do so. He finished the letter thus inadequately:

I shall consider sending my horses and groom. He will be no trouble to you. I shall come down myself in a while.

He signed it *R. Allington* and sealed it up. He thought, Does she even know it is I that owns Castle Orchard?

The Revd Hubert Conway slowly mounted the steps to the pulpit. It was Sunday afternoon, a little early for Evensong, but the time suited the school dinner-hour. His congregation consisted of Mrs Arthur, many of the inhabitants of Orchardleigh and the thirty boys who attended the rectory school. He thought it unfortunate his Sunday sermons needed to be modified and reduced to accommodate small boys – and some of them his own flesh and blood – who haunted him all week with their mischievous habits. *Suffer the little children* . . . Jesus made reference to the innocence of the child, and though the rector knew the child to be innocent – so long as Christened and therefore purged of Original Sin – he did sometimes wonder how small boys could manifest characteristics that seemed so far from innocent. It was, he surmised, the meandering of youth that knew not where it was bound until directed. Not only did the young mind need directing, but he supposed that of every living soul under his care in the parish. It was, undoubtedly, a tall order.

He took as his text *He that is first shall be last.*

'Be content with your lot,' he told the congregation. 'Your reward will be in Heaven. It is as hard for a rich man, remember, to obtain the Kingdom of Heaven, as it is for a camel to get through the eye of a needle. The Almighty has His place for you, and within the bounds of that place your task is to strive for perfection, not to strive for some elevation for which you were not intended. A menial task well done is of as much value in the eyes of the Lord . . .'

Mrs Arthur had asked Phil if he would prefer to sit with the other boys, but Phil declined. He sat by his mother with a vacant expression on his face. Mrs Arthur had heard most of the rector's sermons before, for his repertoire was limited, but the text caught her attention. As a camel never could get through the eye of a needle, it seemed the unfortunate rich man was doomed from the start. How was one to view the rapid reversal of one's position, from comparative comfort, inasmuch as they had enough to eat, to something nearer poverty, needing money to buy Phil boots. Did poverty alter the shape of the camel so it could get through the eye of the needle?

Abandoning any further attempts to listen to the rector, she considered Captain Allington's letter. His attitude to her was generous but he could not be expected to be patient for ever. She lived at his expense, considering the produce of the garden and the home farm were now all his. Even Domino, the fat old pony, was his, though she could not imagine what use Captain Allington would make of him, unless he had a wife and children. It was curious this possibility had not occurred to her before. The set in which Johnny had moved were mostly bachelors, scorning domesticity, but she was not the only wife to be a victim of gambling, and she thought whole families ruined by it. The very notion of a roulette table, faro, and all those other games made her shudder. In which of these terrible pursuits had Castle Orchard passed from Johnny Arthur to Captain Allington? And at which juncture might he return to London and lose the price of it to someone else? As far as her husband was concerned, she knew his debts to have been incurred not only by gambling but also by wild extravagance.

That Castle Orchard no longer belonged to the Arthurs was now public knowledge. She had felt the need, out of honesty, to tell the few servants. She had also told them that Captain Allington seemed ready to keep them. They viewed the situation with mixed feelings – pity for their mistress but without undue disturbance for their own future. Pride, during Captain Allington's brief stay, had appeared so fond of his master, they could not believe much ill of him. It was, as a result, curious how life continued exactly as it had before. She knew she must depart from Castle Orchard, but the lawyer had not answered her letter on the subject of the jointure. She knew there was a jointure. Her father had made it so that if she signed certain documents, the money would be available for her use without the necessity of her being widowed. She had, under duress, signed away a legacy she had had on her father's death, but she had not touched the jointure. How could she decide how she and the children might live without being told her income? She thought they might live in a little house, perhaps just Annie with them, and save money for the education of Phil. The money had been invested, the income reinvested, but why did the lawyer not answer her letter?

She knew she should go to Westcott Park but she barely had the means to travel. She had – temporarily, she supposed – to live either on the charity of the Westcotts or of Captain Allington. She knew the former should be preferable. The only other person with whom she might have had a connection was her mother-in-law, but the old lady had always disliked her and, furthermore, had had a paralytic stroke. To apply to her would not be of the slightest use. She wondered about consulting Mr Stewart Conway. He had written her a formal letter of condolence on the death of her husband which she condemned as hypocritical – but was not much of such things hypocritical, and was she not unfair to blame him for it? She had since not seen him, which made all his hints of undying devotion seem like the kiss of a butterfly on the wind.

The rector came down from the pulpit. She hastily thanked God for her health and strength of mind. Having given her those things, she supposed He expected her to rely on her own resources. She wished she had the deep piety of her late father that had sustained him through troubles. Had he been alive, how willingly would she have surrendered herself and her little family to his care.

On leaving the church the rector took her hand, patted Phil on the head, and said, 'My dear Mrs Arthur, I'm sorry calamity has so overtaken you. I can't believe such wickedness, and keep hoping all is rumour and conjecture . . . insubstantial . . . a fib.'

'It isn't a fib.'

'You will be leaving us?'

'I must, eventually.'

'But to go where?'

'I wish I knew.'

'Not far, I hope. Stewart must advise you. He is clever. He will walk with you across the meadow to Castle Orchard.'

His brother, now coming out of church, seemed ready to walk with her, abandoning the schoolboys to push and shove and scuffle their boots and file away with the undermasters. He gave Mrs Arthur his arm and they went down the path together, past the graves and the innumerable monuments to the Arthurs.

'My husband forfeited his right to a place here,' she said, indicating the graves but looking at Phil as she spoke. 'But then the rights of his heir are forfeited as well.'

'The sins of the fathers are visited on the children,' Mr Conway replied.

'Yes. I always think that very unfair.'

'We aren't expected to understand everything.'

'Now you sound like your brother.'

'I am his brother. I may sound like him from time to time.'

Mr Conway had his sons with him, his twin boys, chubby, flaxen-haired and disconcertingly indistinguishable one from the other. They twittered and chirped between themselves like a pair of yellow-headed canaries, peculiarly incomprehensible. Phil started to play tag with them and they ran about after him as fast as their sturdy little legs could carry them.

'Well, they say the estate is gone,' Mr Conway said. 'Lost in a game of cards.'

'I don't quite know how it was lost, but something of that sort, I suppose. It hardly matters.'

'And the gentleman of the headache is the new owner.'

'Yes, Captain Allington.'

'When does he come?'

'I don't know. According to your brother, you are to advise me.'

'Hubert has great faith in my powers, but I fear it's ill founded. We can't set much store by Captain Allington, a gambling man and without doubt unprincipled.'

'He wrote me a civil letter.'

'One couldn't trust him.'

'I dare say not.'

In silence they opened the little gate in the hedge and entered the Castle Orchard gardens. There was a flight of wooden steps, half-buried in leaves, that led down to a sunken lawn, unkempt and shadowy from the yew that enclosed it. Mrs Arthur looked at her companion. Where were the hints of undying devotion now she was a widow?

She thought Mr Conway would not want to be married to her, now Castle Orchard belonged to Captain Allington. Was he not too practical a man for that? She certainly had no wish to be married to him or to anybody else, yet what might she be driven to do?

Emmy had captured the twins on the carriage sweep. She stood between them, holding them apart, shaking them and then giving each a kiss. They rolled their eyes and said nothing. Though they were a little older than Emmy, she was as tall.

In the drawing room Mrs Arthur offered Mr Conway a glass of wine and a biscuit. She had found in the cellar one bottle of wine left from her husband's last visit. Was it her bottle or Captain Allington's?

'Your brother said you would advise me, Mr Conway. I

wrote to the lawyer asking about the jointure, but get no reply, not one.'

'Perhaps investments failed and he doesn't like to tell you.'

'From the tone of his only letter, I don't think he would hesitate to tell me.'

'You won't be destitute.'

'And what if I were?'

'You will, of course, go to your sister at Westcott Park. Your children would obtain some advantage from it. Mr Westcott must be a man of influence. His property is large, the house grand.'

'But I have no claim on him. Louisa is only my half-sister. It would be a very desperate move.'

'And what of your stepmother?'

'There I really couldn't go. I think she hates me, or something near it.'

'I dare say none of it will be necessary. Why speculate? Nothing can be done until you know your position. In the meantime you will go there, as this now belongs to Captain Allington. It was odd he never said anything at the time.'

'Not at all odd if you consider the awkwardness of his arrival here and the fact that Johnny had made no attempt to tell us or him the truth.'

'I can't think such a man as Captain Allington can have any sensitivity.'

Mr Conway was watching Mrs Arthur. He acknowledged to himself that he had become fond of her, but that fondness had evaporated like the dew on a garden as the sun got up. No, it was not so, he remained fond of her but he was not sufficiently gallant to marry a woman unless he was sure of her income. He was not rich himself. He looked at the curls on her head and wished she would grow her hair that little bit more and let ringlets frame her face. She was not conventional and that would be a serious fault in a wife. Those curls were wild curls and they said something about Mrs Arthur he was not so happy with when he faced reality. She was now watching the children from the window and he went to join her.

She said, 'Jacky and James could escape from Emmy if they would only agree to divide and conquer.'

'When I see my little boys,' Mr Conway said, 'I think of my dear departed wife. They resemble her, you know. It should make me love them more, but I can't forget how they cost her her life.'

Mrs Arthur turned to look at him. She was scornful of his logic.

He said, 'Do they not look like my dear Amelia, whom I shall never replace?'

'No,' she replied. 'They look a great deal more like you.'

He said, judiciously reverting to the original subject, and with reassuring complacency, 'It is as well you have Westcott Park to fall back on.'

Mrs Arthur did not think Mr Conway had given her any advice she had not understood for herself. She was glad when he had left so she might go to her desk and reread Captain Allington's letter. Out of necessity, let alone courtesy, she must reply. Eventually, after much thought, she wrote:

Dear Captain Allington,

Thank you for your letter kindly showing me so much consideration. You seem in no particular hurry to take possession of Castle Orchard but I am afraid this may

*be a politeness on your part. I must tell you honestly
I do not yet know my financial position so I remain
uncertain of what I should do, either to remain here
under an obligation to you or go elsewhere and be
under an obligation to someone else.*

Mrs Arthur, having got thus far, now considered her
removal to Westcott Park. She knew little of the Westcotts
and wondered how she would be received, an impover-
ished, or temporarily so, half-sister of Louisa's with two
children and Annie, but no proper nursemaid. She suspected she would be received with every kindness, but
the idea of arriving like a beggar before the grand portico
of Westcott Park and entering the hall with two anxious
children, an elderly Italian greyhound and barely enough
money to pay the coach fare, was not appealing. There
was also the matter of her poor, tired wardrobe. She was
unused to any sort of society. She could make up the pink
silk Louisa had sent her but it would have to suffice for
every occasion. She then remembered they would expect
her to wear mourning, of which she had none, just one
well-worn grey gown in which she went to church, and
that was only half-mourning. In order to go to Westcott
Park she would need several gowns in black, Phil and
Emmy too. Here, indifferent, she could continue to wear
what she had. Mr Conway would be sure to remark on it.
Perhaps it was as well his attachment to her, under her new
circumstances, was so rapidly cooling.

She looked again at the letter Captain Allington had
sent her. His handwriting was large but neat and perfectly
regular. It seemed out of tune with his habits as a gambler. His letter was nonetheless kind, and as she and her

children were entirely dependent on him at the present moment, she thought his kindness had not only to be recognised but acknowledged.

She ended her own letter with the words:

I should not like to think the presence of myself and my children inhibited your inclinations whether to come here yourself or to send your horses. We presume very much as it is on your good nature, so you must let me know of your intentions. Please recollect we live at your expense. Nothing is quite as it should be here. There was no money at Michaelmas.

She added a few words about the servants and how there was an insufficient number indoors and out, and signed it *Caroline Arthur*.

Phil was down in the boot room and so was Jackson, seated on his upturned barrel, his white clay pipe, forbidden, clamped between his teeth.

'Yer smoked anything, see, if there weren't no tobacco. No money. They'd be months behind with yer money. Yer got it in a lump,' he threw up a grimy fist, 'then 'twas gone. Yer spent the lot. Plenty of wine in Spain. Soldier, did yer say? What's his name?'

'Captain Allington,' Phil whispered, for the second time.

'Never 'eard of 'im. Mind, there's seventy thousand soldiers. Captain Allington? Well, I'm teasing yer. Spanish Allington we called 'im.' Jackson paused and then eyed Phil closely, coldly, with his single eye. He said, 'The sun turned 'im dark as a native, the sun what burned yer to death. The sun and the dust swelled yer lips up till they cracked and blood ran all down yer chin, officers and men alike, none of us was spared. Yer got a green leaf and put it between yer teeth and yer lip. Stopped it, that did. Spanish Allington. Yer don't want Allington at yer back. He'd 'ave the 'ide off yer, boy. What did yer say the name was?'

'Captain Allington,' Phil said, louder, and the other boys laughed.

'He'll 'ave the 'ide off yer, Arthur,' one of them said, in a respectable imitation of Jackson. 'Why is he coming to your house?'

'I don't know,' Phil said. 'It's not our house, it's his.'

'A stickler, Allington was,' Jackson said. 'I 'oped every day a nice piece o' metal would lodge in 'is belly or something of a six-pounder blow is 'ead off.'

'Was he a good officer, Jackson?' Robert Conway asked.

'Follow 'im if 'e said do it, go, kill yerself, wade the river, get in the breaches, whatever, never mind the Frenchies blowing yer to bits, that don't matter, that don't.' Jackson sucked on his pipe. ''E weren't no flogger, 'is bark were worse than 'is bite. A good officer gets yer by without a floggin'. Yer needs a floggin', though. 'Tis the only thing what 'olds yer. Yer didn't give Spanish Allington no lip. I wasn't in 'is regiment, no I wasn't, but 'e were famous.'

'Spanish Allington,' Robert Conway said, 'Wasn't that a bit of an insult?'

''Twas the way 'e looked. Dark eyes. Spoke the lingo. Went be'ind the lines 'e did, the enemy lines, or so 'twas said, lookin' like a muleteer with a stiletto down 'is boot.'

'Was he at Waterloo?'

'Aye. Boney finished 'im there. Cut 'im up like stewing meat, so 'twas said. 'Ow should I know? 'Tis what's said.

151

Knocked 'im silly. Left the infantry and went to the cavalry. I don't know. Get along, boys. Yer wear me out with yer chatter and I wants me rations.'

Jackson took his stick and swished it about. The boys scattered, confused. Was it the same Captain Allington and was he killed or not killed?

Mrs Arthur received a letter from her half-sister.

Dearest Caro,

We had heard rumours but they seemed too incredible to be true. Now it's a fact, and poor little Phil is never to inherit Castle Orchard.

Mrs Arthur paused to consider this. She had known for a long time that Phil was unlikely to inherit Castle Orchard, but she had never said so to Louisa.

Now, dearest Caro, I think you must be very distraught and not know which way to turn. Mr Westcott says you are welcome to the Dower House if you feel it would suit you. He's so kind, I dare say he wouldn't ask a large rent. Pray don't stay a moment longer for fear of Captain Allington's arrival. He can't be a man of principle. We hear all the news from John's cousins, always a little too ready for gossip. Captain Allington is very acceptable in military circles but he is a natural son of the late Lord Tregorn and he makes all his money playing at cards, so I doubt he's really at all respectable, though indeed gentlemen will play cards and lose money more often than winning any. Now

Caro, it is perfectly obvious you can't stay at Castle Orchard if Captain Allington is to come there, even if he were so unprincipled, so little caring of your delicacy, your virtue, to suggest such a thing. Bring poor little Phil and poor little Emmy that they may be safe. Would the Dower House suit? You must come, in the meantime, to Westcott Park.

Your most affectionate sister,
Louisa Westcott

Mrs Arthur laid the letter down. A robin sang in the garden. She went to the window. Phil was standing by the sundial, but she doubted doing anything so positive as puzzling out the time. Did he think about the loss of Castle Orchard? No, his head was filled with swords and battles.

It was now the beginning of November. The lawyer had answered her last letter but only to say the money in the jointure was all spent, as she must know. She had written back to say this was not so. The only money spent was the separate legacy from her father. Though it had been at a particularly distressing time for her, she had been careful in reading the documents her husband had wanted her to sign. Money was obtainable from the jointure with her signature, but not otherwise. The money was safely put away and the lawyer mistaken.

She took up her pen to write to him again. She could not reply to Louisa agreeing to take the Dower House at Westcott Park, for even had she known the modest rent Mr Westcott meant to ask, she had no idea what she would be able to pay.

Annie came in and said, 'The builders are in doing up the lodge, ma'am, mending the window and such.'

'Are you sure?' Mrs Arthur asked.

'Sure as sure, dearie. Mind, it ain't bad, the lodge, only needs a sweep of the chimney and some paint. Do you think he's coming now, the new master?'

'He doesn't say. He says he might send his horses.'

'If he's a fox-hunting gentleman he won't long be parted from his horses, not in November. It must be in his mind to have the lodge filled. The agent spoke to me ever so civil. He was down there instructing the men to do the work. He said Captain Allington was particular, wrote a letter and never missed nothing out of it.'

Mrs Arthur thought his letter to her had missed everything out of it.

Pride, banished to his attic for failing to gain his sixpence, wrote to his mother.

Dear Mother,

You will be interested to learn we is leaving London and moving to Wiltshire, this being an odd place with greyish hills looking like a great smooth coverlet that a giant has gone to bed under. You never would have seen the like, but a travelled man like your son what has been to Spain and Portugal and other foreign places, knows how the world looks. My master has acquired a property. I do think it will benefit him for he likes the outdoors. When we was in the wars he preferred his tent to the billets we got and would sleep in the gardens when he could, though that was also on account of the fleas and the lice which is very numerous amongst those dirty foreigners. Master also says I will do very well

there for there is no gin shop for to tempt my weakness
of which I am not always cured but usually goodish.

My master having property will be a gentleman of
consequence.

Your loving and affectionate son,
Nathaniel Pride

Downstairs, Captain Allington wrote rapidly to Castle
Orchard.

Dear Mrs Arthur,

If you find you must be under an obligation to some-
body, if it was to be me, I should not be burdened by
it. I cannot speak for the other contenders.

As to living at my expense, if you mean you eat my
butter and eggs, I sincerely hope you continue to do so.

You will observe I am having a little attention paid
to the lodge.

Your most obedient servant,
R. Allington

He had received a letter from his stepbrother, which ran
thus:

Dear Allington,

I am astonished to hear you are the new owner of the
Arthur estate in Wiltshire, though why anything you
do should astonish me, I am sure I cannot say. I pray
my son will never part with St Jude for the sake of a
chance throw of the dice, but to give you your due,

I doubt you won the place by chance. I cannot say I approve of this sudden elevation in your position. I suppose you will be looking for a seat in Parliament next and a peerage after that. Ah well, you were always too clever a fellow by half. I shall be up for the opening of Parliament next month and hope I shall see you then. By the way, my brother Thomas is being elected to Parliament, as you may have heard. He will, I think, come in without much opposition. He says if you are still employing Dan, as he is now to be much more in London, he would like him back as his tiger because there never was a more nimble one, even if he could never get him to understand anything.

Yours, etc.,
Tregorn

Allington wrote in return:

Dear Tregorn,

Who taught me to play chess, backgammon, draughts, whist, piquet, cribbage, etc. when I was eight years old? You and your brothers. You must have had remarkably little to do or the weather been bad, though it certainly amused you. I was clever at it, but like Pandora's box, once the lid was off, I was soon out of hand. I sincerely hope not to be in London in December. When I am prepared, I shall invite you to visit me at Castle Orchard. I hope no prejudice at my rise in fortune will make you refuse. Please send my best compliments to Thomas. Tell him I will not part

with Dan because I can make him understand what
I want and Thomas never could. I am surprised at
his wanting to cut a dash with a cabriolet and a tiger.
He will do better to concentrate on his Parliamentary
duties.

> *Your not very biddable stepbrother,*
>
> *R. Allington*

No, he had no wish to be in London in December. He
wondered how Castle Orchard looked in winter. The place
lingered in his mind like a mirage, mysterious as the pleasure dome. Mrs Arthur's phrase 'there was no money at
Michaelmas' also stayed with him. Of course there would
have been no money at Michaelmas, for Arthur would
have taken every penny.

Dan arrived at Castle Orchard in a light fall of snow.
Mrs Arthur saw him from the window, his distinctive
figure astride a bay thoroughbred and leading another of
Captain Allington's hunters. Two days earlier she had seen
the bailiff from the home farm fill the hayloft and deliver
sacks of oats.

He had said, 'Knows what's what, this Captain Allington,
and pays prompt. We won't be pulling the wool over *his*
eyes.' He had looked sadly at Mrs Arthur and added, 'I
hope you are all right, ma'am, and the little ones.'

'We have our health, Stevens,' she had replied. What else
could be said?

She knew she should go but had no idea how or where
to go beyond Westcott Park. She had received another

letter from the lawyer reiterating the first and had written back to ask if he would send her the documents relating to the money, as she had never put her signature to a single transaction concerning it. All she had received in return was a bill for his letter-writing.

Captain Allington had been so long silent, apart from his one, brief page in answer to hers, she had begun to think he was a figment of her imagination, something never to come true, but here was Dan arriving with the snowflakes, a harbinger of his master, but silent. He would smile, nod his head, laugh, but that was all. Had she wanted to direct him she could not do so, but he needed no directing. He laid down the beds for the horses and cleaned out the harness room before deigning to place Captain Allington's saddles and bridles alongside what was there already. He appropriated the rooms over the loft, long since uninhabited, and soon had the stove going and himself snug. He fetched Domino, loved but of no known use, out of the field, tidied his mane and tail, trimmed his heels and oiled his feet.

Sam and Jimmy, employed in the garden and the yard, soon began to tease and annoy him. He seized the elder by the shirtfront and knocked him out.

Annie informed her mistress of this event.

'Serve them right,' Annie said, 'to torment a poor, dumb body, but they learned their lesson. Now he has them out amongst the cabbages, digging as if to save their souls.'

Two days later, a carrier arrived with a bed, a chest of drawers, a wardrobe, a large quantity of books and some pictures carefully wrapped.

Now she received a letter.

Dear Mrs Arthur,

*I am sending a small quantity of furniture. Please be
so kind as to choose a room in which it should go. The
bed, etc. can be put straight in the lodge, but the desk,
the books and the pictures should be in the house.*

*At Christmas I shall pay the staff their quarter,
now my responsibility. I shall pay the arrears when I
arrive at Castle Orchard, if that is necessary.*

Yours, etc.,

R. Allington

Mrs Arthur, folding the letter up, said out loud, 'Which
aren't his responsibility.'

She would very much like to have paid them herself and
thought over the contents of her jewel box, an object she
had hidden away so successfully, for fear of her husband,
she had nearly forgotten about it. She went upstairs and
groped behind a piece of loose wainscot in her bedroom
until she managed to withdraw the box. Were its contents
technically a part of her late husband's estate? The very
notion nearly made her thrust it back in its hidey-hole.
Resisting the temptation, she took the box to the dressing
table, dusted the lid and opened it up, then took out each
thing one by one.

Her engagement ring, a solitary ruby, caused her to
remember, with feeling, the vows of eternal love that had
been proffered with the gift. There were a few bangles, the
sort to be worn over gloves, and some childish pieces of
chain, things she had had as a little girl. Her father had
given her a tiny gold scent bottle, which she supposed
must be worth at least five guineas: she thought of the pain

of parting with it. In the bottom of the box was a necklace, a single strand of seed pearls, diamonds and tiny entwined leaves of gold, the whole light and pretty. It had been a gift from her grandmother. The old lady had said, 'You are like me, headstrong, you will make mistakes.' She had then proceeded to tell of the necklace, but Mrs Arthur had thought, even after the telling, its origins, its authenticity, a mystery, for her grandmother no longer made things clear. The only thing she wore was the mourning brooch, not an article of great value except to herself, a little lock of Matthew's hair under the glass at the back.

If she wanted to sell her jewellery, she did not know how, nor whom to trust. It might mean going to London, and for all she knew of the value of things, the profit might be eaten up on the journey. She put the box back from where she had got it and addressed the other matter of where to put Captain Allington's possessions. She could but oblige him. Why did he not ask her to go or say when he was coming?

There was a little morning room, facing south-east, with a view of the river and the Philosopher's Tower. She and Annie took the dustsheets off the chairs and set about cleaning it, dusting the pictures and washing the glass. When it was ready she sent for Jimmy and Sam to move the desk from the hall, where it had initially come to rest. Dan came in with them and gave his assistance. He looked about the room and smiled and nodded. He patted his master's desk and smiled some more. He shook his head and shrugged over the boxes of books and then he took from his pocket a stub of a pencil and a small piece of paper. Leaning on the windowledge, he wrote slowly and carefully in large letters:

CAPTAIN ALLINGTON SUNDAY

160

With many nods and smiles he gave it to Mrs Arthur. Today was Wednesday. She thought, suddenly stricken with panic, There is a tiny cottage on the estate, at the moment unoccupied. On Saturday we could sleep there.

The cottage was minute, one room downstairs, two up, but it had a roof and a grate. Annie said, 'You can't live here, it's damp. Whatever can you be thinking of? It won't be good for the children.' Mrs Arthur had replied, 'We will light the fire. The children must think we are camping. It won't be for long. As soon as I hear from the lawyer, I'll know what to do.'

On Wednesday morning she got out of bed having slept, out of sheer exhaustion, rather better than usual, and sat down at the dressing table. She was shocked by her own appearance. Annie came up with a jug of water and she said to her, 'I look a hundred years old, Annie.'

'Nonsense, ma'am, you're just a little weary with the worry of it. You have all them lovely curls, and your green eyes what smile so sweetly and laugh of themselves.'

'You flatter me, Annie,' she said, amused. 'My sister Louisa was the pretty one.'

'Your sister, Mrs Westcott, she is what everyone thinks of as a beauty, but you ain't so usual and that's what I like.'

Mrs Arthur went down to the kitchen. She had already discussed the dinner with Cook, who now said, for the seventh time, 'It is a very trying thing to be considering dinners for a gentleman whose tastes we don't know. We don't even know if he will want dinner – and where is it to be served? Not with you and the children. That wouldn't be seemly. I try to get something out of that Dan, but one may as well talk to a post. "Master Dan," says I, "what does your master like?" And I speak ever so slow and loud and careful. It could lead to a misunderstanding.'

'We will be in the cottage.'

'You can't go in that cottage. It's not fit.'

She and Cook went through the store cupboard together and made a list of essential items that were running low. They looked in the larder. Without the home farm they would have been in a dismal plight.

Mrs Arthur went into breakfast. Phil and Emmy were in their places, Phil gently kicking his heels against his chair and Emmy with a doll beside her to whom she was offering scraps of toast and jam. It was a rag doll Mrs Arthur had made herself, large, starey-eyed, but much loved.

As she sat down at the table she found a letter from Captain Allington.

Dear Mrs Arthur,

I am endeavouring to put myself in your shoes. You have every reason to resent me, though whether you choose to blame your late husband or myself for your present situation, I cannot tell. There are many things I cannot tell. I think it inevitable we shall see much of one another, until such time as you choose to depart. You may feel you are a guest in my house, but which retains the essence of being yours, whereas I may feel a guest in a house I have not grown accustomed to call my own. I shall live at the lodge but attend to business in the house, wherever you have put my desk. Allow the children to lead their customary lives, do not decide you should withdraw them or yourself to some distant part of the house that I may never be

162

offended by the sight of you or them, for the children
will not be accustomed to being confined.

Your very obedient servant,
R. Allington

So, he intended to live at the lodge. Her relief was enormous. She had assumed he had intended to put in a lodge-keeper. That very day she had planned to get a little furniture into the cottage. Should she be so beholden to him? Should she move anyway? Having read the letter once, she read it again and then folded it up and tucked it under the edge of her saucer. Really, she would have to read it yet again in a minute, but she decided she must move to that cottage whatever her circumstances. She thought she heard the front door open and shut. A moment later, Annie ran into the room.

She said, breathless, 'What shall we do? Captain Allington is here, and it not Sunday yet.' Overcome, she retreated, leaving Captain Allington standing in the doorway, his hat under his arm. Mrs Arthur noticed the elegant cut of his dark coat and the dandy brightness of his yellow waistcoat.

He said, 'No, it isn't Sunday. Did Dan say I was coming on Sunday? I left on Sunday. That's what he will have meant.'

Mrs Arthur got up from her chair.

He then said, 'I'm afraid I have taken you by surprise.'

'It is for you to come and go as you like,' she replied. 'Phil, shake hands with Captain Allington, and draw up a chair for him. Emmy, run to the kitchen and tell Cook we need another place and more breakfast on the table. I'm assuming you have had no breakfast.' She thought, I must pretend he is just any ordinary visitor. We must be polite.

163

Captain Allington shook Phil's hand and accepted his offering of the chair. He said, 'Yes, I have taken you by surprise.'

'There is a cottage empty. I intended to move there before Sunday.'

'Certainly not.' He spoke sharply.

'We could go to the lodge. I have just got your letter.'

'No. Pride and I shall live in the lodge. That's why I've had the builders in.'

'Then we must go to the cottage.'

Emmy returned carrying a basket of bread rolls. She put them down in front of him and said, 'We had no man at breakfast before.'

Annie followed her with a tray, nervous and upset. She bobbed a curtsey and hastily put the breakfast down.

Emmy, the only one to be not in the least embarrassed, said, 'He can't have coffee. It brings on one of his heads. Tea is all right.' She looked carefully at Allington to see how many heads he might have, before adding, 'Mr Pride said it, when you were here before.'

'Well, Miss Emily, what an excellent memory you have,' Allington said.

'Yes, I do. I remember all my lessons.' She enjoined her doll to eat up and leave nothing on the plate.

Allington then said, briskly, even coldly, 'As for the lodge and the cottage, as I take it they both belong to me, it is surely I that may decide who is to live in them.'

Mrs Arthur poured the tea. She refrained from looking at him. What he said, so bluntly, was true. The cottage was not hers in which to move. How was it she had not thought of that? Why had she not gone to Westcott Park? She had placed herself at the mercy of a man of whom she knew nothing, a virtual stranger, with the gambling habits of her late husband. Surely anything would have been preferable? When she did look at him, she thought he smiled, but of this, she was uncertain.

Phil was watching Captain Allington with round eyes. He was nervous and anxious. He thought his mother was being given a scolding for wanting to live in the cottage.

Allington said to him, 'Do you look after your mother?'

Phil shook his head.

'When I was a little boy I was very managing and I looked after my mother. I would say, "Now, Mother, where are your gloves? They are on the dresser. They've got a hole. I'll fetch your others from upstairs. We'll be late for church. Come along. You're never ready, but we'll be all right, darling, don't worry, hurry with me and I'll get you there before Parson"'. He paused and then asked, 'Are you like that with your mother?'

Phil said, in a tiny whisper, 'I try to look after my mother.' He hung his head, ashamed and confused, for he wanted to look after his mother.

Allington, still looking at Phil, continued, 'As you can imagine, I soon got to think it was I that gave the orders.'

Mrs Arthur tried to see him as a little boy of Phil's age, but nothing like Phil, a shock of dark hair, dark eyes and, even less like Phil, strong. She understood he had, like Phil, been alone with his mother. She said, 'But I find my gloves for myself.'

'I dare say the better way round,' Allington replied. He had eaten a little, she thought out of politeness, and now he stood up.

Mrs Arthur said, 'Is it your wish I should show you over the house?'

'I expect I shall stumble over the different bits of the house as I go along. Don't trouble yourself. Do as you always do.'

Allington spent that day riding round the estate. In the lodge he had laid out every map he could find, to the agitation of Pride, who liked things tidy. Pride had made the lodge comfortable. It was a single-storey building with few rooms, the main one of which now contained a simple bed, a washstand, a chest of drawers, a chair and a table upon which, useful for holding a map flat, was the glass jar containing the sixpences. It had a fireplace and in the little room to the back there was another, in which there were various cooking arrangements. Allington came in late but his dinner was ready. Pride had come to a good understanding with Cook, supplies to be shared between what was now two households.

After he had finished a simple but perfectly adequate meal, Allington sat down by the fire and took a book from his pocket, one he had chosen at random from the morning room, where he now had his desk. He held it near to the candlelight and found it to be the poetry of Robert Burns. He grunted with disapproval at his own choice.

> *Till a' the seas gang dry, my dear,*
> *And the rocks melt with the sun;*
> *I will love thee still, my dear,*
> *While the sands o' life shall run.*

He contemplated the indignities of irrational passion. Ten years previously, and he thought it a long ten years, he had lain in a foreign bed in a foreign house, close to death, and filled his fancy with a pretty, lively girl to whom he never spoke a single word, with whom he thought he could have had no common language.

> *O my luve's like a red, red rose*
> *That's newly sprung in June;*

Was not the colour red a little gaudy? He thought his long past, flaxen-haired love nothing like a red rose. Where was she now? He hoped she was surrounded by flaxen-haired children and with a sensible Flemish husband, a respectable burgomeister.

His mind slipped back to his childhood at St Jude, where the high grey walls of the garden nurtured nectarines. He was not allowed them, but when the gardeners' backs were turned he would scrabble up the walls and run along the top, helping himself to anything he found to be ripe – apples, cherries, figs, peaches, nuts and nectarines. A nectarine on a warm wall was almost too beautiful to be picked, wholesome yet delicate, pale yet flushed with warm colour. Was he not in a peculiar state of mind owing to what could only be described as the love affair he had had that day with Castle Orchard? His heart had warmed to every little copse and meadow, to the woods and fields, to undulating curves and hills, to sturdy barns, white tracks, whole farms and much of a village. There were long stretches of river that were also his, and he remembered those rivers in Spain; remembered himself, young and fit, lean from a combination of exercise and frequent starvation, but in a joyous state of exhilaration and contentment with his uniform faded to rust, patched from top to bottom.

If he had kept his health he would have wanted Castle Orchard and much else besides, but now he thought the estate exactly fitted his needs. His tenants might view him with suspicion and astonishment, he who had won them in a game, but it was of no account, for had he not been able to gain the respect of the roughest soldier? The respect and, he supposed, a grudging affection, for there had always been hands to help him when he was struck with a bout of fever. Some officers were truly loved. He doubted himself in this category.

To love, he thought, one must give oneself away, open locked doors. Had he not addressed the insubstantial little boy who so closely resembled Johnny Arthur, on the subject of care for a mother?

When he finally went to bed, fortified with a glass of hot milk proffered by Pride to make him sleep, which at another time he would probably have declined, his dreams of Castle Orchard were entangled with Mrs Arthur, as though one could not be separated from the other.

Mr Stewart Conway left it a few days before paying a call at Castle Orchard. Mrs Arthur received him in the drawing room but she said, 'I don't know that I should, because it isn't my house. Should I receive calls?'

'Annie showed me in just as usual.'

'She wouldn't have known what else to do.'

Mrs Arthur rang the bell and Annie returned.

'Annie, is Captain Allington in the house?'

'Yes, ma'am, in the morning room.'

'Please knock on the door and inform him Mr Conway has called.'

Annie went away on this mission.

Mr Conway said, 'I had hoped he would be out. I don't wish to know him but I suppose, as a neighbour, it can't be avoided. Your situation is impossible. It will cause a scandal.'

'So it may, but it's very proper.' Mrs Arthur gave a prim smile especially for his benefit.

'The sooner it's resolved the better,' Mr Conway continued. 'May I know, as I stand your friend, whether or not you have received further information from the lawyer?'

As he was speaking, Allington entered the room. Mrs Arthur thought, despite his lameness, he could move swiftly and silently. He must have heard all of Mr Conway's last sentence.

The two men gave each other the briefest of bows that accorded with politeness. They presented a curious contrast to one another, Captain Allington at his least forthcoming and Mr Conway confused.

Allington said, 'And are we to offer Mr Conway any refreshment?'

'It is for you to do,' Mrs Arthur replied.

'In theory it is for me to do, but in practice it is for you to do. However, it is my belief the inestimable Annie, out of habit, will bring whatever she can find in the kitchen she thinks suitable or Pride will furnish her with the bottle of Madeira I brought from London with me.'

'Yes, that is how it will be.'

Captain Allington now turned his attention to Mr Conway. He said, 'You are the brother of the rector?'

'That is correct,' Mr Conway replied.

'And you keep the school?'

'Yes. We have thirty boys and five of those belong to my brother and myself. We prepare them for entrance to

Eton or Winchester. Occasionally one goes to Harrow.' Mr Conway spoke more than he wished, being ill at ease.

Annie brought in a tray with two glasses, the Madeira and a plate of biscuits.

Mr Conway, with an instinctive wish to show upon what a familiar footing he was with Castle Orchard, said, 'How are you, Annie?'

Annie bobbed a curtsey and replied, 'Very well, thank you, sir.'

'But you have brought only two glasses,' he said, smiling.

'Master doesn't take no wine, sir, but Mr Pride says he will eat the biscuits.' Annie looked shyly at Allington and bobbed him a curtsey too.

Mr Conway turned with astonishment to Captain Allington and said, 'You take no wine? That is very singular, very singular indeed.'

'But not a sin,' Allington answered.

'I am an abstemious man myself, but a bottle of wine with our dinner, shared between my brother and I, is not excessive. I suppose you would consider it an impertinence if I enquired the reason for such abstinence.'

'I would,' Captain Allington replied. 'Nor am I accustomed to having my habits commented on by all and sundry.'

'I beg your pardon, sir, I meant no offence,' Mr Conway said, hastily.

Allington helped himself to the biscuits and leaned on the mantelpiece. He was looking about him and at the view out of the windows. He said to Mrs Arthur, 'I like this room.'

'Would you prefer to have your desk here?'

'No, the morning room does me very well, and I may smoke a cigar there.' Allington turned to Mr Conway and said, 'Well, I dare say you have come to discuss with Mrs Arthur the progress of her son at school. I shan't interrupt you further. If I was Mrs Arthur I should want to know why the child was so reluctant to leave in the mornings.'

Phil's reluctance to go to school was unspoken and by Phil himself denied, yet his mother was more than aware of it. She did not see why Captain Allington, who had been three days in the house, knew it too.

Mr Conway laughed. He said, 'I can see you are not used to boys, sir. It is rare for them to wish to start their lessons.'

Captain Allington shrugged.

Mrs Arthur said, 'Phil doesn't like to go to school but never will admit it.'

'There is nothing to worry him at school,' Mr Conway said. 'My brother won't have a cane, though I think myself, under extreme circumstances, it is efficacious.'

Captain Allington, who had moved towards the door, gave Mr Conway a cursory nod and left. Mr Conway, affronted, said, 'He's very abrupt. How can you be in the house with him these three days and not suffer every humiliation, this house in which you should be enjoying comfort and security?'

'But I find him very considerate.'

'You sit down to meals with him?'

'No, certainly not, only breakfast, the day he arrived.'

'All the same, it must make you extraordinarily uncomfortable. What I can't understand is why you don't flee to your sister until such time as your lawyers have come to their senses. Surely your sister would welcome you? You should pack and go this minute. He can't be a gentleman who subjects a woman to such deep humiliation in her own house.'

'But it's his house.'

'So it may be,' Mr Conway said, irritated, 'but that's not the point. Why don't you go?'

Mrs Arthur thought about this. Of course Mr Conway was right, for it was exactly what she should do, yet she didn't do it. He didn't realise, and she didn't choose to tell him, how short of ready money she was. Louisa would lend it to her but she preferred not to ask.

'For all we know, this Captain Allington will assault you,' Mr Conway said. 'The reputation of soldiers, where woman are concerned . . . Think what happened after the siege of Badajoz in the wars in Spain. Three days of rape and pillage. I expect he was there.'

'Don't be ridiculous! That was the troops, not the officers.'

'Why didn't the officers stop them? Answer me that! Because in their hearts they condoned it.'

'I am quite sure that's not true. I don't believe you know anything about it and nor do I. I have perfect faith in Captain Allington not assaulting me.'

'And upon what ground is your faith based?'

Mrs Arthur, who had no idea upon what ground her faith was based, said, 'It is anyway nothing to do with you. I am not a child to be cross-examined.'

Mr Conway was suddenly contrite. He said, 'I didn't mean to upset you. We are, my brother and I, so very, very concerned. Out of anxiety, your conduct may become irrational and we really can't tell what Captain Allington might do. He is a gambler, the thing you hold in abhorrence above all else. He just wants you to stay here to look after the house and servants. He will never be able to keep himself from London and the gaming tables. A little place like this will soon bore him to distraction.'

'I know you mean well. I expect you see it as simple, but in fact it's difficult to leave. What should I do about Phil? Nobody is going to be as kind to me as you and your brother, charging so little. I'll see you another day, perhaps when I hear something from the bank or the lawyer.'

Mr Conway, unable out of politeness to do anything but go, saw himself out. Mrs Arthur leaned on the window. In panic, she thought, What if there never is any money? Her children must go to Westcott Park and she would have to find work as a companion or even a governess. There was, however, money, for she had never made use of it. The little greyhound pressed dolefully against her skirts.

Later that day, Mrs Arthur took Emmy out for a walk. The trees down the avenue were in their full autumn glory. It was overcast, the sky heavy and grey. Emmy ran about picking up leaves and exclaiming at their different colours.

Captain Allington was just leaving the lodge as they reached it. Mrs Arthur could not help wondering if he did not find life dull without the stimulus of the gaming tables, just as Stewart Conway had said. Surely he would tire of Castle Orchard, but she supposed there was novelty in it yet. He started to walk beside her.

'I'm sorry Mr Conway called, but they're accustomed to it, he and the rector,' she said.

'But you may receive visitors if you wish.'

'I have very few. I had the impression you weren't pleased to see Mr Conway.'

'Was I too abrupt?'

'I expect he thought so, but it was his own fault.'

'I can't say I took to him, but if he gives you good advice, I certainly won't object to his coming. I expect he tells you to leave.'

'He does.'

'And where does he think you should go?'

'To my sister at Westcott Park.'

'But you don't?'

'I'm sure they would be kind to me.'

'Perhaps you don't know them well, that you would feel uncomfortable, you and the children.'

'I would feel very uncomfortable. I ought to be in mourning. They would expect all of that. I don't, as yet, know my situation. On the other hand, I oughtn't to be beholden to you, I oughtn't to be here.'

'But I've deprived you of your home. Ought I not to feel something about that?'

'It would have gone, sooner or later – if not to you, to somebody else. Was I prepared, in my mind? Perhaps one never is quite prepared. If you are married to a man who is married to the gaming tables—' Mrs Arthur broke off, remembering the means by which Castle Orchard had changed hands. She then said, 'You have been very kind and considerate, Captain Allington.'

'But,' he replied quietly, 'you have to disapprove of me.'

'I disapprove of gambling in any form. How could I not?'

Allington made no reply. She wondered if he would attempt to defend himself or make excuses but they walked back up the avenue in silence, beyond Emmy's prattling. They parted at the front door.

Indoors, in the hall, Mrs Arthur found Pride, who

174

paid no respect to servants' quarters or backstairs, merely taking the shortest route. He was peering out of the window at Allington's back view and said, with satisfaction, 'Captain has his boat cloak on. I think it's coming on to rain. I shouldn't like him caught in it.'

'Would it affect his health?' Mrs Arthur asked him, seeing him standing there with a cooking pot under his arm.

'It's just if he should get the ague, then he would be ill. The bad head is nothing to the ague. Well, the boat cloak, it's a sad old thing but it still keeps out the weather. Good thick stuff, that, and a baize lining. Belonged to Captain Jameson what was my master's messmate afore he died, that was at the storming of Ciudad Rodrigo that was, a terrible slaughtery place, poor young gentleman. Master was fond of Captain Jameson. He put his head in his arms and cried. When they come to auction Captain Jameson's stuff, which never does seem a pleasant thing, his shirts and the like, what seem warm off him, but they always does it, master bids for Captain Jameson's boat cloak.'

'Did you like campaigning?'

'No, I didn't. Worst soldier in the world, master said, but I'm useful enough in other ways. Terrible wet in Spain or terrible hot, like you burns your fingers on your buttons. Master said you fretted at our living down the lodge. Don't you worry, it's a palace, seeing the places we've been in, pigsties, lice – them foreigners are filthy. Best thing master had was that old boat cloak, what he could wrap himself up in, of Captain Jameson's, poor gentleman, with half his ribs blown off his backbone and he alive for two days with it. Funny old life, campaigning, 'taint fit to tell much of it.'

Pride came to a pause here, realising he was telling it to Mrs Arthur.

Mrs Arthur, mesmerised, said, 'But why ever did you enlist?'

'It was the drink. My pa was a tailor and I was apprenticed under him. I broke his heart, so my ma says. He said I was only fit to be a soldier, riff-raff, so when the recruiting officer came by, I joined up, got a dab of cash, spent it the usual way, an' by the time I was herded up to put me red coat on, and learn the drill, I didn't have nothing but the clothes on me back and a sore head. Trouble is, soldiering ain't sobering. I got into a deal o' trouble through drink. Well, I'd joined a line regiment, part o' what they call the Light Division, an' before I saw any sense I were packed down tight in a transport, sick as a dog, an' the wind contrary. Lisbon, that's where they rolled me out, and a nasty, dirty place it is. My ma brought me up clean an' respectable. She would've thought it a bit of a waste if she could've seen me then. The Light Division ain't no place for the likes of me, I soon saw that, what is the worst soldier in the world, what never could understand the honour of the regiment, all that darting about up at the front – skirmishing, they calls it – dancing with death all the long day. I were so nervous like, I'd never get the ramrod right down the muzzle, an' the damn old thing, the firelock, wouldn't go more than half off. My master wasn't promoted Captain then, but he were in charge of the company, the Captain bein' off sick much of the time. He never were a restful body – like a hare, like a deer, like a cat, stretched tight for action. Later, it were all the more distressing when he were destroyed, broken to bits. It's a hard life though, marching and marching, blistering hot over them rocks and mountains or else plunging about in the mud. Think of the knapsack, three pints o' water in the canteen, sixty round of ball, mess tin, clothes, shoes, brushes, pipe clay, bread, beef what had to last three days, firelock, bayonet, an' once we was issued with tents, you had the tent pegs too an' the kettle to carry when 'twas your turn. Forty to fifty pounds were a terrible burden on a hot day with thirty miles in front of you. 'Cause many got the fever something dreadful from laying out in the dew, an' the tents was meant to save us from that. No, I never was no good as a soldier. 'Tis bad for the others if you're in a funk – catching, like – an' I reckon all them officers hoped I'd get a bullet smack between the eyes double quick. When I became Captain Allington's servant it took me out the firing line. I'd mind the baggage, the mule and what-have-you. 'Twas a privilege I never did earn, but I were a good servant an' I laid off the drink for fear o' losing the place. I soon learned to make the best o' that beef an' such, when we had it. All they little flavourings, rosemary and thyme, just grow out on the rocks for the picking. Master would take his rod and get some fish an' he always spared a fish for me. Now the Spanish make a good-for-nothing fish hook, clumsy thing. Master was always a-begging in his letters home for English tackle. Sometimes there weren't nothing, rations finished, commissariat dropped off the face of the earth, an' I boils a bit o' flour in the goat's milk.'

Pride, grudgingly, came to a halt. He then said, 'I like to do the tailoring now, though I never sewed no gowns, 'twas all gentlemen's stuff. My pa taught me well. He might be a little bit proud of me 'cause I'm a gentleman's gentleman.' He laughed, for he knew he was not a gentleman's gentleman, not like Mr Emill, who had vanished on his master's death. 'Still, he never was pleased with me, my pa, yet I can turn my hand to anything if I puts my mind to it. Master says that, but he also says I talk too much an' so I do.'

They had been standing side by side at the window. Mrs Arthur, aware that Pride was as an open door on Captain Allington's life and more than half-thinking she should not be listening to him, said, 'Pride, those sieges, like the one at Badejos – what makes the soldiers go so mad?'

Pride looked away from her, awkward and uneasy, but he said, 'If a siege is long an' bloody, when the soldiers do get through the breaches, they go mad an' they don't spare nobody nor nothing. They say five thousand men was piled up dead an' then the plunder started. They'll murder any officer what tries to stop them.'

'Was Captain Allington at Badejos?'

'Yes, ma'am. He had a company of Portuguese caçadores. Begging your pardon, ma'am, you don't know what you'll do when the streets is running with blood an' there's Spanish wine in every cellar.'

Allington walked on to the Philosopher's Tower. He inspected the brickwork and peered up at the roof, but he was pensive and abstracted. Eventually he pushed open the door and went inside and up the stairs. In the drawer of the little table he found the bit of paper where Phil had written *Philip Osipher* and other bits of nonsense, in strange, wobbly writing. Allington moved the chair to the window so he was overlooking the remains of the castle and a bend of the river. Was the subject of gambling of sufficient import for the Philosopher's Tower? To him it was, though perhaps it was more a question of morals than philosophy. How could he expect Mrs Arthur not to judge him and certainly condemn him? He could have defended himself; he could have said, 'I am no Johnny Arthur. The risks I take are minimal – I took no gamble.' He could have said all those things, but he had not done so because the underlying lack of principle in his obtainment of Castle Orchard was the same as if he had won the whole thing on the throw of a dice. He could not, with any honesty, regret it, except for the way it coloured him in the eyes of Mrs Arthur: this he did regret. If he had never won a penny, he would be living at St Jude, dependent on the generosity of his stepbrother, as the poor, incapacitated relation. A half-pay officer did not receive sufficient money on which to live, let alone marry and lead an independent life.

He turned his attention to the view. He could see Phil amongst the ruins of the castle, alone, shrugged up in his jacket. He got up abruptly, went down the stairs and back outdoors.

When he reached Phil, he said, 'You are cold.'

Phil somehow interpreted this as a rebuke, that he ought not to be cold. He said, hanging his head, 'I have my jacket on,' as if having taken the necessary precautions against the inclemency of the weather, he could accrue no further blame. He then thought of a circumstance he connected with his jacket and added, 'But it was made by my mother from her cloak and she hasn't another.'

'If you ran about you would get warm,' Allington said.

Phil considered this. He then replied, 'You can't run about by yourself, because you don't know why you are running.'

'Throw pebbles in the river and see how far they go.'

'I don't like the river, I don't like the river at all. Now I want treasure, I don't like the stones, I don't like to turn them over.'

'The river is one thing – it could do you a mischief – but stones are another.'

Phil's eyes were round with horror. He said, 'Vipers, scorpions under every stone. One nip an' they do yer business.'

Allington frowned. He said, 'Where do you get this rubbish?'

Phil, further alarmed at having unwittingly caused Allington to frown, said, 'Jackson in the boot room.'

'If I were you, I shouldn't believe everything he says. A scorpion would never stand the climate here, and as for vipers, they are asleep in the winter. What is it you tell me, you are looking for treasure?'

Phil detected a softening in Allington's tone. He said, 'If I could just find a little treasure I would give it to my mother. I shouldn't want it for myself, except my boots are too small and when my mother asked me, I lied because of there being no money at Michaelmas. Now, the castle must be the place to bury treasure and if I could have turned the stones over, or some of the smaller ones, I might have found some but I remembered about the scorpions and the vipers.'

'What a dilemma,' Allington said.

He started to push the stones about, which were quite large, with his boot, and then bent down and rolled over a few more. 'No scorpions, no vipers. Now get along and look under each stone, even these I've moved already because you must make a thorough search.'

Phil set about doing as he was told, heaving at the stones until he was pink and hot.

Allington returned towards the house. He could see the Conway boys coming in the other direction. They were very warlike, he observed, a tin trumpet and a flag on the end of a stick. He wondered, idly, which belonged to the rector and which to his brother. He had not warmed to Mr Conway; he thought him too intimate with Mrs Arthur, which, he supposed, was none of his business. Children he never minded.

Robert Conway, leading his little brothers and his even smaller cousins, saw Captain Allington. He knew it was Captain Allington, for it could have been no one else. He noted the slight limp, but the upright, soldierly bearing. In his mind's eye he endowed him with the uniform of the 95th and every virtue a soldier could possess, of courage and sacrifice. Had he not been at Waterloo? In a second he found the childish chatter of Stevey, Frankie and the twins unbearable. He thought of making them all run home, but changed his mind. Enraptured, he gazed on the retreating form of Captain Allington until he disappeared under the arch to the stable block.

It was apparent, Allington thought, that the Arthurs had once kept a great many horses. Carriage horses, hunters, covert hacks, hacks for ladies, had all been reduced to nothing – nothing but one fat old pony of no known use, who might or might not have been used to pull a little cart full of babies and toddlers. Mrs Arthur could have no means of escape from Castle Orchard. The spacious coachhouse was empty except for the britchka. She could not, he thought, go even as far as Salisbury, let alone visit a neighbour, had there been such a thing as a neighbour in the remote vicinity of Castle Orchard. His own grey and his two hunters barely redressed the balance, but Dan was busy minding them, gratified to be in charge of so much space. Allington found him in the harness room, which he had swept and tidied. This too was empty, bar the saddles and bridles of his own horses, except for a side-saddle, which Dan had got down and was at that moment examining.

After a few moments the groom raised his sharp blue eyes to Allington's face. Though he had been unable to hear his master enter the room, he had sensed his presence. He put the side-saddle over his arm and strode off with it in the direction of the looseboxes, occasionally glancing back to see that Allington was following him. It was usually easier to do what Dan expected of you than to go through the rigmarole of trying to explain you wanted to do something else, but Dan was intelligent, he could understand most things. Now he placed the side-saddle on the long-tailed grey, peeking down the arch of it to see how well it fitted. Allington looked himself. It was a good fit.

Phil ran as fast as he could towards the house, clutching his treasure to his breast. When he got to the carriage sweep he saw the Conway boys, Robert, Stevey, Frankie and the twins, Jacky and James, standing round the sundial. At the sight of Phil they stepped forward smartly and Stevey, who had a toy trumpet, blew a sort of squeak from its rusted interior and Frankie shook out a flag made from an old piece of blue silk sewed to a willow wand.

'I am the second senior lieutenant,' he said. 'So I have to carry the colours.'

Robert, who was wearing the old red coat of a soldier of the line, said, 'Well, Arthur, we have come to make you our prisoner unless you can run away quick.'

'I'm going indoors,' Phil said.

'Oh no, you are not. That would be cheating.'

'Cheating, cheating, cheating,' Frankie called, twirling his colours about.

'Cowardy cowardy cheat,' said James.

182

'Cowardy cowardy cheat,' Jacky repeated.

'We will tell in school,' Stevey sang out, wiping the mouthpiece of his trumpet on the leg of his trousers.

'What is the French?' Jacky whispered to James.

'I think it's Phil,' James answered, equally puzzled.

Phil eyed the distance to the door.

Frankie said, 'I sticks me bayonet right into 'is belly an' sort o' jerks it up.'

Stevey said, 'An' the bodies in the breaches is right heaped up seven deep, is swollen an' turned black.'

Robert, watching Phil, said, 'What are you holding?'

'Nothing much.'

'Let me see.'

'It's mine. It's treasure.' Phil clutched his hands to his jacket.

'What sort of treasure? I bet it's rubbish.'

'It's real treasure. I found it in the castle, under a stone.'

Having said this, Phil made a sudden dart in the direction of the door but Robert stuck out his boot and tripped him so he sprawled on the gravel. He then rolled him over with his foot. Phil unclasped his hands and displayed a crown piece, three shillings and a sixpence.

Robert took the crown piece and examined it. He said, 'Why, you little silly, it's not treasure. It's an ordinary crown piece with the King on it.'

'It's my treasure,' Phil said, getting up carefully, rubbing his elbows, bruised. The tears started to run down his cheeks. 'It's mine, it's mine. I found it for my mother.'

'If you found it in the castle, then it belongs to Captain Allington. Everything is his now. Your mother will have to give it to him. Hasn't your mother any money of her own?'

'There wasn't any money at Michaelmas.'

'Your mother will have to beg. She will have to go in the street and ask people for money. Her clothes are all patched as it is.'

'You can buy ever so many things with a crown,' Stevey reflected, envious.

Robert handed the crown back to Phil, who hastily put it in his pocket.

Frankie said, 'Ain't you going to keep it?'

'Certainly not,' Robert replied, shocked. 'That would be stealing.'

He turned his back on Phil and ordered his little troop to march. He had it in his mind to inspect the castle ruins for himself.

Phil, from the safety of the front door, shouted, 'Captain Allington was at Waterloo. He was nearly dead. That's what Pride told Annie and Annie told me. He was in Spain for years and then he was at Waterloo. So there! And he's mine, not yours . . . so there!'

As Phil's voice reached a crescendo, all the Conway boys turned, round-eyed. Even Robert could think of nothing to say.

After dinner, Emmy went to bed and Mrs Arthur read *Ivanhoe* to Phil. They sat on the sofa, Phil lolling against his mother, his head on her shoulder. They had lit a small fire.

There was a light tap on the door. Captain Allington walked in. He said, 'I'm sorry to disturb you,' and then went to the fireplace and put on more wood. 'You may as well be warm. There's plenty of wood.'

Mrs Arthur thought how kind he was. She was thinking of the conversation she had had with him that morning.

She wished the painful subject of gambling and of his acquiring Castle Orchard had never arisen; her criticism seemed churlish but at the same time it could not be retracted.

'That side-saddle in the harness room,' he said. 'I was wondering if it was yours?'

'I expect it is. I used to ride.' Mrs Arthur thought of the roan mare that had been her solace in the long, lonely days at Castle Orchard. They could afford a groom then, but groom and horse had all disappeared, after one Lady Day when Johnny had been down from London. He had never said anything – that was not his way – but he would have seen the mare as a means of getting a few guineas into his pocket. She was only surprised he had overlooked the saddle.

'I was wondering if you would do me a favour.'

Mrs Arthur was delighted to think there was something she could do for him. 'Of course. I'm so much in your debt.'

'The agent knows I don't intend to keep him long; it was fair to tell him, but he now doesn't give me sufficient time. I want to get a better grasp on the boundaries between the farms. It occurred to me, if you could ride, you could show me yourself. But perhaps you don't know them?'

'I know them perfectly well.' Mrs Arthur paused. She then felt, looking at his face, which he had the ability to make most remarkably expressionless, a useful thing at the gaming tables, that he had set her a tiny trap, into which she had plunged. She did not feel she could refuse him, but was he not a dangerous man, even more dangerous than Johnny Arthur had been at the age of twenty?

Allington said, 'That saddle fits my grey. He's well behaved.'

'I haven't ridden for quite a few years.'

'Time to start again. You would be doing me a service.'

Mrs Arthur knew she could not refuse him, though she did not see herself as being of the least use to him. She thought of her years of incarceration at Castle Orchard.

She was about to reply when Phil said, 'I must give my treasure to Captain Allington.' He drew out of his pocket the crown piece, the three shillings and the sixpence.

Allington now took the chair on the opposite side of the fireplace, perfectly at home, it seemed, but was it not his in which to feel at home?

Phil went to stand by him, the coins in the palm of his hand. 'My treasure. It was there under a stone. I gave it to my mother but she said as Castle Orchard belongs to you, the treasure is yours.'

'That was a tiresome thing for your mother to say.'

'Yes, I thought that.'

'I most certainly refuse it. I shall give it to you and you shall give it to your mother.'

Mrs Arthur said, 'If Captain Allington won't take it, Phil, you must thank him and put it in your moneybox.'

'But I only went to look for it so I could give it to you,' Phil said sadly.

'In that case, dearest, I shall take it.' Mrs Arthur thought how it was not a large sum but useful. She thought of the journey to Westcott Park – if that journey were to be made – the coach tuppence a mile. She thought, with the little bit she had, it would be enough, but there would be nothing left over and there were other things needed.

Phil pressed the money gleefully into Mrs Arthur's hand.

'Perhaps it should be a loan, Phil,' she said. 'We could write it down: Mrs Arthur owes Philip Arthur eight shillings and sixpence. That would be an IOU but we shouldn't make a habit of it, for we would too easily get into debt.'

'No, I don't want it. It's for you.'

Allington felt enlightened as to exactly how short of money Mrs Arthur was, or she would never have allowed herself to accept it. He wished he was in the habit of carrying a greater sum in his pocket.

Phil said, 'Are you disappointed it's not really old treasure?'

'No, modern treasure is much more useful. It's kind of Captain Allington to let you have it. I expect some antiquarian visiting the ruins, for they do from time to time, flung down his coat on a hot day, and all his change rolled out.'

Allington said, standing up, 'What time would suit you tomorrow? Would the latter part of the morning do? I could have Dan bring the horses round at eleven o'clock.'

'If that is convenient for you.' Though she had not actually agreed, agree she must.

Phil crept into his mother's lap. He wished he was as little as Emmy and closed his eyes to see himself so small, too small ever to grow up. He then thought of his treasure. He had never closely scrutinised any money before and he wondered why it was the King, whom he had thought to be a dressy person, like his father, wore only some leaves in his hair.

He said to Mrs Arthur, 'No shirt, no neckcloth, does he wear no clothes at all?'

'Who, dearest?'

'King George.'

'He wears a laurel wreath.'

Allington looked at Phil. The child was draped in his mother's arms; his thin legs dangled nearly to the floor, exposed from the rucking up of his trousers, and one of his little, heelless slippers was halfway across the carpet. He really was too old to sit in his mother's lap.

Allington said, 'Why are your legs bruised, Phil?'

Phil jumped up, staring wildly at Allington, and then hastily tugged at his trousers to hide his battered shins.

Allington, seeing one of Phil's toy soldiers on a table, picked it up. It was a meagre thing, cut out from card, but brightly coloured. He turned it over in his hand, examining it for the detail of the uniform.

He said, 'How gaudily we go to war, with what splendour of lace, silver and gold, scarlet jackets, pelisses edged with fur, officer's sashes seven foot long. What fanciful trimmings, rosettes, cordings in silk, the gold epaulet with a garter star.'

Phil said, emboldened, 'I want to be a soldier.'

Allington put the toy back on the table. 'You *think* you want to be a soldier. I will tell you how it is. I wore my uniform at certain times, for weeks, even months together, day and night. It was soaked in rain and snow, it was bleached by the sun, it was torn and patched, shapeless, filthy and threadbare, and I, I was half-starved and so were my men.'

'All the time?'

'No. We got into cantonments, we got new clothes, the commissariat caught up with the army. We had our inedible lumps of beef. We even occasionally got paid. I have been down to my last dollar and afraid to spend it.'

Phil was silent for a while and then he said, 'I still want to be a soldier.'

He wished he could say why but Captain Allington did not ask him why and his mother told him it was time he went to bed.

When he had gone, Allington said, 'I should like to discourage him.' He started to quote Bunyan, '"*Who so beset him round/ With dismal Stories/ Do but themselves confound;/ His strength the more is.*" I could have told him more dismal stories than I did.'

'But did you dislike it so very much yourself?'

'No. Though it was not the career I had wished for, I was happy – very happy.'

'But you would discourage Phil. Well, so do I, but I wonder you should.'

Allington thought of how the boy would be at the mercy of his fellow officers, let alone the men, but he did not feel he could say it. Shortly after, he returned to the lodge.

Mrs Arthur watched him go. Was she not keeping him from his own house? She had a letter from Louisa which she now read for the second time.

> *Dearest, dearest Caro,*
>
> *Please, please come. We are so worried about you. We cannot imagine what detains you. Mr Westcott says his coach and horses are entirely at your disposal. The journey takes less than a day . . .*

The letter continued in the same vein.

Mrs Arthur went to the window and opened the curtain a little. There was a tiny flicker of light in the distance that immediately went out; she took it to be the candle in

189

the lodge. She began to consider Mr Westcott's coach and horses, but even more, the tipping of his coachman.

Captain Allington rode one of his two hunters, both gangly, temperamental thoroughbreds with sprightly, uncertain ways, Mrs Arthur supposed least calculated to suit a man with a lame leg. She was pleased to find her riding habit, though a little shabby, still fitted her. Dan had put her up on the grey, adjusted the stirrup and the girth, before mounting the second of the hunters and following along behind. It was sunny and bright. She glanced at Allington and he smiled at her. She thought he was pleased with himself for getting her out, but she couldn't imagine why, for it was soon evident, as far as knowledge of the lie of the land went, he knew everything. Initially, he made a little pretence it was otherwise. As for herself, she had forgotten how it was that Castle Orchard had been her prison because she could go no further than the distance she could walk. Now favourite views, once so familiar, opened before her, the sweep of the downs, the woods all rust and gold, the river and the white chalk tracks. She was also aware that Captain Allington was an agreeable companion. Had she not been restricted to the society of dear Annie and the children, the rector and his brother? She thought he ought to find her dull. Was he not accustomed to London society and gentlemen's clubs?

She asked him how he had come to employ Dan.

'He was born in Cornwall, at St Jude, as I was myself, and always employed there. He wasn't born deaf; he was ill as a small child. I pinched him from one of my stepbrothers. If you employ Pride, Dan is a great respite.'

190

Not only had Allington learned the lie of the land, he seemed to know every secret route, the quiet ways where no one came. They moved silently on the soft turf from one place to another, skirting farms and wayside cottages. She understood he had no intention of their being seen.

Mrs Arthur said, 'You know the land better than I do.'

'I thought you might tell me something more, some little byway I hadn't discovered,' he replied.

She did not believe him but she chose to ignore it.

He then said, 'You learn a lot campaigning. I spent plenty of time behind the French lines.'

'Wasn't that very dangerous?'

'Yes, but less so if you wore your uniform. You wore your cloak over the top, to hide the red of your jacket. There was the initial danger of being shot. Your best hope was to be taken prisoner if things went wrong.'

'And if you hadn't your uniform on?'

'Then a mistake or a betrayal cost you your life.'

Mrs Arthur knew, without asking him, that he had been thus employed. The thought of it was so disturbing she involuntarily clutched at the mane of the long-tailed grey. How could she, as a woman, ever comprehend the horrors that had been daily life to men such as Captain Allington?

The grey horse went along quietly, smoothly. Captain Allington seemed content they should do no more than walk. His dancing, jingling thoroughbred had also settled to a gentle pace.

Mrs Arthur said, 'You must speak good French.'

'I speak French, as you would expect. When I joined up, a mere boy, I knew I would be going with the regiment straight out to the Peninsula. I was ambitious. It had occurred to me that if the Army was to be my career and

I with no money and little influence, I had to draw attention to myself. I arrived in winter, which was fortunate, because it gave me time to study. I had Mordant's Spanish Crammer and Guthrie's for the Portuguese, but I was, of course, able to practise on the natives. I was considered a very dry fellow. Why say I was a boy, when children as young as Phil are officers at sea?'

She said, 'Weren't you afraid?'

Allington laughed. She thought how laughter, like his smile, so lit his face and altered it.

He said, 'What a very feminine approach. Tense, yes, afraid, no.'

'Pride was afraid.'

'Pride was very ill-suited to soldiering.' Allington started, after a moment, to say more. 'One obeys orders, does one's duty, upholds the regiment ... the regimental band plays us into action. As an ensign I carried the colours. How they tug and pull in the wind, enough to send a lad over. They're a target for the enemy, but in those days I was lucky. Some of the men took to religion, very holy and evangelical, but I never could see how they squared it with their duties as a soldier. The need to laugh and joke in the face of death was more appreciated than prayers.'

As he spoke, Mrs Arthur saw this boy he had been, intensely active, over-clever, no tuft of white in his hair, no scars, such as she had glimpsed on his arms when he had rolled back his sleeves to pick apples.

'Sometimes,' Allington said, 'I would reflect on it. I liked to go off on my own, in the peace of the evening, the campfires lit below, the pungent odours of Spanish vegetation in my nose. The donkeys, the mules from the baggage train might set up a serenading. Rather better, the King's German Legion would sing their native airs and tug your heartstrings. The British soldier seems only to be able to sing something coarse when drunk, but the Germans ... I would sometimes think of my mother and be almost glad she didn't live to see me grow up; she would have died a thousand deaths on my behalf. So many companions lost, so many, it made me wonder if the soul flew to its Maker with the swift beauty of a swallow, a rainbow arc of joy ... or whether it flew there at all.' He glanced at Mrs Arthur, turning sharply in his saddle to see if he shocked her, but she was pensive rather than shocked.

As they rode along the quiet, undulating downs in their varying shades of grey and green, Allington said, 'You might not suppose there is any connecting link between these hills and Spain, but I know the wild thyme grows here. I've smelled it crushed underfoot. I liked to course my greyhounds in Spain and Portugal. To get a hare or two added to the comfort of the mess.'

He spoke of the difficulties of the commissariat struggling with squeaking, groaning bullock carts of flour and biscuit, ale or rum for a hundred thousand men, a whole army shifting without apparent rhyme or reason in various divisions from Portugal to Spain and back again, the roads unspeakable. It was easy for a regiment to outmanoeuvre its luggage and supplies, the price of local produce high and the wages in arrears. He said, if you were wounded and had no money for better food, it could be the end of you, but you were in as much danger from fever and dysentery. He told of dust, of mules, of baggage trains and of the unbearable sun.

They started to descend the downs. The chalk track dropped between steep banks, and as they approached level ground they passed through beech hangings red-gold in the mild English autumn.

He talked dreamily of the great golden plains, glistening palely under the powerful light; of earth as red as bricks when turned by the plough; of mountains, one craggy mass of rocks so high whole armies seemed like little crawling flies. He spoke of castles and villages perched on eminences; and of convents full of dark-eyed nuns, imprisoned by grilles that failed to inhibit clandestine whispered seductions in broken, alien tongues. The names of foreign places slipped easily from him. He talked of days of doing nothing, billeted in villages or towns, of theatricals, dances, horse racing and endless dalliance with pretty girls. They lived from day to day. He spoke of beautiful arcaded squares shadowy in the noonday sun; of cathedrals that took your breath away; of corn-ripe stone and cream-coloured churches. He told, without enthusiasm, of Catholic mummery, of tinselled Virgin Marys and decorated saints.

'Ah well,' he said. 'My caçadores . . . Catholic to a man, good and bad, everything done in the name of God. They were touchingly anxious I shouldn't be killed, they had so little hope for my salvation.'

Nearing Castle Orchard there were several places where the river could be forded. Captain Allington already knew them all. His horse plunged into the water and the water swirled about its hocks. The grey followed meekly after and Dan brought up the rear.

She had no conception of fighting in winter but he started to describe the storming of a town in January and a river to be forded, again and again, the ice knocking at the ribs, the clothes frozen solid on the body and the ground rock-like where the trenches must be dug. He talked of marching day after day, of lying down in the rain at night, no cantonments, no bivouac, merely rain-soaked ruts in a field of plough.

He then said, 'I've probably taken you too far. Are you tired? We'll go again another day.'

The Reverend Hubert Conway, though a gentle and unassuming man, had a clear idea of his responsibilities, however distasteful. He said to his brother at breakfast, 'Stewart, it is my duty to remonstrate with Captain Allington. He doesn't attend church, which will set a bad example amongst his tenants. Also there is the matter of Mrs Arthur, poor soul. I fear it will cause gossip, though it is not a subject I feel willing to raise.'

'Mrs Arthur should go to her sister.'

'It may not be convenient for her sister.'

'In that case, what is Captain Allington to do?' replied his brother testily.

The rector could not imagine what Allington should do, short of going elsewhere, or at least further than the lodge. This did not deter him from crossing the meadow that divided his establishment from Castle Orchard and asking Annie if Captain Allington was in.

Captain Allington was at his desk in the morning room, which had now taken on a bachelor air. He had hung his two Cornish seascapes, but the portrait of the Light Dragoon had never been unpacked and resided in the corner with its face to the wall. Allington sat with the window open to disperse the aroma of his occasional cigar. As a young soldier, a cigar smoked under excruciating circumstances of hunger, wet and cold, brought inestimable comfort. Now he thought it a poor habit and one in his changed circumstances he should abandon. He could surely manage without tobacco, especially if it might remind him of Johnny Arthur and his endless snuffboxes.

When Annie showed in the rector, Allington gave him a small bow but said nothing.

Mr Conway, disconcerted, said, 'Mild for the time of year.' He tended to say this when lost for words, whatever the circumstances of the weather. He thought Captain Allington's room very cold with the window open.

Allington asked Annie to bring the rector a glass of Madeira. While it was fetched Mr Conway struggled with a few more commonplaces. Apart from offering him a chair, Allington made no response.

'You will not take a glass with me, I see,' Mr Conway said, forgetting his brother's comments on Allington's abstinence.

'I take no alcohol,' Allington replied. 'Did you have business with me?'

The rector said nervously, 'I have a duty to attend to the souls of my parishioners but they take their example, not unnaturally, from their betters, particularly their landlord. I fear that their attendance at church will slip and slide.'

'My predecessor, the late Mr Arthur, set no such example.'

'Indeed not, the poor, misguided gentleman. Let us hope he found salvation though no time to prepare for it, thrown off the box of a coach.'

'Mrs Arthur sets the example, and while she resides here,

will no doubt continue to do so. Otherwise, it should be your own persuadings, not mine, that get them into church.'

Captain Allington paused here and eyed Mr Conway coldly. He then stood up and went to lean in the open window embrasure. He said, 'I have never met a man in your profession whom I found I could respect. It's as though ordination was sufficient to render a man wise or holy. While I was a soldier there was rarely a chaplain worth his salt, rarely one to go out amongst the dead and dying to administer some little comfort to those who would have welcomed it; no one to brave the stink and pestilence of a hospital to reassure a dying man he had done his duty and could depart in peace. We buried our brother officers in unhallowed ground in shallow graves, and the only prayer we said was that their poor mangled bodies would be spared the ploughshare or the wolves. I can quote the service for the dead by heart, so frequently was I called upon to do it, but I thought myself ill-fitted for the task. As for chaplains, they were only notable for their absence.'

Mr Conway was dumb with horror at the thought of so many bodies so unceremoniously despatched into holes in the ground and the prayers left to Captain Allington.

Seeing Mr Conway made no reply, Allington continued, 'Sometimes troops were drawn up for religious observances, but battles were fought on Sundays – Toulouse on Easter Sunday and Waterloo itself was on a Sunday. During the Peninsular campaign it was frequently necessary to use chapels to house ourselves and our horses, as the only roofed empty space. I dare say you will think it didn't signify because they were Catholic. As for the rascally, fat priests, creeping about in black, we didn't think much of them, so you could be right. You die hard in battle, the soul forced from the body, one second here, next burst asunder, perhaps in several parts and trampled underfoot; yet one moment before, able to think and feel, to write a letter home and contemplate the weather. My view at the time, and I have not seen fit to change it, was that any one of my Portuguese caçadores, despite their idolatrous habits and horrid priests, were as likely when they died to obtain salvation as the rest of us.'

Mr Conway, nervously seated on the edge of his chair, turning his hat about in his hands and occasionally giving a tug to the fine white tails of his clerical bands, endeavoured to picture himself, in the heat of Spain, bending and stooping on the battlefield, even before the cannons' roar had ceased, with words, though what words, of comfort, to those who were not already corpses, and every second in danger of himself joining their number.

He cast eyes of desperate appeal at Captain Allington who viewed him yet more coldly, though he said, with a hint of levity, 'Ah well, I suppose you would have been nothing but a nuisance and forever in the way. Now you come here to admonish me for my failure to attend church and I have admonished you for the failings of the Church. What else did you have in mind?'

Mr Conway, thankful to be removed from the battlefields, said, 'Oh, a very delicate matter and one I hesitate to approach. Mrs Arthur is a woman without protection, no husband, no brother, no father.'

Captain Allington replied, 'It is as well, in that case, is it not, she remains out of harm's way, under what happens to be my roof?' And before Mr Conway could suggest this was not the solution he had in mind, Allington added, 'I think you were quite correct in hesitating to approach the matter. It would have been better not to have done so. I would not presume to discuss Mrs Arthur, so it seems odd you should. It's not in my view the conduct of a gentleman, but I see you meant no harm by it. Let us part company before we fall out with one another.'

Captain Allington showed Mr Conway to the door.

Mrs Arthur met the latter hastening away across the carriage sweep, in his anxiety only just avoiding bumping into the sundial. He said, glancing at the windows, 'My dear lady, Captain Allington . . . you and he shouldn't be under the same roof.'

'I don't think it would be right for me to suggest he didn't use the morning room.'

'But you must leave. You must go to your sister. Captain Allington is a blasphemous gentleman – he's put me into a terrible pother.'

Mrs Arthur could see this for herself. She said, 'As soon as I hear from my lawyer, I shall know, I suppose, what to do. It is most kind of Captain Allington to allow me to stay here while he has all the discomfort of the lodge.'

Mr Conway swept on his way, muttering as he did so, 'Pray leave, leave immediately, dear Mrs Arthur.'

Captain Allington, at this period free from headaches, set about fox hunting twice a week. He would reappear after dark, entirely worn out, content to sit by the fire and endure in silence the discomfort of his lame leg.

'Nothing won't stop him,' Pride said. He was occupied with sewing the long seams of the drawing room curtains, a task in which Mrs Arthur could assist him. Things had not been changed, the same pictures hung in the same places, but Allington had ordered cloth for curtains, as those in the windows, long bleached by the sun, were little more than rags.

Pride smoothed and straightened the mass of fabric. It was a plain linen. He said, 'Master loves his hunting. He don't care a bit it worries me to death. He never did mind that. What I goes through waiting for him to be killed, war or hunting, he never will take into account. Still, when he's hunting, out the way, it gives me a chance to give his uniforms an airing.'

Pride had appropriated a bedroom in the house for various articles for which there was no room in the lodge, and it was here the curtains were being made, for it was also his tailoring department. He went to a chest he kept in a corner and on opening the lid, he said, 'I'm afraid the moth might get them, though kept in cedarwood, so I gets 'em out and looks 'em over. Why do they bugs think it digestible?'

He carefully lifted a uniform and laid it on the table. Mrs Arthur stared at it, the dark blue jacket, the bright facings, the silver epaulettes, the shining buttons. It stirred, she thought irrationally, an elusive memory. 'How gaudily we go to war', is that what Allington had said? And by gazing at his uniform, laying her hand tentatively on the cloth of the facings, it was as though the very garment had seen too much and now clandestinely revealed its secrets, the heart that beat, the lungs that breathed, the effervescent life, there one minute, gone the next.

Pride said, disconcerting her, 'He never wore it much. That's why it's so tidy. The other he had at Waterloo, an' that were the end of it. Looted, see. Fancy looting the clothes, all slashed to bits an' bloody, but it's the lace they are after, real bullion, an' the little precious things in the pockets. Master lost all the bits and pieces he had in his pocket, things he never was without. Fancy shaking a man out of his jacket what's lying bleeding on the ground three quarters dead, but they do, they never think nothing of it. Ah well, a soldier's rights is his booty. I tell you what, them farriers what the cavalry have to have, are the worst. They're meant to help as stretcher-bearers, but 'tis just a pretty excuse to have the officers' watches. The women, they'll be out there with the babes at their breasts before the firing's stopped, turning the bodies up and prodding and poking the poor wounded. My ma, she brought me up a Christian, and I'm sure 'tis no Christian habits they women had.'

Pride reached for the red uniform and laid it out beside the blue. ''Tis smart in the cavalry but he were a thorough-going infantry man, master were. Red jacket, silver buttons – this was his dress uniform. The other wasn't worth keeping. He wouldn't sell it in the hope he could get back to his old regiment. The Portuguese have a dreary sort o' uniform, brown, but still, seemed he were less likely to be shot when he had that on. As for the other stuff master did, that was worse than any battle. I never could rest easy. And in the most part of it, what were master to the French? Just the glint of a spyglass high on a rock. Spoke the languages, looked the part, I don't know what he didn't have to do an' where he didn't have to go, but I never could bear the thought of it, what they'd do to him if he were caught.'

Pride had reduced his voice to something of a whisper, but then he went off on another tack and became more cheerful. He replaced the uniforms and settled to stitching the curtains but his voice went on and on: the sun, the rain,

Captain Jameson, the goat boy, the Duke of Wellington himself, were all grist to his mill.

Mrs Arthur saw in her mind Spain, as Captain Allington had described it, either hot and dry, fragrant with thyme and rosemary, or cold and wet for days on end, and she thought she saw a hundred thousand soldiers, sprawled asleep – even, she supposed, dead – and a very young Captain Allington, perhaps not yet a captain, wrapped in the boat cloak that concealed the tatty, gaudy uniform that, Pride said, hadn't been off his back for days. In another world Johnny Arthur, carefully washed and scented in waistcoat and pantaloons, an ivory snuffbox in one hand and an elegant cane in the other, would be parading down St James's in search of losing his money.

Mr Stewart Conway walked Mrs Arthur back from church. She wished she had mourning as a concession to public opinion but there was no help for it. She wondered about the dyeing of something black, but it did not seem as important as it should. Why should she wear mourning for Johnny Arthur?

There were significant changes to the walk, for the hedges were cut, sharp-edged and neat, and the leaves swept.

'You are cold,' Mr Conway said. 'Why aren't you wearing your cloak?'

'I cut it up. I shall get another, but not yet.'

'Do you hear nothing from your lawyers?'

'Not much.'

'It's shameful. I can't think what they're about. You must have enough money to get a cloak.'

'I am afraid to spend it. What mightn't I need it for?'

After a pause for careful thought, Mr Conway said, 'I shall lend you the money for a cloak.'

Mrs Arthur shook her head. She murmured, 'So kind, but I would prefer not.'

'I am an old friend. You could be beholden to me without trouble.'

'I couldn't.'

'You will only be beholden to Captain Allington,' he said, an edge of sourness to his voice. 'My brother is concerned he doesn't come to church. He says it will set a bad example. He visited Captain Allington, but all he received was a lecture. Poor Hubert was much distressed.'

'Don't you think it would set a bad example if he sat in church with me?' Mrs Arthur asked.

'It would certainly draw attention to the fact you both reside at Castle Orchard.'

'Ah, but we don't, and I don't believe going to church is one of Captain Allington's habits. It's hardly my business to enquire. Let's not talk of him. Tell me about Phil.'

Phil himself had run ahead with Jacky and James.

'What should I tell you?'

'His legs are so bruised.'

'There's a lot of rough and tumble amongst the boys. They are like puppies at play.'

'Sometimes I think it more than that.'

'Mothers tend to think their child victimised.'

'But are you sure it's not so?'

'Phil must learn to stand up for himself. To interfere will only make him less popular than he might already be.'

Mrs Arthur sighed. She was dissatisfied but knew no other approach and Phil himself would say nothing. They arrived at the carriage sweep.

Mr Conway said, 'I shall come no further. I have no wish to see Captain Allington.'

As he spoke, Captain Allington came out of the house. He nodded to Mr Conway and said, 'Good day to you, sir.'

Mr Conway returned the salutation coldly and called his little boys, who took no notice of him for they were in the thrall of Emmy. He had to lose his temper before they could be induced to come, and he thought Captain Allington mocked him. He stalked away down the drive with an arm each of his offspring.

Allington said crossly, 'I don't want you to get cold. Come indoors. Your shawl is worn thin. I hope Mr Conway is of assistance to you.'

'How can he assist me?'

They entered the drawing room together. Captain Allington knelt down to tend the fire himself. He said, 'By enquiring into your affairs.'

'But how could he do that?'

'How could he not? Aren't they too long in coming to a conclusion?'

'Yes, but it is not Mr Conway's business.'

'And he doesn't make it so?'

'No.'

'Though you confide in him?'

'Yes, as much as I can.'

'If Mr Conway won't make it his business, allow me to make it mine.'

Mrs Arthur, uncertain what to reply, said nothing. Allington then said, 'Of course, you can have no reason to trust me.'

She replied, smiling, 'As to trusting you, I am sure I should be advised to do no such thing.'

'You have my word of honour you may trust me. Perhaps that isn't enough. Come, sit by the fire, and tell me your situation. You should have a jointure.'

'So I have. It was some sort of jointure should I be widowed, but I had the means of obtaining it sooner. My father saw all the dangers in my marrying Jonathan Arthur. He was certain he would desert me and leave me penniless. I could soon see the truth of this for myself, but I determined whatever Johnny said, the money should stay where it was.'

'And where is it now?'

'The lawyer says I withdrew it.'

'Does he say when?'

'He says very little, merely that I must know I withdrew it.'

'They should have evidence. Did you have other money?'

'A legacy from my father.'

'And where is that?'

She said, 'I gave it to my husband. I signed it away.'

Allington was silent but then he said, 'You must have had reason.'

Mrs Arthur involuntarily put her hand to her mourning brooch. She started to speak but no words came. She looked round the room as if her little son Matthew might be there.

Allington got up from his chair and went rapidly to the window, turning his back on her, she thought, as if he would escape if he could.

Eventually she said, 'It was the scarlet fever. Phil, who looks frail, had a tenacious hold on life, but Matthew, who was so robust ... Emmy took it lightly. I told Johnny I would have no more children either to die or be ruined. I locked my door. He talked of vows made at the altar but there are many vows at the altar, few of which are kept – none by Johnny.'

Allington returned to her. She was confused at having upset him. Though he had a great measure of inscrutability when he chose, she thought she had upset him. He now said abruptly, 'So Arthur threatened you with the bailiffs while you nursed, or buried, sick children.'

'Yes. He had just obtained the estate, held in trust until he was thirty. I thought he would immediately mortgage it, but he had reasons against it.'

'He bet against it. Your lawyers are Jonas and Scott.'

For a moment she was surprised he knew this, but then she remembered he must have received the deeds of Castle Orchard from one or other of them.

Allington continued by saying, 'I shall call on them. If that doesn't work I shall get our family lawyers, that is Lord Tregorn's, to act for you.'

'But I am unable to pay.'

'It doesn't matter.'

'You mean when I retrieve the jointure, I can pay?'

He shrugged but then he said, 'Yes.'

Mrs Arthur said, 'Sometimes, irrationally, I'm afraid.'

'That the money isn't there?'

'Yes, but it must be there, because I certainly never have had it.'

'Then it's there. I'll attend to it. You must give me a letter of authorisation. I shall take it to London, stating the whole case, which seems not much.'

Mrs Arthur wondered why he never went to London, unless it was the fox hunting that kept him, for surely

London was his spiritual home, a man who had gone from the adventures of war to the excitements of the gaming tables. If he went to London, would he return in less than six months?

Her doubts being evident to him, Allington said, 'Are you afraid to let me go? I am not Jonathan Arthur. The gambler and the soldier have much in common, one gambling with his livelihood and the other with his life, but rest assured I'll return without jeopardising my fortune. Now, suppose by some mishap, you found yourself destitute, would you marry Mr Conway?'

Mrs Arthur said, 'Why do you think it right to ask me such a thing?'

'It is impudent of me. I ask it all the same. You needn't answer.'

'If I were destitute?'

'Yes.'

'Well, it is a very silly thing to ask, because I should have to marry him. However, if I were destitute, Mr Conway wouldn't propose. Even now he is waiting to see the extent of my income.'

'But he's fond of you.'

'Yes, but he's not romantic.'

'Why wouldn't it break your heart to marry him?'

She answered him soberly. 'It would weigh my spirit but not break my heart. I should endeavour to make him a good wife.' Looking at Allington's face, she saw by the very blankness of his expression that she had troubled him even more by what she had just said. Making an effort to smile, she added, 'You now seem the innocent child, if you think things could be otherwise.'

'Perhaps it is I that am romantic,' he replied.

'So should I much prefer to be romantic, but circumstances don't always allow for it. I have children.'

The Conway boys, being free on a Sunday afternoon, adopted Castle Orchard as their playground. Having sought out Phil as an excuse for their trespass and with a vague boyish intent of amusing themselves at his expense, they wandered off to the vegetable garden.

They started, innocently enough, to play where there was a pit of sand, building a castle with the aid of some flowerpots and a seed tray.

'Here is a castle in Spain,' Robert said. 'We will besiege it.'

'What shall we do for soldiers?' Frankie asked.

'Gravel or stones. Phil, you can be the French. You must hold the castle and we will attack you and roll you down the hill.'

'I'll shoot you,' Phil said.

'You can't shoot us all. You may shoot Jacky and James. They probably won't notice it.'

Jacky and James set up wails of protest and fell to thumping each other.

So intent were they at building their castle, they did not notice the approach of Captain Allington.

'These little pebbles are the French,' Robert said.

Allington looked down on them. He said, 'And what's the name of the castle?'

The boys all jumped up. They stared respectfully at their feet.

'Has it no name?' Allington asked.

Robert, not usually short of an answer, said, thinking at

random for a name gleaned from the confused but mesmerising accounts from the boot room, said, 'Badejos, sir,' but he added 'perhaps' in case it was not appropriate.

'You pronounce it as an Englishman would if he saw it written down. You must turn the j into an h, and soften the s into a th sound.'

Robert repeated the word. He was torn between the indignity of being corrected and the excitement of Captain Allington's speaking to him. He now said, 'Badejos, sir,' endeavouring to pronounce it correctly, casually, as if he had known how to do it all along.

'It would take much alteration to turn it into the real thing,' Allington said, 'but I dare say that doesn't spoil your game.'

'Oh, it does.' Robert seized the seed tray and the flowerpots. The twins burst into tears. 'Show us how it was, sir, if you please.'

Allington sighed. 'Flatten the ground,' he said.

Robert and Stephen got on their knees and smoothed the sand flat. Eventually they got it to Allington's satisfaction. He took his cane and made a wiggling line across the middle of it.

'This is the River Guadiana. On one side of it is the town of Badejos, with the castle in this corner, a hundred and thirty foot above the river. On the other side of the town, outside it, is the Fort Paradaleras. Across the river lies the Fort San Cristobal.'

The eyes of the six boys were riveted upon him. Even the twins watched every line he made with his cane, the defences and the town walls, jagged like the teeth of a dragon.

'It is the spring of 1812. The town has a curtain wall

twenty-five feet high and there are eight bastions, that is four-sided fortifications, higher than the walls. Here there is a fortified bridge over the river into the town. The town has a garrison of some four and a half thousand men and a hundred and forty guns. Along the western face the French have built three ravelins, which are triangular fortifications, sown with mines. To the north-east, here, the governor, a clever fellow, has dammed a little stream to make an impassable swamp. Here, to the south-east, is the Fort Picurina, which we capture first, but not without all sorts of difficulties. The approaches were flooded and a siege trench needed to be dug. It rained a lot. As the men dug the earth, it turned to mud and slopped back into the ditches. Much time was lost. Once, while the working parties were changing, the French sent out a sortie of one thousand five hundred infantry who attacked them, filled in much of the ditches and carried off the entrenching tools.

'However, despite all, it was done. Now we can get close enough to pound the bastions with thirty heavy cannons, the object to make breaches in the walls, but while we make breaches in the walls the French, you may be sure, aren't idle. Every night they take away the rubble from the breaches and dig trenches. They mine the approaches and lay down a *cheval de frise*, a plank chained to the ground to which are attached pieces of bayonet and swordblades, all razor sharp and sticking out as much as a yard. Behind that there's a trench four feet deep and wide, and behind that, when it's stormed, the enemy, eight men deep, the first two ranks to fire, the others to load for them. There's an eight-foot slope to be scaled, on top of which are barrels of powder, fused and ready to roll down and explode.'

The boys gazed fixedly at the sand and then at Captain Allington. How childish seemed their games, how babyish their rampages through the wood, and behind Allington's measured tones they could hear in their heads the confused and bloody utterances of Jackson in the boot room.

Robert said breathlessly, 'And then, sir, what happened then?'

Allington again pointed his cane. 'It is the sixth of April. At eight o'clock in the evening the Third Division, about three thousand men, advance and cross the stream. They have scaling ladders and are to climb the walls of the castle and attack the defenders of the breaches from the rear. They go in silence, but unfortunately not unobserved. Some wade the flooded river, others cross by a milldam, but subject to so much fire it is a wonder they manage to get under the castle walls to erect their ladders.

'At about ten o'clock the Fourth and the Light Divisions attack the breaches here. They creep forward in silence, covered by a thick mist from the river. The Light Division go first with the Forlorn Hope. They're the men who have volunteered to lead the assault. They carry sacks of straw to be dropped in the ditches to enable others to cross later.' Allington pointed with his cane. 'They are here, coming from the south-east, and here's the Trinidad bastion they're to attack. The men are curiously enthusiastic for the task, but it's impossible. Remember the *chevaux de frise*, the flooded ditch, the mines, the powder barrels exploding amongst us, the canon, grape and musket, the soldiers cramped in the ditches, British and Portuguese, packed tight together unable to advance, even to move, for the quantity of dead and dying, and the whole place lit up by every sort or incendiary and fireball. From time to time we retreat, reassemble and advance, it is said up to forty times, officers and men flinging themselves forward, ever weaker, ever more desperate.

'The French, amidst the din, taunt us from the walls: "Why don't you come into Badejos?" But we can go no more. In a sudden hush we hear the town clock strike midnight. In the meantime, after much devastation and confusion, the Third Division succeed in scaling the walls of the castle.' Allington pokes the cane at the sand. 'In places the ladders were too short, for the walls were thirty foot high. The men had to climb on each other's shoulders. Where the ladders were longer, the French tipped them backwards or bayoneted anyone getting to the top, and dropped barrels of powder and rocks. All the same, the escalade is achieved. The men tear down the French flag and run up a soldier's red coat in its place, but they are barricaded within the castle walls. Now, look here on the north-west side, where we can see the bastion of St Vincent. General Leith, who has the Fifth Division, has orders to make a diversion to distract the French from the main attack, but he takes ladders and, as that clock strikes twelve, succeeds in escalading the walls, though they are well defended, and gains the ramparts. The French are driven back. The British blow their bugles, which are answered by those in the castle. At one o'clock the French garrison cross the River Guadiana and escape into the Fort Cristobal, which, you will remember, is here, on the other side of the river to the town – but they cannot, of course, hold it forever, and that's the end.'

Allington came to a halt and there was silence.

Phil and Robert were remembering Jackson, down in the dark of the boot room: 'The whole place lit up what with yer rockets and that, yer legs, arms, heads, bodies jumbled up and drowned, chest high, shrieking, the noise was something awful and when yer tried to get ups a ladder or down it, 'tis got the dead hanging off of it upside down, and the muskets going and the cannon, the whole place lit like yer could read yer name if yer 'ad to.'

'So that was the end,' Robert repeated, dazed. 'It was a great victory. Is that not so, sir?'

'The town was taken, that being the object of the exercise.'

'But wasn't everybody dead?' Frankie asked.

'Very many. More than nine hundred of the British troops from the Fourth and Light Divisions and over five hundred each from the Third and Fifth.'

Frankie thought he no longer wanted to go to war.

Robert said, 'And they put the French garrison to the sword.'

'They did no such thing, but the troops plundered the town,' Allington replied.

Robert and Phil still gazed at the patch of sand, and they both saw the piles of corpses and the wicked spikes of the *chevaux de frise*, the ladders and the trenches. The groans of the wounded sounded in their ears and the eyes of the dead looked back at them. They glanced into the face of Captain Allington and thought he saw and heard as they did but he said, 'It's the duty of a good soldier to put aside the horrors of war. To dwell on such things is neither useful nor sensible, for it achieves nothing and puts nothing right. It doesn't mean you must never show mercy or compassion. Guard your honour and you will do as you should.'

Robert allowed unpleasantness to fade and thought of honour and glory. Phil dwelled on the men who drowned in the ditches, the water filling their lungs. He closed his eyes tightly. He remembered something else Jackson had said. He had given a man water from his canteen but, 'it weren't no use for it trickled straight out the hole in his belly.' Phil, hugging his knees, thought, If I were a soldier I would be brave – it would make me brave.

It appeared as though Allington was about to walk away from them. Robert, engulfed by the blindest, maddest hero worship, gasped out, 'But, sir, in all this,' gesticulating at the sand, which still bore the marks of Allington's cane, 'where were you? Perhaps you weren't there.'

If Captain Allington had not been there, he thought, he could kill himself at the disappointment.

'I was at that time seconded to the Portuguese Brigade of the Fourth Division,' and Allington again pointed out on his map of sand the exact position of the breaches. 'I was, therefore, in the last attempt to gain entrance, here. By keeping up such a continuous assault on the breaches, the enemy were drawn away from fully defending their walls from the Third and Fifth, so, though a failure, it served its purpose.'

He walked away from them. The twins squabbled and rolled in the sand. The map of Badejos disappeared beneath their struggles. Robert cuffed them both, but it was too late and everything was spoiled.

Pride was making up a cloak for Mrs Arthur out of a grey duffel.

'Master said you needed a cloak. The cloth was ordered and there it is.'

'But Pride, I didn't ask for one.'

Pride was disappointed. 'Don't you need it then?'

'Why, yes I do.' Mrs Arthur went to the table and absently picked up a reel of thread. She couldn't say to Pride: 'But I ought to pay for it. I can't accept presents from Captain Allington.' She then thought, But my whole life and that of my children is, at this minute, a gift from Captain Allington.

Pride, watching her, read her expression perfectly well. He said, 'It's easiest just to do what he wants.'

'Are you quite sure he meant it for me?' Mrs Arthur had a letter from her stepmother in her pocket.

'There isn't nobody else he would have had it done for, that's for certain.'

Mrs Arthur was less certain. She went away to the drawing room and reread Mrs Templeton's letter. It said:

Dear Caroline,

Louisa tells me of your situation and I must add my pleas to hers for you to come away from Castle Orchard. I never was able to influence you, more is the pity, for you were a very wilful young girl, and in marrying so to displease, you got your just deserts. However, your father loved you and for the sake of his blessed memory I wish you would do nothing to create a scandal that can only reflect badly on your dear innocent sister, let alone upon myself, whom I do not expect you to consider. Are you thinking of your children?

This Captain Allington keeps a foreign actress as his mistress. Of such a man your father never could have approved; he is a gambler besides, no doubt worse than your husband. Please do not tell me any

such nonsense as his sleeping in the lodge, with which
you convince Louisa. A man of that sort will only
have it in his mind to make you his mistress and that
is all, until he tires of you.

The letter carried on expressing similar sentiments for several pages. Mrs Arthur folded it up and put it away as Captain Allington walked into the room. Thoughts ran through her head thus: If he has a mistress he cannot be seeing her often, for he has been here six weeks without going further afield than Salisbury – and that not if he can help. She also thought: If he has a taste for foreign actresses, I can't see why my stepmother thinks he might develop a taste for me, for all he looks at me tenderly from time to time. I dare say he would look on a foreign actress with equal tenderness, if that's his habit.

She said, 'Pride says he is making a cloak for me, but I think it must be a mistake and intended for someone else.'

'No, I intended it for you.'

'But I must pay for it.'

'If you insist, at a moment convenient to you, sometime in the future. As it is, you are bound to catch cold.'

'But why didn't you ask me?'

'Because you must have refused. Where are your warm pelisses?'

'I altered them, turned them. In the end they fell to pieces.'

'You have a very inadequate wardrobe for the time of year.'

Mrs Arthur said, 'Please wait here a moment.'

She ran upstairs and fetched her grandmother's necklace from its hiding place. On returning, she put it into

Captain Allington's hand. He gazed at the seed pearls, the delicate intertwined leaves and the small, sparkling diamonds.

Mrs Arthur said, 'I have no idea if it is real or not. Paste was fashionable in my grandmother's time, but being so pretty, it must be worth something. As you intend going to London on my behalf, please will you sell it for me.'

Allington looked speculatively at the necklace. Eventually he said, 'Was it your mother's?'

'My grandmother's. She gave it to me. She drew me on one side and said, "Your heart rules your head. You are like me, and you'll get into a scrape." I was, you see, engaged at the time. She said, "I will give you my necklace, but you must promise me to tell the man you intend to marry that the diamonds are paste. It's a lie, but no matter." I made that promise to my grandmother because she was old and I loved her. I wore it that evening and when Johnny came to dine, his eyes lit on it. I had resolved to evade a question rather than tell him a lie, but I immediately said, "They aren't real," and I saw how he lost interest. What was that lie I told? A moment of self-preservation? I was ashamed of telling it to this man I loved. The tale of them being rather contrary, I hesitate to think they are real.'

'Rundell's can decide. You will think you should not trust me, but we have already discussed this. Trust me you must. I'll take it to London in a week or so.'

Captain Allington slid the necklace into the large breast pocket Pride always made inside his coats. Mrs Arthur thought he had great dexterity at getting his own way without much argument. If she had a little money from the necklace, such situations could be more easily avoided. She could at least pay for a cloak.

Between Allington's hunting and the uncertainty of the weather, there had been only a few opportunities for Mrs Arthur to ride, but to do so gave her great pleasure. She supposed she ought to refuse, make excuses, but she never did. Captain Allington would tell her when Dan was due to bring the horses round and she would be ready in her riding habit. Depending on which of the hunters needed exercising, sometimes Dan accompanied them and sometimes they went alone. Either way, Allington would always take a discreet route. All they ever saw was some lone shepherd on the downs, or a solitary man ploughing a long furrow, his horse straining at the collar.

The day following that in which she had entrusted her necklace to his care, they were crossing the ford together and she was thinking about the fact that she was allowing him, against her better judgement, to help her. She knew she would be advised not to trust him, yet she did.

As the horses scrambled out of the water, Captain Allington said, almost as if they continued their previous conversation, 'I should like to ask you something. How came you to marry Arthur?'

Mrs Arthur hesitated. She thought, How can I tell him that? She then said, 'You will think the worst of me.'

'Allow me to judge that for myself.'

'I thought him the most magical, the most beautiful, the most original, the most amusing, the most poetic . . . why ever did I think he was that?' For a moment she was laughing at herself, but then she sighed.

'My mother died when I was young. My father remarried when I was ten years old. My stepmother was rigid with correct conduct and household management. I am, at this moment, transgressing one of her rules: no lady should be so immodest as to allow herself to be the subject of a conversation. I was as defiant and naughty as I could be. My father, whom I loved and who loved me, lectured me. I didn't see why he needed another woman in his life other than me. I tried, occasionally, to be good but I was resentful, misunderstood and therefore wilful. As I grew, my stepmother endeavoured, more and more, to take me in hand, to teach me this and that of housekeeping which, though scorned at the time, has certainly been useful since.

'I think, on reflection, I was not so wicked but I ran about like a tomboy, very active – even my hair, such a mass of curls, out of my stepmother's control, though she attempted to batten it down with clips and ribbons and tame it with curling papers. I was inclined never to do as I was told, but in company I was shy, so appearances were kept up. My stepmother used to whisper about me to her friends whilst I was compelled to sit with them, and they would look my way and sigh and shake their heads. I was, I suppose, very unhappy.

'Well, you won't want to excuse me for what followed, but you asked me to tell you, so I shall.' Here Mrs Arthur stopped to look at Allington, but as he said nothing, she continued.

'It was the April of 1815, the year Napoleon escaped from Elba, as I need not tell you. I had a cousin in the Army. He was my best friend, like a brother, seeing I had none. He came to bid us goodbye on his way to join his regiment, with three or four other officers travelling with him. A uniform is a very seductive thing. Some wore scarlet and some wore blue. We dined, there were friends and neighbours; we wanted to dance, which my stepmother permitted. My cousin wanted to waltz but this she wouldn't allow – she was shocked to death – so he contented himself with playing the music on the pianoforte. I didn't know how to waltz. Out of naughtiness and also, viewed from afar, inclination, I went out into the April garden with one of those officers. We could hear the music very well. He showed me how to waltz and then he kissed me. I knew no better; it is what I should have expected. Did I let him kiss me? Yes I did. It is, on the whole, a mutual occupation. As it was, those young officers all went away at the crack of dawn and we never saw them again. I didn't even know their names, though I suppose we were told them at the time. Captain one and Lieutenant another. My cousin Charles was killed at Waterloo. His death expunged everything else from my mind. How terrible it was, to see his name amongst those wounded or killed, all printed so neat in the *Gazette*. Perhaps all of those officers from that night were killed. How it haunted me at the time.'

She said no more. They were riding side by side down the length of a shady lane, old trees knotted and twisted on each side of them and meeting overhead. She glanced at Allington, but he was looking fixedly ahead. Was he shocked, or was it the mention of Waterloo that disturbed him, for surely Waterloo, where he had so nearly lost his life, must evoke, for him, memories best put aside?

At the end of the lane he opened a gate and after closing it he turned to her, saying, 'And then?'

'I told my stepmother of the kiss. I was, you see, really alarmed at my own conduct and extremely innocent.

Can you imagine the sensation I caused, kissing a soldier in the garden? Of course, I was deeply relieved to know my transgression was to bring me nothing worse than dire disgrace. I was totally confined, made a prisoner. My father was wretched, I was wretched and even after we had the sad, sad news of Charles's death, my stepmother didn't relent. She said I would never be married, et cetera, et cetera.

'Shortly afterwards, Jonathan Arthur came into our lives. He was staying with an elderly relation, a friend of my father's who was to teach him estate management, or that was the idea. His father had only agreed to pay his debts on the condition he stayed in Devonshire, out of harm's way, for six months. He had been sent down from Oxford. He burst upon our little rural retreat like a gilded butterfly. I think the fact that I was in disgrace, considered wild, a rebel, was what attracted him to me. I was not allowed to dine anywhere but at home, went to no assemblies, was seen nowhere but, as a relation of my father's friend, my stepmother could not refuse him the house. She didn't make him very welcome, but this he viewed as a challenge. Eventually even she was charmed by his prattle. Now I really was in love, but he never would have married me had not everyone been so against it. His father vaguely hoped I might be a steadying influence, though my own family did not see me as such. In the end, everyone relented and hoped for the best. Besides, he was to inherit Castle Orchard. It was a perfectly good match.'

Their road ran uphill and emerged onto the edge of the downs into the mild, wintery sunshine.

Allington said, 'And how long was it before you realised your mistake?'

'About three weeks. I was, you see, immediately expecting Phil. I was unwell. Johnny went to London. He came back three months later. I was even more unwell. Oh, the wretchedness of those days and months, I can't tell you. My father-in-law set up trusts and died. We moved into Castle Orchard. Johnny came back for that. I thought he might alter but I was eight months' then and I had no appeal for him at all. Once Phil was born, I tried further reconciliation. Sometimes it worked for a while, but really it was hopeless. I settled to make my life around the children and Castle Orchard. It has been lonely but not without its joys and compensations. What I paid for that kiss! My whole life, but that's not really so. I expect I would have married him just the same. What made Eve take the apple in the Garden of Eden? I had always wondered. Now I knew. I suppose soldiers are opportunists.'

She thought, comfortably, it didn't matter what she said to him. She looked to see if she really had shocked him, but perhaps a man who had seen so much of the world was not easily shocked. He merely said, 'Yes, soldiers are opportunists.'

In the dark of the boot room Robert leaned forward and said, 'Captain Allington told us about Badejos. He told us of the escalades and the bastions, the *chevaux de frise* and how the men drowned.'

'Told yer of Badejos, did 'e?'

'You don't say it like him.'

'We can't all be speaking yer foreign tongue. He ain't no business telling of Badejos, not in no foreign tongue, nor in yer King's English.'

222

'Why not? You told us about it yourself.'

'Yer little sisters, yer mothers – soldiers wouldn't spare none of 'em. Can't tell yer what they do, for yer too young. They had us strung up in the streets. Fancy seeing yer mates dangling there and yer too drunk to know it ain't a vision. That stopped us, but we was wore out anyhow. San Sebastian now – burned flat by the Frog Eaters, the Frenchies, only seven houses left upright and they had the sauce to say it was us. Them sieges either kill yer or cook yer, and yer boils right over like yer pan o' milk.'

'Was Captain Allington at Waterloo?'

''Ow should I know? Lost me eye and me leg at Toulouse. Still alive though, more than can be said for some. Spanish Allington, that's what we called him. Yer can't be in the Army without yer leg.'

'Why did you call him Spanish Allington?'

'Speak Spanishy, look Spanishy.' Jackson paused and then said, distinctly, 'He died at Waterloo. They told me that. When the regiment came back. I saw me mates, one or two, and they said he died.'

Robert leaned forward and gave Phil a jerk by the arm. Somewhere a bell rang.

'Get on with yer then, yer varmints, bothering a man.'

Walking slowly towards the classroom, Robert kept hold of Phil – Phil whom he believed had the ear of Allington, who saw him every day.

'Was Captain Allington really at Waterloo?'

'Yes,' Phil said, disconsolate. 'Pride says so. I told you that.'

'We can't tell anything from what Jackson says. Are you sure?'

Phil never thought himself sure about anything, so he

223

made no reply. Eventually he said yes because he thought it was what Robert wanted to hear.

'He must tell us about it, just as he told us about the siege. You must ask him.'

'I couldn't.'

'Why not?'

'I couldn't. He doesn't talk about it.'

'If you don't ask him, I'll—'

They reached the classroom. Robert went in without finishing what he meant to threaten, and Phil broke loose. He ran down the corridor and out of the rectory door. In a moment he was crossing the meadow, clattering down the wooden steps and flying across the garden.

Mrs Arthur found him in the hall clasping Emmy to his meagre chest.

'What are you doing, darling? It's schooltime.'

'I came to see Emmy. The Frog Eaters might have her.'

Mrs Arthur said, 'Now, dearest, if they have a taste for frogs, I don't suppose they would fancy Emmy. If you mean the French, here there are no French.'

Phil would have liked to correct her. Even when he was not himself the French, the French were everywhere, burning villages, killing little girls, putting their bayonets into wounded soldiers. The French hid in the woods by the drive, with their blue coats, their muskets, their fierce moustaches, their cold, foreign eyes and their hairy knapsacks.

Emmy said, 'Bang! You can shoot the French, Phil.' She knew what games the boys played.

'If you shoot a Frenchman, do you know what you do?' Phil asked her, and she shook her head.

'You eat his biscuit. He has biscuits with holes in them

so they can thread on a string. You eat his biscuit and drink his rum, that's what you do.'

Mrs Arthur said, 'Phil, you will miss your lessons.'

Phil went back across the meadow where he met the rector coming to look for him. It was not the first time he had run home. He was comfortable with the rector, who could think of nothing to say beyond telling him he was a funny little fellow.

Mrs Arthur thought Captain Allington gave up a day's hunting to ride with her, but this being so unlikely, she changed her mind.

The day was mild and soft, the river, the woods and the downs half lost in a mist. She said, 'I think it your turn to tell me something.' She thought of the day she had first ridden with him, of his descriptions, so vivid, of Spain and Portugal, that she had lived each second.

Allington said, 'Are we taking turns?'

'You have more to tell than me.'

'How can that be?'

'It's so. My life, though trying in many ways, has been dull, a prisoner here at Castle Orchard, a struggle to make the best of things . . . although once I did a London Season.' This made her laugh and she added, 'What an excitement. It seems a hundred years ago. I am a provincial, know only of country matters and country habits. If it were not for the newspapers, I shouldn't even know that Lord Liverpool was the First Lord of the Treasury and Peel the Home Secretary.'

'But you have read a great many books,' Allington said.

'Needs must when you only have servants and children

for company. You read a book and it whirls away into a pit where are all the other books you have read. I am, all the same, grateful for books. The house is well supplied with them.'

'What shall I tell you? Shall I tell you something I withheld before: I never want to go back to Spain.'

Mrs Arthur contemplated this for a while. She then said, 'But sometimes you will talk of it.'

'Yes.'

'But actually to be there, where all those things took place, all those remembered faces . . .' Mrs Arthur broke her sentence off and finished with the words, 'Today, we won't talk of war. You once told Phil what an overbearing child you were.'

Captain Allington smiled, but it was a grave, almost sad, smile. He said, 'What can I tell you? I was alone with my mother as you have been alone with Phil, but my father had died in action, a soldier. I have no recollection of him. As a little boy I never went to school, but had my lessons with a dear old clergyman – oh, but too old, though I did learn. I think he didn't charge my mother. He told her I was exceptionally clever, but I'm afraid she needed no convincing. What did we live on? There was an Army pension, very small, but what we ate were gifts from the St Jude estate – game, milk, butter, fruit, vegetables, anything in season. We lived in a little house, a cottage, with one servant. My mother cooked. I looked after her, or I thought I did. We had fruit trees, an apple and a damson, not one iota of which was wasted, as you will understand. I wrote labels for jars. I weighed sugar. I did sums. I was vigilant in checking that my mother hadn't been overcharged for groceries or anything else, having learned of this possibility. Now I wonder if I was really useful, or did she just indulge me? How busy I was, running back from my lessons to help her in the kitchen, telling her how she should go on, finding the things she had lost, and everlastingly, telling her not to worry, how we would manage. In the evening I read her books from the lending library, not, you observe, the other way round. Was I insufferable? My mother had long since elevated me to the deity. I was tall for my age. I didn't look like her, for she was fair, delicate, very pretty. Yes, I was tall and I think not plump – skinny, in fact. There, that's a picture of us. Ours was a situation not unlike yours.'

Mrs Arthur agreed, but Phil was no Captain Allington, except in skinniness. She said, 'What did your mother call you?'

'Just by my Christian name. I once looked myself up in the church records to see if I could really have been christened so simply, no saints involved. Even us good solid Protestants are usually called for saints. My name is Robin, which is surely short for something else, but not in my case. For me, it has fallen out of use.'

Mrs Arthur turned the name over in her mind. She saw him as a child and said, 'It's hardly a grown-up name, but your stepbrothers might make use of it.'

'No, they call me Allington. When I was a child, they called me "the little Allington". I was just eight years old when Lord Tregorn's first wife died. He married my mother within a few months. I never had thought of him as much of a threat, being well into his fifties, short, stocky, red in the face, balding. Except as our benefactor, I never thought of him at all. I realised he was very, very kind to my mother. Then my world was topsy-turvy, transported to the Big House, servants, rooms – endless rooms, just one of which could have swallowed our cottage whole – a dining table that stretched as far as the eye could see, with a myriad of glasses and finger bowls, knives and forks and all sorts of niceties to which I wasn't accustomed. It was far removed from my mother and I, with a tray on our knees, snug by the fire or sitting under the apple tree on a summer evening. I was, of course, immediately sent away to school. I think my mother was as mortified as I, but she must have been puzzling how I was to be educated and got on in the world. I went to a small school to prepare me for Winchester. Later my stepfather changed his mind and sent me off to the Army school. I was perfect material for a schoolboy, clever and athletic, but woefully unaccustomed to strangers, let alone other children. My stepbrothers, who you might suppose could have resented my mother and myself, were good to me. They taught me to box. Dan was my sparring partner because he was small. I soon understood the necessity of defending myself, but how deeply I longed for my old life with my dearest mother.

'The headmaster was a little like the rector here. In my second term he called me to his study and told me my mother had died. Of course, I didn't believe him, droning on and on about being released from the cares of the world, happy amongst the angels, the cherubim and seraphim, and making me kneel down to say a prayer. I was confused at not getting my mother's letters any more, confused and suspicious. Nobody came to see me. The headmaster, I later understood, assured them I had taken the information calmly and continued to do well at my lessons. When I returned to Tregorn for the holidays, I ran from room to room, seeking my mother. Where was she? Where was she? I started to shout and scream. I ran amok, threw things, broke things. Nobody knew what to do. Then my eldest stepbrother caught me by the arm and conducted me to the churchyard. He showed me a grave, not yet greened over, and said, "Your mother is there and your little brother too". He then left me.

'The terrible truth dawned, first that I would never see my mother again and second, that she never would have died if I had been there to prevent it.'

Allington turned to look at Mrs Arthur and saw he had brought tears to her eyes. He went white himself. Mrs Arthur, returning his look, thought, as she had previously, that he would escape if he could – the tears of a woman were painful to him; but he had no means of escape.

Allington said, 'I am sorry I upset you. It wasn't my intention. We'll talk of it no more.'

'But why shouldn't I be upset for your sake, for the picture you draw? You are my benefactor, at this minute.'

After a moment he replied, 'That's too difficult a thing to answer. It was all long ago. What made me tell it?'

Mrs Arthur thought, though it was long ago, it was as clear to him as yesterday.

Mrs Arthur caught a cold and gave it to Emmy who, though not very poorly, knew it to be a good excuse for coming downstairs and having a story read to her. She appeared in an old, outgrown dressing gown of Phil's after dinner, when she was usually asleep. At the same time Captain Allington had walked up from the lodge.

Mrs Arthur remonstrated with Emmy, who said, 'Just a little story.'

'I haven't much voice for storytelling.'

This was evident even to Emmy but she sidled closer to the fire and said, 'Captain Allington will give me a story. He has a book.'

'Where is your storybook?' he asked her, sitting down.

'I forgot it. You can tell me a story.'

'I think you overestimate my powers.'

'What do I do?' she asked, puzzled, going to lean on his knee.

'You ask me something too difficult.'

'Read to me from your book.'

'It is not a book for little girls.'

'May I sit on your lap?'

Allington picked her up. She immediately laid her head on his shoulder and he cradled her comfortably enough. He looked across at Mrs Arthur who was watching them. She thought his having Emmy in his arms, her brown curly head on the dark lapel of his coat, her child, an act of seduction.

Emmy said, 'Tell me something from your book.'

Allington closed the book and put it down. He quoted, from memory:

> *In Xanadu did Kubla Khan*
> *A stately pleasure-dome decree.*
> *Where Alph, the sacred river ran*
> *Through caverns measureless to man*
> *Down to a sunless sea.*

Emmy interrupted him. 'What is Kubla Khan?'

'A king – a warlord perhaps, I am uncertain of his history; a man who was always fighting.'

'Like Robert. He is always playing a battle. Phil too, but Phil doesn't like it. Do you know the French put a biscuit on a string like a bead? Alph is a river, is that right? I am not allowed near the river in case I fall in and drown. Phil is afraid of the river. Is this river under the ground?'

'Yes.'

'Tell me some more.'

'*So twice five miles of fertile ground/With walls and towers were girdled round.* How much is twice five, Emmy?'

'Ten.' Emmy, with the help of her fingers, could answer that.

'Sometimes I think I will have those walls and towers placed around Castle Orchard.'

'We have a tower already. What would the walls be for?'

'To keep out all the poachers, but it would be expensive to build – and what should we do when we got to the river?'

'It must be like Alph and go underground.'

'Ingenious child.'

'But it would be difficult to dig the hole, for the water would fill it up.'

'I can see you having the makings of an engineer.'

'Tell me more poem.'

Allington recited the rest of 'Kubla Khan', by which time Emmy was nearly asleep. She snuggled close into his arms but she asked drowsily, 'What is a damsel?'

'A young girl.'

'Like me?'

'Not so young as you.'

'Like Mama?'

'Yes, like your mother, but she is not from Abyssinia.'

'No, she's from Devonshire.'

Mrs Arthur said, 'Emmy, I am going to take you up to bed.' She got up and held out her arms for her daughter.

The following day, Captain Allington left for London.

Phil came back from school, to his mother's astonishment, wearing new boots. 'I went to the cobbler and ordered them,' he said. 'Today they were ready.'

'But the cobbler must be paid.'

'Captain Allington paid him.'

'And you made no mention to me of needing boots.'

'No, but I mentioned it to Captain Allington, that my boots were tight, and a few days after he spoke of it and sent me to order them. The cobbler was already paid.'

Phil looked with deep satisfaction on his new boots. Mrs Arthur was indignant. Captain Allington was so high-handed, yet how could she draw a line between what he might or might not pay for? Yes, if her necklace were worth sufficient money, she would go to Westcott Park, however much she might dislike it, however impossible.

Captain Allington was expected back within the week but he was gone a fortnight. Mrs Arthur became anxious about the gaming tables and her necklace, but when he did return she could see he was ill.

First he gave her a hundred pounds, which was, he said, the value of the necklace. She was so relieved to receive the money she thought it irresponsible to regret the loss, and while contemplating this, forgot to ask him whether the stones were paste. He then went on to describe his visits, on her behalf, to the various lawyers, but without actually telling her much except that he thought it would be several months before they got to the bottom of the riddle and she had best ignore the situation for the time being. The matter was in hand.

As to Allington being ill, he dismissed it as merely a spot of the ague, which attacked him from time to time.

Pride had more to say on the subject. He sought out Mrs Arthur. 'If he's ill, I want him to sleep in the house. I couldn't look after him so well in the lodge. It's a little damp, I reckon, and I need a proper kitchen by. He got that cold you and Miss Emmy had. His chest was bad and he was feverish. I says, "Don't go out in the wet," but he just looks at me and goes out all the same. Sometimes he says, "Think of Spain and Portugal." Well, I do. It would rain and worse, all night, buckets and buckets of it, icy cold. If we couldn't get the baggage up we'd be lying out in it, no rations, no bread, no biscuit, no beef, no rum, bloomin' starving an' wet to the skin, same as the men. The Heavens ain't particular when it comes to rank. Forget? Not likely. What master forgets is his wounds and the fevers. For two years his life wasn't worth nothing, what with one thing and another.'

Mrs Arthur said, 'Make up a bed in the Blue Room.'

'He won't like it.'

'Perhaps it will be my turn to be overbearing.'

Mrs Arthur did not see Allington again until later in the afternoon, certainly looking no better. The first thing she did was to make mention of Phil's boots, a subject she had not had a proper opportunity to broach.

He said, 'Please don't bother me with trifles.'

She was about to say she now had the means of paying for them, but he put into her arms a large shawl, deeply fringed and prettily patterned.

'Allow yourself to remain in my debt,' he said testily. 'We have yet to get the final outcome of your affairs so you don't know how long that hundred pounds must last you. Put that shawl on. I very much dislike you to be so much in want.'

Mrs Arthur laid the shawl, still folded, on her knee. She said, 'I will make a bargain with you.'

'What is it?' he asked.

'That you will sleep in the Blue Room until you have entirely regained your health.'

'I don't wish you to be subject to gossip.'

'Your health is more important to me.' As Mrs Arthur said this she realised it was true. His health was more important to her than anything she could think of at that moment. The idea of his being ill drove from her the decision to go to Westcott Park.

Before he could answer, Phil came in and went straight to Captain Allington and showed him his boots. Allington wished the child were not such a ludicrous caricature of Johnny Arthur.

'Do they fit?'

'Yes sir.'

'Show me your legs. I want to see if those bruises are gone.'

'They are gone, sir.'

'Let me see.'

'I don't like to show my legs.'

'Why not?'

'They are like sticks,' Phil said reluctantly.

'That's of no matter.'

Phil pulled up his trouser legs. Allington said, 'Good.' After a moment he added, 'A very fine leg for a boot.'

Phil's eyes widened, great discs of blue. A credulous smile crept over his face. He pulled his trousers yet higher and contorted himself to take a proper look at his legs. He said, 'Are you sure?'

'Certainly. You will be the envy of every cavalry officer.'

Phil's face was rapturous. He hardly knew himself. Mrs Arthur still had the shawl folded on her lap but as she stood up Allington took it from her and draped it round her shoulders. She put up her hand to stay him but he said, 'I know how to keep a bargain.'

Mrs Arthur suggested to Pride that they should call a doctor.

'Doctors or any of them medical folk, they knows less than I do,' Pride scoffed. 'Master has the fever. He gets it from time to time. I have the medicine. If the doctor comes they'll bleed him, and he won't have it. He doesn't hold with it. They'll drain a man's life away when he's half-dead. As for the fever, it frightens me, but I've plenty of the bark. The surgeons give it, the bark of a tree cooked up in water, though I've known some to put wine with it, it not being very palatable. The bark of the Jesuit tree, that's what it is. A young officer when he had the ague, used to take a hot drink and then gallop his horse. It was meant to drive the fever off, but I'm bothered if I know if it did. Lots died of it. We got it from laying out in the dew. It doesn't do you any good, laying out in the dew. One day for the fever, three or four days better, one day for the fever, that's how it goes.'

Pride was a competent nurse, or certainly as far as his master was concerned. He guarded the sick room jealously and issued orders to the kitchen but it was apparent he was extremely anxious. Allington, despite his care, got no better, each bout of fever progressively worse.

'He wouldn't be here if it weren't for me,' Pride said, when Mrs Arthur came up to the Blue Room. He immediately started to ramble on as only Pride could.

'That Waterloo, ma'am, was the awfulest battle in the world. Soldiers is mad not to miss a battle. Odd, I calls it. Well, it rains all night something terrible an' food is short come the morning. Master gets a pinch o' tea an' a little stir-about. I were that nervous he were cross an' packed me off to the back with his stuff. I fret over Joe, Captain Allington's baggage pony, for he ain't never heard action before but Joe keeps more calm than what I do. Well, he don't know about the French out there, thousands of 'em, ranks of 'em, all a-shouting for that Napoleon what they thinks so much of. I guards that baggage all day. They pesky foreign soldiers what run away would 'ave nicked it. When I was a soldier I never ran away. That frightens you more than staying. They blindfold you an' shoot you in a trice if you desert, but it's my belief nobody wouldn't desert if they got a square meal. At ten o'clock the guns start, the smoke gets up, you can't see a thing and it's listening, listening, listening. The noise, the terrible noise ... won't they ever stop? The wounded start to come by, droves of them, faces black as soot. They're that thirsty they'll drink the water what the wounds are washed in. It's the powder see. You bites the head from the cartridge an' the powder, gets in your mouth. Very drying stuff, powder.

'All day that battle goes, hour upon hour, and nobody knows what's happening. When dusk comes on, it dies away. They tell me Captain Allington is dead and they tell me it's a victory, but I don't care what it is if my master's dead. Night comes on. I'm too low to do much. Nothing to do, no master, no meal to get. The world's empty like, though 'tis full of folk.'

Pride pauses for a moment to prop Allington up in order to give him some water.

'A battlefield is a fearsome thing, but at night it's at its worst, with all the looting and robbing and murdering what goes on. There's no dying in peace out there. The soldiers what ain't dead have dropped down in heaps to sleep. At dawn I creeps out and finds a few men of his company just waking a bit. I wants to find his body. If I don't find that, they might forget he was an officer and dump him naked in a pit. I wants him to have a funeral, a grave, and sweet, solemn words out the Bible. I wants his hands crossed on his breast an' his uniform on, his sword, and I'd stay by and mind that grave as long as I lived – at least, I thinks I would. Nobody cares for him like I do. 'Course the uniform he's wearing would be looted off him but I had his other, same as I keep in the cedarwood chest.

'Two miles each way, that battlefield, two miles each way and forty thousand dead and wounded, let alone the horses. The place were heaped with horses. As for the infantry, you could see the shapes of the squares for the bodies laid there. Carnage you wouldn't credit, but I'd seen it all before – never so bad though – 'cept the breaches at Badejos. The men from his company knows where he is. They tried to get his body off before, but it were too tricky.'

Tears came into Pride's eyes. He wiped them away fiercely. 'I fights for the master, that I do, in my own way. I ain't no soldier, I've told you that, but there's another sort o' fighting, and I done that. Well, when we find him, nobody isn't excited he ain't dead 'cause it's obvious he soon will be. I have that boat cloak of Captain Jameson's on me arm, but oh, you never saw such as sight as he is, slashed to bits, his arms, his chest, his head, he's just one bloody mess, and he's got a dead horse on his legs. They'd taken his jacket an' shirt, his jacket with all his little precious things he kept in the pocket, the little picture and the letter. Still, I was prepared for that. The whole world seems one bloody mess just then, the whole world as far as your eye could see, one heaving, groaning bloody mess. Some of them holes in my master was done when he were on the ground. The French ain't particular that way. They'll take a jab at any man what moves. I never could like a Frenchie, but Mr Emill, he weren't a bad fellow.

'Heave the horse off him, wrap him up in the boat cloak, carry him off the battlefield, working through the bodies, every sort o' thing. Took 'em five days to shift the wounded off. The roads are blocked with carts, coaches, baggage, the wounded, the dying, the dead. Everyone cries for water, but there ain't no water. Every ditch is full of blood. We gets him up in a cart. The journey's terrible rough and we're three hours on the road to Brussels. I walk. I reckon he'll be dead every step I take an' I cry like a baby.

'You've got more chance if you're an officer. Every hospital is full. That Brussels is a pretty place. They put straw in the streets and lay out the wounded, row upon row, French and English side by side and any other sort of foreigner. Funny thing, a war. The women comes out from the houses and minds them best they can. Our first billet is an awful bad place, a bit of a stable. I don't know how to find our own surgeons, what belong to the regiment. I just lie low and mind him myself. As to the wounds, I think what a mess master looks, all gaping, not neat for his grave. You don't want to go to your grave full of holes. I'm a tailor, ain't I? I make a tidy of job it, neaten him up, even his head I shaves and sews up neat. The water for washing and cleaning I boils. Master always says that. Needles and knives and what-have-you. He says, "You don't know what's in the water too small to see." Well, I don't suppose there's anything in it, but I boils it all the same. I knowed of a gentleman what sat on a doorstep and sewed up his own belly but he died as he finished the job. Master ain't conscious, not really, but he'll swallow if I give him something – water, gruel, wine. Then Major Wilder seeks us out. He's come out from England, special. He gets us a real good billet in a merchant's house, sober sort o' folk but nothing ain't grudged. He fetches a surgeon. The surgeon looks at master and says it's a waste of time and to let him die quiet like. Master's leg is bust and he has a musket ball under the knee. I do wonder the surgeon don't take his leg off, for they gets paid for each limb they takes off, so stands to reason they take off as many as they can. Master says it ain't so, but officers don't never admit to that sort o' thing. I wants the surgeon to take out the ball and splint the leg for to make him comfortable, seeing he ain't dead yet, and Major Wilder saying the same, though the man's asleep on his feet, he's kindly, an' does it. Major Wilder won't let my master be bled, knowing how strong he feels about that. Just as well, 'cause they'd not be likely to listen to me.'

Pride paused for breath. He said, looking at Allington, who was asleep, 'Don't seem fair to lose him now. Still, the Good Lord didn't want him then so I dare say He don't want him now.'

Mrs Arthur could see Pride was exhausted, not only by his constant nursing but by all the things he felt a need to say. He believed he, and only he, could keep his master alive. After several days she managed to get him to take

239

a rest while she stayed in the room herself. He made sure there was nothing to be done before slumping down on a truckle bed in the corner and immediately falling asleep. It was with reluctance he temporarily left Allington to her care, but sleep he must.

She had some mending on her lap but it was difficult to concentrate. Pride constantly filled her head with the horrid images of war and her spirits recoiled from them.

Allington opened his eyes. They were bright with the fever. He said, apparently looking at her, 'I love you.'

She could not tell how conscious he might be, but it was not the moment to take him seriously. She wondered in how many languages he could say it. She thought of him flirting with olive-skinned Spanish girls amongst those shadowy arcades and curling balconies, young officers lounging in the hot dusk of a foreign town, of vines, trellises and orange trees. He had told her he had learned the bolero but Pride said the dance wasn't decent.

'In how many languages can you say that?' she asked.

He was so long in replying, she had given up expecting an answer but eventually he murmured, 'Four, maybe five.'

He closed his eyes again. She looked at his white face and thought of nursing Matthew, how his sturdy little form had got less and less, his face wan and thin. She had taken him in her arms, willing her own strength to go from her to him, but he died all the same.

Phil said a prayer in church. 'Please make Captain Allington better. I need him to look after my mother and Emmy. He's given my mother a cloak and a shawl to keep her warm. She wants to pay him some money but he won't take it. Why shouldn't he give my mother a present if he wants? Why is this bad?'

Emmy came to church with them now. She had promised to keep still and she did, she hardly moved a muscle. Her willpower was extraordinary. Phil liked to have Emmy in church but he also liked to have his mother to himself.

Outside, it was cold. Robert Conway came up to Phil. He said, 'Is Captain Allington any better?'

'No. He is sick. He will die.'

Robert clenched his hands together. 'You are lying.'

'Maybe he will die. Pride gives him medicine made from the bark of the Jesuit tree.'

Robert frowned. 'That seems a curious medicine. Does Captain Allington think it right?'

'I don't know. He's too sick to say.'

'He cannot, cannot, cannot die.'

'Captain Allington belongs to Castle Orchard, to us. He's not yours.'

Robert scowled at him and walked off. His father, the rector, was just coming out of the vestry door. He said, 'Well, my boy, you have waited for me, which is an unexpected pleasure.'

Robert walked along beside him, scuffling his boots in the mud. He said, 'Papa, why did we say no prayers in church for Captain Allington?'

'Why, my dear fellow, it is because I know nothing of Captain Allington. He has never come to church.'

'But he must have a soul for you to care for. You say you care for all the souls in the parish, yet you say no prayers for Captain Allington, who is a hero and nearly died fighting for his country.'

'My attempts to visit Captain Allington have borne no fruit.'

'I dare say he doesn't like to be visited. What has that got to do with saying prayers for him?'

'I fear he is not a righteous and godly man, though as a landlord he has proved agreeably efficacious. He's not a man I should like you to emulate, Robert, however heroic he may have been in the past. He's a gambler. You know very well how he obtained Castle Orchard, though such things are not for the ears of children.'

'You said he was a much better landlord than Mr Arthur was.'

'That is so, but I am persuaded he's not moral.'

'Do you say prayers to make him more moral?'

'I have not, dear child. Out of the mouths of babes and sucklings. You surely point me out my duty. I have been confused by Captain Allington.'

'You must say prayers, first for him to get better, or the others might be wasted.'

'Such prayers are never wasted, Robert. You have a mixture of logic and levity in your tone for which I don't quite care.'

'Please, Papa, just pray to make him better.' Robert unexpectedly burst into tears.

'There, there, don't take on so. We shall say prayers for his health and his redemption. He must remain innocent without his being proved guilty, whatever my brother may say.'

'He is wonderful, Papa. I think him the bravest, the most wonderful man there is.'

'I should much prefer you to look up to a man of a more godly disposition.'

242

'And the medicine he has, it is from the bark of the Jesuit tree. Does that make it a Roman Catholic medicine? Roman Catholics are idolatrous. Is that the word? Aren't they very wicked?'

'My dear child, what a muddle. Misguided rather than wicked. It can have no bearing on the medicine, which is considered efficacious in the treatment of certain fevers. It is from the bark of the cinchona.'

Robert was mildly disappointed Captain Allington could not add to his glamour by the imbibing of an idolatrous substance. He renewed his entreaties for his father's prayers which he thought must hold more weight than his own, his father being a clergyman surely having a more direct means of communication with God.

The following Sunday, the rector included Captain Allington in his prayers for the sick, and Allington's fever abated.

It was the tendency of the fever to return every three to four days. Pride said, 'He has been ten days free of it but that doesn't mean it's finished. It's never finished. If he were strong enough for the journey, we should go to St Jude for the winter. It's December now but there's plenty of winter left.'

'For the mildness of the climate?' Mrs Arthur asked him.

'And the sea.'

Mrs Arthur thought of the journey to Cornwall. The britchka could be made very snug. It was possible to travel night and day and to lie down in it with quite a degree of comfort.

'He'll sleep anywhere,' Pride said. 'Got used to it, see.

Dirty little places in Portugal, filthy, you wouldn't believe it, the bugs never gave you a moment. The master preferred the bare ground. I never saw nothing pleasant in marching day and night and lying down on a scorpion at the end of it. The Portuguese, they don't have a notion of comfort – no chimneys, no glass in the windows – miserable, I called it. Now it's my turn to say what's what and I want him down in Cornwall.'

A week went by. Allington started to come downstairs and lie on the sofa in front of the drawing room fire. Meg lay on his lap. He occasionally gave her ears a gentle pull. He wore a capacious dressing gown over a loose pair of trousers, and a rug over his knees. He tied a coloured handkerchief around his throat, made no apology for this state of undress and asked Mrs Arthur to read to him, so she read him *Headlong Hall* and *Nightmare Abbey* to make him laugh.

This led them to discuss whether or not they believed so many things could be discovered from an examination of the head, craniologists being in vogue and Mr Thomas Love Peacock making a mockery of it in his novels.

'We must be made up of our parents and our grandparents, heads and all,' Mrs Arthur said, 'but there certainly seems something very arbitrary about it, when one looks at family resemblances.'

'But when one has no idea of the appearance of one's relatives, let alone their characteristics, one is left at sea,' Allington said. 'There is a mysterious void.'

'You knew no grandparents?'

'Neither father nor grandparents. My parents eloped. For all I know, I may have relatives alive.'

'But have you never been curious?'

'By the time I was old enough to consider the matter, the one person, my mother, who could have enlightened me, was dead. I should have asked my stepfather. He might have known, but I never did. I have always been curious about my father.'

'Had you no likeness of him?'

'No. There was a miniature of my mother . . .' Allington paused and then he said, 'I don't have it. As for my grandparents, they disowned my mother, so I don't forgive them, if they exist.'

He was lying back against the sofa, his hands behind his head, watching Mrs Arthur, who had closed the book on her lap. He said, 'If I die now, if I get another bout, my relatives, if I have any, will be none the wiser, and I don't care in the least. My grandparents must have known of my father's death but they didn't bestir themselves to assist his widow and their grandchild. How cold is the heart that never relents. Perhaps mine is equally cold.'

Mrs Arthur said, 'I don't think it so very cold. There must have been officers, older officers, who served when your father did.'

'There were, and I never said a word, and neither did they. I only have myself to blame, but I was shy of it. It seemed safer to know nothing.'

'Not so courageous,' Mrs Arthur said.

'No, not at all so,' he replied. 'I never ventured to enquire of him.'

They were both silent for a while. Mrs Arthur worried he would tire himself. He was rake thin and very pale. She said, 'Are you warm enough?'

'Yes. I don't want to go upstairs. I'm perfectly comfortable. Are you?'

'Yes, of course I am,' she said, laughing at him. 'It is you that are the invalid.'

'I will have to go to Cornwall as Pride suggests. It's odd to think of a father and absolutely no image spring to mind. I know what he wore, for I know his regiment and I don't believe it has altered much, though the jacket has been shortened. The differences would be in the hat – and of course, officers and men wore their hair in a queue which, I am glad to say, was cut off the moment I joined up, for they took half an hour to dress, all rolled and powdered and greased. So, what is he to me? A red coat, a cocked hat and a queue.'

'But did your mother not talk of him?'

'No. She might say, "Such and such would have pleased your father", or, "Your father would be proud of you". Such things are easily said. I once, and only once, was vouch-safed a view of his most intimate and innermost thoughts, but it was as a page of a book, opened for me, read, and slammed shut; gone for ever, destroyed.'

Allington paused and then he said, 'Now, I'll tell you something. When my mother told me she was to marry Lord Tregorn I knew I was to live at the Big House and have every advantage of education and position. He had promised her he would be a father to me and I should want for nothing. I said, "You will have a maid and two footmen and never have to worry for money or that your gloves are darned. I shan't be any use to you at all." My mother hugged me tightly and cried a little, but I could see the logic of her marrying and was ashamed of my own tears.

'There was a week or so of great change and preparation. On the eve of my mother's wedding day I went to bed as usual. It was winter, just after Christmas, and very cold. My mother was accustomed to come up to bed shortly after me. I lay awake, listening for her, aware of the great closing of one door and the uncertain opening of the next. I suppose I was very uneasy. I listened and listened for her footsteps on our narrow staircase. After half an hour or so I got out of bed and stood on the little landing at the top of the stairs. Then I heard these terrible, wrenching sobs, such as I had never heard before. I tore downstairs in my nightshirt and bare feet. My mother was bent forward in her chair, crying and crying. One by one she was burning letters in the grate and I knew it was my father's letters she was burning and they were nearly all gone. I snatched the last one from her and I shouted at her, I shouted, "They're mine, you can't do that!" and flung myself into her arms and we both wept and wept.

'After a while I made her come upstairs. I put that last letter into my little trunk that was packed ready for our move. I then fetched my mother warm water to wash in and I heated a brick for her bed. She undressed and put on her night-gown. I got into bed with her and struggled to put my arms round her and we cried ourselves to sleep.

'The following morning she dressed herself and, with all appearances of composure, married my stepfather.'

Allington relapsed into silence. Mrs Arthur got up and hastily went to draw the curtains across the windows, for darkness was coming on and she did not want him to see how much this tale had distressed her. When she turned back to him, he had closed his eyes. She pulled the rug up round him and after a while she could see he slept.

Allington insisted on spending time at his desk in the morning room before leaving for Cornwall. He reminded

Mrs Arthur of a leaf, etched by winter to the bare bones – but courage, or the discipline of a soldier, kept him upright.

On the day of his departure he came downstairs dressed for the journey. He had the boat cloak over his arm.

Mrs Arthur said, 'Captain Jameson's.'

Allington sat down on the old settle in the hall. He said, 'Pride tells you too much. I shouldn't allow you to assist him in making curtains. We were mess mates, John Jameson and I.'

The room was filled with portraits of Johnny Arthur's ancestors. Of the man himself, there was none, and had there been, Allington thought he would have had it taken down. It made him think of Phil. Would he, eventually, want to know more about his father, and what could be said of him?

He turned back to Mrs Arthur. 'To be practical, if I have another bout of fever it will probably kill me. Pride, who sets great store by my funeral, will be stowing my uniform into the britchka despite my contrary instructions. He wishes me equipped with a coffin and some clothes. If Pride has his way I shall be six foot under, dressed in all the splendour of a captain of the Light Dragoons. Saint Peter will have no difficulty in recognising my profession. My affairs are in perfect order, such as they are, which is more than can be said of yours. However, they're in hand and it is just a matter of waiting. You don't have to worry. I give you my word no final catastrophe awaits you. I'm leaving Dan here. He will take care of things. Don't go away. Look after Castle Orchard. If I return, it will be with the swallows.'

He stood up as briskly as he could. His stick was to hand. Mrs Arthur accompanied him outdoors. The britchka awaited him, a groom standing holding the hired horses.

Pride appeared with the offending uniform wrapped in a sheet and his glass jar of sixpences.

Mrs Arthur struggled for words but none came. It was unbearable to see Allington so weak, to hear him speak of his funeral with half-cheerful levity and to watch him clamber into the vehicle. He neither looked back nor spoke. In a moment the groom was up on the box and the horses were stepping out.

Dan was in charge of the stables. The outdoor staff at Castle Orchard learned to interpret Dan and viewed the punching bag, which hung in a spare loosebox, with respect. Dan might be diminutive, silent and deaf, but he always had his own way. Mrs Arthur suspected him of exploiting his disabilities in order to do exactly as he saw fit. He brought the long-tailed grey round to the front door and escorted her out for a ride on the days he considered the weather to be suitable. He showed her a piece of paper on which was drawn a clock with the hands at half past one; the grey, distinctive with its long tail; the side-saddle; and a cloud with rain coming from it, the latter with a cross over it. From his sickbed Captain Allington had ordered her life. He knew she spent the morning giving Emmy lessons and then took a little luncheon with her. At half past one she had often ridden out with him. Dan, meticulous in his duties, hastened home with her at the merest drop of rain.

Annie gave her a glass of wine with her dinner. 'He said you was to have it, ma'am. He said, "Annie, look after your mistress and see she has no economies." He mayn't drink it himself, but you are to have it.'

'And how many glasses am I to have, Annie?'

'Now that he didn't say,' Annie replied, 'though he's a managing gentleman.'

'Will he get better?'

Annie sighed. She really couldn't say.

Mrs Arthur reflected on the subject of economy. She and Cook used to struggle with saving the pennies, but as Cook said, they now never had no need to bother their heads, though she wouldn't countenance waste. Mrs Arthur recalled Allington telling her of his weighing the sugar for his mother. Sugar was expensive. He would have known of the scrimping for sugar. She thought of her long hours with the account books and how nothing, now, was required of her but to look after her children, yet she found her life without purpose. When life had been a struggle she had been occupied with the battle of it. The management of the household now ran smoothly on, needing but minimal assistance from herself. Women in her position were, she supposed, used to occupying their time with visiting, but to be ignored by the thin sprinkling of what could be described as society within the vicinity, none of it immediate, she had been long accustomed. She had had no time for making a choice from her scanty wardrobe in order to take tea or play a genteel game of whist in the carefully regulated houses of her far scattered neighbours, all of whom seemed to have viewed her with apprehension and astonishment, either for her temerity in marrying Johnny Arthur in the first place, his reputation being more than poor, or for the scandal of his abandoning her. Only the Conways doggedly persisted in visiting her, one from inclination, the other from duty, but she was alone and their visits did not make her less so.

She received no letters and supposed if Captain Allington wished to communicate he would, unless he was not well enough to write. She thought about it as she clopped along on the grey, the silent Dan half a pace behind her. Dan knew his place. He lived in one silent world and she lived in another. There was Annie and Phil and Emmy, to whom she gave words and attention, but she was solitary, elsewhere, in a sea of nothingness. She was not wretched as she had been when first married, racked, miserable, desperate – that is, until she had learned to manage, to recognise her husband for what he was and to desist from grieving over it. Now she was sad, as if she had been given a glimpse of another world, another sort of life, a door opening halfway before banging shut.

As for money, she chose to accept Captain Allington's word. Had he not said there was no cause for concern on her part? So she assumed, all in good time, she would receive the jointure. When that happened, she must ask Mr Westcott if he had some little house she could take, something less than the Dower House he had already offered. With this in mind she occupied herself in remaking her wardrobe and also the children's. There was an advantage in the delay. By the time she was living elsewhere, there would be no need for her to be wearing more than half-mourning and certainly no need to put Phil and Emmy into black. She asked Louisa to send her cloth in shades of grey and lilac, white for Emmy, with appropriate patterns, dipping into the hundred pounds to pay for it. Mrs Arthur knew how to sew. She had taken apart many an outworn garment to see how it was made. As for the pink silk Louisa had sent her, she still could not see she would have any occasion for it.

Christmas arrived. Emmy received a new set of clothes for her doll, worked by her Aunt Louisa. There was, for

Phil, a puzzle comprising the English monarchs from Their Majesties William I to George IV, to be set in order. Were there no kings before William I? Phil asked.

Annie said, 'How can we be joyous at Christmas if we don't know how the captain is? That Pride could write if he left off talking for once.'

Louisa included, amongst the parcels, a letter for her sister.

My dear Caro,

I quite understand you must look after the house for Captain Allington while he is gone into Cornwall for his health. You are, I see, under an obligation to him. My mother doesn't understand this and thinks it odd. However, his not being at Castle Orchard must be such a relief to you, for never can a situation be so absurdly awkward as yours. What can the banks and the lawyers be doing that your affairs are at a complete halt? It is very odd. John says if you will send him a written note giving your authority, he will go to London. He wishes to know who is your lawyer. Now, dearest Caro, the moment Captain Allington returns, do have your bags packed and come to Westcott Park. From here you can make all further arrangements. You know Mr Westcott says he will send the coach for you. He or John will wish to escort you. It really will appear rather odd if you don't. My mother says it will cause a sensation, and you know how she is when it comes to anything that may draw attention to oneself . . .

The word *odd* predominated.

Louisa's letter went on and on, even to how many servants her sister might like to bring. Mrs Arthur, while reading it, answered things in her head. She could not tell John the name of her lawyer, which he would find *odd*; she found it *odd* herself, but she had never asked Captain Allington the name. Was it Jonas or had he seen fit to employ someone else? If she told Louisa she had put her affairs into the hands of Captain Allington, her sister would be struck dumb.

She wrote *Dearest Louisa*, and then stopped to gaze out of the window where a few lone flakes of snow drifted from an iron sky. She was fond of her but Louisa was so very much the younger and she had but one cause of anxiety in her well-regulated life – that of producing no boy. Mrs Arthur could see this as unfortunate for John and Louisa, as the estate was entailed, but not a disaster as John had four younger brothers.

The New Year was marked by a peculiar incident, or Mrs Arthur saw it as such. Castle Orchard lacked the glories requisite on the public demanding to see it. On no occasion had Annie been required to show strangers the portraits of deceased Arthurs. The most ever requested was permission to enter the park in order to view the Philosopher's Tower and the remains of the castle. Now a card was sent from the nearest post-house with a note to say a viewing of the house would be much appreciated as it was known to be an antique and the owner of the card had been a friend of the late Mr Arthur.

Mrs Arthur's first instinct was to refuse. Who could want to come to Castle Orchard – though it did have its charm, and was certainly an antique – out of anything but base curiosity? On the other hand, the rarity of such a request made her feel it churlish to refuse. The name on the card was Rampton, which meant little to her beyond the idea there was an estate in Dorsetshire to which some scandal or gossip had been attached. She gave permission for the visit, at the same time putting on, without enthusiasm, one of her new gowns. Seeing they declared themselves friends of Johnny's, she supposed she must entertain them. Within an hour a smart travelling coach pulled up at the door.

As the elegantly dressed couple descended from the vehicle, it occurred to Mrs Arthur how neat and orderly Castle Orchard must now appear. For a moment she was proud of it. She herself would appear as a respectable widow, living in quiet retirement, her only article of real finery the beautiful shawl Captain Allington had provided. It then occurred to her that they must know Captain Allington was the owner of Castle Orchard.

Mr Rampton, plump, dark-haired and handsome, wearing a copious neckcloth and a double-breasted green frockcoat with full skirts to his knees, bowed deeply. His wife, slightly the elder, wore pale yellow. Mrs Arthur knew from her sister that waists were back, but as Mrs Rampton was expecting a child, there could not be much of a waist. There was a profusion of tucks and frills about the hem of her gown, however, and she had on a wide-brimmed bonnet covered in bows and trailing ribbons. Under the bonnet was a quantity of fine, pale hair and large, pale eyes. Mrs Arthur thought Mr and Mrs Rampton served a useful purpose in telling her what was the mode, much as Louisa had intimated. She could see why Mr Rampton had been a friend of her husband's, though much younger. They seemed as remote from her life as some exotic creatures from the zoological gardens.

She instructed Annie to send in some wine and biscuits. 'I fear we intrude,' Mr Rampton declared. 'We understood in the village that the owner of the property was absent for his health.' Mr Rampton had made these enquiries, for no amount of entreaties on the part of his wife, who usually had her own way, would have betaken him to Castle Orchard had he thought Captain Allington in residence.

'That is so,' Mrs Arthur replied. She thought some explanation for her own presence was in order, but none sprang to her mind.

'We were passing, you know,' Rampton continued. 'Your late husband was a much valued friend.'

'We have the property of Bell Hill Abbey,' Mrs Rampton said, accepting a glass of wine. 'It is interesting, is it not, to compare properties of similar antiquity?'

'Why yes,' Mrs Arthur agreed. 'But opportunities for my doing so have been limited.'

'Travel, even in a small way, broadens the mind,' said Mrs Rampton.

'Mine must be much confined,' Mrs Arthur replied, 'if that is the case.' She turned to Mr Rampton and said, 'Did you really know my husband so very well?'

'Yes, indeed. His death is a lasting tragedy to me. His circumstances were so unfortunate. I fear it a delicate subject. I had no idea I should ever have the pleasure of conversing with his widow.' Mr Rampton got out his handkerchief as if to dab at his eyes. It was accompanied by an aroma of Attar of Roses, and for a moment Mrs Arthur

255

had the unfortunate sensation of Johnny Arthur himself about to enter the room.

Mr Rampton, feeling more at his ease, continued, 'You must forgive my mentioning it, but the presence of a widow and orphans was not known to society. We all very much idolised Mr Arthur, but he did have his curious ways.'

Mrs Arthur could think of nothing appropriate to add.

'I frown upon gambling,' Mrs Rampton remarked.

'I too,' Mrs Arthur concurred.

Mr Rampton looked uncomfortable but he said, 'I don't allow myself this fashionable indulgence.'

'It is unfortunate when a gentleman gambles,' Mrs Rampton said. 'He has no idea when to stop.'

'No idea at all,' Mrs Arthur consented. She was surprised to find she had so many notions in common with the young vision in yellow before her.

'Allington allows you to continue in residence here,' Rampton said next. 'I dare say it's a convenience for you.'

'It is,' Mrs Arthur nodded, though she thought it more of a necessity than a convenience.

'Not a comfortable fellow, Captain Allington. Too clever by half. He is revered in military circles, but beyond that he never was to be seen anywhere but the Travellers Club and now he's gone altogether.'

'It cannot be pleasant to have your fortune built on other people's ruin,' Mrs Rampton said piously.

'My dear, that is going a great deal too far in Allington's case, especially where Arthur was concerned. Why, people begged him to play, it amused them so.'

'And didn't people lose a great deal of money to him?' Mrs Rampton demanded, roused from her accustomed cool.

'Of course, but why should they not? It's the most diverting of occupations. They are not coerced into losing their money. I am, as you know, far too cautious to indulge, too aware of what is at stake, my love. Pray have no fear.' Rampton turned to Mrs Arthur and said, 'I was, you know, the witness to the game that ultimately cost Arthur this estate.'

'The witness?' Mrs Arthur said, surprised. 'I had always imagined forty witnesses in White's or Brooks's or one of those other places where gentlemen seem to reside on a permanent basis. I don't even know what all these card games are – faro, macao and such things – or are they played with dice? Isn't Captain Allington the exception that proves the rule, that he apparently plays no more, that he *has* known when to stop?'

'I wouldn't call Allington a gambling man,' Rampton said. 'I don't believe he ever played a game of chance in his life. You quite misunderstand him if you think that, but I dare say he never mentions such things.'

'But in that case, how did my late husband lose Castle Orchard?'

'Bound to lose it anyway, if you will forgive my saying so, he owed so much money. He lost at play to Allington and never paid up. An odd way to behave because such debts are debts of honour, you know, and they have to be paid. It was Allington at fault for letting him get away with it. Arthur set Allington to play against him with Castle Orchard as the stake. If Allington lost, he was to forgive Arthur his previous debts, which amounted to a great deal of money. I begged Arthur not to make such a bargain, but he would. He was sure, this time, he would win. We were in his lodgings in Half Moon Street. The whole horrid occasion is etched upon my mind, never to be forgotten.'

'But what sort of game was it they played?' Mrs Arthur asked.

'Chess.'

'Chess,' Mrs Arthur echoed, astonished. 'But of course, Johnny thought himself an excellent player of chess.'

She got up from her chair and for a moment moved anxiously about the room. Her mind was more occupied with Allington than with her late husband. However had she supposed Allington would rely on games of chance to amass a fortune? She had indeed misunderstood him.

Rampton was saying, 'Of course, he would have needed to be a genius to beat Allington at chess. It was the best of three, but as Allington won the first two there was no need for the third.'

'I had never considered it could have been chess,' Mrs Arthur repeated, as much to herself as them.

'I don't see how it could make a difference what the game was,' Mrs Rampton said. As Arthur had been the doyen of what was fashionable, it was no surprise he had kept his wife out of sight for Mrs Arthur's gown was very plain and her hair not properly dressed. She then thought, perhaps it suited mourning, but her shawl . . . that was exceedingly fine, better even than Mrs Rampton's own.

'Allington is a cold, calculating man,' Rampton said. 'My dear friend, the late Mr Arthur, pronounced his sensibilities to be deadened by the horrid scenes of war, the carnage and slaughter.'

'But a soldier's life is noble,' Mrs Rampton interposed. 'They give up their lives in defence of their country.'

Mrs Arthur thought, She is like clockwork, wound up

to give the correct response. She believes what she says but without having considered it.

'Very heroic and all that,' Mr Rampton conceded, 'but in peacetime they have no occupation – and then what is to be done with them? A soldier should be a creature for active service only, and after that he should dissolve like a bubble of soap.' He was pleased with this pronouncement and supposed it worthy of Johnny Arthur himself. He then began to wonder if it were not something Arthur had said to him and he was merely repeating it. He concluded, 'The expense of keeping a standing army is too much, and the presence of barracks around the countryside is wholly unnecessary and a threat to the civil liberties of the people.'

Mrs Arthur said nothing. She thought of the men – sons, brothers, husbands, lovers – who willingly dashed upon the enemy and died, while others were complacent, even jocular, on the subject of their sacrifice. Her own words would be hackneyed phrases falling on stony ground. It occurred to her that Captain Allington would have preferred to leave his bones unhallowed, unburied on some hot Spanish plain, than suffer the tame but endless trials of lameness and ill health.

Impatient with the company, she stood up. 'I am sure you have a journey before you and will wish to delay no longer.'

For a moment she wondered if she should lend Annie to show them the house. She then thought, Captain Allington would have frightened them off the moment they arrived and it was his house. Why should they be spying out the secrets of his life to prattle in some smart London drawing room?

Mrs Rampton said to Mrs Arthur, 'What a remarkable shawl you have. I declare myself quite envious.'

Mrs Arthur extended her arms for the better display of it. She said vaguely, 'Yes, it is pretty.'

'I shouldn't venture to wear such a thing except upon a most special occasion.'

'Would you not?' Mrs Arthur said. 'I wear it to keep warm. You will see the Philosopher's Tower, if you cross the garden, on your way out.'

Thus dismissed, the Ramptons departed only a little wiser than when they came.

Mrs Arthur stopped in the hall to examine the post, searching for a letter from Cornwall that never came. There were only bills from tradesmen which Captain Allington had instructed her to open and pay from the sums he had left for the purpose.

Jackson, having spent the morning shuffling logs into wood baskets, sighed with relief at regaining the sanctuary of the boot room.

'Dunno why they wants so many fires. Dangerous thing, fire. I seed a man drop down 'alf dead from lighting a fire an' 'aving no chimney. They foreigners, yer Portuguese, don't 'ave no chimneys. 'Twas a battle once, Talavera, where yer wounded was shot down in a field o' corn an' that corn caught alight, see, an' burned the lot o' them up. 'Tisn't always pleasant the way yer goes to kingdom come, not when yer soldiering.'

Robert asked, 'Why did you join up, Jackson?'

Jackson was silent for a while. He lit his clay pipe and puffed at it, ruminating. Then he said, ''Twas on account of a girl. Family way, her trouble. 'Er pa were after me to marry 'er. Danged if I knew 'twere my fault. Anyway, recruiting man come by an' I joins up mighty quick.'

'Didn't you want to be married?' a little boy asked.

Jackson shook his head.

'Not ever?'

'I was married the once. Didn't last. 'Twas like this. Corporal Smith 'ad a right useful sort o' wife. There ain't many wives in the Army, six to each company. Draw lots they do, for to get in the boats. T'others 'ave to starve or go on the parish. Well, I says to Mrs Smith, if 'er man goes – gets killed, like – I'll 'ave 'er next. She's willing an' the corporal, 'e goes down in the next action – Salamanca it were – an' I gets the chaplain to wed us. She needs to be wed to go on getting 'er rations, see. Can't say if she fancied me otherwise, but good enough I s'pose. Anyway, didn't last. She would go out after nicking an officer's watch. Horse Artillery, 'e were. I remembers looking at him and thinking he were a bonny lad, though dead as a doornail.'

'But he was English then?' Robert asked, shocked. 'You didn't rob the English?'

'Ain't too fussy. If yer don't nick off o' them, t'others will. Anyways, I says to the missus, "Don't yer go out there till the guns are quiet".'

Jackson came to a halt. His pipe had gone out.

'But what happened?'

'What d'yer think? Bit o' shrapnel got 'er. She an' the young officer were laid down side by side, an' blow me if I weren't right off marryin' after that. She 'ad blood on 'er 'ands. Yer peeked at the poor laddie an' yer thought 'twas a pity 'e ain't stayed at 'ome with 'is mammy. 'E wouldn't never 'ave touched 'is cheek with a razor yet awhile. Brought up

261

delicate, like, it makes yer wonder. I gives such a one me biscuit once. Dead on 'is feet, 'e were.'

The boys, open-mouthed, could not concede of Jackson giving away his biscuit, and Jackson himself, perhaps ashamed at confessing to such weakness, shook his stick at them with more than his usual vehemence, and they scampered away.

Robert took Phil by the arm and half dragged him, half cajoled him, outdoors. It was the end of the school day. They sat on the ivy-covered wall of the rectory garden.

Robert asked after Captain Allington and refused to believe Phil had no idea. Phil was, all the same, emboldened to repeat, 'Captain Allington belongs to us, not you, but he doesn't write any letters. He doesn't care to.'

Robert gazed into space. He said, 'He belongs to England. He is a soldier of the King. If you think he belongs to an ugly little fledgling like yourself, you're much mistaken.'

This graphic description of Phil with his skinny little body and unruly quantity of hair upon a rather outsized head, did not much disturb him. It was better to be an ugly little fledgling than the French.

'Captain Allington will come back and he will describe to us the Battle of Waterloo,' Robert said. 'Remember how he marked in the sand the Siege of Badejos. He will say, 'Here was Hougoumont and here La Haye Sainte, here the squares of infantry, here the French cavalry. Do you think he would tell us all of this?'

'No. He doesn't talk much of battles.'

Phil kicked his heels against the wall. He examined his boots, still new. They were stout workaday boots, for had he not to come across the meadow in the mud? He looked at his legs, grown no heartier, and thought the new size of his feet did nothing for their dimensions, but it was of no matter. Was he not to have a fine leg for a boot?

He said to Robert, 'Perhaps Captain Allington will never come back.'

At the beginning of March, a lad in breeches and boots and a striped waistcoat of blue and green, which denoted his employment with Lord Tregorn, appeared in the yard riding a blue roan pony. He greeted Dan with a familiar smile and took a note from his pocket. Dan studied it for a while before ushering the boy into the kitchen.

'Come up from St Jude with the pony,' the lad said to Annie and Cook.

'Goodness me,' Annie replied. 'What pony?'

'Captain Allington's pony. He got it in Ireland and took it to France with him. It was his baggage pony. Been to Waterloo, Smokey Joe has, an' seen the sights. Joe he's called but we called him Smokey Joe 'cause of his colour an' all the smoke he's seen.'

'The missus will want to see you.'

'Don't spec so. I gave Dan the message what the Captain drew for him. 'Tis a good pony. The captain left it for the little 'uns at St Jude to ride, but even Master Fred is now too big for Smokey Joe.'

Annie made the boy scrub his face and ushered him through the house to the drawing room. He looked about him with cheerful confidence.

Mrs Arthur was making another attempt to write to Louisa.

'This young lad has come all the way from Cornwall with a pony,' Annie said.

Mrs Arthur turned in her chair. She said, 'You mean he has come from St Jude?'

'Yes, ma'am, if you please. Captain Allington sent the pony.'

'Captain Allington, is he well?' Mrs Arthur asked.

'Why, I s'pose he must be, for he's outdoors plenty. He goes out with the fishing boats like he did when he was a little lad, so they tell me. He's mortal fond of the sea, the captain is. Anyway, he asks His Lordship can he spare me to take Smokey Joe up into Wiltshire. He gives me enough money for the tollgates and for to stay the nights and come home on the Mail coach. I'm to stop here one night and Cook will give me supper and make me up a piece for my lunch. Oh yes, and the pony is for Master Phil. It's a good safe pony. I ain't never been on the Mail before and I'd like to sit up on the box, but the coachmen are too grand for lads like me.'

'Goodness, you have got a lot to say,' Annie said. 'Have you no message for my mistress?'

The boy paused and thought for a moment. Then he said, 'Now 'twas something about birds – swallows, I think – but it didn't seem so important as bringing up Smokey Joe, who is getting on a bit, but not too much so, and will be grand for the little boy who don't weigh more than a puff o' dust, the captain said, and what with my catching the coach, and Cook to make me a piece, and I ain't to dally on the road, I can't rightly remember the rest.'

'Oh Annie, take him away,' Mrs Arthur said. 'Find him a place to sleep and give him a shilling to spend for himself.'

'The master must be well,' Annie said, beaming.

Mrs Arthur wrapped herself up in her cloak and walked round to the stable, Meg, beside her. Dan was rubbing the pony down. He touched his hat to her but continued to work, a twist of hay in his hand. She watched him for a while and stroked the pony's neck.

Phil was beside himself at school. He said, over and over again, out loud, 'I have a pony of my own. Captain Allington sent him me and I have written a letter to Cornwall to say thank you. His name is Smokey Joe and he was Captain Allington's baggage pony when he went to war. Smokey Joe was at Waterloo.'

The boys crowded about him. None of the Conways had a pony of their own.

Robert said, 'You are telling a fib. You are a liar.'

'No, I'm not. Smokey Joe carried a kettle and a fishing rod, a water canteen, Captain Allington's boat cloak, his rations, his shirts, his other uniform, his hairbrush, his mirror, his shaving brush, two books but we don't know what they were . . .'

'How do you know?'

'Dan told me. And his neckcloths and a bottle of brandy.'

'How does *he* know? Isn't he deaf and dumb? He couldn't have told you.'

Phil was disconcerted. 'I don't know how he knows, because he wasn't there, but he does. He drew all those things on a piece of paper. I sat in the harness room and he drew Smokey Joe all over with baskets and packages.' He thought about Dan, who had certainly smiled throughout.

'You're a little liar,' Robert repeated.

When school was over Dan appeared with the pony, saddled and bridled, and waited by the rectory gates. It was a dank, raw evening. The boys ran out. They surrounded

265

Smokey Joe, patting and stroking him and saying, 'Isn't he pretty', and, 'Isn't he a little beauty', and 'Didn't he go to war with Captain Allington?' It was, for Robert, too much. Envy ate him up. It was nearly too much for Phil, for they all said, 'Are you going to ride him?' Phil was in a state of wild excitement to think how Smokey Joe was for him, but when he considered the reality of clambering up into the slippery saddle and clutching the reins, then his legs had never seemed so skinny nor his head so large, like Emmy's doll, all hair and stuffing. He was rigid with fright. Smokey Joe was, he thought, bigger than fat old Domino, asleep in the field, who couldn't be got to go anywhere. There was nothing sleepy about Smokey Joe, who had sharp pricked ears and looked all about him. He nuzzled and nibbled at the boys' pockets, looking for titbits.

Someone said, 'Bet you can't ride him, Arthur. Bet he's not really yours.'

To take a rush at what you feared the most having ever been Phil's policy, he flung himself in the direction of the saddle. Dan, with some mysterious sleight of hand, flipped him up into it like the tossing of a coin. Was it luck or management Phil did not continue his flight and come down on the pony's further side? Smokey Joe, used to worse affronts, paid no attention and Dan shoved Phil's boots into the stirrups and gave him a thump in the small of the back to make him sit up straight. Phil was too terrified to do more than sit but he managed a quick, triumphant look in the direction of his schoolmates.

Every day Dan brought the pony to the rectory gates. After the first day he came mounted himself, with Smokey Joe on a string. For five days Phil's ecstasy was combined with terror, but on the sixth day, no mishap occurring to

266

him, he started to imbibe Dan's instructions, for Dan could instruct very well by means of pointing and pushing. Phil started to pick up the reins, delicately, aware of Smokey Joe's mouth with the bit against his soft lips. He had, from the start, light hands, but Dan could not tell him this, he could only grin and nod.

Phil could tell Dan nothing. He could never say he was cold, that it rained, that he had no wish to trot or canter or leap a small log in the wood. Dan was, in Phil's eyes, obtuse, but Dan was far from it. He knew Captain Allington meant him to teach Phil to ride, and teach him he would. He taught him to put on the saddle and bridle, to groom the pony himself, feed it and clean out its feet.

Robert Conway was sick in himself. At breakfast he said to his father, who had watched the darkening of his countenance with increasing dismay and bewilderment, 'I no longer wish to be a schoolboy.'

'My dear child, at your age,' and for a moment the rector had to think what age that might be, 'at your age, one cannot dictate one's life. Of course you must be a schoolboy until your education is complete.'

'Send me to the Military Academy. I'm old enough.'

'Having no connections, it would be injudicious. There might be some purpose in your entering the East India Company, had I the influence to get you well placed.'

'When I'm sixteen I shall enter the Army as a volunteer. Someone will give me a recommendation and I should soon get a commission.'

'Robert, this living isn't rich. Without the income from the school, we would be very poor. How am I to provide you with the necessary means to live as an officer and a gentleman? Then, suppose you are wounded or retired and put on half-pay, your remittance would be meagre. I fear you look to Captain Allington as an example, but you must believe me when I say his position in life is not gained from an officer's pension.'

'He got Castle Orchard by gambling,' Robert said, but sulkily. 'I'm not a baby, I know things like that. I don't care. He was wounded fighting for his country and that's all that matters to me.'

'I am sure his career as an officer was everything that is valiant and honourable. However, it's not my intention you should be exposed to all the horrors of war at so young an age, let alone the fevers of a foreign clime. I believe Captain Allington's current ill health to be a result of his campaigning days. Stephen is the least clever of my boys and, should he want it, he is the only one I should not discourage from a military career, could I get him started. I am hoping for your ordination. It is likely this very living here at Castle Orchard could be yours, for I remain on terms of perfect cordiality with my benefactor. It is possible all could be arranged.'

Robert skulked off to his own room. He thought of Phil and the pony, a pony, though only a baggage pony, which had heard the roar of the cannon and smelled the acrid smoke of the powder while it hung heavy on the hot June air, the smoke of how many muskets, how much artillery? He thought a hundred thousand, but he knew he didn't really know. He then thought how blood smelled and how the ditches ran with it. The air was hot and heavy, smelling of blood and sweat and saltpetre; he nerved himself to think of it, half-exhilarated, half-frightened. He turned to his own treasures, soothed by their familiarity, though nonetheless precious to him: the green shako of the 95th Rifles with the folding-down flap at the front, the green cut feather plume and the cord in black; the three rows of silver buttons; the black lacing; the bugle-horn badge and, most significant of all, the small folding spyglass. Now he wished he had besides some article, even a single button or a thread of silver lace, from the uniform of a Light Dragoon.

In the meantime his father rose from the breakfast table. He wished Robert would not scowl so, but he supposed it was his age. This passion among the boys for anything military was an unfortunate trait, and he would have preferred that they spent less time in the boot room with Jackson.

Phil had time away from school over Easter. He spent much of it in the stables looking after or riding Smokey Joe, but one pony does not take so very much attention and even Phil had to concede when there was nothing more to be done.

The Conway boys, bored, came to watch him. Under their cold scrutiny he lost his competence, dropped things, muddled the buckles on the bridle and slopped the water bucket. Smokey Joe shifted unexpectedly and trod on his foot, but he put the headstall on and led him out to the field.

Stephen said, 'Give us a ride.'

Phil wanted Smokey Joe entirely for himself, but he let them clamber up one after the other and then felt the better for allowing it. With the pony grazing, they wandered off together. It was many days since they had played.

Robert said, 'Let us pretend the Philosopher's Tower is the Castle of Badejos. It's April and the Siege of Badejos was on the night of the sixth. The river runs by it and that can be the stream. If we had a ladder we could lay it across

269

the river in order to get over. Then we must drag it up the glacis and escalade the castle.'

'But the river is too wide,' Phil said. He had no wish for a game that involved the river.

'And we have no ladders,' said Stephen.

Robert, fired with ideas, began to run about the stable yard looking for a ladder. There was one to the hayloft, which was long, but perhaps not long enough. He dropped it down and it fell with a clatter to the ground.

'Dan will be angry if you take it,' Phil said.

'Who's afraid of Dan, who can't hear or speak?' Robert said, pulling the ladder across the cobbles. 'Come on, Stephen, take the other end, and you, Frankie. The twins could do better. Don't mind Phil. He is too much of a weakling ever to do anything.'

They heaved the ladder out of the yard, across the lawn and into the paddock.

'Phil must be the French,' Stephen said. 'He must be in the castle and fire at us with muskets. We will cross the river with the ladder under the heaviest of cannonade but we are so brave nothing will stop us.'

'Yes,' Robert cried. 'We are the Third Division.'

'We are the Third Division,' cried out Frankie, pink in the face and gasping for breath, for the ladder was heavy. 'We will have on our red coats. We are ever so brave as could be.'

'I don't want to be the French,' Phil said, by this time helping with the ladder.

'Then you must cross the river,' Robert said, laughing at him.

'Phil will be wounded and drown in the river,' Stephen said. 'His head will go under and he will go bubble, bubble and that will be the end of him. He will be filled up with water.'

'No, Phil is in the castle. We will escalade the castle and make him our prisoner.'

Phil trotted meekly beside them. He would defend the castle and then he would be a prisoner. He entered the Philosopher's Tower and climbed up to the first floor. He had a stick in his hand which he poked through the window, all the while watching the Conway boys first cross the bridge with the ladder and then find a part of the river narrow enough to take its length. It was too short by about nine inches. They went back and forth, industrious and determined, trying here and trying there, several times in danger of losing it in the current.

Phil narrowed his eyes. He stared down at the enemy and felt his musket in his hand. At last a place was found for the ladder quite near to the tower. He watched Robert lodge it carefully, testing it with his foot. His heart began to bang in his chest. He made the motion of taking out a cartridge and biting off the cap, loading his weapon and ramming down the charge. He was a Frenchman and he was defending the castle. He aimed, Robert in his sights running back and forth across the ladder to show his younger brothers it was safe. He then went back and crawled across, the others following – and at that moment Phil shot him, but he still came crawling on. As if by magic the twins appeared. They ran across the bridge and made to crawl after their cousins. Robert shouted at them to go away, they were too little, but they crawled across all the same. They all came up the slope to the Philosopher's Tower on their hands and knees. Robert ran back down the slope, remembering they needed the ladder for the escalade. He dragged it off the river by himself and started to pull it.

'We are the Third Division and this is the glacis,' Stephen called to the twins.

'The Third Division, the Third Division,' said Jacky.

'The glacis,' said James.

'And Phil is the French. He is defending the castle.'

'Phil is the French,' said Jacky.

Up they came, up the glacis with the ladder through nettle and bramble. Phil fired and fired with his musket, each time reloading. He saw the English soldiers in short scarlet jackets. They put their ladder to the castle wall. He shot them and shot them but they never died. He was wild with the excitement of it. The French were brave, they were not cowards, Captain Allington had said, and was he not a Frenchman defending the castle while the English crept up the walls.

Captain Allington jumped down from the britchka at the lodge gates. It was a perfect April, a perfect day, and Castle Orchard was before him. He was in good health, such good health it surprised him, yet his heart lifted but little at the sight of the familiar drive and the tall trees of the wood, now flushed with green.

As he walked towards the house he started to argue with himself, to put out the opposing forces that beset his mind. His inclinations, his honour, his sense of logic, were vedettes, Light Dragoons, opposing forces prettily skirmishing with one another, yet it was his sense of reason, of logic, that always won, that declined to lie down and die. Instead of feeling elated at his return to Castle Orchard he was wondering why he had been born or why a French sabre had not spliced his head more effectively, if nothing was ever to end satisfactorily.

Of late he had thought it better never to return to Castle Orchard, yet return he did.

The swallows would soon be skimming over the river – and he had pledged to return. The drive, the wood, were now orderly and trim, the undergrowth no longer spilling forth. He reached the carriage sweep with the sundial in the centre. It was half past three. Here, on this spot, Mrs Arthur had watched the britchka drive away and he had not even said goodbye. He had needed to come back.

It was at that moment, while he stood by the sundial, that he heard Phil scream. It was a scream of terror but also of despair. Allington immediately started to run in the direction of the river. It crossed his mind how well he recognised the very nature of the scream, for he had heard such screams before, from women and children caught in the labyrinth of war. For a short while, in running, he could conquer his lameness and move as a sound man.

The three older Conway boys were on the bridge, leaning over the balustrade, clinging to Phil by his boots and ankles. Phil was hanging upside down with his head a few feet from the water. His hands were tied behind his back with a pocket handkerchief. He made little movement, just the feeblest jerks of his body.

Robert was white. It was a game that had run away with them. He thought of letting his brothers hold on while he waded into the water and caught up Phil from below, but Stephen and Frankie were only nine and eight years old, they might not be strong enough to hold Phil on their own, and between the three of them, they were unable to pull him up, to undo what they had done. He could call to the twins but what use were they, playing on the bankside as if nothing were happening? Robert was on the verge of panicking as he weighed up what they might do and the consequences of failure. The river was not particularly deep, but the current was swift and none of them could swim. He did not hear Allington's footsteps until they were nearly upon him and then, when strong arms hoisted Phil back over the balustrade Robert was at first weak with relief and then, with terrible mortification, he saw it was Captain Allington who had rescued them.

Allington busied himself with Phil, who was limp and pale. When his eyes opened he started to weep pathetically, covering his face with his hands. Allington shook him. He said, 'You are all right.'

Phil muttered, 'But I drowned. The water drowned me.'

'No, it didn't drown you, silly,' Frankie said. 'You are not even wet.'

Allington looked at the Conway boys. His cold eye fell on Robert and he said, 'Well?'

Robert said nothing. He was sunk, reduced, and fought within his mind for some desperate means of redeeming himself. He considered, yet more mortifying, lying, or putting a different light on their game that had not really been a game, but there was the telltale handkerchief that Captain Allington had unknotted from Phil's skinny wrists.

At last Robert said, 'He was too heavy, though he doesn't look heavy at all.'

Allington propped himself against the parapet of the bridge. He did nothing further for Phil apart from allowing him to bury his face in the folds of his coat.

Stephen said cheerfully, artlessly, 'He was our prisoner.'

'And how did that come about?'

'It was just as you told us. There was the Castle of Badejos, there was the river. Robert knows its name. We laid the ladder over it and we all crossed it that way, even Jacky and James, though they are too little. Robert called to them but they wouldn't stop. They never listen. We nearly forgot the ladder but Robert went back for it. We needed it for the escalade. We pulled it up. It's ever so heavy and it got stuck in the brambles but we got it there.'

'And Phil was the French?' Allington said.

'Oh yes, we always make him to be the French. The ladder was long enough. Robert got through the window but we went round by the door. Robert said we were to take the enemy from behind. So, you see, we made Phil our prisoner. We tied him up.'

'And then you didn't know what to do with him?'

'Phil is afraid of the river. We didn't mean to drown him.'

'I dare say not, merely to torment him.' Allington turned his attention to Robert. 'You, I suppose, were the captain in charge of this company?'

Robert said quietly, 'Yes, sir.'

'Your conduct,' Allington said, 'is unbefitting an officer or a gentleman. If you were a grown man and I your senior, I would have your sword removed and I would place you in arrest, pending a court martial. As it is, you are a boy, but not too young to understand that the torment of a younger child should be as foreign to you as to an officer allowing the torture of a prisoner in his care. Take the ladder and put it back where you found it. Don't come back.'

Allington took Phil by the shoulder and started to walk towards the house.

Phil, trotting along beside Captain Allington, could not refrain from clinging to his coat with one hand, the terror of the river still with him. At the same time he was ashamed of himself, ashamed of having been so frightened.

He paused by the sundial. He gave Allington's hand a tug and whispered, 'I mustn't upset my mother, nor tell tales.'

'And how is that to be managed?' Allington asked him.

'When I can't tell truly, I don't tell at all.'

They went indoors.

Mrs Arthur, having seen the britchka and spoken to Pride, had composed herself to meet Captain Allington, but the sight of Phil's white face distracted her. She half-stood up and then sat down again, saying, 'Phil, whatever has happened?'

Phil went to his mother but did not quite accept her embrace. He glanced anxiously towards Allington before saying, 'Nothing much. You know I don't like the river and the river gave me a fright.'

'But you aren't wet. You can't have fallen in.'

'No. Just a fright. I was silly, I expect.'

He looked at Allington again, who said, 'Yes, he had a shock. He was nearly in the river.'

'But I'm all right now.'

'He needs a cup of tea,' Allington said.

Phil said, 'I shall go down to the kitchen and sit in the chair by the stove. Cook will give me a cup of tea. Then I shall be better.' He would go away from his mother, and Captain Allington would answer the questions.

Mrs Arthur let him go, a little reluctant, a little suspicious. 'What did happen by the river?' she asked.

'I don't think I should tell you what Phil isn't prepared to tell you himself. That would be dishonourable.'

'Oh, gentlemen and their honour,' Mrs Arthur replied, exasperated, and then, looking at him carefully, she said, 'You are better?'

'Yes, I am better.'

'We would like to have known how you were.'

'The agent would have told you if I had died.'

Mrs Arthur, nonplussed, hesitated before replying. She then said, 'Are you truly better?'

Though he looked well, she felt something not right.

'Yes,' he said, 'I am better than I've been for years.'

'Cornwall suits you. Perhaps you wish to live there.'

'No. I wish to live here. This suits me perfectly well.'

'And my affairs, are they completed? You must be ready to have Castle Orchard to yourself.'

'At the end of the month everything we need to know, every last bit of the puzzle, will be in place. I haven't troubled you with it.'

'And is it so much of a puzzle?'

'It's not a puzzle to me, but it is to everybody else.'

'It has been so kind of you to take so much trouble. I shall be very relieved.'

'So you must be. You have been in a state of limbo. You will be free to leave Castle Orchard.'

Mrs Arthur looked at him, uncertain how to reply. How could she possibly want to leave Castle Orchard? In the end she said nothing, turning her back on him and going to the window. She was wearing, he noticed, the faded blue smock over the gown she had worn when he had seen her under the apple trees with Emmy, the day he had come to Castle Orchard the previous autumn. He had been filled with poetry and all things he could express only in his head. He joined her at the window but he was silent. Mrs Arthur still wished to make some sort of reply, but the suddenness of his appearance, Phil and the river, nothing being as it had been, deprived her of words.

Captain Allington then said, 'I'm watching the wagtails on the lawn, bobbing up and down, their tails too long for their bodies. They remind me of young officers struggling to manage their swords.'

He might, she supposed, have been going to say something further, but the door opened and Emmy ran in. She held out her arms and Allington scooped her up and kissed her. She said, 'Well, you are bad and naughty. You wrote no letter. Say me a poem.'

Allington said:

> 'So we'll go no more a-roving
> So late into the night;
> Though the heart still be as loving
> And the moon still be as bright.'

Emmy was not satisfied. 'How is that? It's half a poem.'

'Half a poem is enough for today. I have a lot to do.'

He put the child down and left the room.

Mrs Arthur waited in the dining room with Phil, who she thought very pale. She said, thinking he had been too nervous to speak in front of Captain Allington, 'What did give you such a fright?'

He replied, 'Only the river, but I didn't get wet.'

Annie put jonquils, spring flowers, on the table, to celebrate Captain Allington's return.

'You all like him,' Mrs Arthur said, something she would never have said to the other servants.

'We know where we are,' Annie replied. 'He's fair, but I never would leave you and the dear children.'

278

Mrs Arthur knew when Annie said fair she meant more than that, but Annie would not know how to put it into words. It was the power of a good officer who could make his wishes theirs.

Annie said, 'Cook is cross. She wanted to do something special to send down to the lodge but he gave us no warning. I don't know where gentlemen think food comes from, that's what Cook says.'

When they had had dinner and Annie was clearing the plates, Captain Allington returned.

He said, 'Excuse me, I'm disturbing your evening but I wanted to say something to Phil.'

Mrs Arthur said, with an uncertain smile, 'You need not apologise for entering your own house.'

'I suppose I need not,' he replied, but with an unaccustomed vagueness. He turned to Phil and said, 'Every day you will hit the punching bag in the stable. When you can hit it hard, Dan will teach you to box.'

'But I don't want to hit anybody,' Phil said, startled.

'I dare say not, but nevertheless, you must learn it. My stepbrothers will go fifty miles to a prize fight, but it's not of the least interest to me. For a boy, as an accomplishment, it's invaluable.'

'If you want me to do it, then I will.'

Allington glanced at Mrs Arthur. He said, 'Of course, if your mother doesn't wish it, we will think no more about it.'

Mrs Arthur thought her opinion on the matter entirely immaterial and that she was consulted only out of politeness. Captain Allington seemed, at that minute, to calmly assume the role of a father.

Phil was tired and went to bed early. He slipped away,

trying to see himself in the role of a Jackson or a Belcher, prize fighters, but it seemed unlikely.

Mrs Arthur said to Allington, 'I hope you will take tea.' She went into the drawing room. There was a gown of Emmy's she was lengthening. 'I wanted to thank you for sending the pony for Phil.' She thought how he had reappeared, like the genie from the lamp. Whatever had occurred to so frighten Phil had done away with explanations and formal greetings, but he had altered.

Annie brought the tea in earlier than usual. She said, 'Cook and me didn't think you ought to be late, seeing as you've been travelling, sir. That Pride thought you'd be cross, but 'tis only for your good, Cook and me says.'

Allington said, 'Thank you, Annie.' He turned to Mrs Arthur. 'Phil may as well have Joe. My nephews have outgrown him. I brought him back from Waterloo, or somebody did. Major Wilder brought his baggage pony back from the Peninsula for his niece, so I suppose I grasped that idea. Joe is old now.'

Mrs Arthur made the tea and Allington took the cup from her, relapsing into silence. He sat down by the window. There was still daylight left and he seemed absorbed by the garden.

Mrs Arthur, wondering if they were ever to speak again, said, 'Tell me what you are thinking.'

'I was thinking of the sundial. What times will it tell by moonlight? I should be able to calculate that.'

'Perhaps it goes backwards.'

'That would suit me very well, forward in the day and backwards at night, like Penelope unpicking her tapestry, time suspended, the hourglass turned and turned so the sand never ran out.'

'Are Emmy and Phil never to grow up and am I to be altering this hem for ever and ever?'

'Yes, but you should not need to alter the hem if Emmy is never to grow. Well, time won't stand still and we shall continue to wind the clocks.'

'If time had stood still, you might still be in Cornwall. It's the place of your childhood, so perhaps home.'

'Yes, that is so, but it is also the place of illness, of being too feeble to do more than lie and look out of the window at a distant strip of the sea. If I'm to be so ill again I should prefer to die. I'm too much reminded of Brussels. I lay day after day, in a house there, a respectable merchant's house. My room was white, the bed was white and the hangings were white. There were no pictures. The window looked on to the street but I could only see the windows of the opposite house, which appeared to be unoccupied. They never altered. How well I remember that room, every fold in the hangings of the bed, the single chair, the table, the washstand, the medicines. My hostess was dutiful. She grudged me nothing, but I never saw her smile. There was a young girl in the house, some sort of cousin, about fourteen years old. No, older, I suppose. She had a long, flaxen plait and used to skip in and out, running errands. I fell madly in love with her. She was a cheerful child, light-hearted, and in her exuberance inclined to knock over the few things in the room. They were always saying "Hush, remember the poor, wounded soldier." At least, I believe that is what they were saying. I was too ill to grasp the language.'

Allington came to a halt.

Mrs Arthur, after a while, said, 'And did she reciprocate your affections?'

'I never spoke to her nor she to me. I believe she spoke

no French, the only language we might have had in common.' Allington smiled. 'I don't think I can have been at my best, my head shaved and bandaged, my arms bandaged, my chest too, my leg in a splint. There I lay, often delirious, always in pain, waiting to die but never quite doing so, quietly teasing myself with a passion for this girl.'

Mrs Arthur thought of this flaxen-haired girl he had so oddly loved.

'I expect,' he continued, 'she is now a matron with her hair arranged on top of her head, and several blond babies. Time will not have stood still.'

He got up and said abruptly, 'I wish you good night.'

After he had gone, she laid down her sewing. She thought of him with those Spanish girls, with this Flemish child. Was he trying to tell her how transitory were his affections? From the window she could see him walking down to the lodge in the half-light.

Robert Conway found no consolation in the uniform. The three rows of silver buttons, the velvet facings, mocked him. Captain Allington's words, 'unbefitting an officer or a gentleman', returned to him at every moment of the day. His uncle, now long dead, who had once shrugged his living form into the tight green jacket, would never have forgiven him. Sometimes he tried to shift the blame, to accuse his brothers or Phil, but he knew those terrible words would haunt him for ever. He repeated them to himself again and again.

The rector noticed that his son was in a state of disharmony and, as the rector was not accustomed to observations so close to home, he became uneasy and addressed him on the subject. 'You are out of sorts, my boy. You are growing too fast. Why are you not out of doors? Do not the woods, the river, the meadows of Castle Orchard beckon you?'

'I can't go to Castle Orchard,' Robert said sulkily.

'My dear boy, why not? We may not have become much acquainted with Captain Allington, but he has not forbidden more humble folk the benefit of his park.'

'He has me.'

'Don't be ridiculous. He has only just returned. You must have misunderstood him, or been engaged in some childish prank. I am sure he meant no permanent ban.'

'Yes, he did.'

'Pray, tell me why.'

'No, I can't. It was silly. It was nothing.' Robert flung this at his father as he made a retreat, hastening outdoors into the rectory shrubbery for fear of being forced to tell the truth. Here he crouched on the ground beneath the laurels and plotted enlisting as a common soldier. A few tears spilled down his cheeks. He would go as a volunteer and get his commission and be killed. Robert, his mind running away with him, saw a hundred ways in which he might redeem himself, death being the most satisfactory.

Mr Conway, giving up any thought of the duties he had intended for the morning, walked to Castle Orchard and sent in his card, begging Annie to plead his cause with Captain Allington in allowing him a few minutes of his time. He saw that his nephews, Jacky and James, had followed him.

'Run home, little boys,' he said. 'Uncle is busy.'

Allington, who had just been seeing the agent, received the rector's message.

'He begs just a few minutes, sir,' Annie said. 'He is a kind gentleman, Mr Conway is, and means good.'

'But is he useful, Annie?'

Annie thought about this. She then said, 'Seeing we must have a rector to remind us of our Christian souls and to say our prayers and love our neighbours, why, then he must be useful, sir.'

'And we can't do this for ourselves?'

'And we must be married and buried and baptised, sir,' Annie continued, ignoring his questions and thinking her arguments in favour of the rector conclusive. 'He is a good man even if he doesn't understand ordinary folk too well.'

Allington had the rector admitted and sat down opposite him in the morning room into which spring sunshine streamed and there was a fine view of the river.

'What may I do for you?' he asked.

'It is my earnest wish to be on cordial terms with you,' the rector started. 'Of course the rectory living ought to be yours, but the late Mr Arthur, of whom I can't bring myself to speak, sold it as quick as he could. Nevertheless, for myself as the rector not to be on good terms with you, the landlord, let alone yourself as my neighbour, would, I feel, be injurious to the parish, and my first consideration must be the parish.'

'And mine too,' Allington said, 'seeing how much of it I own. The care of their souls I must leave to you, seeing you have the better authority in that department.'

Emboldened by Allington's conciliatory manner, Mr Conway said, 'It sets a better example if the landlord regularly attends his place of worship, meaning by this the church.' He added nervously, 'I have mentioned it before.'

'Should you not plead with me to attend church for the sake of my soul rather than merely as an example?'

'That too, of course.'

'I feared you were putting the example first.'

The rector, confused, said nothing.

Allington said, 'I don't object to attending church. Where should I sit?'

The rector immediately saw a dilemma. Each pew in his church was allocated and jealously guarded by the occupants, even if only tenant farmers and their wives, except for the ones at the back where sat the poorer parishioners. Mrs Arthur continued to use the Castle Orchard pew but she ought to give it up to Captain Allington.

Allington gave him a quizzical look and then said, 'You came to see me about something other than this?'

'Ah yes, my boy Robert. He is very out of sorts. He tells me you have forbidden him your grounds. I could not imagine this to be so, the people always having been allowed in the park.'

'The people are allowed in the park, or to cross it, which is as much as they ever seem to do. Otherwise it is so. I have forbidden all your sons my grounds.'

'May I ask the reason?' the rector said, agitated.

'What reason did they give?'

'It was only Robert to whom I spoke. He gave no reason.'

'If he has not given you his confidence in the matter, it would be most wrong for me to do so. I will tell you nothing he is unwilling to tell you himself.'

'I see it is more serious than I thought.' Mr Conway was about to embark on the difficulties of fatherhood when the door was unceremoniously opened and the twins came in.

'Oh, naughty boys, what are they doing here, bursting in without a by-your-leave and I told them to go home? They never heed anyone. I must apologise, sir.'

Jacky and James crossed the room at a trot and went

straight to Captain Allington. Simultaneously they tugged his sleeve.

Jacky whispered, 'Quick.'

James whispered, 'In the river.'

Allington leaped to his feet. The boys ran and he followed them, soon overtaking them, across the garden to the river.

Where the river bent round the Philosopher's Tower a willow tree leaned into the water. There stood Phil, up to his waist, one hand desperately clasping a branch and with the other trying to hold on to Emmy and to keep her above the water. Allington plunged into the river. He scooped up Emmy and put her over his shoulder. Phil he took by the hand and said, 'Now Phil, I am holding you steady. Walk out of the water with me.'

They reached the bank safely. The twins had vanished. Emmy spluttered as Allington laid her over his knee and shook the water from her. She started to scream. 'Where is Dolly? I want Dolly. Jacky and James threw her in the water and I went to get her.'

Allington thought Dolly had met a watery grave. He said, 'Never mind Dolly. You are lucky to be alive.' He stood Emmy on her feet and gave her a bit more of a shake. 'Now, miss, there is a rule that you may not go down to the river. The river is deep and you are small. You have broken that rule and you are punished for it.'

He hastened them up to the house to get out of their wet clothes. They were met by Mr Conway, who had never understood why Captain Allington had departed from him in the first place.

'Dear, oh dear, they have fallen in the river and Jacky and James came to say so. The river is not safe for children.

Are they all right? They will catch their deaths and what will poor Mrs Arthur do then?'

'They will not catch their deaths. Go to Annie and get her to make up a fire. Where is Mrs Arthur?'

'Annie says she went to the village to see the black-smith's wife who has just been confined with another baby girl. Dear, oh dear. What an occurrence. I shall fetch Mrs Arthur.'

In the house Annie soon had blankets, a fire and warm drinks. The children sat there in silence, like two little mummies, shocked. Allington withdrew and watched them from a distance. Seeing Mrs Arthur running towards the house, he pushed the casement up and called to her, 'Don't be too alarmed. They are both safe.'

Mrs Arthur hastened into the room. She embraced both children in turn, holding back her tears of relief in order not to alarm them. She asked, 'But how did you get in the river?'

Phil said nothing but Emmy burst out crying. 'Jacky and James threw Dolly in the river. I went to get her, but the water is deep. Captain Allington says I am punished for I was naughty to go to the river.'

Mrs Arthur looked at Allington. He spoke severely. 'That is what I said. By her disobedience she nearly drowned herself and Phil as well.'

'Phil came in the water and held my head,' Emmy said, between her tears. 'Dolly is gone, she is drowned. I won't never go to the river again, I promise, I promise.'

'Phil, darling, is that what you did?' Mrs Arthur asked.

'Yes. I went in the water.'

Mrs Arthur put her arms round him and now she wept as much as Emmy.

Phil said, 'Don't cry. I'm all right.' He spoke stiffly, almost awkwardly, slowly sipping at the warm milk Annie had given him.

Allington left the room, left them all alone together and went himself to change before continuing the business of the day. It came on to rain.

Mrs Arthur stayed indoors and played games with the children to distract and amuse them.

Phil played the games to satisfy his mother and occupy Emmy, but he was subdued. He knew his mother thought he was brave and that he had done the right thing, but his mother could be relied on to think well of him. Captain Allington had said nothing, so should he have done something less silly as he was both afraid of the water and unable to swim?

Captain Allington did not return but he came in after dinner as he had the previous evening. He sat down at the table. He had with him a piece of paper and a pencil and straight away began to draw a map and talk to Phil at the same time.

'Here is France, here is Spain, and here is Portugal. Here, to the north-east of San Sebastian, further up the coast, the Bidassoa spills out into the sea. On this side of it is Spain, on that side of it, France. We have spent the months preceding October 1813 pushing the French north through Spain, but now we reach the Pyrenees, where we don't wish to winter. It's too high, too cold. The Bidassoa is a formidable barrier at its mouth. The French believe it impassable. They concentrate much of their defences elsewhere, but the Spanish shrimp fishers have been consulted and we are informed exactly where, at low tide, the river may be crossed. The Fifth Division conceal themselves behind an embankment here, opposite

Andaya. Spry's Portuguese and Lord Aylmer's Brigade are posted in the ditch, here at Fuenterabia. There are further troops concealed higher up, above the broken bridge of Behobia, here.

'Our tents have been left standing and our campfires burning so as to deceive the enemy. At seven o'clock in the morning on the seventh we leave, in stealthy silence, our places of concealment. There is half a mile of sand which we traverse in two columns. Not a sound is heard. We cross the low-water channel. A rocket goes up, here, from the steeple of Fuenterabia. It is a signal for the artillery, here at San Marcial, to open fire and cover the troops who are to ford the river higher up, above the bridge of Behobia. Seven columns now go forward all at once, some plunging straight into the river, others still snaking across the heavy sands.

'The river is icy cold and chest high. Muskets are held above the head to keep them dry. Not a shot is fired by the startled French until the further banks are safely reached. The Fifth Division, at least, have crossed from Spain to France.'

Allington paused to look at Phil's face. He said, 'Now *there* is a tale of crossing a river, a mixture of courage and ingenuity. The latter is as much of importance as the former, but the most dangerous position in the field is the most sought and the greatest honour attached to it.'

Phil allowed himself to breathe out. He thought of the soldiers wondering, all the while with the current a-tugging and pulling, when the French would see them and shoot them all down in the water. Their bodies would have tossed and turned and gone out to sea, so much red coat and red blood for the fishes to eat. Despite that, it was possible to be courageous and do one's duty, to go in the water to rescue Emmy. He smiled at Captain Allington.

Emmy appeared in her dressing gown. She went straight to Captain Allington and said, 'I want to ask something. Why is it wrong for me to go in the water to get Dolly and not wrong for Phil to go in the water to get me?'

'I dare say your dolly was precious but your mother will make a new one. You we can't replace.'

Emmy clambered determinedly onto his lap. She said, a little sleepily, 'The new dolly won't be the same as the last. Say me a poem.'

'Certainly not. You should be in bed.'

Emmy knew he was no longer cross with her.

Phil thought, Emmy is never afraid and she charms Captain Allington. It's because she looks like Mother, ever so much, though smaller and rounder. I have to get in the river before he approves of me, and who do I look like? I look like my father and he wasn't any use at all.

Mrs Arthur said, 'Come along, Emmy. I will take you up to bed. Captain Allington will want his cigar.'

'This evening,' Allington said, after they had left, 'it is my intention, Phil, to take a glass of wine with you.' He immediately poured half an inch of wine into a glass and gave it to Phil, before pouring out an equally small amount for himself.

Phil, suddenly realising his intentions, said, shocked, 'But you mustn't drink any wine. It will give you one of your heads.'

'Perhaps such a small amount won't affect me. I intend to take the risk. It's in tribute to you.'

'No, please, you're not to do it. All right, you must drink so little wine you hardly taste it.' Phil dipped his finger in the glass and dabbed it against Allington's lips. 'There, that's all you need do. Now I will drink some of mine . . . why, it's quite disgusting.'

He gazed at Allington with his wide blue eyes and Allington was reminded of Johnny Arthur, but Arthur would never have gone in the river to rescue anybody.

Phil said, 'You won't take any more, will you? I should very much dislike it if you did, though I understand it was to please me. But I'll tell you something. I am not so afraid of the river as I was. I mean, it didn't drown me this time, did it? I felt that it could.'

Allington said, 'You must respect it. Why don't you learn to swim?'

Phil thought if Captain Allington would teach him to swim he would learn it. Was he not hitting the punching bag every day with his hands in Dan's gloves and riding Smokey Joe and making him canter?

By the time Mrs Arthur returned, Captain Allington had gone back down to the lodge.

Phil said, laughing, delighted, 'Captain Allington took a glass of wine with me.'

April was passing by. The hunters had long since been put out to grass. Dan had little to do but occasionally saddle one up so he might escort the long-tailed grey for the sake of taking out Mrs Arthur. Captain Allington did not go with them. He spent hours at his desk in the morning room. It was as though he had set himself some particular task, to be completed at a given time. If he came up in the evening, it was to return to work. Mrs Arthur thought he withdrew himself from their society inch by inch.

She tried to contemplate her future, to think of Westcott Park.

Pride said to Annie, 'Asking for trouble, the master is. No rest, no rest, no rest. It's not good for him.'

In the last week of April, Captain Allington went to London. Though he did not say why he was going, he told them he would return for May Day. Orchardleigh had a maypole in the meadow; May Day was celebrated with a feast, consisting of a roasted pig and a barrel of ale, provided by Castle Orchard. The children from the village practised their steps for the maypole dancing. Emmy ran off to join them, seizing a ribbon for herself.

Phil was a hero at school, which astonished him. 'I couldn't let her drown, could I, my own little sister?' he would repeat. He went off in the mornings willingly. Robert Conway evaded him. It crossed Phil's mind, though without any feelings of enthusiasm, that he could hit Robert just as he hit the punching bag, though Robert was bigger than him. He now hit Dan as well as the punching bag, and Dan pretended to be very much hurt.

At length Robert did approach him, just as he was going home, on the very last day of April. He thrust into Phil's arms a large, awkward parcel and told him it was his. He said, 'I can't keep it now. It hurts me to look at it. I never want to see it any more. It's as my father preaches in the pulpit: the first shall be the last and the last shall be the first. Well, I'm last now, so you can have this.'

Puzzled, Phil laboured back to Castle Orchard and was just entering the house when he saw the britchka on the carriage sweep and Captain Allington stepping down from it.

Phil said, without preliminaries, 'Robert gave me this.'

'But do you now know what it is?'

'No.'

They entered the hall together. Phil put his parcel down on the table and undid the strings. There was the jacket of rifle green, with the black velvet collar and cuffs, the elaborate swirled and curled corded silk; the three rows of spherical silver buttons, the crimson sash, the shako with the cut feather and the glass in the leather pouch.

Allington watched Phil's reverential gaze, the tracing of his finger over the convolutions of the cord, his delicate counting of the buttons and the touching of the whistle.

'But I can't keep it,' he said.

'Is that what you think?'

'Yes.'

'Then pack it up and send it back.'

'Robert said it hurt him to look at it.'

'He is punishing himself,' Allington said. 'Doesn't he deserve to be punished?'

'Not so much as this. Anyway, it was my fault for being so afraid of the water.'

'No, he behaved disgracefully. I am glad to think he knows it. It was not only that he bullied you, he might even have killed you. What would your poor mother have done then?'

Phil said, 'Yes, I need to be here to look after my mother.'

The evidence being scanty for Phil ever having looked after his mother, Allington thought of that other child and mother. *Don't forget your prayer book. Where are your gloves? Here are violets to pin on your gown. I picked them in the hedge.*

Sadness stole over him. He watched Phil, his gaze now returned to the uniform and said, after a moment's thought, 'Perhaps this is not really Robert's to give away. It may have been given into his care but it belongs to the family. Conduct such as his should be nipped in the bud. There is a type of officer who bullies his fellows, anyone who will be bullied, and he bullies the men. They're insufferable. But Phil, one should not reject what amounts to an apology. Keep the glass. That will be punishment enough. You could take the whistle, but that is part of the uniform whereas the glass is not. Tell him from me it's not too late to mend his ways.'

Phil took the telescope from its pouch and going to the door, put it to his eye. He said, 'Think what was seen – the enemy, tiny-wee in the distance, the Eagles of the French . . . the bayonets shining through the cornfields . . . Mother and Emmy are picking flowers.'

Mrs Arthur came downstairs, prepared to attend some part of the May Day festivities, which would commence in the evening, and found Mr Stewart Conway in the hall.

'You are a stranger here,' she said, taking him through to the drawing room.

'I'm not welcome, as you well know. I see Captain Allington has returned. He doesn't encourage visitors – even the children are banned.'

'For that there was good reason.'

'But what was the reason?'

'I don't know.'

'But you choose to believe in it?'

'Absolutely.'

'Because Captain Allington said so?'

'He is not the sort of man to tell a fib. Either way, your boys, Jacky and James, feel themselves exempt.'

'I came to apologise for their naughtiness, throwing

294

Emmy's doll in the river. If your children had drowned because of it, what would I have done? I never could have forgiven myself. It's made me think how out of hand they are. They need a mother and I must marry. You know perfectly well I've long wished to marry you, but lack of means has prevented me.' Mr Conway rushed headlong into his theme, unable to sit though Mrs Arthur was offering him a chair and sitting down herself.

'Now, I think, with the school doing quite well, and you being bound to have something of your own, we surely could manage. I've given the matter a great deal of thought, for one cannot always permit one's heart to rule one's head, but indeed, I don't think I could allow anyone but yourself to take the place of my dear Amelia. You must know how I have loved you for many a year, though it was more a sin than anything else, while you were a wife rather than a widow.'

Mrs Arthur said, 'But what if I have no money of my own?'

'But you will have. When are you to know?'

'Now, today, tomorrow. Captain Allington told me he would have the details at the beginning of May. He returned from London yesterday, but whether or no he went on my behalf, he never said.'

'You are too trusting. He may take what money you have. We know nothing of the man and I deeply regret your long sojourn under his roof. I see how it came about, but it was wrong. A woman's virtue, her reputation, is her armour. A respectable marriage to me will cure it all. Of course I regret the gossip, but it will be forgotten. I know he lives in the lodge, but who would believe it?'

'The slippery mire of scandal and gossip . . .' Mrs Arthur sighed. 'Johnny had already exposed me to it in a manner more painful than anything Captain Allington has done. I dare say I was unwise not to go to Westcott Park, yet I can't regret the decision.'

'Nor I, for it would have taken you from me.'

'I would have been less conveniently placed, it is true,' Mrs Arthur replied.

'Now you're teasing me. It isn't the moment.'

'I suppose a woman should always be flattered by a proposal.'

Conway stepped forward and endeavoured, without quite succeeding, to seize her hand. 'You are crying,' he said, noticing that her eyes had filled with tears. 'I don't see how that could be necessary. I so wish to make you happy. I don't believe you have ever loved me, but you will grow to do so. We are not children. Of course, it would be a worry if you disliked me.'

As he spoke they both heard the rapid step of Captain Allington – rapid, yet with that slight unevenness, as he approached via the stone-flagged passage that led from the offices.

'How lame he is,' Conway said, an edge of bitterness in his voice, mortified at the interruption.

'Not very lame and an honourable wound,' Mrs Arthur replied.

Allington could be heard crossing the hall and then he entered the drawing room. Mr Conway thought of the affront, that he had the right to enter any room at Castle Orchard without so much as a polite knock at a door.

Allington glanced at Mr Conway and gave a slight bow, saying as he did so, 'You were thinking of escorting Mrs Arthur to the maypole, I dare say?'

'Indeed not,' Conway replied. 'My brother doesn't allow

the boys to attend so I certainly can't do so myself. The rector cannot be sure the festivities attached to the First of May are not too pagan in origin to be tolerated.' He spoke gravely. Captain Allington should not fluster him.

'But perhaps the festival is attached to the Virgin and therefore Catholic,' Allington suggested. 'Either way they could turn young heads from the straight path of moral rectitude.'

'Quite so,' Conway said stiffly.

'You will not allow your little boys to go? However, that will not prevent them going if they wish it.'

Mr Conway, perfectly aware of the truth of this small jibe, stumbled for words, muttering something about Jacky and James doing as they were told.

Allington said, 'Well, you will wish to be off. Your brother will need assistance in penning in his charges lest they escape and take up idolatrous habits.' He turned to Mrs Arthur and said, 'Where is your shawl? It will be cold later,' and on seeing it lying on a chair, 'there – I will take it for you.'

Mrs Arthur thought of him with his mother. *Where are your gloves? Where is your bonnet?*

Stewart Conway, unable to do anything else, made his bow and departed. Mrs Arthur looked at Allington, who immediately relaxed his expression. She said, by way of a comment on his absence, 'You have been very busy.'

'Yes,' he said.

'And as for Mr Conway, you are so unkind to him.'

'Wasn't he causing you distress? What right has he to do that?'

Mrs Arthur wondered how much he understood of how distress was caused.

They left the drawing room together and went outdoors.

'I know it's not my business, but I'm always afraid you may marry him,' Allington continued as they started to walk across the garden together.

'And should I not? There are circumstances under which a woman must marry whether she wishes it or no, a woman with children. I have told you that before.'

'Those circumstances will not be yours.'

'Sometimes, I still fear the worst.'

'No, no. You need not. I shall put all the documents out for you tomorrow. You will know exactly how things are.' He spoke briskly, almost cheerfully, but she still thought there was something not right, unexplained, even should she have the jointure.

He asked her where were Phil and Emmy and she told him they always spent the evening with Annie, who took them away before too much ale had been consumed.

They started to walk towards the meadow and there they parted. Mrs Arthur watched him go, remaining by the gate, reluctant to step forward into the jolly little crowds that half-filled the meadow. What would he do? He would move swiftly through his tenants, stopping to speak to each one, never forgetting a name. He still had her shawl over his arm, but as yet she had no need of it. The inhabitants of Orchardleigh were already set to enjoy themselves. There was a pervading smell of roast pig. She was accustomed to the yearly ritual, but was it not time to say goodbye? She would certainly have the jointure. How many days would it take her to pack her few possessions, her clothes, hers and the children's? She would go to Westcott Park, for there she could go immediately, but she need not stay. She could find a little house to rent, with a small garden and an orchard, where she could be alone with Annie and the children.

Now she stepped determinedly into the meadow. She would speak to the farmers' wives as usual, the women from the cottages in Orchardleigh, and then she would seek out Annie. She found her and Phil watching the children wind their ribbons up and down the maypole to the squeak of the fiddle. The evening sun sent long shadows to dance on the meadow. Emmy was nowhere to be seen. She was chasing Jacky and James who were running through the crowds, hither and thither, like two plump little fishes slipping through water.

As dusk fell, Captain Allington rejoined her. She had been aware of him, never too far away, her shawl over his arm, as if he held her to ransom with it. He stopped to speak to the fiddler. The ribbons on the maypole hung limp; the children had gone, but the fiddler played on. Phil and Emmy had departed, Annie having an exact sense of when the evening was getting out of hand, losing its innocence.

Captain Allington had the same notion. He said, 'Here is your shawl. Should you have had it earlier? I shall walk back with you. I assume the celebrations will become Bacchanalian from this moment hence.'

They went through the gate and entered the yew square where, at some moment, he had had a bench placed. He indicated, without speaking, they might sit for a moment but as he did so the fiddler in the meadow turned from playing jigs and struck up a waltz.

Mrs Arthur sat down. Abstracted, she was listening to the music, which had swept her back to another garden –

her father's – and to another time, another place … the lilacs in bud, the dusky shadows of an April evening and the sound of the pianoforte.

She turned to Allington and said, with conviction, 'It was you, that April, 1815, long ago.' She supposed, when he had stopped to speak to the fiddler, that he had requested that tune.

'Yes,' he replied starkly.

For a long moment she could say nothing.

Allington then said, 'I didn't tell you.'

'Why not?' She thought, why had he not told her?

'You had forgotten. I hadn't. Besides, you thought it didn't abound to your credit. It certainly didn't abound to mine. You were rather a wild little thing, though innocent. I took advantage of you, graceless scamp that I was.'

She thought, How could I have forgotten him, the sharp dark eye, the rib-hugging midnight blue of the jacket? She said, 'Do you ever forget anything?'

'Certainly not that.'

'My Cousin Charles, those other young officers – did you know them all?'

'No. I knew one of them. He knew your cousin. We had met by chance and decided on travelling together. I was on my way to Cornwall to say goodbye to my stepfather. As for forgetting things, the thing people really want to ask but in my case don't usually have the temerity, is my experience of Waterloo. Of that, I remember little.'

'Perhaps you prefer to forget it.'

'Maybe, but battles are confusing things. One would need to have climbed a hill to see the two square miles of Waterloo. The smoke obscures your vision. We were very wet that morning. We had had no cover and there

300

was little to eat. Plenty of jokes and laughter; trying to get a fire to go, clothes sodden, Pride trying to get me to change my shirt. There is a bit of a mist but the sun will break through. I had always been fond of the sight of an army first thing in the morning, the slow stirring of a great beast, lines of horses, the stained-glass colours of uniforms, scarlet and blue, the black of the Brunswicks, the green of the Ninety-fifth, the Scots in their petticoats. We go to our deaths very well dressed, but rather less so when we've lain in our clothes all night. I say to myself, "I shall never see this again. This is the end." Well, the end it was, but not as I foresaw it.'

He came to a halt.

Mrs Arthur said, 'You mean you thought you would be killed?'

'Yes. Soldiers get such premonitions from time to time. In my experience they are usually right. One of my fellow officers is beside me, crouched over the fire, getting smoke in his eyes, trying to light a cigar. I can see him now. His groom is just behind him holding his charger, the steam rising from its wet back. There is a deal of noise all down the line as the infantry test their weapons. I say, "This is the end." He agrees. He says, "We'll win, and all of us soldiers will be put out to grass as surplus to requirements." It was odd I chose to speak to him. He had never liked me much, mistrusted what was known as my cleverness. I said, "That may be so, but I shan't live to see it." He reprimanded me, tried to rally me a bit, but it was he, not I, who died that day.'

Mrs Arthur, sitting beside him, the May Day revelry, the fiddle, alive in the meadow behind them, thought of waltzing in her father's Devonshire garden with this veteran, youthful soldier, so soon to be facing his probable death. It was no wonder he lived as he did, kissing the passing girl.

Allington said, 'It was then I thought of the letter. I always carried in my pocket my mother's miniature and the letter my father had written her, the one I saved from the fire. It may seem strange, but I had never read it – it hadn't seemed my business. I knew my pockets would be rifled. Battlefields are strewn with letters – did you know that? The last letters from home all lying about in the mud, trampled. I suppose I hoped that letter would make some mention of myself.'

Allington paused before adding, with a deprecating smile, 'Ah, but the previous Captain Allington had a lyrical pen. The mention of an infant would hardly have become it. I wished I hadn't read it, such a passionate love letter to my mother. I lost it with her miniature in its seed-pearl frame, but I remember it.'

He then said, more briskly, 'But of Waterloo itself I know little, a blank space in my head. I remember opening my eyes in the middle of the night and looking at the moon, the clouds racing across its face, so that it came and went. The battle was all over. I don't even know how I came to be there. I'm certainly in a great deal of pain and a horse, mine or someone else's, is straddled across my legs. From time to time it struggles. There's a Frenchman close to me. He's sitting up with a pistol on his lap. I can see he's a cavalry officer, a cocky-looking fellow. I say – God knows why I say it, amidst the massed horrors of the aftermath – 'Is this honour?'

'Why yes,' he replies, in perfect English, and then, after a moment: 'I have looked you over, your wounds are such you will not recover. Did you hear our soldiers cry "*Vive l'empereur*" and the noise of our drums? Could you hear those from the English lines?'

'I'm in Spain,' I reply. 'The Emperor is not in Spain.'

'He says, "Nor are you, my friend."'

'I take a while to digest this and then I say, "Would you be so kind as to kill this horse? It too can't live and it causes me much discomfort in the meantime".'

'The Frenchman doesn't hesitate. I can't recall his wounds. He crawls to my side, one way or another, and in the most masterly way he puts his pistol to the head of the horse, careful to get a correct angle, and shoots it. It subsides on top of me, but at least it is still.

'I say, "You're truly my friend, but maybe you should have applied that bullet to me".'

'He is thoughtful, but then he says, 'I doubt I could do it. I was actually keeping it for the plunderers, who will be with us shortly, and now I have no more powder.'

He starts to search the trappings of the horse for a powder horn and that's the last I remember of him. Of course, he's right, the looters come – Brunswickers, to the best of my belief. I don't care to remember it. They want my clothes and the contents of my pockets. I am buffeted and shaken about, shaken without mercy. All soldiers loot. It's their bounty. I should be more tolerant of it, but they are rough and think nothing of murder. That Frenchman died beside me, knifed and stripped. He would defend himself and that is certain death.

What do I regret? Not my uniform, had there been much of it to preserve, but the miniature of my mother and the letter. At that exact moment it was of little importance, however.

Mrs Arthur said, 'Because you were going to die?'

Allington said, '*Half in love with easeful death*.' He laughed. 'That's an understatement.'

Robert Conway leaned out of his bedroom window. He could see in the moonlight the party in the meadow, the maypole unattended, the ribbons discarded; the village people, his father's parishioners, dancing, swaying, hopping, swinging the women with liberated shouts and stamping of feet. Somewhere out there, Jacky and James were doing as they pleased.

Robert looked for Captain Allington. It was too dark to see him but he supposed he would have done his duty and gone home.

The dark green uniform of the 95th lay folded on Robert's bed. Suddenly he turned from the window, stripped off his clothes to his shirt and started to dress in the trousers and jacket. The legs of the trousers were too long; he had to fold them up. He fastened the round silver buttons with infinite care. The black velvet collar was high under his chin. He took the candle and moved to the mirror, shuffling a little in his stockinged feet and pushing back the cuffs of the sleeves. He placed the shako at a rakish angle on his head, but when he moved it tipped, absurdly, over his nose.

Suddenly he was angry with the uniform, that it didn't fit him, and he was angry with Phil for giving it back to him but keeping the glass. The loss of the glass in its leather pouch would ever remind him of his mortification and disgrace. That, he supposed, was the intention, and without the spyglass, the uniform lost its magic.

Robert took the uniform off and put his own clothes back on. He then remembered the message Phil had given him.

It is not too late to mend his ways.

Robert slid the window higher and climbed onto the outer sill. Seizing the stems of the vine that grew against the wall, he manoeuvred himself to the ground. It was not difficult – he had done it before.

He crossed the rectory garden, giving a kick to the cricket stumps as he went, and entered the meadow. The May Day celebrations continued, but they were no longer for the benefit of the maypole and the children. The fiddler played on. A young man was kissing a girl in the dew-soaked grass.

Robert slipped from one group to another, looking and looking, but avoiding his uncle who was doing the same thing. His uncle would not know how to find Jacky and James. You needed to look under tables and inside bushes. Where was the girl who was meant to mind them? A woman laughed and seized his arm, but he hastily pulled away, starting to skirt the bank and the hedge.

Jacky and James were huddled together, fast asleep, against the bole of the chestnut tree, an empty mug in Jacky's hand. Robert removed it from his loose grasp and sniffed it suspiciously before chucking it to one side. He took each twin by the arm and shook them awake before marching them in the direction of the rectory. They dragged their feet, but they went with him, sleepily, biddably.

A figure rolled towards them, bore down on them. It was Jackson, emerged from the boot room. Robert asked himself, Where does Jackson sleep?

'Got they little ones, 'ave yer? Scamps, they is. Boys is soft as butter nowadays.'

Jackson swayed over them, his breath heavy with drink.

'Go as yer volunteer, they will. Funny thing, yer volunteer, eats with they, fights with us an' there ain't nothing fancy about that. They all be young gentlemen, some o' them near young as yerself, Mr Conway, sir.' Jackson slurred the word *sir* with drunken insolence. 'They dies usual, but if one gets by without 'aving is 'ead blowed off, 'e becomes yer officer an' orders yer about, dang 'im.'

'Jackson, you are drunk,' Robert said, his voice frigid but at the same time sounding exactly like his father's.

'An' why not, me young fellow – *sir* I should say? Why not? I what laid down me leg an' me eye, dang it, why can't I enjoy meself, same as yer officer what has the best claret? Spike the Frenchies in the guts for the honour of yer regiment, young fella.'

Jackson poked a menacing finger in Robert's chest and the boy hastily tugged at the twins. As they moved away they could hear Jackson muttering, 'Why should I be cleaning they boots, I what 'as laid down 'is life for 'is regiment's glory?'

The front door was open. Robert hauled his charges laboriously upstairs. In their dormitory, half-lit by moonlight, he made them take off their clothes, which they did in a shambling daze. He hauled their little nightshirts over their heads and put a nightcap on each before tumbling both into one bed. They fell instantly asleep, wound together like puppies.

Robert wrote a note for his uncle and left it by the candles on the chest in the hall. He then went to bed himself, feeling grown-up and righteous. After a while, lying very still and gazing at the pattern the moonbeams made on the wall, he decided, when he was a man, he wouldn't throw his life away on being a soldier. Was it to be the Church? The prospect had no charm.

Captain Allington had given Mrs Arthur his arm and they had walked the short distance up to the house. They were silent. She thought everything that he could say had been said. In the hall he had lit her a candle and told her he had a little more work to do, a letter to write, and that it was his intention to lay out all the documents pertaining to herself on the table in the morning room. He wished her good night, his manner now formal, even brisk, as if he was glad to part with her.

Upstairs, slowly preparing for bed, she again contemplated what sort of house she could find, how she would educate Phil. And intermingled with these practicalities were the images with which Allington, and also Pride, had filled her head – the little boy with his mother, soldiers in the Peninsula, brutality and gallantry, boat cloaks, colour and want, gaping wounds and hideous pain, struggling horses, fleas and dirt and fever . . . but Allington's account of Waterloo overrode them all.

She then thought about Captain Allington's mother. Had she not been alone with her child, worried and struggling to make ends meet, fretting over the future of her little boy? She had known, oh how briefly, enduring love. She had done the mundane, the sensible thing, sacrificing the memory of it to secure the future of her son. There, Mrs Arthur surmised, they parted company. She herself had nothing to sacrifice but pain and bewilderment, a confused sense of longing and of emptiness.

When she finally slept, her dreams were filled with those letters fluttering about the battlefield, lying in the mud (and, she knew, though he had not said so, the gore), those letters epitomising the abrupt severing of the loved from the beloved.

She woke rather early, unrefreshed, and lay in bed trying to dispel the images that had beset her mind. Captain Allington had said he would lay out her papers in the morning room. She may as well dress and at least learn her true state, hers and Emmy's and Phil's. Did not their whole future depend on those papers? He had constantly reassured her, yet she would remain in ignorance until she saw it all for herself. It would be another hour before the household stirred. She dressed, scooped up her little old dog, half-asleep in her basket, and went downstairs. She opened the front door and put Meg outside. It was a beautiful day.

Closing the door again, she crossed the hall and went inside the morning room. There were indeed a few papers on the table. Dominating the room was a portrait of a soldier that had not been there before, on the wall facing the windows. It was large, on a dark ground, and striking. The young man, in the uniform of an officer in the dark blue of a Light Dragoon, stared out of his own picture with indignant impatience. The artist had captured the peculiar fiery intelligence that emanated from his face, little more than a boy's. How old had he been then? She thought twenty-two or -three, with no white in the hair that covered the wound to his head. This was how he had been, how she might have remembered him, had he not altered. Yes, he had altered, but she could still see his present self with perfect clarity within the image. Why had he chosen to hang it there? Was he finally laying his proper claim to Castle Orchard?

She turned to the papers on the table. They were very few, considering the time that had been taken by the various lawyers to produce them. There was a letter addressed to herself in Captain Allington's own hand. Beside it was the pouch in which she had placed her necklace when she had given it to him to sell for her. It was still there, so what of the hundred pounds? Bracing herself, she now opened the letter, unable to anticipate its contents to the slightest degree.

Dear Mrs Arthur,

Your late husband often used to say he would be hanged. His words came back to me that day you told me your signature was required to release the money provided by your father. Forgery is a capital offence, so I do wonder that he risked it. I suppose risk is what he liked, though it certainly tormented him. Jonas and Co, in a fit of the sulks, had chucked all the Arthur papers, several hundred years of them, into a huge tin trunk. It took many a threat of a legal nature to get them to unearth the necessary documents and then to trace the witness. There was only one to trace, for the other, Sir John Parkes, is dead. Arthur's own French valet was the second, and he, having absconded with the remains of his late master's wardrobe, was unanxious to be traced. When run to earth, he agreed to having witnessed Arthur sign the document. He was only bound to witness what Arthur wrote, a signature, albeit not his own.

Of course Jonas should have been suspicious, but he pointed out that you had signed away one legacy already. There is really no redress. The money is gone. I have therefore put the deeds of Castle Orchard back into your name. You will find them there on the table. I leave behind my portrait but I will send for the rest of my belongings at some more convenient time

Your most obedient servant,
R. Allington

Mrs Arthur's first reaction was one of disbelief. How could he possibly suppose she would allow him to make such a sacrifice? He might have acquired Castle Orchard in an unorthodox manner, but it was his, and she knew he loved it, the place where he might come to rest. Had he told her that? No, but she knew it. Where was he now? Not, she also knew, asleep in the lodge. As if shaking herself awake from a dream, she hastily crossed the hall and went out-side. Meg was waiting for her, trembling on the doorstep. She scooped her up and half-ran across the lawn to the stable. A cursory inspection confirmed that the britchka was gone.

But Dan was in the yard, methodically strapping the long-tailed grey. She thought, He never said what were his plans for Dan, and would Dan know them?

Dan turned round to look at her. It was pure chance that he did so. When Mrs Arthur considered the blank wall that was Dan, she thought it like the final trick that fate could play on her. Dan, if he knew, could tell her nothing.

He pulled his hat off and surveyed her quizzically. He had sharp, bright eyes, like a robin, and he did indeed cock his head and observe her every move as she stood helpless before him. He dropped the wisp from his hand, patted the grey on the rump and walked off towards the harness room. He then stopped and looked back at her. She could see she was to follow him.

In the harness room he was hurried. He made a little soft whistling noise between his teeth, the only sound he ever made. He sat up at a three-legged stool and pulled open a drawer. It was filled with bits of paper covered with all the strange little drawings and ingenious hieroglyphics Allington so patiently executed in order to communicate with his servant.

Dan produced a piece of paper and a pencil. She thought, If I can think how to ask him where his master is, he wouldn't think it proper to answer. Had not Allington left deliberately? She looked at Dan with despairing eyes.

He thrust the pencil further in her direction, she thought irritated by her slowness to respond. He then took the paper back, folded it in two and wrote carefully and very slowly, yet neatly, on the outside,

Capt. R. Allington.

He then gave it back to her and she realised he would take a message. She clutched the pencil tightly, as if her life depended on it, and then she thought her life *did* depend on it – and she had no idea what to say.

Dan reached for another pencil and started, impatiently, to draw pictures of clocks.

She wrote, *Please don't leave me.*

Dan took it and put it in his pocket. He reached down a saddle and bridle.

Meg whined and scratched with a feeble paw at her skirt. She walked away across the yard. In a moment Dan passed her on the grey. If she wanted to call him back, he wouldn't hear. She considered the things she ought to have written to Captain Allington, had she been able to tell Dan to wait. But she had spoken the truth. It was an acknowledgement of what she felt – all she felt. There had been no time to dress it up or arrange it. In that one short phrase she had risked as much as Johnny when he had settled to play his last game of chess.

As she came face to face with the rambling old house, she felt no sense of possession, only the deeper conviction that Castle Orchard belonged to Captain Allington, whatever the deeds might say.

Indoors, she asked Annie to give the children breakfast. She said she would go and lie down because she had a headache. There was a letter from Louisa to read and also one from her mother-in-law, but how could she concentrate? She opened the latter first, though in a desultory manner, for such a letter was a rarity. The old lady's handwriting had deteriorated since her stroke. The address was written in another hand, she assumed that of the paid companion, Miss Blakeway.

Dear Caroline,

I wish to speak to Johnny on the subject of my will, but he never could be bothered with correspondence. He is too lively and writing letters doesn't amuse him. I dare say he comes to Castle Orchard from time to time so you must see if you can influence him towards paying me a visit.

Miss Blakeway is a little mad now, but for old times' sake, I try to look after her. She will say Johnny died in an accident but I would have heard about it, had it been so. The creature does go on and on, but I humour her.

Now get yourself some fresh gowns for the summer, something utterly fashionable and absurd. It is no good expecting Johnny to be an attentive husband if you are not up to the mode. No man likes to see his wife in what was new two seasons previous. It is that sort of thing that drives them to take mistresses, though sometimes I wished Johnny's father had taken a mistress as it would have turned his mind away from what he considered my extravagances. Now Johnny is extravagant and talked of going to Paris, the naughty creature . . .'

The letter dribbled to a halt mid-sentence and the old lady had then signed it. Mrs Arthur shook her head in bewilderment. It was curious to be receiving such a letter just now. Ought she to write back, stating the truth about the death of Jonathan Arthur? Certainly not.

Louisa's letter ran thus:

My dearest Caro,

I suppose Captain Allington has not returned yet. John is very anxious on the subject of your affairs and is inclined to be hurt you don't confide in him. I have told him I know you will come just the minute Captain Allington returns from Cornwall and I have written the same to my mother.

Now, Caro, I don't want you to be offended with me but you must know it really will look strange if

313

you stay at Castle Orchard after Captain Allington
returns. My mother said things most unpleasant
which I know aren't true, concerning yourself and
Captain Allington. I know you are good and innocent
and go to church like you always have, despite that
wicked Johnny I wish you had never married.

I believe it is shyness and the uncertainty of your
affairs that has kept you away from us until now.
That is what John's father says, and I think I have
been insensitive in pressing you so hard.

Your ever loving and affectionate sister,
Louisa Westcott

Dan returned not that day but the next. He nodded and
smiled at Mrs Arthur, but she thought he looked disturbed.
He brought no message with him, but if Captain Allington
had anything further to say he could have used the Royal
Mail like anybody else. Dan came round to the front door
the day after that with Allington's grey and the side-saddle
as if nothing had altered, expecting Mrs Arthur to take
her ride. She thought, while Dan was employed, Captain
Allington still had control of her life, for Dan could never be
redirected nor did he ever show the slightest inclination to be
redirected. His continued presence remained unexplained.

While out riding they met the agent doing his rounds.
He doffed his hat and remarked that Captain Allington
had told him to refer to her, but everything had been left
in such order and every possibility allowed for, he could
think of nothing to ask her. He then said he thought the
climate of Italy satisfactory for the Captain's health but he
ought not to stay once it became too hot.

Mrs Arthur, after making a few polite rejoinders, rode on. The weather was beautiful.

Annie complained of the abruptness of the master's departure. Phil and Emmy asked where he was. Mrs Arthur said nothing or pleaded ignorance. How could she tell them she had no idea whether he would ever come back? She saw to Emmy's lessons and took her for long, slow walks, dawdling at the pace of the child. Emmy filled her pinafore with wild flowers. Time was no object. They went without hats even when the sun was hot. Emmy took off her shoes and stockings and did exactly as she pleased. Meg was garlanded with daisy chains.

Mr Stewart Conway visited Mrs Arthur one evening, after Phil had gone to bed.

He said, 'I can never get to see you. I understand Captain Allington is away. This abrupt coming and going, it's very inconsiderate. I suppose it's what soldiers are accustomed to. Annie tells me there is a splendid portrait of him hung in the morning room. She is quite in love with it. It's the uniform. What dandies these soldiers are.'

'What will you do, Mr Conway, if Jacky and James should wish to be soldiers?'

'I never suggested it was not an honourable profession, merely that too much is made of it.'

'But suppose Bonaparte had invaded England?'

'I am sure we would have been glad of all the protection the Army could give us. I believe I would have volunteered myself. However, I think the likelihood of it exaggerated.'

'Why did he build all those boats, if that were the case?'

'Well, I dare say it was his intention, but it is not what I came to discuss. You are again in charge of Castle Orchard. It is a great convenience to Captain Allington. Is it not time to put a stop to it? Trying as you are, teasing a fellow with questions and answers, it is my most earnest wish to look after you.'

Mrs Arthur thought, If I married him, Castle Orchard would pass from myself to the Conways, and this he doesn't know. Why, as a married woman, could she not hold property for herself? It was the law. If she stood at the altar and married Stewart Conway, at that very moment he would become the owner of Castle Orchard, the house, its farms, its villages, the bends of the river, its meadows, its ruin and its Philosopher's Tower. As it was, she had no need to marry him.

He said, 'Last time I spoke to you we were interrupted. You told me your affairs were now in order, but I think you were yet in ignorance of them. I told you, or I intended to tell you. . .'

Mr Conway was lost for words. Mrs Arthur looked at him gently but there was no encouragement in her face.

She said, 'I think it much better you should tell me nothing. My affairs are at last in order and my income sufficient for my needs and those of my children.'

'So I am not required?' he said.

'I have been grateful for your friendship.'

'Friendship is not of what we talk,' he said.

'No, but I don't want to talk of anything else, at least, not at the minute.'

'But you will move away?'

Mrs Arthur wished she knew what she would do. Would Captain Allington agree to take Castle Orchard back? It seemed unlikely. She was sure there must be other women better qualified to make Mr Conway happy. He now took her hesitation and confusion in answering as a refusal to confide in him. After fruitless further discussion he went away in a dudgeon.

Mrs Arthur, after he had gone, wondered if he would court her for the rest of their lives and whether he would feel her refusal to marry him some denial not only of his natural right to be in possession of herself but of Castle Orchard too.

She could yet write to Captain Allington and send the letter via Lord Tregorn. Sooner or later His Lordship must know the whereabouts of his stepbrother. Had he gone to Italy as the agent had suggested? She started several letters but finished none.

The weather broke. The glorious, warm May sunshine was replaced by mist and drizzle. Phil bobbed his way across the meadow to school under a huge umbrella which swayed above him. When the wind blew, he and it tussled together like some little ensign with the regimental colours.

Mrs Arthur stepped out of the front door for the purpose of ascertaining the weather. Coming up the drive at a smart trot were a pair of bay horses and a landau with the hood drawn up. Puzzled, she hastily withdrew into the house. Who could possibly call on her now? After a moment's thought, she decided it must be her brother-in-law, though the vehicle had not looked like his. The man on the box had been wearing a greatcoat so had he been dressed in the Westcott Park livery, she would not have seen it.

She went into the drawing room to await events. What did she have on? Not one of her fresh-made gowns with which even John could not find fault, but John, under all circumstances, was dependable. He might find it difficult to approve someone so unwise as to have married Johnny Arthur, but she could tell him the truth. Captain Allington had given her back Castle Orchard and she was loath to take it. He would point out to her that she had to take it, having no other means of support, which was true. He would say it was Phil's inheritance. Phil's inheritance had been forfeited by his father. He might also think out some compromise. He would help her for the sake of Louisa.

She went to the window and sat down to wait, folding her hands in her lap to compose herself. Annie would show John in at any moment now. After a while her mind wandered. What a curious life was hers and how alone she was.

Eventually it occurred to her she had heard no voice, neither Annie's nor John's, no slam of the front door. She got up and returned to the hall. It was empty. She looked out on to the carriage sweep. There were no bay horses, no landau. Had she imagined it all? Was she going mad? She then saw a figure coming slowly up the drive, from the direction of the lodge, a cooking pot under one arm. It was Pride.

Mrs Arthur reached for her shawl and stood out by the sundial, waiting.

As soon as he came up to her, he said, 'Cook will be after telling me off, we do everything so unexpected, and I've been in a deal of trouble lately.'

'Oh, Pride, I didn't recognise the landau.'

'He changed it. A gentleman in the yard at the White Hart was admiring the britchka. Master said, "I'll change it for your landau if you'll agree to it this minute." Said he

318

was going to be a family man and the landau was more appropriate.'

'But Captain Allington – is he all right?'

'Middling, I'd say, but what can you expect when he does everything so sudden? I'm to tell you he's gone down to the river, he's gone to the tower.'

Mrs Arthur crossed the garden, passed the apple trees alight with blossom and greenery, and made her way to the Philosopher's Tower. The door was ajar. Captain Allington was, she knew, there. She climbed the staircase and walked blindly into his embrace.

Below them, Phil walked with the younger Conway boys along the river as far as the bridge, where the mist hung. They could be seen and heard from the window, which was open. Stephen was holding Jacky and James by the hand: they were now all a little afraid of the river, as if they had glimpsed what it could do. Phil was, perhaps, the boldest. He had conquered the river.

Frankie was heard to say, 'Robert wouldn't come. He doesn't want to play any more.'

Stephen said, 'We can play.'

'Not the same games,' Phil said. 'Not those. When I grow up I expect I'll be a soldier but I'm not going to be one now. We had better go away from the river. Jacky and James are too little. I'll get Smokey Joe and we'll take turns.'

The boys turned back towards the house. Their voices diminished. Their footsteps left trails in the long grass, the dew.

Captain Allington and Mrs Arthur smiled at one another. When she came to examine his face, it blazed

319

with that fierce, impatient intelligence that made him look like his portrait, stripping the years from him. It shocked her. How was it she had engaged the attention, let alone the affections, of such a man? He also appeared extremely white, in fact not particularly well, but she thought him happy, very happy.

He had on the table the little note she had written, that Dan had delivered.

He said, picking it up and smoothing it out, 'I viewed this as a proposal. The man is meant to ask, but as I didn't, it must do.'

Mrs Arthur said, 'But you could have asked.'

'You might have accepted me.'

'Of course.'

'But you might have accepted me for the same reason as you were prepared to accept Mr Conway.' As Allington spoke, he restlessly paced the room, which was really too small to contain him. Mrs Arthur was aware that though he spoke seriously, he was absurdly light-hearted.

She said, 'It wouldn't have been at all the same. And Castle Orchard, you will have it back.'

'What of Phil?' he asked.

'When the time comes, you will do what is best for Castle Orchard. Time will tell what is best for Phil.'

'I thought you might never forgive me.'

'I have nothing of which I need to forgive you.'

'Gaining Castle Orchard from Arthur by the means that I did.'

'While you were away, I received a visit from the Ramptons. I learned a lot about you then. Why didn't you tell me?'

'The principle is the same.'

Mrs Arthur thought about this. Maybe he was right, that the principle was the same, but had he not been owed the money? She said, 'I'm at a loss for words but I have nothing to forgive and nothing to condone. In fact, quite to the contrary. Could it be a sufficiently weighty subject for the Philosopher's Tower?' She then added, smiling, 'If you told me every detail of what made you act as you have, I should make excuses for you.'

Together they went downstairs and out of doors.

She said, suddenly anxious, 'Where have you been? You don't look well.'

'No further than the White Hart at Salisbury. I couldn't go any further. I had the worst one of my heads, as Pride and the children would say, that I think I've ever had – but maybe I always think that. Pride was cross with me for going off so abruptly. He kept muttering, "Stand to your arms one hour before dawn when in the face of the enemy." When we reached Salisbury he got so drunk he couldn't look after me, so the arrival of Dan was opportune. He stayed with me until Pride was sober. In fact, I dismissed Nat.'

'But he hasn't gone.'

Allington laughed. He said, 'No, of course not.'

'You would tell me, wouldn't you, if you had had the fever?'

He took her arm and looking down at her he said, smiling cheerfully, 'I don't think I'll ever have that again. I killed it the last time. As for my not looking well, I just got up too soon. We'll walk across the meadow to the rectory and ask to have the banns read. Neither brother will care for it much, but that can't be helped. Would you like to do that? It's a little wet. You look very pretty. You had better wear a cloak.'

The weather cleared again. Castle Orchard settled down in lazy warmth to await the summer. Pride, who had been busy moving things between the lodge and the house, now sat at the window of what was to be his new quarters, a pen in his hand.

> *Dear Mother,*
>
> *We are stopping here. Your Nat ain't going to know nothing but fields and cows and what. The master has come over sentimental, but it's for the good. I can see him now, off for a walk, arm in arm, hand in hand, and little Miss Emmy scampering about picking the buttercups. You might think as he's to be married, if he should turn sickly when I were away visiting, it wouldn't be of so much account, but it's not so . . . .*

The letter proceeded on, the usual series of small lies and ingenious fibs designed to convince his aged parent he was indispensable. Behind him, on the mantelpiece, was the glass jar holding the sixpences.

They all wrote letters that day. Captain Allington wrote to his half-brother.

> *My dear Tregorn,*
>
> *I am going to marry Mrs Arthur. Three weeks for the banns. Will you come?'*

He wrote the same to Major Wilder, but more fulsomely.

He then took out his pocketbook and wrote in that: *Happiness. Contentment. They were not so bent on eluding me as I had thought.* He then added, arbitrarily, *A pair of greyhounds. Use the landau. Take the children, J. Arthur's, God help me, life is curious.*

Mrs Arthur wrote to her sister.

> *My dear Louisa,*
>
> *Captain Allington has asked me to marry him and I have accepted him.*

She stopped to consider the vague inaccuracies of this statement. It was not difficult to visualise the consternation it would arouse in the breast of Louisa.

> *Come to Castle Orchard. Bring the little girls and let John give me away. Let him not be shocked. I have nobody else to ask. Tell him Captain Allington was prepared to give me back Castle Orchard. If only we had crystal balls, we wouldn't make mistakes, or not so many, but for this I need no crystal ball, so you must believe me, dear Louisa.*

She paused again. The crystal ball told the future, not how to evade it, but perhaps there was not the need to complicate the matter by pointing this out. It was as hard as ever to write to her sister.

As to the more distant future, Phil received a small independence from his paternal grandmother, the old lady dying intestate. As his mother had in her heart foreseen, he never did inherit Castle Orchard. He joined the Army and went out to Canada, where, in winter, the tears can freeze in your eyes – to fight the rebels in Montreal.

You may still go to Castle Orchard, if you can find it, up that lane and down this . . . and ask to see the Philosopher's Tower. Allingtons live there to this day. Captain Allington's own eldest son, being successful at the Bar, entered politics and was elevated to the peerage. Being an impudent, clever fellow, he had a rook or a castle inserted into the family coat of arms.

Acknowledgements

I wish to express my gratitude to the late Nick Robinson, without whom this book and my last would be languishing in a drawer at the bottom of my desk.